monsoonbooks

THE FLAME TREE

Yang-May Ooi is a Chinese-Malaysian author, story performer and TEDx speaker, who grew up in Kuala Lumpur. She read English at Oxford before practising law. She currently combines creating performance work for the London stage with writing. She lives in London with her partner.

Learn more about the author at *www.YangMayOoi.co.uk.*

T0154786

ALSO BY YANG-MAY OOI

Mindgame

The Flame Tree

Yang-May Ooi

monsoon

monsoonbooks

Published in 2014
by Monsoon Books Pte Ltd
71 Ayer Rajah Crescent #01-01, Singapore 139951
www.monsoonbooks.com.sg

ISBN (paperback): 978-981-4423-90-8
ISBN (ebook): 978-981-4423-91-5

First published in 1998 by Hodder and Stoughton.
This updated edition published in 2014.

Cover design by Cover Kitchen.

National Library Board, Singapore Cataloguing-in-Publication Data
Ooi, Yang-May.
The flame tree / Yang-May Ooi. – Updated edition. – Singapore : Monsoon Books Pte Ltd, 2014.
pages cm
ISBN : 978-981-4423-90-8 (paperback)

1. Malaysians – England – Fiction. 2. Women lawyers – England – Fiction. 3. Construction industry – Fiction. 4. Malaysia – Fiction. I. Title.

PR6065.O4
823.914 -- dc23   OCN874967666

Printed in United States
15 14   1 2 3 4 5

To my parents, with love and gratitude

ACKNOWLEDGEMENTS

During the long course of writing this novel, I turned to many people for advice, support and encouragement and their enthusiasm helped pull me through many of the difficulties along the way. In particular, Helene Nowell, Terry Bailey, Fiona Cutts, Rosanna Moskovitch and Alex Jukes-Hughes. My father, together with Alex Wood and Simon Charles, gave me detailed advice on the business and legal issues. Janet Cook filled me in on geophysical background. Thanks, all, for everything! Any inaccuracies that appear in the story are, of course, entirely mine.

Thank you also to Beatrice Oh Siew Chew and Sue Oh Siew Yoong for their help in preparing the manuscript for this edition.

I am deeply grateful to my parents and to Yang-Ming and Yang-Wern for their generosity, encouragement and belief in my. I am indebted to Tim and Alice Renton for their spirited confidence in me, which helped bring this novel to fruition.

Finally, to my angel, who gave me courage to embark on my life as a writer and who has stayed by my side through it all - all my love and heartfelt thanks.

AUTHOR'S NOTE

This is a work of fiction. Names, characters, place and incidents are either the product of the author's imagination or used fictitiously. Any resemblance to actual events or locales or persons living or dead is entirely coincidental. Without prejudice to the generality of the above, 'Kampung Tanah' and its surrounding region is a fictitious place. The 'Kampung Tanah (Special Development Area) Act 1996' and the related 'planning review' with its procedure and committee are entirely invented by the author. They are not based on any Malaysian statute, procedure or body, nor meant to reflect in any way whatsoever on Malaysian law, policy or official.

Yang-May Ooi

PART ONE

YANG

Yang

The masculine principle. It is the animus that gives us logical reasoning and proud strength. It is the ambition that drives us to power, the restlessness that goads us to achievement.

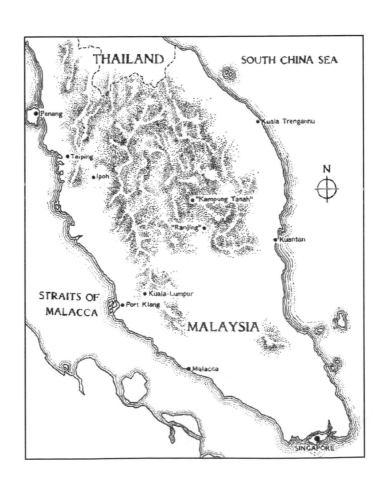

1

Jasmine Lian settled herself into the roomy Club Class seat on the Malaysian Airlines flight for Kuala Lumpur. Through the porthole window, she saw that the summer drizzle had started again, darkening the tarmac where the laden baggage-cart was snaking to the hold of the jumbo 747. Somewhere beyond the bustle of Heathrow, she thought, Harry would be just arriving at the sleek, modern offices of De Witte Cootes, a small but aggressively rising finance house where he was a broker. She pictured his confident stride and sparky grin that he would invariably flash at the female staff. Always the flirt, she thought, but she smiled in spite of herself. Always the flirt, but he was devoted to her alone. She thought, almost with awe, there would be only one Mrs Harry Taunton and it would be her.

But, all too starkly, she remembered creeping out of Harry's bed back in his house in Fulham earlier that morning. He'd still been asleep, his hair over his eyes, his face like a young boy's. Quietly, she had dressed and slipped away to come to the airport.

They had always been the perfect couple. Was she risking everything by taking this trip now? Ever since she'd known Harry, he'd made life seem so special, as if they were charmed youth. If he knew her as she really was ... Jasmine was afraid to think of the consequences. At Oxford, Harry had been older than most undergraduates, his work experience in the City after Harrow having turned into a two-year job. To Jasmine, he was the more glamorous for it. She remembered the summer balls a few years ago at Oxford, complete with champagne hamper and the right group of friends, she and Harry the dazzling centre of it all. Others watched them with envy from the periphery, glanced back as they passed. Even those women in Harry's crowd slid their covetous gaze ever back to him. Jasmine would be elegant and graceful in a red *cheongsam*, the formal evening dress of her Chinese heritage, its tailored slits showing off her long, slim legs. Harry, as ever, looking gorgeous in black tie, all angular, athletic lines, his square-jawed features softened by a blond fringe falling into his eyes. Harry, always needing a haircut and having eyes only for her.

She could hardly believe that of all the many women he knew – all of them wealthy, confident and attractive – Harry had chosen her to love. Once, five years ago, at a garden party in Kensington, she had stood by the sumptuous buffet and stared at all their friends, well-dressed, good-looking people who had taken her into their fold, accepting her as one of them because Harry was one of them. Harry had just come down from Christchurch after a four-year degree course. He had gained only a third in Classics but had been snapped up by De Witte Cootes. He'd been twenty-six then and poised to make his first million in the City within the next ten years. Jasmine had been exhilarated to be in the company of all these high-flyers – management consultants, brokers, designers, bankers, some with inherited titles – and more than a little intimidated.

Marietta Asquith, a glamorous blonde in her mid-thirties, had come up and taken her by the arm. "Don't be shy with us, dear," her husky voice had soothed her. "I want to know all about you."

They took a turn round the garden, arms linked. At twenty-three, Jasmine had just started a new job as a trainee solicitor at a firm in Lincoln's Inn, having gained a double first in Law at Corpus Christi and a distinction in her Solicitors' Finals. Marietta was an interior designer and her family had known Harry's since he'd been a boy. Her husband was something in the Foreign Office. Jasmine never knew what he did, only that he was often away. He was not there that afternoon.

"My dear," Marietta said, "you've been so good for Harry these last three years. I can't tell you how he's changed ever since you've been a part of his life. You make him so happy. Like no other girl he's ever gone out with."

Jasmine blushed. "How has he changed?"

"Happy, you know? Like a puppy. He adores you. Raves about you – so sweet, so innocent, not like coarse English girls, so delicate, and on and on. What potion have you slipped him?" Marietta's laugh pealed across the lawn as she squeezed Jasmine's arm affectionately. They had become fast friends.

The 747 taxied onto the runway.

In the aisle, a petite Malay stewardess in a batik *sarong kebaya*, the figure-hugging Malaysian national dress, was going through the motions of the safety procedure. A smooth male voice gave the instructions in Malay and then in impeccable English. Jasmine found herself listening fondly to the Malay, which she had heard only a few times over the ten years she had been in England. She was pleased that she still understood most of it.

She had wanted to tell Harry the truth this last weekend. They had been down at Oaklands, the manor house and estate in Sussex which had been in his family for generations. Harry's father and his second wife were in the South of France for the summer and Jasmine and Harry had had the place to themselves. Since their engagement two months before, she had been waiting for the right moment to tell him. The unseasonable June rain had eased as if miraculously for their weekend idyll. The sky was bright and cloudless, and the gentle slopes of Sussex green were lush and teeming with butterflies and ladybirds.

"Darling ..." Jasmine had begun.

Harry lay on his back on the tartan rug, gazing up at the sky through the branches of the ancient oaks that sheltered their picnic from the midday sun. He had the broad shoulders of a long-time rower and the muscular build of a rugby halfback. Stretched out on the rug, he seemed a giant at rest beside Jasmine's delicate build. The wicker hamper lay open, smoked salmon, duck terrine, strawberries and champagne spreading across the rug in antique china and fluted glasses. Jasmine curled across Harry's chest, teasing his cheek with a cold strawberry. As she looked up at him, she could just see the house across the meadow of buttercups beyond his tousled head. The tennis courts were above his right ear, the lawns and banks of flowers like a crown across his golden hair.

"Mmm?" Harry turned and drew the strawberry into his mouth, toying his tongue around her fingers.

Her breath caught in her throat. She sat up and made herself go on, pulling her hand away. "There's something I ..." She hesitated. She stared at Harry. This was the happy ending she had always longed for, wasn't it? The perfection of this glorious day that Harry had bestowed on her gave her a sense of watching her own life as if in a movie. They were lying together, happy and in love, in an English glade in summer and the credits should be rolling. Only, the house lights were coming up too soon and she was back in the old Lido cinema, *kacang* shells crackling underfoot, the groundnuts' salty residue in her mouth and, all around, the air stale with the garlicky sweat of the tropics.

"What is it, my love?"

Jasmine looked away and took a sip of champagne. "Nothing, really."

Harry reached up and stroked her black hair. He caught her in his hazel-green gaze. His flirtatious tone belied his words. "Not having second thoughts, are you?"

"No." Jasmine laughed a little too quickly.

"Then what is it?" He smiled, as if at a child.

"It'll be perfect, won't it?"

"The wedding? Of course." Harry eased himself up and kissed her lips.

"No, I mean us. Our lives. Once we're married."

He drew her into his arms and she let herself sink into their safety. "Of course," he murmured. She felt his lips on her hair, touching her ears, resting on her brow.

Harry had believed the story she had told him. Her parents had been killed when she was eight years old, she had said. Their Bentley had crashed one night on the Singapore – Kuala Lumpur highway. She had waited up for them all night. "But I fell asleep," she had said. "Perhaps if I hadn't given up on them, they might still be alive." She had been brought up by a tutor, she had told him, all her practical needs taken care of by employees paid for from a trust fund her parents had left.

Jasmine had entwined her fingers in Harry's. "You are my family now," she had said, wanting it so much to be true.

In the aircraft, Jasmine felt the throb of the jet engines change. A sudden burst of propulsion pushed her back into her seat and the horizon tilted from the window. The air popped in her ears and a dizzying vertigo shook her as the airport below fell away. Rushing up, a panorama of fields and trees encroached with buildings and roads that were the outer London suburbs. These, too, bottomed out as the plane thrust up into banks of cloud.

Jasmine found herself breathing rapidly, a chill making her shiver. She hadn't been able to tell him.

On that sunny afternoon she'd said, at last, "I have to be away on business on Monday."

"Day after tomorrow?" Harry looked surprised.

"Yes. I have to go to Kuala Lumpur for some meetings." Her heart was beating hard.

"You didn't tell me this before."

"Darling, I did. Two weeks ago."

"I don't remember." Harry frowned. "What meetings?"

"That bid for the new university in Malaysia. I act for one of the tenderers – the British company."

"Yes, Jordan Cardale." Harry nodded but she could see that he could not remember the conversation.

Jasmine went on quickly, "There are some preliminary issues to settle and they need me out there for a few days."

Harry took in her words and said nothing. She watched him anxiously. Finally, he shook his head. "It must've slipped my mind." There was a hint of annoyance when he next spoke. "But do you have to go? And at such short notice. The wedding is less than a month away."

"I've got it all under control. Anyway, the event company is doing most of it."

"Yes, but you're the bride. You shouldn't rush off now. You need to be here – available. What if – what if there's a problem?"

"Darling," Jasmine stroked his hair, soothing him, "I'll only be away a few days. It'll be fine."

"But –"

"I've left all the details with Marietta. She'll be in daily contact with them."

Harry looked doubtful but she could see he didn't want a quarrel. Then he said, "What about me?"

"My darling ... is that what you're really worried about?" Jasmine drew his head towards hers, showering his face with kisses. "Sometimes when you're working late, and I'm working late, we don't see each other for up to three or four days. Just pretend next week is one of those weeks."

"Do you *have* to go?" But he was pouting, teasing now, like a child who knew how to get his own way.

His old trick made her laugh. "You're too charming for your own good. It's not fair – you know I can't refuse you anything when you give me that look!"

He gave her a strong dose of sulky James Dean and Ralph Fiennes from beneath his lashes. He smiled slyly. "So don't refuse me."

"Oh, my darling, if only I could stay. You know how important a client Jordan Cardale is to the firm. And to me." It was because of the work she did for them that she was now the youngest corporate partner at Carruthers. "If they want me, I have to go."

"But it was I who introduced you to the senior partner at Carruthers." Harry played up the theatrical intensity, making her giggle at the incongruity of his words and manner. He broke into a laugh and then pulled a serious face, back in cinematic brooding mode. "I am your Svengali" – a strangled Slavic accent –"I made you who you are, I formed your tastes, showed you how to behave, what to wear, who to be seen with. You are mine, my creation! You belong to me and I command you to stay!"

He finished with a flourish that entangled her in his arms. They were laughing as they rolled and tumbled together on the grass.

After a while, their laughter subsiding, Harry gasped, "Will I be able to reach you?"

"Why? It's only a few days."

"I might want to hear your voice before I go to bed."

"I'll be at the Shangri-La but there may be an on-site meeting in the hills – you might not be able to get me there."

"You'll have your mobile phone with you, won't you?"

"Yes, but in the hills I don't know what the reception will be like."

"Faint heart – or faint phone signals – never won fair lady," Harry had said, waving his arm in a mock-gallant bow, even though he was lying on his back.

And now Jasmine was flying back to Malaysia to keep a promise she should have forgotten long ago, the secret she had kept from Harry. Jasmine found herself twisting her ring. Her engagement ring. She looked down and saw the single blue-white diamond, two carats, set in platinum. From Tiffany's, she remembered proudly. Like the flat in Chelsea he had chosen for her, its interior made over by Marietta, it symbolised who she had become.

So why could she not let go of a duty from an old life? Her new life with Harry was what mattered. It was all she had wanted in the world, wasn't it? She had it now, so why was she putting it all at risk by rushing to a past she should have left behind?

Jasmine closed her eyes and listened to the roar of the aircraft engines.

They had driven back to Harry's house in Fulham late on Sunday night. Jasmine remembered lying in his arms, the covers thrown off in the heat. The night is seldom dark in London and she watched him drifting off. The window was open and above the yellow haze of London lights, the full moon seemed cold and alone.

"Are you happy, my love?" Harry murmured dreamily.

"I have never been so happy," she lied.

On the upper slopes of the tropical highlands of Malaysia, dawn was still a few hours away. The air was chill and fresh. Stars glittered like frost over the dark jungle on the hills. Here and there were clearings cultivated with vegetables and fruits. There were strawberries, lettuce, carnations and temperate flowers, too, which would not have survived in the heat of the lowlands. These were the smallholdings scattered around the market town of Kampung Tanah – the Village of the Land.

In the town's high street, Wong sat in his office below his family's living quarters. He was in his mid-forties, chubby from a few years of good business. His office was a partitioned area in the storehouse at the back of his general goods shop. He sold the items he trucked in from the lowlands – dried spices, salted fish, video games. On journeys down to the cities, his trucks carried fresh produce from the hills for the supermarkets.

As Wong worked on his accounts, he heard a car pull up in the back parking lot. Its engine gunned before subsiding to stillness. A car door. Then footsteps – taking their time – crossing the tarmac. Wong squinted towards the hinged door at the rear.

A dark figure of a man stood in the doorway. The solitary desk lamp made Wong an easy target where he sat.

"So this is Wong Keng-wi," the man said, in Cantonese. "Yes?" Wong began to get up. "Who are you?"

"The businessman? Chairman of the Kampung Tanah Business Association? Member of the town committee?" the man sneered.

Wong nodded. He moved to the light switch on the wall.

"No!"

Wong froze.

"I am your friend," the man said. Wong's hand searched for the telephone.

There was a sound. Metal scraping on metal. Wong stared at the switchblade in the man's hand.

The man gestured and Wong moved away from the phone.

"Call me Good Friend." The man took a jambu from a bushel of the local fruit. He made Wong sit with him on crates by the open door.

Staying in the shadows, the man sliced his jambu. "You're an influential man in this village."

He was matter-of-fact, his knife occupied. The ordinariness of their seating reassured Wong and he began to relax.

The man was saying, "People do business with you because they trust you. You're doing well."

"Business is OK," Wong said, cautiously.

Suddenly, the man flicked the knife onto the crate between them. It thudded into the wood. Wong started.

The man began to talk. He knew everything about Wong – his business, his wife and his family. "Your son, Jimmy, he's your favourite. Seven next month. Loves cars and fancy gadgets."

"H – how did you know?"

"Knowledge, my friend. That is the key to business success. The world is changing." The man took out a wad of cash. He peeled away two thousand ringgit and let them fall on the crate. "Progress is like enlightenment. We are on the path to a better state of existence. I am a Buddhist. Are you?"

Wong stared at the money. He nodded.

The man said, "I go to the temple. I pray to the spirits and gods. They are like my friends. They are enlightened beings."

He toyed with the knife, watching Wong. "They control things we do not understand. But they want to help us. Like I want to help you." He paused to let this sink in, then went on, "Many farmers have been selling – they've got good money for their land. There's going to be a big development here soon."

Wong took the bait. "We see people from KL coming and going. Testing the soil. Surveyors, engineers. All kinds, men in suits. What's the development? Holiday condos? Country club?"

The man spoke quietly, drawing Wong in closer to catch his words. "University – top class. New life into this dead place, heh, what do you think? Businesses will follow, tourists will come to see this new wonder of Asia. There'll be condos and country clubs, restaurants and malls, casinos, even, maybe – bright, beautiful lights flashing up the night, big fancy highways zooming us all up and down to KL, to Kuantan, anywhere you want, everything you want."

"New customers with money. They will need a big store." Wong stared out at the dark morning beyond, as if into a rich future. "Also a good transport service – minicabs, maybe even limousine service. I can give them that."

"You believe in the future." Good Friend laughed.

Wong held the money in his hand. It could do him no harm to hear out this man. It might even gain him an advantage. He acted tough but he seemed reasonable.

The man went on, "If I perform my obligations to the gods, they grant me success in business, long life, a happy family. In return, I give them my loyalty. Like we expect loyalty from you, my friend."

"We?"

"I have associates – rich men. Like you, they believe in the future. We need you to be our representative here. We want everyone in this town to be our friends – and you and others we are contacting will help us."

"What do you want us to do?"

"You will know in good time. For now, remember this. I am always loyal to the gods. If I'm not, they can grant me terrible misfortune. Maybe, one night, a short circuit in my storehouse and everything is burned to the ground. Or my son, say his name is Jimmy, like your son, maybe he disappears and weeks later they find him dead, his body mutilated. Again no reason."

Wong blinked, his mouth dry.

"I shall burn an offering for you when I go to the temple." The stiletto blade glinted yellow from the lamp, flashed grey from the embryo dawn outside. "I would not like to lose your friendship, Wong."

"You have my friendship – I swear it, Good Friend."

The man closed the blade. He laughed, the confident laugh of a patron pleased with his protégé. "We will share good fortune together."

Wong followed him out onto the steps. The man kept his back to him but he could see the brown suede jacket and jeans in the dim light. They looked expensive. Wong saw the money bright in his hand. Instinctively, he brought up the wad and sniffed its rich fragrance.

There was a red Mazda sports cabriolet in the empty parking lot. The man swung himself in.

Wong understood the deal. But it would not be so difficult to be loyal to this new friendship, he thought. After all, there was no gain without risk – and there was much to gain.

The car squealed away in a thrust of power.

It had no number plates.

Wong slipped the money into his shirt pocket.

*   *   *

As the 747 hurtled eastwards over India, Jasmine dozed uneasily. She had stretched out in the reclining seat, a blanket drawn up close around her.

She had not had the nightmare for a while. This time was like all the other times – except for the face. She had not seen it those other times. It always began with the sound of weeping. Through murky blackness, Jasmine stumbled towards the sobbing. Fragments on the floor cut her bare feet. She crashed against unseen objects. The weeping lured her on. And then, she saw the room again.

Shadows shaped themselves into a table, chairs, a sideboard. Shattered glass and broken objects lay everywhere. There had been a struggle. It was night. By the jagged window, the woman wept. A weak light filtered in from behind her. Where her face should have been, Jasmine saw only an infinity of darkness. The sobs filled the room. It was the end of everything. Nothing but despair lay ahead. The weeping drained Jasmine's heart. She felt cold.

She could not move. She could not speak.

She saw the blood. A black stain on the woman's sleeve. It fanned up onto her shoulder, down across her chest. Seeping through her fingers, which now covered her face. Jasmine screamed but no sound came.

The woman looked up and raised her arms in a plea for help. Jasmine stared at her face but only darkness stared back. The metallic stench of blood was suffocating. "Save yourself," the woman said. "Leave me."

The outstretched arms turned and kept Jasmine at bay. Go, run as far away as you dare, they said. The woman spoke again. "I must wait here but you can escape. You have a chance."

"Come with me," Jasmine called out. "I must stay. Save yourself."

Jasmine wanted to help the woman but she could not. She wanted to escape from the dark and the blood and the faceless woman but she could not leave her.

"Go. If you stay here with me …" The woman's voice trailed off.

Jasmine turned and ran. Her legs were heavy, as if she lurched through mud. She looked back and wished she never had. The woman was watching her, her face now ashen in the eerie light. Jasmine looked back and saw what she had always known. The face was her own face.

She woke up, gasping for air.

For a moment, she did not know where she was. The roaring hum of the engine unsettled her. She stared at the seats looming like sentinels across her vision.

Then she remembered she was on the flight to Malaysia. Slowly, she sat up. She tried to still her heaving breath and pounding heart. She touched the dampness on her cheek and stared at her fingers. There was no blood, only sweat.

*   *   *

It was nine in the morning and the temperature was already 30 degrees. Jasmine stepped out of the tunnelled walkway from the plane into Subang International Airport, Kuala Lumpur.

How it had changed since she had last been there ten years ago! Back then, she had been about to take her first journey overseas and the shabby little airport had seemed huge. She had been eighteen, clutching her passport and a suitcase full of homemade clothes. There had been no one to see her off. Now there was no one she knew to witness her return, reinvented stunningly and dressed for respect. The refurbished airport had two new terminals and shining floors as far as you could see. It had the opulent look of a new nation that had made good and knew it.

In spite of the air-conditioning, her lightweight Yves St Laurent suit felt too dense. Jasmine prided herself on her designer wardrobe, the internationally recognised labels like talismans of her new identity. In her beautifully tailored clothes, Jasmine felt empowered, charmed with glamour and good fortune. They hid the frightened girl she had once been. She caught an image of herself in the smoked glass partitions along the polished corridor of the transit lounge – a graceful, elegant young woman in her late twenties with silky black hair, classical Chinese features, and the confident manner of a Western woman.

The Chinese and Malay businessmen in the terminal were in short-sleeved shirts. The few executive women looked cool and stylish in silk blouses and cotton skirts, and Jasmine spotted some in designer names. A Muslim woman strolled by in a colourful *baju kurong* – a loose tunic over long, matching *sarong*. Jasmine took off her houndstooth jacket and draped it over her luggage trolley.

Outside, the heat enveloped her with a physical impact. She had forgotten its suffocating humidity. She slowed her pace and sauntered to the Avis counter where she rented a BMW Clove-tinted smoke of the *kretek* cigarette trailed from a group of chocolate-brown young men as they passed. The aroma caught Jasmine like a memory of everything she had missed about home. Home. This was home. This heat was home. These dark-skinned, slight, friendly people were home. Jasmine stood, unable to move, taking in this world that had lived only in her memory for ten long years.

The car-jockey came up with the keys to the BMW. Rousing herself, Jasmine loaded her overnight bag and leather briefcase into the boot. The engine started with a roar and, pulling out onto the highway, she followed signs to the city centre. The air-conditioning blasted cold air but the glare of the sun burned through the tinted glass. She passed royal palms and bougainvillaea, then rubber plantations and oil palm estates.

Soon, the KL skyline loomed and she stared in amazement. The last time she had been here, there had not been a skyline to speak of. Now, sleek buildings of glass and steel gleamed in the sunlight. The centrepiece was the Post Office tower, a spire impaling a flying saucer of office suites. Downtown, she gaped like a tourist at the sprawling shopping malls – Yow Chuan Plaza, KL Plaza, Sungai Wang 'river of money'. She could not match the wealth of what she saw with the hazy picture she had held in her mind of a much smaller and less imposing capital city. She felt a buzz from the energy and bustle she sensed all around. This was a city of money and new prospects, racing to catch up with its more mature cousins in the West. She cruised towards the international hotels jostling for space – the Regent, the Hilton, the Istana and, finally, the Shangri-La.

She pulled up and had the car-jockey hold the car. Inside the Shangri-La, marble floors and icy air welcomed her to a fantasy palace. Suddenly, her nerve failed her. What if someone recognised her? Saw through her veneer of breeding. Saw who she really was. Jasmine looked furtively round her. A few men were giving her admiring glances but nothing more.

"Can I help you, *mem*?" The young man behind the reception desk inclined diffidently towards her.

Jasmine floundered. Then, she drew herself up and walked over to the desk.

She checked in but did not wait to see the room. She hurried back to the car, not wanting to think about what she was doing.

She kept her mind on the road and on the drive ahead. She did not contact Seng & Mustafa, her firm's associate offices in KL – they did not know she was here. She did not contact her client – they were in London. The client and project were real enough. But there had been no meetings arranged in Malaysia.

She had lied to Harry.

Not a lie, she corrected herself. Just, well, not exactly the truth. Not just yet. She *would* tell him. He would know everything when she got back to London. She *would* make sure of it.

Manoeuvring through the traffic, she found her way back to the highway and headed north to Taiping. The clear stretches of tarmac sped her through vistas of tracts of rubber and oil palm. In the east, the blue of the Titiwangsa mountain range filled the horizon, its highest peaks enshrouded in mist.

That last journey alone to KL airport, she had taken the bus – six hours along the old trunk road, single file all the way, its diesel engine spewing black smoke. She had been crammed between a fat old woman, with a loud, betel-stained mouth, and a young man, whose cheap cologne steadily soured into rancid sweat. Six hours of watching timber lorries scrape by and trying to hold down her nausea and her nervous excitement, knowing always that her life was about to change forever.

Now, speeding smoothly along this new highway, Jasmine thought how strange it was to be back after so many years. The landscape she remembered had been filled up with concrete and tarmac, veneers of progress. But she knew intimately this glaring sun and its bright sky, the palm trees and, here and there, the uncleared mass of jungle. Other, forbidden memories crowded the corners of her mind, tumbling against the backdrop of this tropical landscape, summoned as if by her return.

Her mother had told her never to come back, but Jasmine had made her a promise. Her mother had replied, "You'll wish one day you never promised me anything," but Jasmine had sworn it in spite of her protests. And now she knew that her mother had been right.

Jasmine had trained herself to forget all that had come before Oxford. But where she had succeeded in mastering her future, she had failed in taming the past. She had been glad to leave the sweltering heat as if leaving the claustrophobia of her servant class. And here, amid the swamps and jungle, her emotions had been wilder, more unsafe, her passions unsubdued. She had thought them becalmed in the cool of her English life but she had been mistaken. They had begun to prowl again the evening that Harry had asked her to marry him.

Three hours north of KL, just outside Ipoh, she searched the landscape for the limestone hills whose caves for generations had housed dwellings and sacred temples. In the ten years she had been away, cement and chalk factories had arrived to devour the limestone. There remained only gouged-out cadavers of hills and the debris of dead forests. Relentless blasting for chalk had drained the land of holiness and life.

It seemed to Jasmine, suddenly, that she saw before her the landscape of her heart.

2

Malaysia runs the length of the exclamation mark extending southwards from Thailand with Singapore as the dot on the end. A range of hills forms a central spine dividing the West Coast from the East. The South China Sea on the east sweeps in clear waters and fresh trade winds, bringing good fishing, Vietnamese boat people and pirates. On the west, the sweltering Malacca Straits collects the debris of commercial tankers and the waste of both the heavily populated West Coast and the many islands of Indonesia.

In the humid fertile soil of Malaysia itself, lush vegetation creeps to inhabit every untended inch. The jungle is all pervasive, dank and impenetrable still in large tracts of the interior. The history of the nation is the history of the struggle to win territory from the rainforests. Spice farms, *padi* fields, rubber and tea plantations, tin mines and factories, cities and suburban gardens have all been hewn from the wilderness. But, in time, the jungle always reclaims it, relentless and without mercy. Even today, those hikers who stray a few metres from known forest tracks will find the trees closing in on them, each tangle of green indistinguishable from the next, no markers in the perpetual emerald twilight to lead them home.

On the West Coast, the capital city of Kuala Lumpur has tamed the tropical wilds with tarmac, tower blocks, shopping malls and air-conditioning. Highway arteries link its wealth to other centres of commerce and industry – Johor Baru to the south, Ipoh and Penang to the north. The soaring temperatures of global industrialisation have brought unusually dry weather in recent years. Long aridity has parched the soil, cracking seams in the red earth, searing thirsty vegetation to crackling brown. The jungle's one essential sustenance

– moisture – is losing its hold. Many today believe concrete and tarmac might win now against the wilderness where generations of agriculture and mining have failed.

Three-and-a-half hours' drive north of Kuala Lumpur, the small town of Taiping nestles in the foothills of Bukit Larut – Larut Hill. It was once the administrative centre for the British Empire's tin-mining operations in the state of Perak. In the nineteenth century, transplanted English society strolled in its orderly streets, shopped at department stores, sipped papaya sodas at the soda fountain, played cricket on the *padang*, dressed up to go to the races. But the tin ran out, as it was always bound to, and the whites moved on. They left behind their colonial buildings – the town's museum, its district offices, its Anglican church – and the most beautiful public gardens in the country.

The Lake Gardens were created from the debris of the tin mines, its fathomless lakes formed from the results of open cast mining. Now, more than a century after the land was replanted, huge rain trees arch over the perimeter road to touch the water's edge. Lotus blossoms bloom in still ponds. Bamboo groves and ornamental gardens speckle the undulating landscape. Pagodas dot islands, hillocks and the lakes themselves. Bridges – arching, curving, zigzagging – playfully span stretches of water.

From every point in the town, the hills can be seen. Their thronging life and waterfalls are part of all who live in Taiping. The amassed bulk of the hills used to bring rain every day, brooding black with the colour of the storm. But in the heat of the recent dry weather, they take on the nature of the sun, glaring bright through the steam from the dank jungles. But they also give relief – amid the sheltering trees, only a few metres up the hills, the air is fresh and cooled by mountain springs.

Some miles off the new highway, Taiping is overlooked, these days, by those rushing between Kuala Lumpur and Penang and is yet undiscovered by tourists. It is like an old relative that has been forgotten by the young. Content in its own home, it carries on in the quiet meditative way of the very old and very wise.

*   *   *

Half an hour away from Taiping, Jasmine drove into the town of Simpang, named for the crossroads around which a jumble of old wooden buildings had gathered. She had come off the highway and approached from the south on the old trunk road. Ahead, she saw the intersection with the east-west road inland from the coast towards Taiping. Suddenly, her energy seemed to ebb.

She pulled into the kerb by a coffeeshop just before the lights. It proclaimed itself in both Malay and Chinese to be Sing Kee Coffee and Eating House. Metal tables and chairs cluttered the floor and spilled onto the walkway above the monsoon drain. Ceiling fans, blackened with grime, circled in the heat. The hawkers on the perimeter had sold off their noodles and roast meats and were swabbing their counters. Groups of men sat around smoking and finishing their meals. Families passing through ate without energy, bleary-eyed from their journeys. All of them turned to stare as Jasmine walked in.

Among those Asian skins darkened by the sun, she felt pale as cream. The men's cheap shirts and scruffy trousers were of the same fashion as those she remembered from her childhood. She froze under their stares. A chill came back to her that she had not felt in a long time. A rough-looking man took a toothpick out of his mouth as he looked at her. She started – a reflex from a time she thought she had left behind. Would he speak to her? Would he make a move towards her? *You're Tommy's daughter, aren't you? Come and give your uncle a kiss, little girl.* The man looked away and picked up his glass of beer.

One by one, the locals around her returned to their food and conversation. Jasmine realised she'd been holding her breath. She sat down at an empty table and tried to recover her composure. She made herself look calmly around the coffeeshop. The women there, she noted, had done what they could with their limited budgets, dressing simply and cheaply, with little make-up. All their money had gone on their children, who were got up in baseball caps and jeans and colourful tops. Everywhere, she saw bad skin and the scars of mosquito bites.

The impassive proprietor asked for her order. She stared at him for a moment, noticing his stained T-shirt, dirty slippers and shorts. She ordered *kopi peng*, strong local coffee sweetened with condensed milk and poured over crushed ice. She felt her alarm subsiding and a strange sense of being home begin to emerge. And yet, she was acutely aware of her immaculate make-up, her brightened lips. She had left her jacket in the car but she still seemed overdressed. Too well dressed. People were still flicking stares and whispering to each other. She made out that one table thought she was a Hong Kong movie star but they could not remember which one.

She had been so desperate to escape the life that had waited for her here in Malaysia. If she had stayed, could she have been any more than 'Tommy's girl', leered at and cat-called for favours? She remembered how she used to envy women like these drab wives. At least they were wives and mothers, they had a place in life and husbands to honour them, she used to think: no decent man would want Tommy Fung's daughter.

The coffee arrived and she took a long sip. The cloying sweetness surprised her like an old friend. In London, she drank her coffee black and without sugar. She smiled. It seemed an emblem of how much of herself she had changed, how she had taken care of every detail.

She stared at the plastic Peter Stuyvesant poster on the cracked wall. Why had she come back? Why had she not forgotten her promise? Why could she not merely live with the memory of it, live on into the future she had made for herself?

It was not too late, she thought. She could get into the car now and turn back. Go straight to the airport and back to London. Tell Harry that the meeting had gone well, that all the outstanding issues had been resolved. Settle back into her life in London and look forward to being his wife.

She buckled on the armour of her logical, legal mind. After all, she made herself argue, what more did she owe her mother? She had repaid *Ah Ma* in full – and more – with all the money she had sent over the years. Jasmine was still now telegraphing her large sums every month, securing her old age and anything she could possibly want. Every week, for ten years, Jasmine had written home and every week she'd go to her post office box, hoping for her mother's reply. But she never got any letters. Her mother had never written to her in all these years. Not one letter. She owed *Ah Ma* nothing more, she said to herself without conviction. The promise had been made in a moment of heated feeling. *Ah Ma* herself had warned her not to make it – surely, she would not hold Jasmine to it now, after all these years.

But the truth was something simpler. Jasmine had always known it. This anxiety and indecision was only the web she had often woven for herself to stop that very simple thought. Jasmine breathed out a long breath and felt her mind go quiet. It was simple. She was tired – tired of the masquerade, tired of her desire to escape, of her duty to escape. She wanted to go home.

Jasmine paid for the coffee and walked to the car. She pulled out into the traffic and, at the lights ahead of her, turned right, following the sign towards Taiping.

* * *

Mrs Fung filled the tiffin-carrier with vegetables fried in *belacan* (a spicy shrimp paste), curry kapitan (chicken curry made with lemon grass and coconut cream) and steamed fish. With a bamboo pole, she lifted it onto one of many hooks high on the ceiling. Each was labelled with the name of a customer.

At three ringgit a time, she made a good income from her meals-you-collect service. She would have enough over the next years for a comfortable retirement. The gods were continuing to be good to her, she thought, with surprise.

Mrs Fung was almost sixty-five, but a lifetime of disappointments had not bowed her. She carried her small frame with dignity and her soft bright eyes looked out at the years of struggle that came and went. She still wore the old-fashioned Chinese tunic with its high collar and snap buttons trailing diagonally across her breast. It was stiff with tapioca-paste starch and immaculately ironed. She wore her hair, which was still dark and abundant, in a tight bun. Her only indulgences were black tailored trousers from the supermarket on Kota Road and a jade bangle.

She lived on the edge of Taiping beyond Night Soil Bridge from where, only twenty years ago, the night-soil bearers would empty their urns. On the far side of the Chinese cemetery, her house was wooden, dating back to 1898. It sat back from the road down a narrow rutted lane. On all sides, the garden and compound protected it from enquiring eyes.

Her garden was the daughter and also the sons she had lost. It burgeoned with a profusion of beautiful plants – red hibiscus, violet bougainvillaea, fragrant white gardenia. The bleeding heart creeper speckled its red and white flowers across the fence. Along the verandahs hung orchids, the white moon orchid and the dappled tiger.

And above all this towered the flame tree. Its smooth limbs reached out to the sky, its abundant green spreading high above the house. In the wind, its leaves sprinkled the garden in a flurry of jade and ochre. In bright sunlight, the translucence of its canopy against cotton clouds gave it a yellow glow.

Mrs Fung carried the organic waste out to the compost heap. She lingered among her cherished plants, smiling at their fragrance. Over the long, difficult years, she had found comfort in this, her only deep delight. With little money to spare, she would sneak cuttings from the Lake Gardens or woo seedlings from friends. But once a year, no matter how tight her budget, she would allow herself the pleasure of buying a plant from Wee's Nursery.

Those were occasions she hoarded like miser's gold. She would walk among the shrubs or potted saplings she coveted, deciding and deciding again on the one she would have for her own. And on the day she had enough in her biscuit tin behind the stove, her heart beating as she handed over the money, she would point to the plant she yearned for and take delivery of another dream.

She would never forget the year she bought the sapling that had now grown into the flame tree. She paused by the simple shrine at the foot of the tree. Kneeling, she removed the burned stubs of joss-sticks from in front of the red-painted tablet. She poured away the bowl of tea she had laid there early that morning. In the evening, she would pay homage again.

Across Asia, homemade shrines dotted the landscape. They honoured the spirits of the trees and rivers and forests. They remembered travellers killed in accidents on the road, pacified demons who lurked at the edge of the known world. Shrines honoured the dead of a family at the ancestral altar in the home, pampered the god of good fortune at doorways. Mrs Fung tended her shrine more dutifully than most and now, beyond her expectations, she had begun to reap the benefits in the late years of her life.

The *ang mo* would be coming again to see her that afternoon. She smiled. The white man came whenever he was back in town. When he was not, he would take the time to make a special trip just to see her. Today, she had made him his favourite dish of pork fried with potatoes and a dash of Lea & Perrins.

She listened for the sound of him at the front of the house. It was past two in the afternoon. He was late.

The last time he had been here, the neighbourhood had gathered to watch her command over this white man, whose forefathers had been their masters. He was mending her fence, stripped to the waist and tanned. Years in the outdoors had streaked sunlight through his brown hair. Absorbed in his task, taking down the rusty netting, setting right the posts, putting up the new wire mesh, he had not seen them at first. The little crowd gathered in the neighbouring gardens and stared from windows and porches.

They stared at her where she stood in the shade of the verandah – like the *memsahib* his mother used to be. They commented on his skin, how it was so unlike theirs, pinkish gold and furry with hairs bleached to whiteness in the sun. He caught her eye and grinned. They had forgotten that he could understand them.

Now, she tied on her broad-brimmed farmer's hat against the sun. She would have to water her garden again this evening, laboriously carrying the watering-can back and forth. She squinted at the clouds. The last rain had been a faint drizzle two weeks before.

Mrs Fung squatted and began to weed a flowerbed.

When she finally heard the verandah door swing shut and footsteps over the wooden floor it was almost four.

"Ah, you've come at last," she called, without turning. "I've been waiting so long."

*   *   *

Mrs Fung's words froze Jasmine in mid-step. She stared at the figure of the old woman squatting by the sunflower bed.

How small the garden looked, after all these years. And how frail her mother seemed.

Jasmine had walked through the familiar house, trailed her hand over the worn furniture she had known since childhood. Finding the house empty, she had come out into the garden. A rush of panic and claustrophobia and love swelled against her will. Now, these words, so casually uttered, had the force of an accusation.

Jasmine took a shuddering breath. The old woman looked round. They stared at each other. A tumble of emotions crossed Mrs Fung's face. She stood up with difficulty, trowel hanging in a soiled hand. Finally, she said, 'Jasmine. It's you."

Tears blurred Jasmine's vision. A band constricted her throat. She gave in to the grip of the past. She sucked in a breath with a sob. "*Ah Ma* – Mother."

They moved awkwardly towards each other. Mrs Fung studied her daughter. She was appraising the confident poise, the expensive clothes. Jasmine knew that the look of success stood before her mother and she smiled when *Ah Ma* nodded in triumph.

"You're getting married," her mother said.

Jasmine gasped. "How did you know?"

"For ten years, we've been dead to each other – as it should be. Now, you're here. There can be only one reason." Mrs Fung moved to embrace her child but stopped, her soiled hands hovering above Jasmine's pristine blouse.

Before she could withdraw, Jasmine enveloped her in her arms, breathing in the familiar smell of her mother and finding comfort again in the feel of her. Mrs Fung held Jasmine against her. She continued, laughing through her tears, "I told you to forget the promise. To forget me. But you didn't. You truly are a good daughter."

They spoke in Cantonese, the dialect of the girl Jasmine used to be. She closed her eyes. She *had been* a good daughter. Now, she felt ashamed. She felt ashamed of this old house and the memories it made her face, the father she had never mentioned in almost twenty years and the stain she could never wash clean. She was ashamed of the little old lady in old-fashioned Chinese dress, who could hardly speak English, who smelt of garlic and rose-water scent, whose ambition for Jasmine had changed her daughter's future. And, most of all, she felt ashamed of what she had come to say to her mother.

She had promised, that day long ago, to come back for her mother when she was getting married. Her mother would meet her husband, as was proper. *Ah Ma* would come to live with them, Jasmine had said fiercely, as was right.

"He'll know everything about me," the girl she used to be had declared. "And he'll still love me. Or he will not be the kind of man I want for my husband."

Her mother had smiled and stroked her hair. "It's better not to make this kind of promise."

But, after all these years, the old woman had remembered her daughter's words.

And she was proud of her. Proud of the integrity she thought Jasmine had retained and of the kind of man she thought her daughter had chosen.

* * *

Mrs Fung made Jasmine sit down on the sofa while she scurried about in the kitchen. Her excited voice maintained a constant chorus. "I think about you every day. Waah, how you've grown up!"

Mrs Fung brought a glass of iced lime juice for Jasmine and sat down opposite her. Jasmine tasted the sharpness of the limes from the garden and the sweet fragrance of the *pandan* syrup. It was the taste of her childhood. She sighed. Mrs Fung laughed.

The silence was awkward.

Jasmine noticed the patchwork coaster her mother had placed proudly on the cheap table in front of her. There were patchwork headrests on the chairs. By the screen door to the verandah lay a mat made of coloured off-cuts tied into an old gunny-sack.

Now that she looked, she also saw the egg cartons, reincarnated into seedling trays. A bunch of flowers bloomed from an old coffee jar. Through the screen door, she could see the flame tree, now grown so tall and shading a red-painted homemade shrine. This was home, and it was a past that could destroy the future for which she and her mother had sacrificed so much.

* * *

Jasmine thought of the sleek modernity of her flat, and Harry's house that declared his wealth and status. He displayed antiques from Oaklands, manly and European. Her interior designer had used modern decor from Heal's and Liberty's – Jasmine had not wanted anything old. "No second-hand goods," had been her instructions. Everything new, nothing from the past, not even someone else's.

She tried to imagine transplanting her old life and identity into her untainted Chelsea flat and could not.

"Tell me about this boy," Mrs Fung said. "The one you're going to marry."

"Well, he's English."

"Does he love you?"

"Yes. Yes, he does."

"Does he love his mother? You can tell he's a nice boy if he loves his mother."

"I think he does."

"What's his name?"

"Harry."

Mrs Fung repeated, "Hallee."

Jasmine looked down. She saw the glitter of her diamonds. "This is the engagement ring he gave me."

Her mother's eyes widened. She exclaimed, as she took Jasmine's hand, "Waah! It's real! Waah, Jasmine, he must really love you!"

After all these years, Jasmine felt a child still – like the day she had come running home with the results of the Oxford scholarship. She had not let her mother down. The sacrifices of the past had not been squandered.

"I've succeeded, *Ah Ma*, just like you always wanted me to."

* * *

Jasmine looked out at the flame tree. Her mother had planted it the night her father had walked out. It had been a thin sapling then. Now it arched high above, embracing them all in its protective calm.

Jasmine remembered the raised voices of that night, long ago, the sound of fist against flesh and bone. The frenzy and terror of that final row. The shame of what he had tried to do. And then the door had slammed, her father screaming his usual curses all the way down the path. "I should've left long ago. This time it's for real. You lousy bitch, I don't need you." And this time he had meant it.

Her mother had waited, pacing, pacing. The hours of the night ticked by. And suddenly, her garden saved her. She was out there in the darkness, clearing the patch at the bottom of the garden, pouring her years of sadness into the soil of her home, working feverishly, planting a life in the moment she had lost everything.

It had been more than twenty years since that terrible night. They had never heard from Jasmine's father again.

Jasmine suspected that he had gone to Bangkok where he always used to go "on business", staying for indefinite periods and returning only when he had run out of money. For once, his "business" venture must have thrived.

She could hardly remember him now. The last time her mother had spoken of him had been when Jasmine had won the scholarship to Oxford.

"You have a chance to change your destiny now," Mrs Fung had said. Her voice was matter-of-fact. "Your father is a gambler, a drunkard and a whore-master. He owes money everywhere he goes. He's travelled all over, always trying to do "business". Everywhere his name is bad. The name of Fung is rotten like he is.

"I took his name when I married him, as a wife must. Look at what it has done to me. I used to be a Lian. Lian Mei-ling. I could have had a good life. But I went against my parents' wishes for love. I took a man and a name from the sewer. That's where the name belongs. With that name, you'll always be in the gutter.

"You have a chance for a new life. You will have a new name that is related to wealth and success."

Jasmine Lian.

Her mother's gift of her maiden name had had the power of a charm.

It had taken her ten years to inhabit the transformation. No one ever knew the truth. That the wealth she had displayed had been bought with endless toil. She would skip lectures to work in the kitchens at the Randolph Hotel, making up with late nights in the Bodleian Library.

When term was over, in the anonymity of London, Birmingham and Manchester, she worked at two jobs, unrecognisable among the cities' foreign workers. And always, there were the sums trickling in from Malaysia, pitifully small after the conversion into sterling.

She had a copy of *Debrett* and a book on English etiquette, both well hidden. She mimicked the manners and speech of those with whom she wanted to be seen. She joined the Oxford Union and debated with men and women who later entered the Foreign Office, the City, the Inns of Court, the government. She pored through *Vogue* and dressed stunningly in clothes she could hardly afford.

No one even thought to ask if she was who she said she was. The past was gone. There was only the future.

How splendid the tree looked. In the years without her father's curses and his violence, it had flourished. There it stood now, its strong, smooth limbs reaching out to embrace the future. Its leaves were rich and fresh with life.

But Jasmine had never seen its blossom, that colour of blood and fire she had heard could set a forest ablaze. Her mother had longed for that flame tree. She had talked and dreamed of the scarlet canopy that would transform their little garden.

Jasmine wondered if, in all those years her mother had waited alone, she had ever seen the tree bloom.

*   *   *

Mrs Fung did not know how to behave with this successful young woman. She did not know what to say to her. Her daughter seemed a stranger even in her own country. Jasmine's clothes were too heavy for the climate, her hair expensively cut, her mannerisms unafraid, like those of a Western woman. Her voice was strong and confident and, wherever she was, she was not afraid of taking up space. Like the *ang mo*. And in the house she had kept her shoes on – as must be the custom in the West, Mrs Fung thought, but not here.

When Jasmine showed her a photograph of the man she was going to marry, it was like looking at the picture of a movie star – someone beautiful and powerful, who could conjure a multitude of dreams. This was not a man to whom she could be mother-in-law. "*Ah Ma*," Jasmine said. "Why haven't you been using the money that I've been sending you every month?"

She nodded sideways, only slightly, but Mrs Fung saw the nod encompass the whole house, its shabby contents, the garden and compound, her own clothes, herself. She shrugged. "I've been saving it."

"Why not use it?"

"I'm saving it for when I'm old. Or an emergency."

"But I'll be there for you."

"You've been a good daughter," Mrs Fung said. "The sooner you leave this old life behind, the sooner you will be free. I am an old woman who has lived out her life. It's *your* future you must look to."

Jasmine could not meet Mrs Fung's gaze. It was as if her mother had seen into her heart.

They sat there, both searching for something more to say. And then they heard the voices – laughter and chatter – coming down the pathway. "He's here!" Mrs Fung said.

She hurried out to the front verandah, leaving Jasmine to follow.

3

As he strode down the pathway, the neighbourhood children swarmed around him. He was in his early thirties and had the stroll of a man comfortable in rough terrain. His khakis and hiking boots were dusty and well worn. A white cotton tunic of Indian origin caught the breeze as he moved, fluttered against the lines of his torso. He was tall and lean, and had the healthy strength of an outdoor labourer. At first, he did not see the women.

He was tanned from years of working in the sun. As a boy he might have been described as pretty but maturity had etched complexity into his features. At rest, his face might have seemed too serious but now, as he laughed at a boy's joke, it was animated with warmth.

On the front verandah, Jasmine stood very still.

Mrs Fung slipped into her sandals and hurried down the steps into the courtyard. "You're here! Look who's come home!"

He looked up towards Mrs Fung. His eyes were so clear you could see the sky in them.

"Luke," Jasmine murmured. And then she closed into herself, watching without expression.

He broke away from the children. He called to Mrs Fung, using the old Chinese name he had always used, "Fung *Cheh* – Older Sister Fung."

Leaning down, he enveloped her in his arms. He spoke to her in Cantonese, greeting her in the traditional way. "Fung *Cheh*, have you eaten?"

"Silly boy, don't be so formal with me! I hope *you* haven't eaten – I've made your favourite dish."

"I've been dreaming of it. All I've had to eat in Sri Lanka was curry and more curry!"

Jasmine watched them approach. They seemed so relaxed together. He had his arm around her mother as if he were her son. The old woman had lost the edginess she had had with Jasmine. She laughed with the young man as she used to do long ago with her daughter. Jasmine stiffened, unable to control her jealousy. There was something else too, a lightness in her spirits suddenly that she preferred not to acknowledge.

"See who's come home," her mother was saying.

Luke glanced up, smiling. His gaze focused on the elegant young woman on the verandah but he did not recognise her. His smile became polite. And then he knew her and his look changed. It was only a moment, a flickering of emotion wavering over his features. And then his smile was wide and friendly. It was only a moment but Jasmine had seen it: the tightening of the lips, the hardening in his eyes.

Or had she? She looked hard into his face as he came up the steps – his expression was warm.

She smiled back. It felt to her like a grimace.

She could see the day-old stubble on his cheeks and the crumpled state of his clothes. A sheen of sweat filmed his skin. He smelt of his long journey and that familiar hint of musk and spices.

"Jasmine," he said. "Welcome home."

She braced herself for his bear-hug.

He reached out his hand to shake hers. It felt rough.

"Aah, it's so nice to have you both here," Mrs Fung fussed. "I'm such a lucky old woman. My daughter and my good boy, here together. Come, come."

Luke took off his shoes and followed Mrs Fung barefoot into the house. Jasmine realised only then that she had been wearing her shoes indoors. She quickly slipped them off.

"I'm sorry I'm late," Luke was saying. "I had to go straight from the airport to a meeting with new clients. They wanted the best consultant they could get."

"Which is you!" Mrs Fung beamed.

"Yup."

"What about your trip to Sri Lanka? You haven't told me anything yet!"

Luke laughed. "Slow down, I'm back now for a while ... Hey, how's the fence standing up?"

"Good. Come, I show you." Mrs Fung took his hand and led him out into the garden.

Jasmine had no place here, not in the chatter, not in their lives.

She did not go outside with them. She needed these moments alone. Seeing her mother again had been more difficult than she had imagined. And then Luke – scruffier, older, but still the same. The same. Was she still unchanged, too, in spite of all she'd been telling herself? Jasmine leaned against the wall. She felt drained.

*   *   *

The red Mazda cabriolet pulled into the courtyard of the Buddhist temple on the edge of the shopping district of Kuala Lumpur. The roof was up, and behind the tinted windows the air-conditioning was on. Its legitimate number plates revealed that it was registered locally.

The temple was one of the last in the city centre, most of the others having been demolished to make way for office blocks and shopping malls. It had once been a residential house but layers of renovations had added annexes for altars, statues and prayer rooms. The roof teemed with dragons, clouds and gods.

It was late afternoon.

The Mazda parked askew across two spaces. Ronnie Tan emerged into the hot afternoon. There was a swagger to his manner. His early-morning visit to Wong up in Kampung Tanah had gone better than he had hoped. He had not had to use the switch blade.

He was in his late thirties. His features were angular for a Chinese, his eyes narrow and hard. His short black hair was brushed back with a touch of Brylcreem. He was small but moved with the confidence of a street fighter. He was now dressed in grey slacks, blue Ralph Lauren shirt and a Paisley tie. A row of pens emerged from his breast pocket. His non-prescription Alain Delon glasses gave him a serious, office-bound demeanour.

He owned a security company offering personal and property protection, surveillance equipment and profile investigation. He was an intensely religious man and contributed an impressive sum every month to the temple. A figurine of the Buddha graced his dashboard. A shrine occupied a corner of his office downtown. In his house in Bangsar, the recently developed residential district for the recently wealthy, an altar table stood in the hallway.

The feudal hierarchy of Chinese society was moulded into Tan's life. In his relationship with the gods and spirits – as with his family and business associates – there were levels of dues to be paid and favours to be bestowed. Gifts cemented friendships, oiled the wheels of business. Red packets of money given by father to child, elder to younger, superior to inferior confirmed duty and obligation. A favour granted was a favour owed in return. Nothing came for free.

Tan took off his expensive American shoes and left them amid the pile at the temple door. A sign on the wall above said 'Beware of Shoe-thieves'.

In the main hall, Tan bought joss-sticks, lit them with his Zippo, then padded across the tiles and stood before the ornate altar. It bore brass urns of joss-sticks burning out. Wooden tablets with prayers in Chinese characters stood like sentinels across the surface. Devotees had left offerings of tea, fruit, cups of liquor. He shook his joss-sticks with both hands in obeisance to the gods and bowed. Then he stabbed a few sticks into one of the urns. He repeated the ritual until he had distributed his clutch of incense.

He went over to the cash counter by the side of the hall. A woman was paying for a jar of fortune sticks to ask the gods for guidance. An old man rented two mussel-shaped fortune-counters to seek advice. Tan paid for prayers to be said for his current business enterprise. For an additional sum, he also arranged for offerings to be made. As an afterthought, he gave the monk five ringgit for prayers to be said for Wong.

"Wong Keng-wi," he repeated as the monk wrote the name on a slip of yellow paper.

Outside again in the muggy heat, Tan waited to cross the busy road to his favourite coffeeshop. He pressed an autodial combination on his mobile. He did not introduce himself when the line picked up. He spoke in English. "Initial contact made."

"How many?"

"Six out of the ten. Wong only a few days ago. So far, all positive."

"Good. And the other four?"

"Maybe ten days."

"They are the most influential – ah – subcontractors there. We must have them. Wong's position in the Business Association makes him our most useful contact."

"Now he is part of our project, contact with the others will be quicker. So far, they all like the – um – fees. Their philosophies make them receptive to our proposals." Tan dodged the cars and jogged up the steps to the row of shophouses. "The remainder won't be any trouble."

"Excellent. Any information on those who might be ... of a different philosophy?"

"Some of my contacts have referred to them. I can find out more."

"Our sub-contractors will help us with those others. That is why we are contracting them," Tan's client said.

"Understood."

"Send me your interim invoice. There'll be a bonus for your fast work." Tan rang off.

The two-storey shophouses were the remaining buildings from the last century.

Elevated above the ground and enclosed by deep monsoon drains like moats, each shop overflowed its trade onto the five-foot covered walkway. Tan skirted grocers' baskets of dried goods.

The coffeeshop was just opening after the mid-afternoon lull. The hawkers spread their food on their stalls around the premises – roast duck, fried *kway teow* – "the best flat noodles in town" – beef ball noodle soup. Tan swapped gossip with the hawkers as he sat down at his usual table. He ordered a Carlsberg and treated himself to a selection of dishes. The boy, in singlet and shorts, called his order to the cooks. "And hurry it up! Mr Tan looks hungry today!"

"It's hard work doing business." Tan laughed. "Don't you love it?"

* * *

Mrs Fung served her customers in the kitchen but did not mention her daughter. She had the skill for silence of those whose life is owed to endurance.

Jasmine and Luke ate at the old stone-topped table in the living room, closed off from the kitchen and away from the windows. Luke handled his bowl and chopsticks like a native. Since Mrs Fung had left them alone, they had hardly spoken, busying themselves with the meal. In spite of herself, Jasmine glanced at Luke each time she thought he wasn't looking. It was nice to see him again, she allowed. And it was nice that he was being nice to her mother. So why could she not stifle the irritation that gnawed at her?

He seemed distant now they were alone, formal almost, as he passed her a dish or reached for the soy sauce. Did he still hold a grudge from their last quarrel all that time ago? She decided she would not let the silence unnerve her.

She looked up and found him staring at her. She stared back, mustering all her self-possession. A grin threatened to crease his cheeks. And his gaze was growing impertinent, as if he found her amusing! She looked away and pretended to ignore him. At last, he spoke, and the appreciation in his tone caught her off-guard. "You're looking very good," he said, in English.

She took in his tunic, his unshaven crumpled state and his rough hands. She was aware of her own expensively cut clothes, her immaculate hair and makeup. She tilted her head back in defiance.

"I know," she said.

Luke broke into a grin, as if she had said the funniest thing. He seemed to relax then.

He sounded almost happy. "You haven't changed."

The words stung Jasmine like an accusation of failure. They mocked her ten long years of transformation. They told her she was still just a pimp's daughter. She said coolly, "I see you're still slumming it among the natives." She indicated his tunic.

A flicker of surprise crossed Luke's eyes. And then he smiled. After all this time she still had not forgotten. He would give her the game she wanted. "Of course I've gone native." He waved a hand at her designer image. "Adapt to their customs and habit of dress and the locals are more likely to treat you as one of their own. You've gone native quite successfully over in Old Blighty. I'm just doing what you're the expert at."

"That's different."

"Is it?"

"I perfected my English to succeed." The old fury caught her full throttle at last. She let it carry her, fuelling the momentum of her battle. "I went to Oxford to succeed. I dress to succeed. You? You're just playing at Third World living."

"Playing?" Luke raised his eyebrows. "I was born here and I grew up here. You know that. I live here now – it's my home."

Jasmine laughed without humour. "Your mother used to hate it out here. I'm sure you're making her very happy."

For the first time, Luke looked annoyed. She had hit a nerve. But his tone was calm when he replied, "I don't think my mother cares much what I'm doing these days. My parents are back in San Francisco and she's too busy worrying about the Big One." He grinned. "She probably wishes she were back in this 'god-forsaken hole' as she used to call it. At least, there are no earthquakes here."

Jasmine was in the grip of anger and not yet ready to be sidetracked. She asked, in a conversational tone, "Since when did you get so friendly with my mother?"

"You went away. She was on her own. I'd come by whenever I

was in town. It became a regular habit. She was always more of a mother to me than Mom."

"Yes, I know."

"She misses you a lot. Talks about you all the time."

"*I* miss her."

"How long has it been? Ten years?"

"What are you getting at?"

"It's been a long time, that's all."

"Are you saying I don't care about my mother?"

Luke scrutinised her for a moment. "Sore point, is it?"

"Why, nothing of the sort. It's none of your concern anyway – how we arrange our lives, my mother and I! You're not part of this family. Whether I come back once a year or once every ten years – or never – has nothing to do with how I feel towards her!"

He put up his hands in a calming gesture but his smile infuriated Jasmine more. She went on, "What about you? You're still rebelling against your parents – no, against your mother. You always wanted to hang around us off-white people just to spite her. It's easy for you – anytime you get bored you can get a ticket out. We have to claw our way out of here – no easy escape and cushy life waiting for us over there." She stood up. "I created a chance for myself out of nothing. I got out. It wasn't easy to do that. I changed my life. I had ambitions and I achieved them. Just look at yourself. What have you achieved? What have you done with your life? I knew you would never amount to much. And I was right." She paused, gasping for breath. Her heart was pounding and she was flushed with anger.

He was staring at her in astonishment. His stunned silence filled her with satisfaction. Then he burst into laughter.

"What are you laughing at?" His laughter rolled at her. "Well?"

"Hell, I've missed you." Luke held her gaze in the blue of his eyes. "No one can give a good fight like you could. I bet you're a damn good lawyer."

He sat back in his chair and appraised her with a lover's eye. His smile was one of pride and respect. It was as if she were a prize that he had won. It outraged her. But before she could retort, he said, "Do you remember how you fought for the reinstatement of that kid at school? That punchy speech you gave Dr Han that got the PTA mobilised?"

"That was a long time ago."

"You spoke out for the kid. He would've accepted being expelled. His parents were too afraid to do anything. And the teacher would have carried on terrorising the weaker kids. You were only twelve at the time. You haven't changed – you've just got better." Luke beamed with old admiration.

Jasmine felt her anger slinking away. Why had she flown off the handle at him? In her confusion, she just wanted to get away from him but she said, "You egged me on."

"Yes, but only from the sidelines – I didn't have the same teacher, it was easy for me."

"Yeah." Jasmine couldn't stop her smile. "I was quite a hot-shot lawyer even then, huh?"

"You bet! Remember how you were always talking about what was fair and unfair? How it wasn't right that kids who were smaller or people who were poor or couldn't speak up for themselves always got bullied."

"That's why I wanted to be a lawyer."

Jasmine suddenly moved away. Why talk about all this now? It was all finished with long ago. She said, "My mother's taking a long time."

"So when are you coming back to open your own practice, like you always wanted?"

"I was young and idealistic back then," Jasmine said, deliberately harsh.

"You know what's happened to the kid you got reinstated?"

Jasmine shook her head.

"He went on to the agricultural college in Serdang and now works for the Ministry of Agriculture advising local farmers on new techniques and best management. I've worked with him a few times."

She did not answer him.

"Jasmine? You made a difference."

Making a difference. Jasmine looked at Luke. His eyes had always been the windows to the flame that powered him. He always used to talk about making a difference. She used to laugh at him. Don Quixote, she used to call him. Then, in England, she had made herself forget how much she missed him.

"That was all a long time ago," she said.

4

Luke left Mrs Fung's house as the sun began its descent behind the hills. Driving across the Lake Gardens, he turned towards the Waterfall at the foot of Bukit Larut.

Before Independence, Bukit Larut was known as Maxwell Hill. It stood at the outskirts of Taiping, a part of the ridge of hills that winged the eastern side of the town. It had been open to whites only and, in the nineteenth century, the English *memsahibs* were carried up the steep tracks in sedan chairs hauled by coolies. After the British left, the old hill station was still a hideaway retreat. The steep single-track road had now been tarmacked but its steep gradient meant that it could only be accessed by four-wheel drive. The local council ran a Jeep service from a base at the foot of the hill for non-residents.

When they were children, Luke and Jasmine would hike up to a clearing on the slopes and spend the afternoons with a picnic prepared by Mrs Fung. This was their favourite place. On a clear day, they could see the town and the rice fields and plantations all the way to the sea. In the evenings, fireflies came like faerie familiars to dust the darkness with light.

Luke found himself thinking about Karim, the boy who had been expelled for attacking a teacher. Jasmine had been twelve. Up there in Firefly Clearing, Luke had watched her forging the prototype of the fierce and successful lawyer she would become. "It's not fair!" she cried to Luke. "Ranjit was bleeding. Karim stopped *Encik* Adnan beating him. Mr Adnan's not even being told off! And Karim is expelled. No one's doing anything to make it right!"

"You could do something," Luke said.

Jasmine wrote down what she had seen. She persuaded her classmates to sign the petition. She went to the headmistress. She canvassed the members of the PTA. But the adults met her with complacence. "Karim's a bad hat," they said. "Don't worry about him, girl."

"Don't give up," Luke said, on a bright still afternoon. He was fifteen and his American father had instilled in him a belief in the power of the individual. "All you have to do is try. It's ordinary people who change things. People like you and me."

She stood on a rock, looking out over the slopes. The air was cool and fresh. The plains below stretched out, flat as glass. Looking up at her towering figure, Luke saw her passion stir. She said, "Anything is possible, isn't it?"

Tall against the glaring sky, it was as if, in that moment, she discarded the role of the powerless petitioner. In its place stood a fighter with a cause and an arrogant spirit. She said, "If *we* feel what they did is wrong, there must be others who feel the same. They just don't know it yet."

Jasmine went to the Treasurer of the PTA, Dr Han, whose daughter Mei, was in her class. She caught his attention: "Maybe he's beating Mei also but she's too scared to tell you."

"That stopped him!" Jasmine recounted triumphantly to Luke. They huddled on the back steps while Mrs Fung wiped down the kitchen surfaces after dinner. It was night and in the semi-darkness, Jasmine's excitement had the power of magic. It seemed to Luke then that, together, the two of them might hold the world to ransom.

"What did he say?"

Jasmine made a face of shock. "'Ha? Mei? What's happened to Mei? Are you telling the truth?' Then Dr Han looked at me like this, his eyes so narrow. 'You're Tommy Fung's daughter.' I could see what he was thinking – same as everyone always thinks." She turned away, bitterness in her voice.

"What did you do?" Luke asked.

Jasmine pulled herself straight, and when she turned back, she was strong and vibrant. "I said, 'Yes. I'm his *daughter*. I'm *not* him. I'm different from him.' And then before he could say anything, I rushed on. I told him everything, and then I just couldn't stop."

"'I am the top student in my class. If I'm playing the fool now, you can report me to the head teacher and I sure can get into trouble. I don't need to stand up for a boy who's nobody in the school. But it's like ... You always go to the PTA meetings, Dr Han. You don't have to go but you want to make the school a good school for Mei.'"

"It was like – I wanted him to believe in me. Me. You know? If he believed in me, I just knew he would believe in what I was telling him. Then I said, 'You don't have to do anything about Ranjit – maybe someone else can do it. But what if no one else does? What if everyone believes the teacher's version and doesn't ask us? There are no parents there at school to see. How do you know what they tell you is the truth?'"

The next week, Dr Han called an emergency meeting of the PTA and the district school inspectors were summoned. *Encik* Adnan was suspended and Karim came back to school a hero.

After school that day, Luke's laughter rang out in Firefly Clearing. "You changed things!"

For the first time, Jasmine seemed to recognise her gifts – intelligence, instinct and, most of all, passion. She was elated, a far off look in her eyes. He grabbed her. "You can achieve anything, overcome any obstacle!"

"I'll never forget seeing Karim walk back into class," she said. "I'm going to be a people's lawyer. I want to speak for them and fight for them."

As their excitement ebbed, they perched on the high rock, looking out over the plains. Jasmine began to speak, almost to herself. "When somebody hits someone else, it's ... You can never forget such a thing. When you've lived it, it's like a ghost always there even though the person's gone. You always remember the sound of a beating – a fist against bone, a slap, a kick in the stomach. You get to know the different sounds. When I saw the teacher hitting Ranjit, I was so scared – I couldn't move, I couldn't do anything. My father's gone, almost four years now, but I still get the nightmares. As if he's still there. I hear him cursing her, I can smell the brandy. And the horrible sounds of … of … And I hear her, trying not to cry so I won't hear. But it's going to be different now. I stopped *Encik* Adnan, didn't I? I won't be quiet, I won't shut up, I'm going to speak out from now on. I can change things! And I will, I swear it!"

Luke touched her, his palm resting on her back. She jumped, brittle with a pain he did not then understand. Her eyes were shrouded, as if they looked inwards at memories she rarely spoke of. Luke heard himself saying lamely, "Are you okay?"

Jasmine seemed to shake herself. Her face softened and she laughed. "Hey, I'm hungry!"

She nudged him off the rock. He spread out their picnic of coconut buns and curry puffs, and poured out tumblers of guava juice. He cried, "A toast! To the most amazing girl on earth, spunky little titch and lawyer *extraordinaire*. Look out, Oxford, look out, world!"

She tackled him, grabbing at his plastic cup. "Titch, huh?"

In the bright sun, her hair was glossy with streaks of light. Her creamy skin was soft and warm to the touch. They wrestled and shrieked with laughter. She smelt of honey and sweat.

As they munched buns, Luke fished out a well-thumbed paperback of Robert Frost's poems. "The foremost poet of America speaks to you."

It was a familiar moment. Luke loved Frost and Whitman, Wordsworth and any ballad. Jasmine loved anything short that rhymed.

He began to recite "The Road Not Taken", hardly glancing at the page. The poem described how a traveller came to two paths diverging in a wood. He walked the one that seemed to have been less travelled by others and it was that which made the difference to his journey.

He smiled. "You did something when no one else tried. You

took the road no one else did and –"

"And it made a difference. "Jasmine took his hand. "You were right – ordinary people, it's us who make the world we live in."

*   *   *

In those days, Luke's mother had already closeted herself in the air-conditioned cool of her room. Every afternoon, Mrs Fung would make him go to her. "You no argue. She mother," she would say in English.

The chill of the room made him shiver. The bedroom smelt of cigarettes and sherry.

"Darling, is that you?" Mrs McAllister lay in bed with a flannel over her eyes. She lifted a corner. "Lord, you look a mess. I've told you to wear your shoes in the house – do you want to turn into a bloody little native? And stop skulking by the door, you're as bad as the servant. Come and give your poor mother a kiss."

Luke did as he was told. Her arms closed around him and he pulled away.

"Sit on the bed by your mother." But he moved across to the dressing-table stool. She sighed. "You're so grown-up now. You used to like to cuddle, do you remember? You're getting just like your father. So strong. So silent. That's what I fell for in your father – the rugged outdoors type, so different from those chattering chaps back in Surrey. No doubt you'll make the girls swoon, too, when you're older. You'll bring back some poor little thing to this god-forsaken hole. That'll be such a lark, hey, darling? You men off doing whatever you men do and we girls waiting for you at home, wasting away in this heat and bored as hell!

"I'm sorry, darling. My temper's frayed these days. It's too hot, don't you feel it?"

Luke shook his head. "I like it."

"Your father's been gone for two weeks now. God knows when he'll be back. What keeps him away for so long, damn it? Tin mines are just hideous contraptions sucking up dirt and spewing out sand the other end. What's so complex that it keeps him away for months on end?"

"Mom, he's a mining engineer. He travels to different mines, it all takes time."

She scrabbled for a cigarette. "You'll be leaving me to go to high school soon. San Francisco! I was there in fifty-nine with your father – it's not bad for an American city. You'll be staying with your grandparents, which won't be so lovely. At least you'll be getting out of this stinking hole."

"Mom, I like it here."

"I, of course, wanted you to go to Winchester. But, no, your father wants you to grow up an American. Promise me you won't forget your poor mother, left alone in this ghastly hole?"

"Mom ..." Luke rolled his eyes. He should have gone to America two years before to start high school but his mother had been unable to bear the parting. His parents had argued again, his father torn between Luke's future and his love for his wife, his mother turning away from his father to appeal to Luke, *You'll catch up at school, won't you, darling? You're a bright boy. It won't do you any harm to stay here just a little longer, will it?* He had seen her terror and loneliness and he had nodded. Shrugged and nodded. And his father had given in.

"Promise me you won't forget me?" Mrs McAllister pleaded. "Life's so difficult for me ever since I married your father. Promise you won't forget me?"

"Yeah, sure. I got homework, Mom." He put the stool back. "See ya." In one fluid move, he pecked her on the cheek, strode across the room and was gone.

"See you," she said softly.

Luke's father had married his mother for her beauty and her laughter, like a peal of bells. "Don't be angry with your mother," he would say to Luke. "You should've seen her in those days. She could have had lords and she chose me. When we move back home to the States, I'll make it up to her."

John McAllister was a shy man who loved the solitary nature

of his work. In his twenties he had worked with mining companies in South Africa. Malaysia had been his first posting after their marriage.

Whenever his contract came up for renewal Luke's mother nagged him to apply for a promotion out of fieldwork. He would promise her the world, then stay on where they were. "A suit and an office. That's not for me. Maybe in a couple of years."

"I know he loves me," his mother would sigh. "But not enough to give up this damn tinkering with crankshafts and what-have-you."

Luke had seen his father's technical drawings, their delicate detail showing the skill of a craftsman. Imagining them into the giant steel and strength they would become, Luke saw the sum of his father in his work. It was more than just tinkering and it meant more to him than the love he had for his wife. It was who he was. His identity and his spirit were founded in what he did. In the moment of drawing, and out in the mines, he forgot himself in the dedication to the work and, in that same instant, he owned who he was. His wife envied him that.

Luke dimly remembered a time when his parents had been in love – when their delight in each other had been in their voices and eyes and smiles. Now, they played out a script, like actors in a play that had been running for too long. And then they would retreat backstage again – to the solace of work for him, and blame, for her.

It was to Mrs Fung that Luke would go with his successes and failures, hopes and worries. She laughed at his jokes and she knew the nicknames of all his friends. She had been with his family since he was six and by the time he was eleven, he was speaking to her in accentless Cantonese.

Luke and Jasmine would go fishing after school or lie reading in secluded shade. They left notes in secret places, using a special code. "The road less travelled" was the signal of important business, giving their jaunts an exciting buzz. "The road less travelled leads you to two coconuts in the waterfall", and they would meet at two o'clock by the coconut trees on Waterfall Road without fail.

They always had with them Mrs Fung's picnics – fresh watermelon juice or iced tea, curry puffs, pork dumplings, bean-paste rolls. Luke rode his shiny Raleigh and Jasmine raced him on the gardener's bicycle, standing on the pedals through the crossbar.

They swam in the network of streams at the Burmese Pool, sliding down the range of mini-falls. In the forests, they stalked bright birds and monkeys and, in rare moments, caught sight of mousedeer. They played with the children from the *kampung* nearby, amid the coconut groves and raised wooden houses.

In the evenings, if his father was away, Luke ate with his mother in the dining room beneath the circling fan. Mrs Fung served them between eating her own meal in the kitchen with Jasmine. He would listen to their quiet voices, watch for their shapes as they passed the doorway.

Increasingly his mother took supper in the cool of her room, and he would eat at the kitchen table then with Mrs Fung and Jasmine. He loved those nights in the glare of the fluorescent light, eating with chopsticks while the geckos ticked overhead in the fanless air.

When his father was home, or when his parents entertained, Jasmine helped her mother to serve, silent and without expression. His mother would be vivacious again, perfuming the night with Chanel No. 5. Their guests were other expatriates on a visit from Ipoh or Kuala Lumpur. They pined for their home countries and swapped jokes about the locals. The men talked about the money-markets and the women complained about the weather and their home help. Their children were all at school abroad, among their own kind.

His father was considered an eccentric in letting Luke attend the local school. "You liberal Americans really believe in brotherhood and equality, don't you?" the expats would laugh.

Luke sat, encased in socks and shoes and smart clothes, glancing always to the freedom of the kitchen and straining to catch Jasmine's eye. Those nights, she would never return his gaze.

Later, when Luke was studying in America, he would return

each year during the summer vacations. They tried to preserve the friendship of their childhood but there was a strange awkwardness. As if they knew that soon the road they travelled on would diverge and nothing would be the same again.

In America, Luke did catch up, working at his studies as if possessed. He excelled in the sciences at school, especially Physics and Chemistry, loved Geography, played baseball, wrote for the student newspaper. At college, he majored in civil engineering and graduated *summa cum laude*. His postgraduate masters was in Environmental Sciences and Development.

"Why don't you want to live in America?" Jasmine asked Luke when he was back in the first summer vacation. "When I go to England, I'm not coming back. *Ah Ma* will live with me in London in a big white house with railings round it. In London, everyone is dressed smart and they all talk smart. Like in *The Avengers*."

Luke laughed. "I like it here. It's hot and I like the jungle. The food's not so good in America, not so much taste." He shrugged. "I was born here. This is home."

Whenever he was back they hiked up to Firefly Clearing. Wherever he was, his memories always led him back here, to where they had both been happiest.

Another time he said, "I'd like to make this place ours forever."

Jasmine said, "This is one place in Taiping I'll come back to – once a year, no matter where I am or what I am doing."

It was his first year in college and two summers before she left for England. She was almost seventeen, the boyishness of her childhood evolving into simple grace. Her hair was soft and thick on her shoulders and the face of a woman had emerged from the cocoon of the girl. Her pleasure at being with him again showed in every move and look and smile. She was so close he could smell the honeyed scent of her.

He put his arm around her. "It's our place, huh?"

"Nothing's ever going to change that."

"I'm going to build a house here one day," he said. "It'll be here on this slope –" He paced out the shape of the house " – with these rocks on the side, and the verandah would stretch along over here. So we can sit out and look over the treetops and down into the plains."

"And on a clear day, we'll see the ships out at sea." Jasmine laughed. "Will there be a swing on the verandah?"

"Sure."

"We'll sit and sway back and forth –"

"And drink your mother's iced lime juice –"

"And read poetry and talk about philosophy and justice and books and all the things we love."

"You got it." Luke smiled and watched her walk through the imaginary house, naming the rooms and intoxicating him with her delight.

*   *   *

Driving past the foothill station of Bukit Larut, Luke shifted gears down and set his Land Rover up the winding incline. The jungle soared above him on either side, singing with cicadas and humming with birds and insects.

Seeing Jasmine again, poised like a fashion model on the steps of Mrs Fung's house, he felt as if the ten years of their lives had never come between them. She pervaded every memory of his childhood, and now he suddenly knew that in those missing years, she had accompanied him in all that he did. Her physical presence that afternoon had moved him like the incarnation of a secret hope.

The light had deepened to velvety green as the day faded fast. Luke turned off the track into a concealed private entrance and wove through the thickening layer of bush. The track was narrower, simply paved with stones, winding upwards still.

He remembered their last meeting there in the clearing. Jasmine had been almost eighteen, about to leave for Oxford. Their excursion had begun with such hope, the increasing tensions between them laid aside for that one last time. He remembered how he had longed to touch her then, to reach out and stroke her hair, feel the softness of her cheek with his fingertips. But he had not, and when she had told him she was never coming back, everything changed.

"What do you mean? Never?" he had said, in disbelief, when she'd told him the plans she and her mother had made. "Your mother wants you to do that?"

"She made me promise."

"What?" Luke did not believe her. "What about your ambitions? To be a people's lawyer? I don't understand you any more. In the last few years all you've talked about is making money, getting rich, getting ahead. You were never like this before I went away. Why won't you come back? Why not stay on here? I'll be back in a few years after college. We can still –"

"We can still what? Be the same? You, the little master, and me … what? Nothing, no one, still in the gutter waiting to be bought! I am your servant's daughter." Her voice rang into the empty sky. "And Tommy Fung's daughter."

"I don't care. It's never mattered to me, you know that."

"But it matters to *me*. I don't need your permission, little master, to feel what I feel."

"That's not what I meant! To me, you're just you."

Jasmine raised her hands, a furious growl surging from her. "Don't you get it? These are the facts. I'm Tommy Fung's daughter and everyone knows it – even as far away as KL. Everywhere I go, men ask me for favours. Every job I try to get, all the people there know – the women think I'm a tart already, the men bet on how much I charge and what I can do. If I stay I'll never be anything more than what they want to make me. Why can't you understand? Or maybe that's why you want me to stay, little master – sit, stay, beg, fetch, open your legs!"

"Stop it!" Luke shouted over her. He had to yell it again and again before she stopped. He was shaking with rage, staring at her in frustration. There was so much he wanted to say – to tell her how angry it made him, the way people treated her, how he didn't care who her father was and she shouldn't either, how he wanted to help her against them all. But he didn't know where to start. Or how to start. He wanted to tell her how he felt. But what did he feel? They'd been such close friends, almost like brother and sister, and now ... What was she to him now?

"Jasmine ..." he began. He was almost twenty-one. He had dated a few American girls at high school and college but suddenly none of them seemed to matter. All he could think of was he would never see Jasmine again. He had imagined that nothing would change and that when he came back for good in a few years, she would still be there. He had not thought what their relationship might become – only that she would always be a part of his life. Perhaps, in spite of every ideal he held, Luke thought, he was just the spoilt little master she said he was. "Jasmine, don't be like this. Let's talk. I know things look easier for me and maybe I take things for granted."

"There's nothing to talk about," Jasmine said. Her face was hard but her eyes watched him with pain. For a moment, she seemed to gather her strength for the final assault.

Luke opened his mouth to speak, his next words rushing up to startle him. *I love you.* They hovered unspoken on his lips. He'd never said those words to anyone before. Caught off-guard, he stared at Jasmine, light-headed and speechless.

She rushed in, baiting him, "Things don't just *look* easier for you, they *are* easier. You've never had to work for anything in your life. Whatever you want, it's there – nice house, respect, the best education in the world. You don't know what it's like to scrimp and save and fight every inch of the way for what you want –" She faltered. She seemed to hesitate over her next words but she recovered, pushing on icily, "You're just like your mother – whining, self-pitying and helpless without your servants."

"That's below the belt!" Luke cried. But he caught himself. He mustn't allow this raw nerve to distract him. Jasmine was furiously rooting around the picnic spread, collecting her things – a book, a water bottle, her sun hat. She did not look at him. She was going and he didn't know how to stop her. He tried again. "Why are you being like this? Let's talk ... Don't go with this crazy fight like the last thing we ever –"

He went up to her but she pulled away.

She said, "I have to go." She kept her face averted and started to move away.

"Wait! Jasmine, I –"

She snapped round. Her eyes were bright but her voice was held in tight control. "I'm going to Oxford and I'm going to succeed. No one will know me so far away over there. I don't need you, I don't want you in my life. Just leave me alone. Over there I can be who I want to be. And I'm going to be somebody. I'm going to be rich and powerful. I'll show them. I'll show you. I promise." And she started down the hill.

He stared at her back as she strode down the path. She had been happiest here, he thought incongruously, she'd told him so. And he didn't know how to stop her walking away.

He felt the stinging hurt of her words. He wanted to yell after her, hurl abuse just to see the barrier she had pulled between them crumble into tears. But he couldn't. He wanted to go after her and tell her that he loved her, that they'd work it out, he'd protect her, give her everything she wanted, make it easy for her like it was for him. But something stopped him. A horror and a dread of what they might become on the hopes of such a promise. A resentful, unhappy invalid and a distant, disappointed man – wavering images of his parents flickered through all his memories.

Exhausted, suddenly, he slumped on a rock. He sat there for a long time.

*   *   *

Seeing her again in her expensive clothes and Italian shoes, Luke knew that Jasmine's ambition had hardened into success. She had the same lithe figure as the girl she had been at eighteen but each of the passing years had traced itself about her – in the firmer set of her jaw, in her poise, the steadiness of her gaze, her authority, her forgetting of her Asian self.

She was more beautiful than he had ever remembered.

He arrived home just before the sudden darkness of the tropical night. The forest opened into a clearing and, in the brief twilight, the shape of the house emerged from the wilderness.

It was built in the style of the Malay longhouse, borne off the ground by stilts of brick and stretching one room nestled against the next across the gentle slope. The frame was wood, unpainted but varnished against the elements. Tiles of olive green cloaked it against the background of trees. Natural rocks dotted the cleared area round the house but it was difficult to tell where the compound ended and the forest began. The verandah looked out over the folding hills, and far below, the lights of Taiping shimmered like starlight on water.

Jasmine had never seen this house. Luke had invited her to visit as he left but she had declined. "I'm on a busy schedule, thanks all the same."

Luke's weekly housekeeper had remembered his return today. The house had been aired and the lights were on. A wood fire burnt low in the brick fireplace in the main living area. Now the sun had gone, the air was chilly. Luke removed the fireguard and stoked up the flames.

He poured himself a shot of Jack Daniel's. It was good to be home.

He picked up the telephone and dialled his voicemail service. There were two messages. The first was from Susan. She was a lecturer in Development Economics and Sociology at the Science and Economics University in Penang where Luke occasionally taught. They had been in a casual affair for the last three years. "Hey there, welcome home," she said. "Dinner tomorrow night? We've two months to catch up on."

The second was from Dr Kenneth Chan. The doctor had called the urgent meeting earlier that day. "I'm very happy that you agreed to advise us," he said now, from Luke's electronic mailbox. "Let me know when you want to start your survey of the Kampung Tanah region, the sooner the better. Our budget is tight and we can't pay travel expenses. But you can stay with me and my wife – she's a very good cook!" He gave his contact numbers and rang off.

Luke put Zoot Sims on the old gramophone, and as the rich tones of the saxophone crooned into the night, he hauled his tote bag into the study. He began to unpack – notebooks and papers, a Dictaphone, a torch. Feeling in the inner pocket, he pulled out a Smith & Wesson .22 revolver. He had been licensed by several Asian countries to carry a gun. His environmental recommendations to government bodies and Third World development agencies could cause anger among those with vested interests. Private companies faced financial losses where their dams or factories or logging projects would have to be redesigned or abandoned. With anger came repercussions.

The week before, in Colombo, he had been tailed by two men on a scooter, petty thieves or more sinister agents, he did not know. He had managed to lose them in the bazaar. It had not been the first time he had been followed on that assignment.

But so far, he had been lucky. There had been incidents on other assignments – shots fired from a car in the Philippines, a roughing up in the streets of Jakarta. He prided himself in his integrity, and these attacks only fuelled his determination to finish his job without deviation from the truth.

He had never yet used the gun. Still, as usual after every trip, he unloaded and cleaned it, checking every detail. When he finished, he reloaded it and went through to the bedroom. He unlocked the drawer by his bed and slipped it in beside the box of ammunition.

There was an old photograph at the bottom of the drawer. He pulled it out and looked at it for a moment. Tucking it into his breast pocket, he slid the drawer shut.

Outside on the verandah, he settled into the swing, the bottle of Jack Daniel's on the table beside him. In the darkness before the moon rose, he watched trails of light bobbing near the rocks. Jasmine used to call it "the dance of our own private starlight". Did she remember it still, this wonder at the light of fireflies? Did she remember this place, this clearing of fireflies, their own special place?

He looked down at the photograph in his hand. In the waxy light from the windows behind him, he could see the laughing young man and girl. It had been taken on that last picnic here in the clearing, on that rock to the west. They had not yet had that final acrimonious quarrel.

He had set the camera on the self-timer and they had clambered up to face it. They keeled to the side, arms entangled in a flurry of tickling. Jasmine's hair streaked across her face. They were screaming with laughter.

He'd sent her a copy soon after their quarrel, to the post-office box address in Oxford. She had never replied.

Their old laughter in the picture was infectious and Luke smiled. The moon was rising now, low on the horizon. It seemed swollen and yellow, as if awakened from sleep. Luke stared out at its slow ascent over the lights of Taiping and saw only his memory of Jasmine.

Had he really known this girl he'd never been able to forget?

5

Tan poured more brandy into the two glasses and added ice. His brother reached out for his drink and continued his story. "So the gun is there on the table in the scarf I brought it in. I count the money and it's two grand short."

Tan settled back in the leather armchair. It was almost three weeks since he had made contact with Wong. Tan and his brother were in his study at home, cooled against the tropical night by German air-conditioning. The whole house was air-conditioned. Inside its sealed atmosphere, there were no mosquitoes or geckos. Noises of his family elsewhere in the house were muffled in the electric hum. It was civilised.

"I say, 'Pay up. The price is fifteen thousand ringgit.' The punter says, 'A friend of mine thought that was too much.' So I say, 'You doing the deal with him or me?' I put the money in my pocket and pick up the gun. I play with it, you know, like just idling away time, and then I put the bullets in." Kidd gulped some brandy and guffawed. "And the guy he just stands there. So then I point the gun at him and ease off the safety. I say, 'Your smart friend, where is he now, ha?' Whoa! He's shitting himself. Says he doesn't have it on him, tries to say he's having money problems. I touch his face with the muzzle – ha, you should've seen his look. Like 'Wah!'" He made a comic face of terror.

Tan interrupted, "So he paid."

"Yeah. I dunno what he wants the gun for – what a pussy bastard." Tan's brother swallowed more of his drink and waved impatiently. "And you know what I said? I said, 'Anyone try and trace this piece – or me – and I'm gonna come and blow your fucking brains out.

You open your mouth to anyone and you don't sleep afterwards and you grow eyes behind your back – 'cos I'll come for your blood.' Ha! Right up in his face like this, my voice real low and I roll my eyes a bit. Scared the shit out of him!" Kidd roared with laughter.

Tan said, "What the punters do with the weapons after the deal is up to them. But we don't get involved in killing. That was close to the line."

"No, man. I wouldn't have pulled the trigger. It was just to frighten him."

"He might have tried something. A struggle – the gun goes off. Ease up on these deals for a while, a few as favours. That's how it started and that's how I want it to stay." Tan sighed. "How many times have I told you? Discretion. Low profile. That is why we are successful."

Kidd made a face but said, "All right, stop nagging, man."

When the brothers had been in their teens, Tan had got into calling him 'kid' and somehow the tag had stuck. Kidd was now in his late twenties and wore the name like a battle scar, spelling it with two Ds as if it might be an American hero's. It sat oddly with his street-boxer's physique and hard, mean face.

It was Kidd who controlled the hit-and-run transactions – supplying a single weapon that could not be traced, a one-off intimidation of someone's wife's lover. Behind the taxable profits of their security company, these favours for well-off clients were a lucrative sideline. They were kept within the family members whose trust could be depended upon. Tan, his brother Kidd, another brother and several cousins. Tan himself did not like matters involving personal affairs. Revenge, jealousy, anger, hatred – these were unstable factors that made customers unreliable and ultimately dangerous to his informal business.

He preferred the long-term commercial matters that he handled for selected associates. He liked their simplicity. There was no room for unstable passions. The objective was always the success of the associate's enterprise: last year, his prolonged intimidation of an auto dealer's rival led to the folding of that rival's business and the continued profit of Tan's client's monopoly; the favours granted to the businessmen of Kampung Tanah would yield lucrative results for the company paying him. The sums at stake in such matters were millions and sometimes tens of millions. These networks could be stable over a period of many years. Those involved had too much to lose to act unpredictably and this containment of disharmony appealed to Tan's sense of the inherent order of things.

Their security company had grown out of their father's tiny locksmith's shop where old Mr Tan had huddled over his tools for more than four decades. Tan had left school at ten to help with his father's business. In the eighties, Malaysia and South East Asia boomed with the rest of the world, and as the populations grew richer they acquired more things that needed securing. With the public face of their business, Tan's company offered additional services: on top of the standard fare of grilles and sliding gates, chains and padlocks, they could provide home security assessments, electronic surveillance and movement detection equipment, uniformed patrols with guard dogs. A spate of kidnappings – children of millionaire tycoons snatched on their way to and from school, birthday parties, private lessons – opened up the market for personal bodyguards, and Tan could provide the most reliable and most discreet service. Over the years, he expanded to Indonesia, the Philippines and other countries in the region where his clients needed him.

It was time to call his client. He went out onto the balcony. The night air was humid after the cool of the study. The house occupied a quarter-of-an-acre plot on the side of a hill. The lights of KL glittered before him. As he waited for the line to connect, Tan switched on the spotlights to illuminate the side of the house.

The original kernel of the house lay within an ornate shell of extensions that stretched disproportionately over the plot of land. The house now went on right up to the boundary fence. What little yard remained was paved with stone tiles. The architectural style was an ostentatious mix of Florentine balconies, Greek columns and modern Americana. Tan took in the scene with pleasure. His father had brought them up in a cramped apartment above his locksmith's shop in Pudu, a downtrodden area that was still undeveloped. The old man had lived a few years to see this new house. It made Tan proud to think of it.

"Hello," the voice said, on the other end.

"Nine sub-contractors are now awaiting instructions." Tan spoke in English.

"Good. Number ten?"

"Kamaruddin. I recommend that he is not involved." Kamaruddin was the town councillor. "The fewer officials we have to deal with, the more secure the project."

"What are his views on progress?"

"He is in favour of anything that can bring economic improvement to his community. He'll be persuaded by the combined business interests of our sub-contractors."

"What about those others?"

"The town doctor. A Christian. Western-educated, mainly English speaking. A do-gooder with firm principles. Dr. Kenneth Chan. He's engaging an environmental adviser."

"What for?"

"To assess each proposal. And to advise on protest action, campaigning – things like that."

"Hm. Any others?"

"He has a few allies. Ibrahim, the head teacher of a local school, and Sarojaya, a young lawyer."

After a thoughtful silence, his client said, "Our sub-contractors can start earning their fees. As his trusted neighbours, they will persuade him to embrace progress."

"They should offer indirect advantages to him and his allies. Chan won't be interested in an outright fee."

"Exactly. And if that cannot persuade them, well, with men of principle, other, ah, inducements than fees may be needed."

"I understand." Tan hung up. He leaned on the balcony. His client had been referring to intimidation. Extra payments would be involved. Sometimes, Tan thought, men of principle were good for business.

* * *

The offices of Messrs Carruthers had been in New Square in Lincoln's
Inn, London for almost two centuries. Unusually for solicitors, the
firm had managed to grab a toe-hold in the prestigious Inns of
Court, the preserve of barristers' chambers. Over the generations,
it had grown to occupy a whole stretch of the square, of which a
velvet lawn was the centrepiece, dappled with flowers and shaded in
blossom trees. A stone fountain splashed in the sunlight. Inside, the
offices smelt of polished wood and parchment. Creaky staircases
punctuated the building, their steps worn by generations of
lawyers.

This was the England that had made history for a thousand
years and whose people had once ruled over much of Asia. Jasmine
could never forget that this was the world from which, not so long
ago, someone like her – an Oriental, a woman, the daughter of a
servant – would have been excluded. And this was the world to
which she now belonged.

Carruthers had become her family. Her colleagues were her
social circle. The men were articulate and charming, the women
confident and forthright. Arguments were settled with words
and an English detachment that always amazed her. Theirs was
the civility of a culture as far removed from the world she had
known as English meadows from a jungle landscape. Once a year,
her department and the construction-law department went on
a weekend retreat in Cumbria to refresh their bonds of common
enterprise. Now that Jasmine was a partner, she was also invited to
the partners' conference held at a castle in Scotland every summer.
Here, she participated in the policy making and social life of the
inner sanctum of the family. And, in return, she devoted to her firm
the best of her energy and spirit.

Jasmine's office had the feel of an artist's studio, with its
slanting ceiling and large windows. Filing cabinets and bookshelves
ranked along one wall. An oil painting of Venice looked over the
mahogany conference table. At the far end of the room, Jasmine

was at her desk. It was uncluttered but for the one file she was working on. This minimalist concentration projected calm and utter control. A computer terminal sat on the side desk.

Jasmine had been back in London now for over a week. In this place of order and reason she could almost imagine that her connection with Taiping had never existed.

The law, with its rules and regulations, its orderly progression of logic and theoretical argument, had been a bastion over the years against the contradictions of her life. It was orderly and precise, a sanctuary of certainty, drawing lines and boundaries against the unreasonable, bringing neatness to the chaos of human interaction.

But even as she tried to focus on the complex work before her, the days back in the world of her past intruded into her mind with an intensity she could not dispel.

She stood up and crossed to the window.

The night before she had flown back to London, neither she nor her mother had slept. Jasmine could not stop the memory of that evening embracing her. They had sat together on the sofa like they used to, Jasmine curled against her mother as the old woman stroked her hair.

"Have you seen how the flame tree has grown?" Mrs Fung said softly.

"Mm-hmm."

"So many years."

"Have there been flowers yet?"

"The flame tree takes many years." In the light of the old moon, they could see the ghostly shape of the tree brooding over the garden. Mrs Fung's voice lulled into dreaminess. "The first bloom may come only after twenty years. At first it will be a sprinkling of colour. Then, with each season, the red will be richer and the blossoms will spread thicker. Slowly, over the years, the flame will creep over the tree.

"This is the tree you plant when you believe in the future, my little one. You know why? You have to wait – almost one quarter of a century to see what you dreamed of when you first put the sapling in the ground. Twenty-five years – that's long enough for your own child to grow up and have children of her own." Mrs Fung stroked Jasmine's hand. "After those many years, the tree will be the most beautiful you will ever see. I thought my life was over the night your father left. But I planted this tree that night. You have to have hope to plant this kind of tree. Hope that you'll still be here to see it bloom twenty, twenty-five, maybe even thirty years into the future."

"And once it's planted, hope keeps you faithful. From each day to the next, you wait for it to take root, you hope to see the new shoots. You hope to come out into the garden and find the trunk thicker, harder. You fear to see it wither. You worry about bad soil, not enough rain, parasites. You hope and wait. And then, day by day, you know you have survived."

"No, it hasn't flowered yet. But soon. Soon it will. And I will be here to see it. I have waited so many years. It makes me frightened almost, to think we are now so close. Maybe something will happen and I'll never see it." Mrs Fung laughed softly. "You have a silly old mother, don't you?"

Jasmine squeezed her mother's hand. "You're not silly."

"The neighbours think I'm a foolish woman," Mrs Fung said. "They told me so. They said I chased your father away."

"He walked out! He beat you."

Mrs Fung continued, without hearing Jasmine, "They called me a bad wife. They still watch me in the morning and in the evening, I know they do, when I go and pray at the shrine under the flame tree. They say to each other, 'She is sorry now, look at her praying to the gods to bring her husband back, offering them sacrifices to watch over him. She is still waiting for him,' they tell people, 'and so she should be'."

"*Ah Ma*, it's been twenty years. They can't expect you to wait like this."

"It's not them who make me do these things. I have to pray at the shrine. I do it because I have to. That is the way it is."

"But it wasn't your fault."

"We cannot change what has happened. But we can pray for the future." Mrs Fung caressed her daughter's cheek. "You are the future. My precious one, I know you came back to keep your promise and take me to England to live with you and your husband." Jasmine stared at her. The blood pounded in her ears. In the last few days, it had become clear to her that her past had no place in her bright future.

She had been afraid to tell her mother that she could not – did not want to – keep her promise. Her own betrayal had kept her from sleep, tossing and turning through her mind the excuses, the justifications.

"*Ah Ma*, there is something we need to talk about –"

"Let me finish speaking first." Mrs Fung ran her fingers over Jasmine's lips. "Then you can say what you want to say. If you still need to."

"*Ah Ma* –"

Mrs Fung smiled. "I cannot come with you, my precious one. Look at me, I am too old to change my habits and live in a new country. This is where I belong. This is where I must stay."

"*Ah Ma* –"

"Shh." She laughed gently. "My English is no good. How can I live with people I can't talk to? I couldn't even go to the market by myself!"

"I could help you."

"Hush, my little one. My life is here. In Taiping. In this house. I always told you that you could escape and now you have – shh – that is enough happiness for me. I cannot leave here. That is not your fault. You cannot change how it is. Hush, now, listen to your mother, go back to England, go back to your life. You are free. Live your freedom."

Mrs Fung took her daughter's hand. "Now, my little one, that is all I have to say. Now, what is it you want to talk about?"

For a long while, the silence of the dark was punctuated only by the intermittent call of the tok-tok bird. When at last Jasmine spoke, her voice was hoarse. "It was nothing," she said.

Her mother had given her face, Jasmine knew that. In clinging to her life in Malaysia, Mrs Fung had released her from the promise. And she had saved face for herself by avoiding the humiliation of rejection.

Looking out now into New Square, Jasmine felt relieved. She had kept faith with the past but she could now also live free of it. And yet, the guilty shame clung to her like an odour.

Luke laughing at her. The memory slapped her in the face. How she had hated him laughing at her. He was so morally superior, wasn't he? Preaching to her about her mother.

And then there was the way he had looked at her. His clear eyes invading her, prying as if into her heart. His confident appraisal of her, approving, appreciating. As if she belonged to him.

She shook her head to clear her mind. She reminded herself she was back in London, far away from the clutch of the past. Here, she was safe.

Luke. She had not seen him again since that afternoon at her mother's house. She regretted declining his invitation to see his house. One morning, she had driven to the Jeep station at the foot of Bukit Larut on the impulse that one of the Jeeps could take her up to his compound. But, after idling there for a few moments, she had skidded round and driven back to town.

They had been friends. Luke and Jasmine. Jasmine and Luke. Just friends. And it had been a long time ago. Jasmine stared out at the lawn. Their lives had moved on. They had each become what their childish ambitions had drawn them to. And they had each turned out not at all as the other had hoped. Luke, with his teasing smile, his bright eyes. He lived still in a world of ideals and good deeds. Jasmine smiled. It was touching and, in some ways, she envied him his trust and his hope.

She was a realist. Life is tough and you have to make your own destiny, she would say.

And what would he reply, she wondered. Perhaps some lines from Wordsworth about daffodils and the beauty of nature. She laughed and shook her head. Luke. Quoting poetry and making a difference.

Then the silence caught her and she turned away from the window.

6

"It was rumoured that you had a heart but I never believed it." Nick Roberts strolled into Jasmine's office. It was seven thirty a.m.

He was in his early thirties and had been made up to partnership at the same time as Jasmine. He had sandy hair and his steely eyes assessed the world through Armani horn-rims. Jasmine thought him vain for a man and guessed that his grooming made up for an insecurity to which a man more sure of his standing – like Harry – would never have given in. Roberts wore Thomas Pink shirts, Hugo Boss suits and the ubiquitous braces of those lawyers for whom the gung-ho Eighties had not ended. He continued, "And now taking time off to shop for a wedding dress – you're losing your edge, my girl." Jasmine had not told the firm that she had been to Malaysia. Instead, she'd said she had taken time off to discuss wedding plans with Harry's family. Nick was the firm's young-gun litigator and had been trying to corner her for several days.

"There are times when a woman's touch can win more points than that macho horse-shit of yours," she said amiably. "And I'm not 'your girl'."

Nick roared with laughter. "Congratulations on your engagement. When's the wedding?"

"July fifteenth."

"You'll be in the thick of that Jordan Cardale project. What with wedding preparations and the honeymoon the timing's not ideal. JM won't be pleased."

JM was Julian Masters, the senior partner. One of his favourite sayings was that a lawyer's worth is measured in the revenue he brings into the firm. Jasmine recalled with amusement that her biggest client was among Carruthers' top ten income-generating clients and Roberts had been wanting a slice of the Jordan Cardale portfolio for some months. He had handled a few contentious cases for them but he did not have any profile with the CEO and controlling shareholder, Bill Jordan, who dealt only with Jasmine and the senior partner. It was Jasmine, in practice, who handled all the company's major international transactions, those routinely bringing in six-figure fees.

Roberts was saying, "Had lunch with JM while you were away. This is an important deal for Jordan, isn't it? He's missed a few chances to up his interests in Malaysia. This is the big one for him. He needs full back-up from us."

"He's got it. JM's not the worry-wart you like to make him out to be."

"I'm just offering to lend a hand. It's a major deal, coinciding with an important time in your personal life. I can keep things on the boil for you while you're away." Roberts smirked. "Contrary to what you think, I know about love and romance – I can be quite the New Man with my wife. So, just say the word."

"You're too sweet. But there's no need."

"Look, a court hearing I had tomorrow morning has been rescheduled. I could sit in on your meeting with Jordan – ideal chance for him to meet me, get my perspective on the issues. Then I could cover for you any time you need to take off."

"I covered all the bases before I went on leave. The construction aspects have already been reviewed by Benson Lee. His team will be dealing with those matters within Malaysian jurisdiction."

Benson was one of the partners at Seng & Mustafa, Carruthers' associate firm in Kuala Lumpur. Jasmine's role as leader of the legal team was a coordinating and supervisory one, bringing together the construction, finance, taxation and international-law strands. Exceptionally in the staid legal world, Jasmine had been made a partner at twenty-eight, three years after qualifying as a solicitor – the earliest that a lawyer could be given partnership. Roberts was almost five years older and had been JM's rising star until Jasmine had usurped him.

"My section here is full of capable lawyers who'll work with me on this. And there is *no* litigation perspective." Jasmine laughed. "Besides, non-contentious work is too subtle for you – you know, achieving consensus through an iron fist in a velvet glove, that sort of thing. Your 'bull-fighting in a china shop' approach really wouldn't do."

It was well known in the firm that Roberts enjoyed high-risk tactics and flashy showmanship. In his private life, so the office gossip went, he was riding a lucky streak, and his gambling instincts were keeping him in style. He'd bought a new Porsche last month with cash, and an ostentatious diamond bracelet for his wife. They went on trips to Hawaii and the casinos there. His wife had stopped work and he'd installed her in their enormous new second home in Oxfordshire. They were trying for a baby, Jasmine's secretary had heard from Roberts' secretary. As a lawyer, he won large out-of-court settlements for his clients but the partners knew that he skimmed close to the boundaries of professional ethics. So long as the boundaries remained intact, Jasmine thought, his continuing success would buffer him against any complaints from the others.

Roberts grinned. "The day will come when you'll beg me to help you out. Then we'll see whose approach will get you out of trouble."

When Roberts had gone, Jasmine finished dictating a letter. Since her return, she had been coming into the office from early morning to almost midnight. As a partner, she had to deal with administrative matters and supervise junior lawyers. As well as the Jordan Cardale deal, she was running four other major transactions. Newly appointed to these managerial and team-leading roles, she was keen to prove herself. She was in first, and the last to leave and took files home with her. This morning, she worked with stern efficiency, dictating faxes and memos, drafting and reviewing contracts and speaking with clients and other lawyers.

Those under her supervision queued up to discuss pressing

matters with her – the flotation of CompuNat on the stock exchange needed her senior input, Blinfield Industries was under threat from a takeover bid and her assistant needed her guidance. On her own matters – a client was acquiring a series of new factories, another was expanding operations into Australia, yet another was contracting for the purchase of new plant and machinery – she caught up with the back-log of the last few days.

Jasmine was entirely focused on her work. In her concentration, she had no other reality but the here and now. She had become again the powerful lawyer, certain of her opinions and without emotion.

She wrangled with opponent solicitors, pacing behind her desk and addressing their disembodied voices on the speakerphone. She charmed, cajoled, bullied them. Her weapons were her formidable mastery of the law and her commercial sense. She fought on the main issues, driving down her adversary with relentless logic. She conceded minor points – and in exchange, she would win the battles that mattered.

This was the part of her work she loved – to fight with words and wits, thinking quickly over a wide range of issues. An adjustment to the structure of a deal could have expensive taxation consequences. The reworking of a contractual clause to meet present needs could lead to long-term difficulties. It was the lawyer's role to find the right solution.

She knew that some junior solicitors called her arrogant. She preferred "confident in her own abilities". She had no patience with "paper-pushers", those average-grade lawyers who had made it more through tenacity than brilliance and who were slaves to textbook precedents, nor with "sharks" – those who loved to hold meetings and blustered their way through deals.

A good lawyer, she would say, makes the deal happen and makes it work, on paper and in the real world. On paper, she must be economic and elegant. In the real world, she takes no bullshit.

In the afternoon, she set aside time to draft a consortium agreement. Afterwards, she worked on an article for the *Commercial Law Digest*. At five o'clock, she dealt with the outgoing post, reviewing that of the lawyers under her supervision and signing her own. By five forty-five, the clatter of word-processors and the jangle of phones quietened to stillness. An hour later, the offices were almost empty.

Jasmine stretched, and cleared her desk of the last file. Outside, the sprinklers' *tchktchk-tchk* could be heard in the evening stillness. There were a few lawyers left – ambitious senior assistants and the younger partners. The senior equity partners would have mostly gone by now, at the wheels of their BMWs and Mercedes on their way to wives and children in Surrey and Hertfordshire.

Jasmine stretched and picked up the phone. She had not seen or spoken to Harry since her return to London several days ago. Whenever she phoned his house, the answering machine picked up. At his office, she was told he was in meetings or out with clients. They had so far communicated only through messages.

His last had been the night before. "Yah, hello darling, I don't know if you can hear me, it's bloody noisy in here." There was a pause as he took a swig of his drink. "Look, darling, dinner's off, I'm afraid – we've got some clients over from Germany and it's the old wine-'em-and-dine-'em routine. Bloody boring, I'd much rather be with you but work, work, work. Hell, you know what it's like."

He had sounded drunk. The message had made Jasmine irritable. She saw Harry in a pub in the City with a gang of rowdy men in suits. He drank far too much and it usually made him loud – loudly uproarious with his drinking companions and loudly sentimental with her. "It's part of the business." He would shrug, flashing her his lop-sided grin. "How to do it, how to win it. Oils the old cogs of the network, darling, you know how it is. You do it, everybody does it – dinner, Ascot, a box at Wimbledon, best seats at the opera house, a piss-up down the pub, it's all the same thing."

She dialled his office but the switchboard had shut down for the day. She tried his direct line – the voice-mail picked up. Same again at his house. She did not leave a message on either. She'd done so earlier in the day and she didn't want to seem the nagging wife already. In spite of herself, she tried his mobile phone but it was switched off. Finally, she called her own answering machine, but there were no new messages.

She had hoped to see him that night. She needed to see him. After her visit to her mother and seeing Luke, she needed to be rooted again in her life in London. Throwing herself into her work had helped but she longed to be with Harry again, to be reminded of how much a part of her life he was and how much she meant to him.

She went to the pantry and made some fresh coffee. She had a lot of work to do, she told herself, and tonight was as good as any to tackle it. A steaming mug to hand, she settled at her desk for another long night.

It was after midnight when she got back to her flat. She had made the cab stop outside her favourite all-night Chinese restaurant in Wardour Street to pick up a carton of sea-food noodles. She ate it hungrily while leafing through the mail.

After a hot shower, she climbed into bed, relishing the soft designer sheets, the smell of early morning through the open window. She was asleep as soon as she had settled into the pillows.

The nightmare came again. The same dark room and the same sobbing figure. The old terror let loose again in sleep. Her own face looking back at her in anguish.

*   *   *

The offices of Jordan Cardale PLC occupied the top five floors of a soaring glass and steel tower in the London Docklands. The meeting room where Jasmine sat beside Bill Jordan was on the top floor, commanding a view of the Thames westward to the City. It was eight a.m. the next day.

Jordan had gathered the design-and-build core for the Malaysian tender bid – the architect, the quantity surveyor, the structural engineer – and the civil engineering team for the infrastructure. Representing Jordan Cardale PLC were Bill Jordan and a junior director, Viscount Edward Danesleigh, a tall elegant man in his mid-forties.

Jasmine was the only woman among the seven men. She had been stiff and tired from her restless night but a brisk jog round the block before a rushed breakfast had helped. Looking round the boardroom, she reflected how such gatherings of men used to intimidate her. She would feel their eyes on her, that assessing look of male egos. Back then her reflex had been to appease them – at turns apologetic, ingratiating and over-respectful. Now, however, she knew how to use her gender – and her looks – to her advantage: how to flirt and charm to disarm a male opponent – that worked a dream – but if such apparent guilelessness still failed to win her what she wanted, she'd go in for the kill, ruthless and armed to the teeth with legal know-how and commercial strategy.

Today, the men round the table were part of the team she headed for the tactical briefing on the tender bid. She had worked with them in the past and they treated her now with respect – at least to her face, and that was all that mattered. It was irrelevant to her what jokes they would trade at her expense in the pub, as she knew men did to counteract the "bruisings" inflicted by tough female colleagues or opponents.

Jasmine had been the main lawyer retained by Jordan Cardale PLC for most of her career. Her advancement within her firm had been due to the sensational growth of this client over recent years: the fees she had earned from her work for Jordan had won her the partnership.

Bill Jordan presided over the meeting. He was in his late thirties and beneath his Gucci suit, he was hard and muscular from workouts in the gym. He had reddish gold hair and pale lashes. His eyes were cold and blue. He sat back in his chair, but his relaxed posture hid an impatient alertness.

He had been born in Peckham, his father a self-employed builder, and he had the pugnacious determination of a man who had made good – damn good – in spite of his circumstances. His driving will had built Jordan Cardale into an international player and his personal assets included a yacht, several Porsches, a penthouse in

Chelsea Harbour and houses and apartments around the world.

Danesleigh's title lent breeding to Jordan's construction and property management business. His function was to perform all the duties that Jordan himself had little time or respect for: he attended public relations events, wooed and entertained clients. He sat in on strategy meetings to consolidate his PR brief but had no decision-making power.

Jordan Cardale was one of six tenderers to bid for the construction of a new university town in Malaysia. There were two Malaysian bidders and the others were Indonesian, German and Korean.

"We're now eight months into the tender process," Jordan was saying. The site investigations and surveys had all been carried out. The core team were now finalising the design and costing aspects and reviewing the legal issues. "Bids will have to be submitted in September, still two months away."

The invitation to tender had been issued by a conglomerate of wealthy Malaysian business interests. It was led by Dickson Loh, a property tycoon, and included members of Malaysia's old monied families, who had made their fortunes in tin and rubber. There was also newer money, from men who owed their millions to the eighties property boom and speculation on the international money markets. They called themselves Consortium 2000. They proposed to launch a university for the twenty-first century, the first Asian university to rival the reputations of Oxbridge in England and the Ivy League institutions in the United States. Its curriculum of business, economics, politics, science and technology would be the envy of its Asian neighbours and, more importantly, of the West. Its students would be among the best in the world. As a private university, its revenue would come from fee-paying foreign students and international contracts for Research and Development services to industries and businesses. Wealthy benefactors, ranging from multinationals to private individuals, would be attracted from around the globe to bestow impressive endowments.

The design of the university, town layout and infrastructure had been thrown open to the tenderers. The contract would be awarded to the developer with the best design and most cost-efficient capabilities.

Jordan's original company, Jordan Construction Limited, had grown over the last decade through a combination of lucrative contracts and the acquisition of other construction companies. It expanded to international status when it took over the ailing Cardale Brothers conglomerate two years before. Jordan looked to the Asian markets just as the property bubble in England burst in the late eighties; while the building industry collapsed at home, he rode the crest of the Asian boom.

His Asian offices were in Kuala Lumpur to take advantage of Malaysia's advanced infrastructure and sophisticated financial markets. From there, he controlled projects in Indonesia, India, the Philippines, Thailand and Vietnam – hotel complexes, office buildings, shopping malls and condominiums.

"All our developments so far count for peanuts. Any jerry-builder worth his salt can put those up," Jordan said. "We should now be beyond that level of the game. We should be producing first-class top quality developments, the kind that people talk about and want a stake in – and will pay big money for."

He had not yet secured a large-scale high-profile project in Malaysia in spite of several ambitious attempts.

"To win in Malaysia's highly developed economy, you have to be a world-class player," Jordan said. "Malaysia is where we have to be seen if Jordan Cardale is going to amount to anything. Once we get in, we'll be among the best in the business. And we'll have put down the first marker in Jordan Cardale's Asian empire."

In world history Malaysia was a young country. In its infancy it had been known only as a British colony, producing tin, rubber and spices, named the Federation of Malay States or Malaya. Its labour force was made up of Malays, Chinese and Indians, all under the government of the British Empire.

The humiliation of the British under Japanese occupation during the Second World War coincided with growing nationalist feeling in the region. Shortly after the war, India gained Independence, and the Empire began to disintegrate into the Commonwealth. Malaya followed, reinventing itself as Malaysia and transforming its cheap labour into masters of their own fortunes.

In the decades that followed, the country grew from an agricultural and natural resource base to a manufacturing and industry economy. The new generations of Malaysians – descended from labourers, coolies and farmers – were educated as lawyers, doctors, accountants, bankers and industry chiefs. In the 1970s and 1980s, many went to the United States, Britain and Australia for their education and returned home with First World expertise and sophistication.

In the 1990s, the first Malaysian-manufactured car, the Proton Saga, was launched internationally and Malaysia graduated from being a developing country in economic terms to a developed one. The country currently enjoyed double the economic growth of Britain and a minimal percentage of unemployment.

Malaysia's success was part of a dynamic growth within the Asia-Pacific region. Singapore had surged upwards since Independence to a GNP *per capita* of almost one and a half times that of Britain. It was poised to inherit Hong Kong's thriving markets after 1997. Vietnam and China were becoming the new economic frontiers, embracing capitalism with a vengeance after decades of war and communism. The world was on the brink of a shift in economic and political power balance away from the West and towards South East Asia.

"The university project is our ace," Jordan said. "Anything it takes to win, we'll do it. This is the gateway to the big time. No one is going to stand in my way."

The site was located 400 kilometres from Kuala Lumpur, up in the hills of the Titiwangsa Mountain Range.

Jasmine watched the huge digital screen which hung on one wall. It was linked to a multi-media computer terminal and displayed a site plan of the proposed university and its town – *Bandar Universiti Titiwangsa*, Titiwangsa University Town. Two existing towns could also be seen: Ranjing in the foothills and, up on the slopes, Kampung Tanah.

Over the months, Jasmine had worked on the legal documentation and knew the site only from plans and drawings. For the first time, the vista opened out beyond the volumes of legal work to reveal the grandeur of this project. She watched with a rising tumult of mixed emotions. Until now, the likelihood that her work might throw her up against her buried identity had been academic, safe as she had been at her desk in her office in London. But she had already dangerously blurred the boundaries by using this project as an excuse to Harry for going back to Malaysia. In the months to come, her work for Jordan would take her back to Malaysia physically and mentally and the alarm she had been suppressing began to stir. She reined in hard on her emotions and forced herself to focus dispassionately on the facts that were being presented to the meeting.

David Scott, the architect, tapped a command on the keyboard and a computer-designed image of Titiwangsa appeared, precision mastered for colour, depth-of-field and quality of texture. This was the vision that Jordan Cardale would offer to the Consortium in a CD-ROM package accompanying their tender bid.

At the summit plateau, the university buildings stood high against a clear sky and flowed down the western incline. The town of Titiwangsa was further down the slopes, along the natural contours.

There were shops, restaurants, hotels, houses and apartment-blocks in a mix of neo-classical and post-modernist design. Large tracts of land were given over to wealth-creating recreational activities, flattening the hills for golf courses, riding and a themed adventure park. The Consortium would control the university and some of the commercial and residential sites but much of the land set aside for the new town would be available for sale to other developers. There would be phased development over a period of ten years. The infrastructure and Consortium-owned sites would be constructed by the winning tenderer with the university buildings as part of Phase I. Phase II – the construction of recreation facilities and hotels by other developers – would occur at the same time.

Jordan said, "We will conquer the jungle for the next millennium. The Empire might be dead but we Brits can still thrash 'em all. We'll civilise the wilderness, like we've been doing for centuries."

The screen showed a tower soaring high on an escarpment. It was the Titiwangsa Tower which would house the Science Faculty. Scott said, "The final adjustments to the design have now been incorporated as you require, Bill."

"Excellent."

The tower flew up from the mountain precipice in a futuristic incarnation of power and technology, entwining steel, granite and glass to command the earth below. "This will win us the contract. It will be the tallest tower built on the highest site in the world." Jordan turned to the rest of his team. "Until recently, the twin Petronas Towers in Kuala Lumpur were the tallest buildings in the world. Just after they were completed, the Shanghai World Financial Centre in China snatched the record from Malaysia. Imagine the blow to national prestige.

"We are going to give back the pride to Malaysia with the Titiwangsa Tower. Above the offices and science-faculty facilities, the Satellite and Space Observation Unit will be located on the upper floors and roof. The tower will be so tall that terrestrial static and telecommunications systems will not interfere with the transmitting and receiving equipment. There is no way the Consortium can resist such a prize."

A waterfall flew over the edge of the rocky cliff while above it the immense tower loomed up to the sky. Jasmine stared at the spectacular vision on the screen.

She understood these people who made up Consortium 2000. She understood the ambition that yearned to own the tallest building, the biggest yacht, to be known as the best lawyer, the richest developer, to control the largest empire. Once, in medieval Europe, merchants and self-made men built the landscape of a continent – the villas and churches of Italy, the castles of Germany, the *chateaux* of France – and became respectable. This was the Renaissance of Asia, and the new rich were purchasing their stake in the landscape of history. They would be respectable. As she had now become, because of Harry, because of the facade of her life in London. But, in spite of herself, the anxiety began to awaken again. With an effort she focused her attention on the screen and tried to ignore the knot tightening in her stomach.

A new six-lane highway would be built from Kuala Lumpur to Titiwangsa, a long straight stretch driving inland to the foothills. The tenderers had a choice of two routes from the foothills to the summit plateau, almost three thousand feet above sea level. The longer route meandered further eastwards and would bypass an area already inhabited by Kampung Tanah and surrounding farms. The shorter route came directly into the market town then passed up onto the higher ground and into Titiwangsa. Jordan Cardale would submit on the basis of the shorter route.

"So the Kampung Tanah residents will have to be relocated," Jasmine said. In her mind, she saw bulldozed homes and shell-shocked families watching amid the rubble.

"The shorter route cuts more than an hour and a half off average car journey times to and from Kuala Lumpur," Jordan said. "It's the only feasible alternative for such a development."

"The residents will be incorporated into Titiwangsa?"

"No, to this valley here below the escarpment," Scott said. "New Kampung Tanah will be built as part of Phase I. A proportion of the local residents will then be relocated. The rest will be moved over four further phases. A minor road will link it to the highway."

Jordan said, "The main town is prime development land set aside for luxury housing and business premises. There'll be plenty of property developers looking to get a piece of that action. The local residents won't be able to afford any of that land."

Jasmine said, "The development must benefit the local people."

The region had been designated a Special Economic Development Area by a recent statute. This was to ensure that the local people and the country as a whole benefited from the project through job creation, wealth distribution and the prevention of monopolies. "'Benefit' is not defined," Jasmine went on. She was picturing homeless masses by a sleek new highway, glaring resentfully as the rich zoomed by. "It may be argued against us that relocation like this does not benefit the people there."

"The locals will get spanking new model homes and a town hall thrown in, which they don't have at present. Why would they make trouble?" Farul Zain, the quantity surveyor spoke up.

Jordan said, "They won't."

"The statute provides that the winning design is subject to approval by the planning authorities within eight weeks of the contract award. There's a detailed and complex procedure you'll have to follow as the winning contractor who applies for the approval. The authorities may require modification, taking into account whether or not the local people 'benefit', including submissions by the residents."

"There won't be a risk of the planning review not going our way," Jordan said. Danesleigh interjected anxiously, "The PR angle could be difficult to handle. I'll need a full briefing if the locals kick up a rumpus."

"They won't."

Jasmine persisted, "I know you're confident that the short-term issues are tied up. I'm looking at the long-term. Jordan Cardale will still be involved after completion – you're bidding for the management contract of the Consortium-owned properties."

"So?" Jordan was impatient to move on.

"Well, these people may be from a small hick town but they aren't stupid. Once business in Titiwangsa is in full swing and the punters aren't bothering to turn down that minor road to bring their spending money to the local residents, someone may try to invoke the statute and bring claims for retrospective compensation based on their loss of 'benefit'."

"How likely is that?" Zain said. "Once they've missed their chance at the planning review stage, that's taken to mean that they agreed to it and can't change their mind, isn't it?"

Jasmine shifted mentally into high gear. The hours of preparatory legal and factfinding work she had put into this project before today's meeting now came to the fore. She moved from her instinctive knowledge of these people, whose lives were in Jordan's hands, to objective, commercial analysis. "My research shows that in recent years there has been an increase in cases brought by grass-roots local groups against major developers. There's greater awareness of environmental issues and the rights of minority groups. A judicial review could be called to assess whether your application for planning was conducted properly. The press is hotting up on their coverage of such issues. This is one of the reasons for the 'local benefit' provision in this statute. It will be a particularly sensitive issue where the developer, who will also be the manager, is a foreign – and white – company. Echoes of colonial exploitation and all that. It could be very bad for your image not only in Malaysia but in the region as a whole."

She could see the men mentally calculating the cost of court cases, compensation and public-relations damage control. She would let them stew a moment before coming to the rescue as a good lawyer should. This was a problem she had diagnosed late at night in her office the week before her secret trip to Malaysia. Everyone was assuming that the development would be safe once they had successfully navigated the planning review – as if the statute had been drafted merely to pay lip-service to the caring environmentally aware nineties. This was the sort of point average lawyers missed.

The knack to foresee a potential conflict, to isolate a problem before it even occurs – that was what made the best lawyers different from the rest, she thought triumphantly. With foresight comes knowledge, and knowledge is power. This is what the best lawyers could give to their clients, power in the corporate game and an edge on the other players. That was what justified their enormous fees.

But suddenly, her mind went blank.

The men waited. Farul Zain was of Malaysian origin and his

smooth brown face was tense as he mulled over her words. He had been with Jordan for eight years and would be the project manager on this development.

Did he know about her past through his connections in Malaysia? It was an anxiety that had gnawed at her ever since they had first worked together several years ago. She had made a point of making sure early on that he knew the story of her dead parents that she always told with touching bravery – the hidden pain and quiet sincerity never failed to convince. So far, Zain had never behaved in any way to indicate that he might know or want to know anything more about her background. She kept her distance and, for the most part, had been able to dispel the old anxiety.

The knowledge nagged her that this project would require regular trips back to Malaysia for meetings and site visits. Ever since Jordan had first talked about his intention to bid, Jasmine had been jumpy. She could not have refused to act back then, and now it was too late to pull out without jeopardising her career as well as her secret. So far, she had handled her fear of being exposed by not handling it. Now, all of a sudden, her fear leaped up to paralyse her. She found herself staring at Zain. Would he be tempted to probe? Would others enquire about her past? Would someone recognise her? Jasmine reeled from the rush of panic.

The rest at the meeting were now debating among themselves. Danesleigh looked lost without a brief on the potential crisis. Jordan and Scott leaned across the table in a tense exchange. She had lost control. She flicked through her notes but all she could think about was her mother. The old woman waiting to see the flame tree blossom, refusing to move to a better life, refusing to use the money Jasmine had been sending her, waiting for a husband who would never return. Stubborn. Like the people of Kampung Tanah.

"I suggest a two-pronged solution," Jasmine said at last, but her voice faltered.

She understood the people of Kampung Tanah. That was how she had been able to see the problems attached to the relocation.

The solution she had found had also come from the depths of this understanding. But now she felt as if her ideas had taken fright at becoming reality and she floundered in a void.

She forced herself to control the panic. She raised her voice and repeated what she had said. This time she got the attention of the meeting. She was master of her professional self again. The fog of confusion dispersed. But, even as she spoke, it felt like a betrayal.

"First," she said, "Jordan Cardale, through a Malaysian subsidiary, purchases the New Kampung Tanah land from the Consortium. You can reduce the tender price by a sum representing the purchase price of the land – this has the effect of making your bid more attractive and also, taking the problem of the local residents out of the Consortium's hands. The Consortium won't care what happens to the local residents, so long as the short-route highway can be built. They'll be only too pleased to wash their hands of the new town."

Jordan was attentive now. "Go on."

"You now control the land. What money has to be paid out to the residents as compensation for the loss of their original homes can be recovered through a part-exchange funding scheme. Such a scheme is not disallowed by the statute. The locals are getting an all-mod-cons new home for their old hovel so it's not unreasonable that the value differential is taken into account in the transfer."

Danesleigh said, "So – we can reduce the tender price, which means we're more likely to win. And because we're giving the locals a more expensive new house in exchange for their old one, we get them to pay us the difference in value – like when you trade in your old car for a new one. This way, we recoup some of the compensation we'll have paid out for relocating them in the first place."

"Precisely." Jasmine met each of the seven gazes. "But we'll have to handle the valuation just right and tie up the legal drafting so it's not staring them in the face. It'll take a damn good lawyer to see the full picture and they won't be able to afford a 'damn good' one. So, you squeeze some profit out of this aspect and, also, the subsidiary is staffed and fronted by locals. The residents think they are dealing with their own kind. The spook of the foreign devil is defused.

"Now, my second and main point. By controlling the land, you can control your relationship with the residents directly. As part of the deal for their new properties, we incorporate provisions whereby they have no come-back regarding any misconception as to what 'local benefit' means to them. They acknowledge that they are fully satisfied with the 'benefits' of the relocation, that they accept fully that they are relocating of their own free choice. They are presumed to have full knowledge of all matters and consequences pertaining to their new location and they waive rights to further compensation. We take it out of the arena of public law and into private law. Throw in a few exclusion-of-liability clauses and we have them stitched. "

Jasmine stopped speaking and a tense silence prevailed.

Then Jordan slapped his palm on the table. "I love it! You're as sneaky as they come, Lian. We can win the tender, make a profit out of the locals and stop them from causing a stir later on in one fell swoop."

Jasmine said, "Correct on all counts. We'll have to make sure that they have the advice of lawyers from the outset so they can't cry, 'Foul'. But I'll easily run rings round any they may employ."

"Gentlemen, this is the winning spirit that I'm paying you lot for. The advice I get from my lawyers is worth every damn penny they take off me." Jordan winked at Jasmine.

Jasmine smiled. Damn right, she said to herself – but the words seemed hollow.

She usually loved this part of the job. Her skill in manoeuvring through the legal minefield could secure the best interests of her client where a lesser lawyer might fail. It often gave her an adrenaline rush. It was why she had become a lawyer, she liked to think.

But today, she felt an emptiness even as she received Jordan's praise. The thought nagged her that the people of Kampung Tanah were the kind of people from whom she had come. She thought suddenly of Karim and the difference she had made then. What was the difference she was making now?

But Kampung Tanah's interests were not her concern, she was not their lawyer. Her job was to look after the best interests of her own client. In any event, she told herself, whatever she did, she was part of a new era bringing progress to a backwater community. These people were getting a damn good deal, they had to expect some sacrifice of their rights.

Damn right, she said to herself, and this time she felt the conviction in her mind.

7

Harry was late.

His secretary had reserved a window table at Bibendum on the Fulham Road and Jasmine had been there for more than an hour. At the other tables, confident couples and designer-sleek groups lounged in the oversized armchairs. She was alone and it seemed as if the stained-glass Michelin Man was laughing at her.

She ordered another Martini. Tonight would be the first time since her trip to Malaysia that she would be seeing Harry again. After the frustrations of trying to contact each other over the last few days, this final hour of anticipation was almost unbearable. She couldn't wait to see his smiling, handsome face again and feel his warm gaze on her. She imagined for the hundredth time his pleasure at seeing her again.

She liked it when he was happy. She still tried hard to be the girl he'd first fallen in love with but so much had changed since then. Jasmine knew that Harry had not been pleased that she had gone abroad for a few days, even if he had masked it in jokes. She had not been very good at making him happy in the last year, she thought, preoccupied as she'd been with her work and career. And now, this fake business trip. She'd make it up to him, Jasmine promised silently. She thought with chagrin how good he had always been to her – not only a charming and adoring lover but also like a kind, loving father, teaching her how to behave, making her into the confident woman she'd become, spoiling her, looking after her. She'd do everything from now on, she swore, to make him happier than he'd ever been.

She felt an urgency in her need to see him, to be reassured that her present life had not changed in the time she'd been away. She glanced at the doorway impatiently.

She thought with shame of how difficult she had made it for Harry to contact her in Malaysia, leaving her mobile switched off, never giving him a land-line contact number for any office. She would phone him from her mobile as if between meetings or late at night after a long hard day. Chatting lovingly – but briefly. And all the time, had there been something in her voice or an evasiveness that had made him suspicious?

A shiver ran through her.

Did she have the courage after all to tell Harry the truth? It was not just this one lie, she thought, there had been ten years of lies. Ten years of making him fall in love with someone she had never been. Actually, darling, she imagined saying, I'm the daughter of a pimp; and your family and friends, the Tauntons of Sussex, Lord Beauchamp, the Honourable Lucinda Wickham, Mr Fiennes Harrington MBE, they'd be so proud of you for being so egalitarian and modern in marrying not only a foreigner but beneath your class too. A coolie they might have called her in an earlier generation.

But if he loved her he would understand, wouldn't he? What was so wrong with wanting to get out of the pit into which her father had cast her? She herself had never been a – she faltered on the word – a whore. So why the big song and dance? She fancied him saying, "I love you, that's all that matters, I love you, I love you." But she felt cold and her heart raced painfully in her breast.

Jasmine looked up and saw Harry. His broad frame filled the doorway as he scanned the room. He had not yet seen her. His mouth was a tense, thin line and his eyes seemed distant as they swept the tables. It was the look he had when things were not going well. Perhaps the deal he'd mentioned, with the Germans, had fallen through. It was more a hope than a thought – the alternative was that his tense manner had something to do with her, and the possibility frightened her.

But when he caught sight of her, the old pleasure swept over his face and he moved quickly towards her. With a laughing embrace, he drew her out of her chair, making her squeal with surprise as he showered her brow and cheeks and lips with kisses. "My darling, how I've missed you," he said, with feeling. She could smell the whisky on his breath. She tousled his hair, leaning in to kiss him back.

Happily, Jasmine and Harry settled into their seats. The waiter, hovering with menus, approached. The other diners had turned to watch and smiles still lingered on their lips as they went back to their conversations. Harry ordered a Scotch on ice.

"Mineral water for me," Jasmine said.

"Not drinking tonight?" Harry sounded disappointed. "I thought we'd have champagne later to celebrate your safe return."

"Champagne, yes – later. I've just had two Martinis and they've gone straight to my head." Jasmine laughed, making a silly tipsy face.

Harry dismissed the waiter with a nod and took Jasmine's hand in both of his. He grinned and brought her fingers up to his lips. "I've missed you so much."

"Me, too. How are you, my love? How did the German deal go?"

"Splendidly. I got the account!"

"I'm so proud of you!"

"We took them out to a club to celebrate last night. As team captain, I had to be there – you understand, don't you, darling? It's a capital funding venture for an electronics plant they're setting up in Croatia – the new Silicon Valley, they're hoping. They're going to be one of the first in there and De Witte Cootes is making it happen. That's one hell of a feather to my cap, huh? Our cut of the deal could take me into six figures by the end of this financial year!" Harry leaned back in his chair with a bark of satisfaction.

Their drinks arrived and Jasmine toasted Harry's success. She was beginning to relax now, seeing him so happy. He gulped his and slapped the tumbler on the table with excited energy. If she paced the evening right, she thought, she would be able to tell him everything later, back at her flat.

Harry ordered another Scotch and looked around anxiously. "Is this table all right? I told my secretary to get us their best."

"It's fine."

"I don't know, that girl can't do anything right. The amount the company pays her ... can't type and not much of a looker either."

Jasmine adopted the soothing tone that usually worked when he was agitated. "This is wonderful, Harry. Really it is."

"I just want it to be perfect for us." He leaned forward and gazed into her eyes. "Do you remember, this was the first restaurant ..."

" ... you took me to when I came down to law college? How could I forget? I was so nervous, just a student still and you were this smart, gorgeous grown-up in your suit and the maître d' recognised you and it was like you were royalty."

He smiled. "This is our special place."

"We celebrate everything here, don't we?" It occurred to Jasmine that over the years this exchange had become almost a catechism.

Boisterous laughter and the rattle of Japanese voices broke into their space. At the far corner of the restaurant was a table of Japanese businessmen. "Goddam Japs." Harry frowned, glancing at the distraction. "Like performing bloody monkeys, aren't they? Peasants in their bloody rice fields one minute, the next, they're making widgets and, bang, they think they fucking rule the world. Filthy coolies."

Jasmine flinched. She tried a watery smile. He was tired and easily riled, that was all. She picked up the menu and made a show of reading it but she couldn't take in anything. Harry's drink arrived and he took a swig as he ordered a bottle of Krug 1984 and a third Scotch. When he turned back to Jasmine, he seemed relaxed again. "So, how was your trip? You didn't say much over the phone."

"It's so nice to be talking face to face."

"What's the site like?" Harry leaned forward, fully attentive, as he always did whenever she talked about what she'd been doing. Jasmine thought ironically how proud she usually was that Harry was so unlike the men that her female friends complained about: he always wanted to know everything she'd been doing, paid careful attention and never forgot anything.

"Oh, you know, at this early stage …"Jasmine flailed, not wanting to compound her lies with yet more. "Tracts of jungle, a few markers. Not very dramatic."

"Why did they need you out there?"

Jasmine kept her tone light. "On site the legal eagle might pick up something everyone else has taken for granted."

"So what did you pick up?" Harry was smiling. Was she imagining it or was his smile fixed and tense?

The champagne and whisky arrived. Harry drained the tumbler as the waiter poured the champagne and hovered to take their order for dinner. "Dammit, we'll tell you when we're ready." Harry dismissed the man with a jerk of his head.

To Jasmine, he raised his glass of champagne and said gently, "Welcome home, my darling."

She clinked his glass with hers. "Here's to your success."

Harry took a long swallow and poured another glass. "Go on. You were telling me about the site."

"Well … it's a good site. Dramatic –"

"But you said it wasn't dramatic."

"Did I? Yes, well, the location's dramatic but not the site – yet. The location – great views, great potential, beautiful scenery."

"You sound like a brochure."

"Well, it's all true." Was she sounding too defensive?

"I'm sure it is. There's no need to get defensive. I'm just interested in your work, that's all, like the good husband should be."

"I know … I'm sorry –"

Harry slumped back in his chair and stared balefully at Jasmine. "It's always the same problem, isn't it?"

"What do you mean?"

"This. We talk but we're not really talking."

"But of course we are."

"Dammit!" Harry snapped, startling them both. He stared at her a moment, hesitated. After a gulp of champagne, he decided to continue, but he was becoming more agitated in spite of himself. "Look, it's not you I'm angry at – it's our whole situation. It's just ... Ever since you got the hope of partnership, we haven't really, well, connected. We hardly see each other. You're always working late, going abroad for meetings, going out to client functions. And now you *are* a partner, it's got even worse. I mean, just weeks before our wedding, you get hauled off to an overseas meeting. Enough is enough. You've got to learn to handle your clients, darling, you can't just jump when they click their fingers."

"Harry ..."

"You don't open up to me like you used to." The words came out hard and accusing. Harry drank more champagne and softened his tone. "You remember how you used to talk to me about your work, ask my advice – and me not even a lawyer? Do you remember? What's happened? We used to be so close."

"My love, things *have* been better recently," Jasmine found herself pleading. "Ever since we had that long talk a month ago and now we're engaged – I've been trying so hard and you *have* seemed happier again. Haven't you?"

"Well, yes, I suppose – since our engagement." It was a reluctant concession.

"Then I let this – this trip spoil it all again. I was too weak to say no this time but after we're married, it'll be different." Jasmine knew she should stop but she couldn't. She wanted so much to make it up to him, to see him happy again, and lies were her only hope. "It was a last-minute thing, Jordan needed a legal tangle sorted out, I had to go. But now, it's over. And after the wedding we can be perfect together again, I promise. If only we could've seen each other sooner than tonight. I've missed you so."

"I want to believe you." There was a returning anger to his tone, blurred with alcohol. He'd had three whiskies and several glasses of champagne by now – on top of what he had drunk before he arrived.

Jasmine struggled on, "The important thing is that you're here at last and we can spend a special evening together."

Harry stared at her. "What's that supposed to mean?"

"Mean?"

"'The important thing is you're here at last'," he repeated harshly. He looked defensive. "You saying I've been avoiding you? Giving you a taste of your own medicine?"

"No, I was just –"

"Who's avoiding whom?" The tense line was forming again on his lips. His voice rose. "Who's always off on business trips? Always in a meeting. Can't be contacted. Too busy to talk."

"But I've just explained –"

"Explained or covered up?"

Jasmine gasped. "What?"

"You say it's work, you always say it's work. It's your every excuse. I don't know whether I believe it any more."

"But it's true!" Only this time it wasn't true. Jasmine stared in horror at the abyss beneath her.

"Is it?" Harry's temper caved in. He leaned unsteadily towards her, almost on his feet, his chair grinding back. "You've just said the meeting was a last-minute emergency. You said at the weekend that you'd told me about it two weeks ago. Which is it? Two weeks or last minute?"

Jasmine blinked. What had she told him and when? She drew herself straight and said, "A few weeks back, I said I *might* have to go if the local lawyers couldn't sort it out. So it was last minute because they couldn't. All right? Is the third degree over now?"

Her heart rang in her ears. A hot shame began to spread up her neck and face. Another frightened lie to unravel later. She set her expression into one of indignation. Harry was silent. She could see he was deflated. She wished she could rewind the whole dialogue and start afresh, make it go the way she had hoped instead of getting them mired in their familiar pain.

Harry set his jaw. He did not move. His face was close to hers, pink spots on his cheeks. Everyone in the restaurant had turned curiously to them again, distracted by Harry's sudden movement from his chair.

Harry said, in a ringing voice, "Is Jordan your client in more ways than you're letting on?"

"*What*?" Jasmine was breathing hard, taken by surprise. Anger and horror spun in her head. Churned her stomach. The restaurant was still. They were all listening, the waiters, the Japanese men, the beautiful people. Her voice was shaky. "Harry, you're drunk!"

Harry ignored her. "What do you really do for him? Hmm? Tell me! Why don't you tell me about your 'work'? Maybe I can give you some tips, help you service him better!" Jasmine stood up. She stared into the ugliness in his eyes. Her hand was drawn back, instinctively coiled to slap the drunken leer off his face.

But something she saw in his eyes stopped her. It chilled her. Seeped like miasma through the crack of all her defences. She felt weak, afraid. It was only a moment, no more time than it took to draw a breath, then it was gone, slithering back behind the camouflage green of his glare.

She pushed her way out from behind the table and ran across the room. Outside, it had started to rain.

Harry caught up and grabbed her arm. "Where are you going?"

"Home. Let me go." The cab she had hailed pulled up. Harry was still holding her. "Don't you walk out on me again." He turned her to face him. "Do you hear me?" Caught like a rabbit in the glare of his eyes, she nodded. She began to tremble, tears shattering her control.

She was aware of Harry still standing there. But the fight seemed to have gone out of him. He let her go.

Blindly, she climbed into the cab. Harry stood forlornly in the rain as the taxi pulled away.

*   *   *

Jasmine sat in the darkness of her living room watching the rain. The light of the streetlamp cast a waxen pallor into the room.

The phone rang for the sixth time that night. Again she did not answer it. The answering machine picked up. Harry's voice drifted towards her. "Darling, I know you're there, please pick up the phone. I need to see you. Please, I want to make it up to you. I don't know what came over me. I've missed you so badly. I wanted us to have a wonderful evening. It's been bloody awful without you. Now look what I've done. I didn't want to hurt you. You're the most precious thing I have, I'm just so scared of losing you – it makes me crazy."

His voice was cracked with tears. Jasmine pulled her cashmere wrap closer. She heard him sigh and then the phone went dead.

His malice lingered with her. She had never seen him like that and it frightened her. In the past, he had been moody, easily provoked. But she had known how to handle him then, how to contain his tantrums – she had never thought of his moods as anything more than that. Tonight, that vicious anger, that was new.

Why had she risked everything she had with Harry by rushing back to Malaysia? For a promise? She hadn't even kept it in the end, she thought bitterly.

Had she hoped to see Luke again?

It startled her, this thought from the secret darkness. With an effort, she forced it beneath the surface again. Struggling. As if to drown the girl she used to be. It was over. Had been for those many years. Had never even begun, she corrected herself.

She held the thrashing thoughts down below the surface till there was deathly stillness again. Only an echo haunted her.

She was to blame for what had happened this evening. Harry must have sensed something was not right. He must have sensed it for as long as they'd been together. He was right, they had never really connected. How could they, her secret like a sword between them? Poor Harry, he was trying so hard to make a connection with her. And all she'd given him were evasions and lies and more lies. No wonder he had lashed out in frustration, to hurt her as she had been hurting him.

The phone rang again. "Jasmine, if you can hear me, will you look out of the window?"

Jasmine glanced up. He went on, "You don't have to speak to me. Just go to the window. Please?"

Rain washed the pane like tears. She looked into the empty street below. The trees in the square shuffled with the beat of the deluge. Under an arching lamp, Harry stood staring up at her window. Rivulets ran from his drenched hair down his face and cheeks. Rain and tears. His trenchcoat was soaked. In one hand he held a mobile phone to his ear. In the other he cradled a bunch of flowers. When he saw her silhouette appear, he broke into a smile.

"Thank you, my darling," she heard from the answering machine behind her. "I just had to see you."

She touched the cold glass where his cheek would have been. He looked like a little boy. His handsome face was filled with such relief and pleasure at seeing her there. Her heart ached at what she had done to him. She was to blame for what had happened. He was in love with her, she could see that, and his jealousy was only natural. She had stoked it up with her evasiveness. And there he stood in the rain, taking the blame, loving her still. Her heart went out to him and, suddenly, she knew it would all work out somehow and they would find a way out of these painful rows.

She let him in and he enveloped her in a sodden embrace. She tasted the rain and tears on his face. They did not speak as the passion of remorse engulfed them. On cushions and soft rugs strewn across her living room, they made love in the dark, shadows of raindrops patterned on their bodies.

He told her how he loved her, how much he had missed her. "My Jasmine, my love ..."

She lost herself in his burning touch, gave herself up to the embrace of his strong powerful body as he held her to him. His lips and tongue tasted her frantically. His urgent hands caressed her hot skin. She arched back, breasts aching for his touch, her nipples round and hard. She abandoned herself to desire, thinking of no one, remembering nothing, living only in that moment.

*　*　*

Jasmine awoke to find Harry watching her. The sun streamed in through the windows, the morning beyond clear and fresh after the rain. He lay beside her on the cushions and rugs on the floor, half leaning on his elbow. A duvet was draped over them both – Harry must have fetched it from her bed during the night, tucking her up like a child.

She smiled and reached out to touch his cheek. "Morning, my sweet darling."

He leaned down to kiss her. "You're so fragile when you're asleep. I love watching you."

"Oh, Harry ..."

"I don't know what happened to me last night. It was like something snapped and I just couldn't stop myself. I was a bastard, can you ever forgive –"

Jasmine placed her fingers over his lips. "Don't let's go over all that."

"But, my darling, I can't forget what I did, how I behaved." He looked wretched. His bare chest was broad and powerful and she could see the muscles hard in his arms as he leaned and gestured. Yet, he was so vulnerable in that moment, a young boy whose whole happiness depended on her. Jasmine felt a surge of tenderness for him. He said, "I can't forgive myself – not if you still hate me."

"My love, I don't hate you, don't be silly, please." She drew him down towards her, kissing him. "I forgive you, of course, I do."

"Really?" His relief was evident. He looked at her hesitantly through his lashes, that shy James Dean glance that always charmed her.

She nodded and he hugged her, rolling her on top of him as he lay back on the rugs.

They were laughing and playing like pups.

"Oh no," Jasmine said suddenly. "What time is it?"

"After nine."

"I'll be late for work."

"Do you have to go?" he nuzzled her breasts, making her giggle. "You're a partner now, a boss. Aren't you allowed to be late?"

"Well, I suppose –"

"Didn't you mean what you said last night?"

"Mean?"

"You promised – things'll be different now, you said. Kowtowing to your firm, it's all over, you said."

Jasmine nodded slowly. "Yes ... of course, I meant it."

"So ..."

Jasmine tousled his hair as she got up. She laughed. "You always know how to get your way, don't you?"

"That's part of my charm."

She called her secretary, her tone incongruously business-like as she stood by the phone in the nude. "I won't be in till after lunch, I'm working from home this morning. Don't put any calls through, I'll deal with them when I get in later."

They spent the morning cuddled together on their makeshift bedding, sipping hot black coffee. Jasmine heated up some frozen croissants and they munched them among the cushions, picking crumbs from each other's bare torsos. It was all going to be all right, Jasmine thought with relief, just as she had hoped. She should tell him now, when the glow of making up might cushion him from the pain. But seeing Harry so happy, and feeling the magic of the moment, she could not bring herself to break the spell.

"It's going to be pretty damn good, isn't it?" Harry sighed, leaning back on the cushions and drawing Jasmine into the crook of his shoulder.

"What is?"

"Us. The future. With this Croatia deal in my pocket, I'll be on the up and up at De Witte's. Did I mention we've been invited to a private ski chalet at Klosters this winter?"

Jasmine's eyes widened.

"Impressive, eh? Reichman – one of the senior vice-presidents of the German company – it's his chalet." Harry grinned. "Won't you love that, darling? New Year in the mountains."

"Mmm."

"Last year, you had to rush off to Hong Kong at short notice for some banking client. You won't let that happen again, will you?" he nibbled her ear.

"I'll try."

"You let your work intrude so much, darling. We've had to cancel so many engagements over the weekends because you've had to work. And last Easter, we had to drop everything so you could go to Paris."

"Lyon."

"Whatever. My point is, well, you don't have to be at your firm's beck and call so much now. I'll soon be making more than enough for the two of us and you'll have the choice whether you want to carry on working or not."

"I love my job, you know that, Harry. You used to be so proud of me. I thought you understood how much it means to me."

"I'm still proud of you, darling. All I'm saying is you have a choice now. I'm not forcing you to do anything you don't want to – what do you take me for?" Harry twisted up so he could look into her eyes. He looked hurt. "I just care about you and I want to look after you. Is that so bad? I know I've been on at you about your job but that's only because I love you. Surely you can see that."

Jasmine felt mortified. She had become so defensive, she thought, she couldn't even appreciate his kindness any more. She kissed him and nodded.

Harry lay back again. "But things can be different now. Just think of it. You won't have to give up travelling abroad – there are likely to be more foreign trips on the table for me and we could both go together. No more lonely separations and disjointed telephone calls. No more crazy rows over nothing. Don't you think it would work? These Germans are based in Munich and I'll be expected out there at some point. A long weekend of Bavarian fairy-tale castles – what do you think?"

"Wonderful."

"Or how about Rio and Mexico City? Or Indochina? I've got my eye on the emerging markets for my portfolio. South America and Asia – there's unbelievable expansion there and the time to get in the thick of it is now. What do you say, darling? Wouldn't it be bloody brilliant? You could come with me on my trips, we could have a ball. The honeymoon would never be over. It'll be just like falling in love all over again."

Jasmine smiled but said nothing. She didn't want to spoil the moment. Harry rolled onto his side to look at her. He seemed to expect her to say something. Instead, she kissed him. He responded warmly and shifted closer. "Think about it," he said. "You *could* come with me. We *can* be perfect again, my love, you know we can."

* * *

The monkeys loped along the telephone wires, wide-eyed babies clinging to their mothers' fur. Boisterous males scampered on the pavement and up on the cables of lights that circled the park. Mrs Fung and Luke paused on their evening stroll through the Lake Gardens.

Joggers pounded by. On the lake, paddleboats meandered aimlessly. By a bamboo grove, a Tai Chi class was in progress. Mrs Fung chuckled with glee at the antics of the monkeys. On evenings like this she could almost forget the recurring pain that had plagued her in recent months. It had flared up again last night. The honeysuckle-stem medicinal draught she had prepared had not been strong enough. The cramps simmered still in her abdomen.

They strolled on towards the lotus-blossom lake. She was seeing more of Luke now as his current project was in Malaysia. He had been on site visits to Kampung Tanah and divided his time between writing up his reports at home and teaching seminars in Penang. He had many friends but he always made time to see Mrs Fung. He was telling her about his latest assignment, speaking enthusiastically as he always did about his work.

"Kampung Tanah doesn't know what's hit them," Luke said. "Imagine a market town about half the size of Taiping. For generations it goes about its business, off the beaten track. Suddenly, the outside world arrives on its doorstep. The Consortium has been sending up surveyors, geophysicists, civil engineers to map out where the university town will be. Each of the tenderers has their own team of architects and technical people checking out the site to prepare their designs for the bid. I'm going round with my equipment and instruments and asking the locals all these questions. What a circus!"

"Can you help them?" Mrs Fung enjoyed listening to Luke talk about his work. Luke nodded. "The locals want me to help them look at the technical side of the six designs submitted during the tender process. Then I prepare a report to the planning authorities for them on the one that wins. I look at the environmental impact of the development on the local area. What economic and social effect would there be? How does that affect what the local people want?"

"So you can help the locals get the right development for them."

"The planners look at everything, including what the local people want, and they can make the developers change parts of the design."

"So the local people can make a difference." Mrs Fung kept her voice steady but the pain had returned.

"Malaysia is starting to realise the importance of environmental issues." Luke was animated now. He did not notice Mrs Fung's face tightening. "I feel Malaysia could be the leader in responsible development – it's no longer just another Third World country but a developed and democratic nation where different interests live and work well together. There are already many laws dealing with environmental issues and this special law gives the local people a say from the beginning."

"You're the one who's going to say it for them." Mrs Fung squeezed Luke's arm. They were by the edge of the lake now, the lotus blossoms spreading across the surface before them. She said, with an effort, "You and Jasmine – so clever at school, now with such important jobs."

Two children waded in the shallows, fishing out frogspawn with nets. "We used to do that," Luke smiled. "Jasmine always had to collect the most, or the biggest!"

"And she'd sell the frogs as pets to the other kids at school!"

"I let mine go." Luke laughed. "That was the difference between us. Still is."

They made their way to the red and white bridge that zigzagged across the water. A pagoda floated at its centre and there, Mrs Fung liked to sit among the lilies and dragonflies to watch the evening deepen. She said, "Jasmine was so proud. It was the first money she earned. She was seven."

The planks creaked beneath their feet as they followed the bridge's meandering path. Black and gold carp glided up to take the air. Mrs Fung went on, "It's the custom that with your first pay, you should give a dinner to honour your parents. Jasmine took me to the night market. She carried the money herself and ordered and paid just like a grown-up. I had beef noodle soup and *kopi peng* and she had satay and a Fanta grape soda. I'll always remember. It came to four ringgit ninety, and she left a ten-cent tip. It was all the money she had."

"I didn't know," Luke said, almost to himself.

The cramp wrenched her gut like a twisting vice. Mrs Fung stumbled against Luke, closing into a ball of pain. Cold sweat chilled her. Through the ringing in her ears, she heard Luke call her name.

*　*　*

Luke held Mrs Fung's thin, still figure, his anxiety turning to relief as she began to stir. She gasped, "'S nothing. Rest. Sit. I'll be fine – a moment."

Luke carried her to the bench in the pagoda. She leaned against him, gulping air. The cramp had passed, leaving her trembling.

"What is it? Let me take you to a doctor," he said, peering at her pale face.

She fished for her handkerchief and turned away from him as she put it to her lips. "No need. Just a little cramp." The handkerchief came away stained with saliva and bile. Flecked with brown blood.

She tried to hide it but Luke had already seen. He grasped her arm. "How long have you had these cramps? You must see a doctor."

"I am having treatment." Mrs Fung saw his anxiety. She took his hand. "The pain comes and goes but it's nothing serious."

"Let me take you to the hospital."

Mrs Fung made a face. "That place is like a mausoleum. It smells of chemicals and death. White everywhere, the colour of the dead. I never want to go there."

"But –"

"I am taking medicine. I have a course of treatment. The gods have been good to me."

"Does Jasmine know you're ill?"

"No!" Mrs Fung said sharply. "And you must not tell her. It's not serious. I don't want her worrying, rushing back here, trying to be the good daughter. She must live her life."

"Why don't – ?"

Mrs Fung tightened her grasp. There was an intensity in her look. "Promise me." Luke knew then that, in spite of her words, Mrs Fung was seriously ill. She held his stare with imploring desperation. "Promise me!"

"I can't –"

"Listen to me. I know you think that Jasmine is selfish and hard. You judge her for closing her heart from her life here. You are ashamed of her for chasing all the prizes that, for you, are no more than trinkets. You think she should come back to her roots, embrace her heritage."

Luke was silent.

"But her heritage is disappointed hope," Mrs Fung said. "I wanted her to have everything I never could have. I made a wrong choice and I have had to live with the consequences. I married for love, I never went to school – that was for my brothers only. I am the past. She is the future. I want her to forget where she came from."

"She wrote to me every week for ten years but I never replied. She remembered a promise I would have preferred her to forget. Her spirit will always be generous and her heart will always love. Under her fine clothes and education, she is still the daughter she has always been."

"I know you are angry with her for wanting the things which take her away from here. If you are angry with anyone, it should be with me. I gave her the ambition. I told her not to come back. I wanted her to forget. Before my time comes, I want to achieve one success to make up for all my hopes that failed – that she should live the life she was meant to live."

Luke looked out over the darkening hills. Mrs Fung's voice was weak but she spoke with a passion he recognised. He had heard it before in Jasmine, in the girl he had always known and in the woman she had become.

"Don't be angry with her," Mrs Fung said again. "I know she hurt you that last time you saw her."

"You knew?" Luke turned to her.

"Yes. I knew how she hurt you. It was the hardest thing she ever did. She cried the whole night. Like her heart would break. It pained me so much to see her. I took her in my arms and rocked her but she just couldn't stop. 'I made him hate me,' she kept saying. 'He hates me now and I hate him. It's the only way.' If I could have taken that agony from her, I would have. I've lived with it all these years. To see your child sacrifice everything she loved because she loved you more, how can a mother bear such pain?" Mrs Fung was almost in tears.

After a pause, she went on, her voice hoarse with emotion. "There was no going back. In this life, you come to places where the only thing you can do is go on. Maybe you can never understand if you've never been through what I went through. After – after what I lived through ... the only safe thing was for Jasmine to leave and never come back. I made her go. She had to escape. Don't be angry with her. She hurt you because she had to. She didn't have the strength to leave you any other way. She made herself go on and not look back. I am to blame, not her. And now she's so strong because she's had to be. But it's only strength on the outside. Inside, she's still my good girl, that's why she came back."

Luke drove his fingers through his hair, staring out at the deepening dusk. He could hardly take in everything Mrs Fung had said. Every nerve in his body felt raw. He saw Jasmine up in Firefly Clearing, her face hard. He heard her cold voice, hurling taunts and insults. And all the time, her eyes – he had seen it in her eyes that were bright with suppressed tears: he had seen her pain and he had let her walk away. He had let her words – her whole act – erode everything that he knew about her. Luke squeezed his eyes closed, dropping his head into his hands. He had not had the courage to tell her what he had felt for her. He had been too caught up in his own confusion to understand what she must have been going through.

"Goddam selfish idiot!" It exploded from him as he shot to his feet and stalked across the little pagoda. Leaning against a post, he rested his head on the wood. He was breathing hard, the old confusion and tumult of emotions spilling through him.

He looked back at Mrs Fung's shadowy figure in the twilight. She seemed so frail. Throughout her life of serving the whims of others, she had maintained an awesome dignity. Such strength and endurance, Luke realised, she had passed to her daughter.

For the first time, Luke thought he understood Jasmine. Her single-minded courage and that of Mrs Fung's came from the same source. It was as if, for each of them, love knitted her very being together, a love between mother and daughter that held no conditions.

"My time is coming soon," Mrs Fung said. "Then there will be no more secrets. Jasmine will be free. When I am gone, she will be alone. She lost me once when I made her leave, soon she will lose me again. She's had so much pain and sadness and she's still so young. I don't want her grieving before it is time. Especially now when she is about to start a new age as a wife and mother. Now is not the time for her to divert her life to the past."

"If she looks back now because of me, then everything that she and I have sacrificed over these long years will be like ashes in the wind. This man whom she will marry, he has believed everything that she has told him. He will not be able to bear the burden of the truth. If, because of me, she lets the truth slip out, she will lose her future – and then my life will have been for nothing."

"Can you understand now why she must not know that I am ill? Promise me you won't tell her."

For a long moment, Luke remained silent. He was calmer now but he still could not think clearly. But how could he refuse such a request? "I promise."

Mrs Fung stared intently at him. She was exhausted now but there was one last thing. Gathering her breath, she said, "When I am gone, you will be the only family that Jasmine will have left. She will need you then to help her through my passing ..."

"That is still far in the future."

Mrs Fung shook her head. "Listen to me. It is time. I don't know how long. But soon. Hush, let me finish ... I am old. What is one year or five years to me now? Jasmine's future is soon secure. I am ready."

"Ssh, don't talk to me about hospitals and doctors. I will live my life to the end. I will not give my body and will to men in the colour of death. I will not lie in wait for death, siphoned with tubes and poured with chemicals. I will live until my time comes. That is the old way. We cannot hide from the natural course of life."

Night comes suddenly in the tropics. In the thick darkness, the garden's strings of lights reflected on the water like fireflies. The call of cicadas beseeched them from the shore. Mrs Fung's voice drifted out of the night. "Jasmine will be alone, far away from who she is. She will have to hide her grief. Be with her. You will be the only one left who truly knows her. She will need you then. Look after her. Look after her for me."

The smell of evening swam in Luke's senses.

Jasmine alone, Jasmine trying so hard to fulfil her mother's dream. She had pursued the things which had taken her away from her home. And from him. He felt again his anger at her betrayal. And a new shame that he had let her dupe him into blame and resentment.

In the years after she left, he had drifted through casual affairs. He thought of Susan, tall and English, whose placid reasonableness charmed him. Like all his other relationships, theirs was without expectation and, so, safe from betrayal. He had drifted for three pleasant years with Susan. Susan, who like all the others, had demanded so little of him and who had never engaged him.

Jasmine fighting him, Jasmine making him laugh, Jasmine fierce with passion and determination. What of her own dreams? Was she happy living out a life that did not belong to her?

He had never been able to forget Jasmine. He knew then that he never would. He felt a confusion of pain and exhilaration. He saw Mrs Fung's dark shape waiting for his answer.

"I promise, Fung *Cheh*," he said. "I'll be there for Jasmine. Always."

* * *

Jordan's penthouse flat in Chelsea Harbour overlooked the Thames, and the dawn light flooded into the open-plan living space. He sat in an armchair at the windows that spanned one wall of the flat but he did not notice the panoramic view. Files and dossiers were spread across the oak coffee table in front of him and his concentration was focused on the work.

His mobile rippled its electronic call. He grabbed it and blipped it on. "Yes."

"Everything going as planned," the voice said, at the end of the line. It was Tan. He was cocky, almost.

"Go on."

"My people have set up the International Business Development

Foundation."

"The name's a nice touch."

"Thought you'd like it. Incorporated in Gibraltar, all legit office-holders – well, as legit as you and me."

Jordan laughed. "I'll start channelling through the funds for our 'contractor's expenses'."

"Usual procedure." This was a complex chain of fund transfers routed through Guernsey and shell companies in India, which would confuse the trail back to Jordan or any of his business interests. The Foundation was to be the technically legitimate body that would front Jordan's web of influence in Kampung Tanah. Through it, the residents of the town loyal to its call for progress would receive their carrots of "contractors' fees" and "expenses". Tan and his family firm would provide the sticks to beat any waverers. So far, no sticks had had to be deployed.

Jordan said, "The contractors understand what's expected of them?"

"I've got them eating out of my hand. Lingam, the lawyer – he's got the biggest practice in the KT region – he's doing all the paperwork for setting up the KT Business Development Committee, offshoot of the Foundation. He's wetting himself at being so close to the 'circle of power' as he calls it." Tan barked a laugh. "And there's Lee – he owns the main hotel in KT, Lee Hotel. He's reporting back on any stranger who comes into town, like he's scoring Brownie points over the others. They're all like fucking kids! After my anonymous visits, I let it be known that I'm 'Dunstan Khee, Vice-President of the Foundation', and they bought it! They act like I let them touch my bloody crown jewels, man."

Jordan crowed. "And you're sure there's no way to link the Foundation to me?"

"Dead sure. I've got a whole paper-trail history to show that it's a – let's see, here we are – 'a group of non-political business interests with the charitable object of promoting local economic success through international co-operation'. All that global-village shit."

"If I didn't know any better, I'd believe it. Who wrote up the bumpf?"

"I got a cousin who's a lawyer – fancies himself as a writer."

"Dr Chan and his allies. Any progress on shifting their position?" Jordan got up and moved to the window. The sun was rising, dispelling the grey dawn.

"I put Lee onto Ibrahim, the school teacher. They got kids in the same school. Early days yet – little chats after school, maybe a Sunday family outing. They're just sniffing each other out. And Lingam's got his order to soften up that young legal kid, Sarojaya – the boy's ambitious and hungry, he'll be easy."

"Chan?"

"Wong's got that job. We made him chairman of the committee. But the doctor'll be a hard, slow climb. He's sharp – and suspicious."

Jordan glared down at the river. "Don't let me down on this one, Tan."

"Hey, no way. Give me some credit." Tan sounded offended. "I promised you Chan by whatever inducements necessary – and so long as you're paying, I'll deliver. But he'll squeal if we go in like thugs, you know that, so I'm putting on my soft gloves. That's why you like my work. I know when to use the light touch and when we need the big boots."

"I'll wait to hear from you, then."

Jordan rang off. He stretched for his coffee mug. He and Tan had a working relationship going back over a number of development projects but none as important or as risky as this one. So far, Tan had never fucked up. Jordan gulped down the last of the cold coffee and made a face of disgust. He squinted out at the sun rising behind Battersea's skyline. Tan had better not fuck up this one.

8

L uke walked down the track with Dr Kenneth Chan towards the farmhouse three miles outside Kampung Tanah. With them were the Indian lawyer, Horatio Sarojaya, and Abdul Ibrahim, the Malay head teacher of the local school. It was late June.

Early morning dew hung in the deep blue light. It was dawn behind the range of hills. Terraced steps of vegetable gardens and orchards covered these shadowed western slopes. At the edge of the cultivated land, the forest began. The call of monkeys whooped across the sky.

Dr Chan and his two colleagues were the informal leaders of the diverse group of local people concerned by the proposed development in their area. Dr Chan was a clean-cut man in his mid-forties, outspoken and touched by missionary zeal from his Presbyterian upbringing. He was the conscience rallying the locals. Ibrahim, in contrast, was a thin, cautious man of the same age, tempering the doctor's energy with his calm. Ten years younger, Sarojaya had a bookish enthusiasm for his legal vocation. He had recently set up his own practice, consisting of himself and his secretary. He had offered his services free on this case in the hope that his public-spirited involvement would raise his profile in the community.

In the yard of the farmhouse, the men sat on makeshift chairs with local farmers and representatives of the small Orang Asli community. The farmers wore gumboots and overalls, their broad-brimmed rush hats and canvas gloves beside them. The aboriginal people were dressed in T-shirts and slacks, distinguished from the other locals by their soft curly hair and a reddish-brown complexion.

Ibrahim said, "In these modern times, change is inevitable. But the question is, what development is right for us?" He spoke in Malay, the common language among them all.

This was the final stage of Luke's preliminary investigations. He had already gathered the geological and site-survey data on previous visits. As part of his routine fact-finding, he used a video camera stored in the boot of his Land Rover. The images, transferred digitally onto his computer, aided geographical analysis and projections as well as acting as a visual *aide-memoire*. He was now familiar with the terrain and topographical history of the area. Today, he was on a reconnaissance to understand the concerns of the people who would be affected by the development.

"If there's a bigger town here, our farms got more business," Leong, their host, said. "We can supply direct – better than to truck produce up."

An older man sighed. "I got an animal farm, pigs, chickens, ducks. City people disturbing everything, cars everywhere, no good for my animals, man."

"Our young people all go to the cities now, more money there. If better business here, then they got a reason to stay. You all can see, in the last two years, Widecom, that cellphone network company, got the go-ahead to spread their cover to this area. Now, even the loneliest farm can make cheap cellphone calls up here in the hills. We have to move with the times or slowly die out."

"Mobile communication base stations don't take up much land."

Murut, the leader of the Orang Asli community, spoke up. "I hear they want golf course and theme park – like Disneyland. Where will they put these things?"

"They clear the forest and dig up our people's graves," a young man interjected. "The forest is our provider. Then they make us earn our way sewing bead trinkets and carving toys for tourists. That is not life."

"The jungle is an ancient spirit-place," Murut said. "Human

needs reverence to enter or he will be devoured. What do these big city people want from this place they do not understand? Let them stay in the world they know."

Another voice said, "If we live looking backwards, our community will die."

Fierce debate rang out across the yard. Uncertainty and anxiety fuelled tempers, goaded neighbours against each other.

Dr Chan let the energy exercise itself, then asked for quiet.

Luke spoke in fluent Malay, raising a ripple of respect from his listeners. "This is what I hear you say. This land provides your communities with food, wages and spiritual life. But for the farmers, there is now competition from other markets and you may not be able to survive very long. For the Orang Asli community, the modern world is encroaching and your old skills may not be enough to face the challenge."

There was a murmur of accord. This white man had spoken what was in their hearts and, in spite of his pale eyes and complexion, there was an affinity with them in his manner.

"You don't want progress at any cost. For farmers, a new market nearby for your produce will revive the community but there must be careful development to safeguard the quality of the soil and the elements. For the Orang Asli community, a balanced recreational development might be, say, a nature reserve instead of a theme park. Your forestry skills can then translate into work as forest rangers and guides and forestry management. Your craft skills can contribute to house-building and furniture-making for the new local market."

These ideas excited Luke's listeners. Their balance and harmony appealed to an ancient Asian yearning. A modern world had goaded these men into the singular choices of "either-or" and its strain had shown in the earlier flaring tempers. The mood shifted towards possibilities and hope.

Dr Chan clapped Luke on the back. "I knew you were the right man to help us."

"I can only work with you to express what you want. I can

show you alternatives but the submission to the planning authorities will contain what you all ultimately desire. Then it is in the hands of the authorities."

"Can they reject it?" Leong asked.

Sarojaya, the lawyer, said, "They may implement all, some or none of our submissions. In deciding, they have to consider the environmental impact and also, what 'benefits' us. But they are, nonetheless, committed to approving a viable development." He flicked through a thick phone-directory sized statute. "I have it here at Sections 145, 289(c) and 347-359 of the Kampung Tanah (Special Development Area) Act 1996."

"We won't give up without a fight," Dr Chan said. "Whatever your law book says, Horatio. Whatever big business says."

*   *   *

Back in Kampung Tanah, the consensus was the same.

Luke and his companions sat at a table on the covered walkway in front of an Indian coffeeshop. The midday glare bleached the hills but in the shade where they sat, the air was cool. A spread of fried chicken and assorted curries was piled across the table.

The coffeeshop overflowed with merchants, craftsmen and market traders. They all offered their views on the development, raising their voices across the tables as they ate.

From his store, Wong noticed the crowd spilling out onto the walkway. Leaving his daughter to close up for lunch, he made his way down the street. He found a stool in a corner of the coffeeshop. He ordered a drink.

Wong watched the white man. He had the confident bearing of one who was certain of his own mind and unafraid to stand by his principles. That was the way with these whites, Wong thought, arrogant and opinionated.

Luke talked about how development and local concerns could work together. There would need to be careful planning for buildings to take account of the hilly terrain. Soil erosion and air pollution would need to be addressed by natural prevention such as restrictions on tree felling. Measures for traffic control would have to be implemented. "But most important of all," he went on, "is the involvement of local people. Local skills, local knowledge of the land, local labour. Everyone has a stake, no one is alienated. Not just for short-term gain but for future generations.

"I've seen many places with thriving communities, long-term potential, valuable resources over-developed by outsiders for quick profit. When it's developed too fast and too much, all the resources are depleted, the local people displaced, there's no more money to be made. So the developers and money-makers move on and do the same somewhere else.

"But with proper management and co-operation, I think there's a chance here to do things differently – so everyone benefits."

"Not just the developers," Dr Chan interjected, "but us also and our children. And our children's children."

There was loud agreement. Wong sipped his coffee.

"I heard they're going to relocate our town!" someone shouted. "For the highway."

"We don't want that! We want our town here. Like it is!" another voice called. Someone else said, "If our views are not favoured, we can start a protest campaign. Like your environmental group, Mr McAllister, Green Action Direct – you hold protest campaigns to save the rainforest and to stop dam-building and so on. Your group can help us save our town."

Luke had to shout to make himself heard. "I am not a member of Green Action Direct. And I have no association with them or any political campaign group. I am an independent consultant. When Dr Chan contacted them, they gave him my name from a public directory of environmental consultants. I have no connection with them."

While Luke cared deeply for the protection of the environment, his independent stand was fundamental to his work. He was fiercely protective of his personal and professional integrity. Association with any party or political agenda would compromise that. He continued, "Green Action Direct have their own agenda. That agenda may not fit in with what *you* all want. They are outsiders – just like the developers. Just like me."

The people around him were quiet. He was not sure that they understood – or wanted to understand.

He said, "I'm here only to find out what you want and to give you technical advice. What goes in the submission to the planners is what you all want for this town."

The meeting absorbed Luke's words. He was telling them that they had to take responsibility for whatever decision they came to. It was not a position they were comfortable with.

"There are Western environmentalists who are like Victorian missionaries," Luke went on. "They come in with their own agenda to take up a local cause and twist it to fit what they think is best for you. You don't need that. Only *you* know what's right for you." Luke trusted passionately in individual integrity and personal responsibility. Facing the people in the coffeeshop that afternoon, he believed that the town would be able to steer the course for their own future without interference.

Wong finished his drink. He thought the young man typical of these greenies he had heard about – full of nice ideas but laughably unrealistic. Profit was everything and anyone who didn't know that was a fool. The town listened to the white man now because they still clung to their old familiar lifestyle. They would not care so much for balance and working together and environment, Wong thought, when they saw what new lifestyles the future could buy.

*　*　*

Some days later, in Susan's fifteenth-floor condominium in Penang, Luke went over the economic data on Kampung Tanah with her. As colleagues at the same research university, they had worked together on numerous projects, Susan's sociology and economics background complementing Luke's environmental expertise. The bright sea lay beyond the window and a breeze brushed through the open terrace doors.

Susan was a slim brunette, tanned from windsurfing, tennis and hiking. She was pretty in a conventional way, her pleasant smile and amiable manner attracting many admirers. Until recently, her affair with Luke had been comfortable, friendly. They had been realistic about their hopes in this casual relationship, their commitment to their careers taking priority. Luke had found in her a mutual support and companionship. For the most part, it had almost made him happy.

But in the last year, Susan had begun to talk about a future together. Luke had drifted with her plans but it was a commitment that she had structured. He had been evasive of any decisions and reluctant when she tried to press him. "We're wonderful together as we are. Let's not change things for the sake of change," he had said. But the directionless course of their affair was making her restless.

And now something had happened.

He leaned over the computer terminal where Susan sat. She was switching windows between graphs and statistical tables, summarising for him her analysis of the impact of a large-scale development on Kampung Tanah's market-town economics and human sociology. In her soft tones, she outlined competition differentials, capital-labour ratios and income distribution.

Luke suddenly moved away and slumped into a chair. He said, "Don't you ever wonder about these individuals who make up your charts and statistics?" His voice expected a fight.

Susan looked at him. "You wanted me to analyse the impact of numerous new individuals moving into an established community," she replied calmly. "I can only do that by looking at mass movements."

"But don't you *care* about their hopes and ambitions and fears?"

"That's what economics is about – people's motivations. Only on a large scale."

"But don't you care?" Luke leaned forward combatively.

Susan scrutinised him. He'd been back from Sri Lanka for

three weeks and ever since an underlying irritation prickled his manner whenever they met. In their professional lives, Luke had begun to take issue with Susan's academic views as if for the sake of provocation. Unsure of how to confront him, she would shrug and wait for his mood to pass.

"It's irrelevant," she said now. He gestured impatiently.

She had never seen him like this. She attributed his edginess to fatigue from a heavy work schedule. Last semester, he had been supportive to her throughout the first segment of her doctoral project. She resolved to take his moods in a reciprocal spirit. But the memory of what he had told her some weeks ago bothered her.

Luke had told her about his encounter with an old friend, a woman he had never been expecting to see again. It had been a passing anecdote but in his speaking about her, there had been a warmth in his voice that Susan did not recognise.

He was saying now, "Things happen – world events, whatever – because people feel passionately about something. I've never seen you passionate about anything."

"Why are we having this discussion?"

"I don't know." Luke shifted sulkily. "You're always so ... rational. So sensible."

"And it bores you?"

Luke said nothing.

"We never used to quarrel. Now, recently it seems ... I'm not quite what you want."

Luke frowned. "That's not –"

"You're still in love with her."

Luke stared. Her voice had been without recrimination. He made a face and turned away. There was no need to clarify who Susan meant. "We were just friends," he said, after a long pause.

"When did you know her?"

"We were kids."

"Was she a foreigner, too?" Susan asked, thinking of the expatriate white community in Malaysia.

Jasmine in her heavy European suit and high heels. A stranger to her past. "You could say that."

"Is she 'passionate'? Is this what this is all about?"

Luke stood up. "Stop analysing this scene and get involved in it!"

"There was a time when you didn't want involvement. That was what you liked about me."

Luke looked down. He was quieter now. "Seeing her again made me wake up. Made me feel again ..."

He fell silent. Susan murmured, "Feelings you could never have for me?"

Luke hesitated. Then nodded. "I'm sorry."

"What are you going to do?"

Luke prowled out onto the sun terrace. The glare from the sea and sky was painful. The heat blanketed the day like the jungle on the surrounding hills. The breeze gave no relief

Susan joined him. They did not look at each other. She said, "It's over, isn't it? It was over even before Sri Lanka."

"We used to want the same things from this relationship. But –"Luke searched for the right words. Finally, he said, "Well, I'm not a family man."

Susan smiled. "I'll be all right, you know. It'll be awful for a while but, hey, I'd rather that than be your easier option."

In the sun-drenched bedroom, they made love with the tenderness of saying goodbye. Afterwards, as they dressed, they watched each other and smiled.

Susan said, "She doesn't know how lucky she is. What are you going to do?"

"Work. Write – that book on grass-roots developments I've been talking about."

"You know what I mean. About her."

"She's getting married in a few weeks."

"So?" Susan stared at him expectantly. "Aren't you going to stop her?"

Luke laughed. "This is real life, not a romantic novel! I can't go rushing across the world and shout, 'Stop the wedding!'"

"Why not?"

Luke groped for the words.

"What are her feelings for you?"

"I don't know."

Susan burst into laughter. "Here is Mr Passion himself, too fiery for the sensible rational life – now too sensible and rational to go and get the woman he loves!" Then, more gently, "What are you afraid of?"

Luke thought of his mother, her English beauty sodden with alcohol, her fine manners wasted in the sweaty tropics. Empty days and mud and mosquitoes instead of the witty conversations in stylish drawing rooms and shopping and lunch in Bond Street. He thought of what had become of the hopeful young lovers his parents had been. He thought of Jasmine in his arms, by his side, taking his hand, slipping her arm round him. He ached with hope but all he saw was his mother's disappointments in her eyes.

"She couldn't live in Taiping," Luke said. "Her ambitions are for power and money and all the things I've fought against all my life. My work is about curbing the destruction that power and money can cause. How are we to make a life together?"

"That's what's driven you apart?"

"I couldn't live with her in London. Me in my old khakis, flying in from some 'godforsaken hole,' as my mother would put it, straight into a nice little power-dressed cocktail party to swill Martinis and gossip about the people that matter? No, I can't see that."

"But aren't you even going to try?" Susan cried, in exasperation. "You – who's always talking about passion and being true to yourself and making a difference. Are you giving up already? What about making a difference in both your lives?"

Luke stared.

Susan said, "She's not your mother, you know."

Late that afternoon, Luke drove to a deserted beach on the windward side of the island. Walking barefoot across the creamy sand, he stopped near a grove of palm trees. He felt restless but drained. The stiff evening breeze whipped sand, stinging, into his shins. The crackling of the palm fronds roared above the rhythm of the waves.

Stripping down to the waist, Luke began the motions of *silat Minangkabau*, an ancient Sumatran martial art. His fists rammed from his spirit-centre at shadow opponents, he twisted and kicked, high and sideways. At first, his movements were unfocused, graceless, the turbulence of his angry mind scattering his energy. He went over the sequences again. And again.

He remembered the words of his fighting master. "*Silat* is a gift from the tiger. In defence and attack, the man controls his body like the tiger does," the old man's gentle voice came back to him. "Tiger-spirit and man-body become one." Luke relinquished his mind and emotions to the strong, swift gliding of the tiger.

A calm began to propel the fierce movements. His energy stilled into powerful intensity. He worked the sequences over and over, till the transformation took him – till the sunlight and dark of the tiger's markings fused in the sinuous gold and shadow of his muscled body, and beyond, into the rippling light and shade of the sea. In that moment of unity, when spirit and animal and elements focused into infinity, Luke held within him knowing and not knowing, being and not being, all things and nothing. It was a release and a containment. Stillness and acceleration.

The tiger's dance concluded at last in a gesture of anticipation and acceptance. Although he had worked out vigorously and a sheen of sweat glistened on his torso, Luke was breathing gently. He made his way to a promontory of rocks on the edge of the bay.

There he clambered up to a perch jutting out over the sea. He stayed for a long time, staring out at the sea and sky.

He remembered Jasmine as he had known her long ago. He thought of the beautiful, confident woman she had become. He heard again Mrs Fung's voice coming out of the darkness in the pagoda.

He had always loved Jasmine and he always would. He knew then that it did not matter whether she loved him in return. It was enough that he loved. It freed him, suddenly, this knowledge – as if a part of him that had been long dead now awoke.

9

The humping rhythms of "Wild Thing" blared through the smoke-filled bar. The men cat-called to the sullen peroxide blonde prowling the stage. Her skin was white against a studded body harness. Rhythmically, she slapped a riding crop against her thigh-high stiletto boots. All that was left to come off was a rubber G-string.

After work in the City, in the Grog and Garter Tavern, Harry drained his third shot of whisky and slapped the tumbler down among the pint glasses and plates of chips. His party of colleagues and clients smoked Davidoff cigars and waved money, competing to shout the worst obscenities.

Harry wandered over to the bar with his newest client contact. "Have to say, Bill, I can't get excited over a Nazi bitch."

Bill Jordan nodded. "They don't make 'em like that out East." They settled onto bar stools and ordered double vodkas.

"Hey," Harry savoured the spirit burning his throat, "you hear the latest thinking on the Philippines?" Harry had recently secured an introduction to Jordan through his contacts. They had played squash, and drunk together at various City watering holes – all at Harry's instigation and expense. His ostensible motive was to offer Jordan opportunities to raise capital for the venture in Malaysia.

"The Philippines are looking good for an economic recovery. If the Government pulls it off, there's potential there for high rewards. You should move your personal stocks out of Japan to Manila – the risk-reward equation in Tokyo is looking drab. The Nikkei's been flat for a few years now …"

For a while, the men talked stocks and the emerging markets in

Asia. Harry was smooth in his patter, business-like and intimate at the same time, as if he and Jordan were old friends.

Apparently matching Harry drink for drink, Jordan remained detached and alert. He let the toff woo him, feeding him enough to encourage but slipping out of his reach when it counted. Jordan despised the hoorays and he thought this one particularly lazy, proud and stupid. He knew why Harry was ingratiating himself and it amused him. Especially as Harry had thought he was being subtle.

Harry did not want Jasmine to know of his new friendship with her most important client. "She's not my keeper," he had said to Jordan. "What I do is my own business."

Jordan had complied with Harry's desire for secrecy. He could see nothing to gain or lose by it for now. Secret knowledge was always a weapon and he liked to update his arsenal. There was a reason why the fiancé of Jordan Cardale's best lawyer was wooing its CEO in secret – just before Jordan's most important construction bid in Asia. Jordan intended to find out what it was.

The stripper gyrated in her finale and swaggered off the stage. The next performer was a lithe Thai girl, made up in the 'eastern exotic' look, and wearing a dragon on her head.

Harry and Jordan watched, savouring her satiny *cafe crème* skin.

Harry murmured, "That's more like it."

"Asia's the last frontier for money-making adventurers like you and me, eh?" Jordan ordered another double for Harry. "Nobody worries about rules and regulations. A favour here and there – all part of the Asian way of life. Money changes hands, no one asks too many questions."

"Keeps the cogs of business oiled." Harry clapped the other man on the back.

"It's like the Wild West, mate. The Gold Rush. Great opportunities to make it big. But you got to be a street fighter, know what I mean? No place for fine manners. Rough and ready, live or die by your wits, mate. The people out there aren't very sophisticated," Jordan gestured at the writhing Oriental girl just out of the paddy fields. "They know how to make money, like, it's in their blood, but we can run circles round them. We got a lot more civilisation behind us. No way can a few wog peasants outwit us, mate. They're not that bright – they let us colonise them once before, didn't they?"

But Malaysia had proven otherwise. Jordan had bid in previous high-profile tenders there – the new five-terminal airport near Kuala Lumpur, a multi-million commercial development in Johor across the causeway from Singapore. So far, he had failed in all of them.

The other South East Asian countries where he had a presence had been easy. Malaysia had a more sophisticated political structure on top of its superior economic dynamo. Together with its educated elite, these gave the country a greater leverage and discernment in attracting the best contractors for their projects. It riled Jordan that he had not been considered good enough by what was, after all, only an Asian country. The Malaysians had not been impressed by him, these wogs, jumped up in their designer labels and buying their way through Oxbridge and the Ivy League. Jordan scowled. They weren't going to keep him out. He had the money to make sure that, this time, he would be a front-line contender. His tactics were risky: if things didn't go as planned, if the people he relied on played beyond his control, he would lose a lot more than just money.

He said suddenly, "Bill Jordan does not lose."

"I'll drink to that."

"I'm stealing your wife away right after the honeymoon, mate. The first big meeting in KL on the university tender – all the legals, surveyors, engineers, the lot."

Harry glanced sidelong at him. "The legals?"

"Both the London and KL teams together for the first time."

"First time?" Harry had turned from the stage and was watching Jordan now. "Don't be a bad sport, mate. Jasmine's the best bloody lawyer I've got. We need her out there."

"No other meetings out there before?"

"Sure, we have. I didn't do the site survey from here!"

"I mean, legals and so forth."

"Nah." Jordan laughed, but he was watching Harry watching him. "Your fiancée's charge-out rate is too expensive to fly her round the world for any old meeting. She's my big guns, know what I mean? We roll her out for the big battles. Haven't had any of those yet."

Harry nodded, with an attempt at nonchalance. But the colour in his face had deepened. Jasmine had told him she was going to Kuala Lumpur for meetings on the Jordan Cardale project. She had told him about a site visit to the hills. She had disappeared out of his life for almost a week on the basis of this lie. The muscles in his jaw worked to contain his fury.

The Thai girl finished in a contorted posture of servitude to the delight of her white audience.

Perhaps it was Jordan who was lying. Or both of them. Harry narrowed his eyes. He thought of the wild, impulsive accusation he had thrown in Jasmine's face at Bibendum. He had wanted to hurt her as she had been hurting him but he had not really believed her capable of such a thing. A horror at what he might be opening up crept through him. And then anger, suddenly, at how he had been duped. He rode the anger, driving it hard inside, while on the surface he laughed and bough Jordan another drink. One way or another, he would find out the truth.

* * *

In the week before her wedding, Jasmine worked eighteen hours every day. She would be away from the office for two weeks on her honeymoon, and afterwards, there was the tender meeting in Kuala Lumpur. All the work on the Jordan Cardale tender and four other major deals would be covered by the time she left the office on the eve of her wedding. She would brief her senior assistant so he could deal with practical issues, but there would be no crises in her absence that would require another partner taking over the flies: she always made sure of that.

The arrangements for the wedding were well under control in the hands of the event company.

It was dark by the time Jasmine stepped out of the office on the Wednesday night before her wedding. Lights were still on in some of the barristers' chambers around the square. In the warm summer night, she felt as if she were back in the courtyard of an Oxford college.

Jasmine searched the shadows for someone. She did not know why. As if she had sensed him before she saw him. Luke was waiting for her by the porter's lodge.

She saw him ease away from the wall into a frame of light from a window. It was as if an unacknowledged hope had slipped into reality. His familiar smile waited for her. His eyes were bright against the tan of his features. He stood confidently at ease in his Western clothes – jeans and a cotton shirt the colour of red earth.

The shock of pleasure made her laugh out loud. The weariness of the day drained away as she found her pace quickening towards him. There was no need for thought, no doubts to paralyse her and she caught herself grinning and breaking into a run. He swept her into his arms.

"Luke!" She was laughing, feeling him hold her closer. "What on earth are you doing here?"

"I had a conference in Brussels. Thought I'd stop by and see the great lawyer at work." His voice was warm in her ear.

She gathered herself and moved out of his embrace. "Well," she said, taking him in with her gaze. Looking away. "Well, this is where I work."

"I know."

"I was going home."

"I know."

They grinned.

"Is there anything you don't know?"

"Shall we walk a little? Before you go home."

She hesitated, wariness creeping back. What if Harry saw them?

Luke said, "Your mother told me. No one knows about your past. They won't find out through me. I just wanted to see you again."

She looked up into the eyes she knew so well. The warmth she saw there drew her in as it always did. She felt afraid of what might happen but she nodded.

They strolled through Lincoln's Inn Fields towards Aldwych. There was little traffic at this time in the evening and, for a while, it seemed to Jasmine that she walked in a dream.

She could not stop herself from talking, as if she was afraid of what he might say into the silence. She talked about the wedding. About Harry's family and how wonderful they were. She talked about Marietta, the interior designer to whom Harry had introduced her, who had been so kind, who had welcomed her into Harry's circle of friends: they were the best of friends now, going shopping together, doing lunch and Marietta had been so good about helping with the wedding. The wedding – it was going to be so special – Jasmine talked about who would be at the reception, what gifts had already arrived, how much she adored Harry.

"What's so funny?" she demanded suddenly.

Luke was watching her with a smile. "I make you nervous, don't I?" Jasmine opened her mouth to retort but could think of nothing to say. "I was right to come," he said, with a relief she did not understand.

"What are you talking about?"

They had crossed the Strand onto Waterloo Bridge. Luke stopped and faced Jasmine. He said, "You're making a mistake with Harry."

"Excuse me?" Jasmine gasped. How could he know such a thing? She felt winded.

"You're making a mistake marrying Harry," Luke said. "You know it."

"Harry's wonderful!" Jasmine recovered. She thought of all the reasons why she loved Harry. "He's so generous and he's done so much for me. He adores me."

"You?"

"I adore him, too! Harry's the best. He has everything – good looks, charm."

"Money and connections."

Jasmine felt it like a slap. "How dare you?" She turned and hurried away. He had thrown the truth in her face. The vista across the Thames opened out. To her right, the Houses of Parliament and Big Ben glowed up-river. On her left, the pale dome of St Paul's rose like an early moon out of the cluttered City. Wisps of light shimmered on the water far below.

When Luke caught up with her, she snapped, without breaking step, "Have you come all this way to insult me?"

"No. Not to insult you."

Luke blocked her path. Her momentum propelled her into him. He steadied her. She shook him off. "Listen to me," he said.

She tried to sidestep out of his hold. He was firm, forcing her to look into his eyes. She would not at first. Could not.

"Jasmine."

Something in the way he said her name held her. She took a breath and faced his gaze.

"You don't love him," Luke said quietly. "You love all the baubles that he can give you."

"That's not true." But her protest was half-hearted.

"You're marrying him because you're afraid."

"I'm not scared of anything."

"You're afraid of living your mother's life. You're afraid of failing all her ambitions. You are living out *her* dreams because you're afraid to have any dreams of your own. I'm afraid that if you do, you'll destroy the one thing she lives for."

Jasmine felt cold. She began to tremble. "I don't know what you're talking about."

"But you're the one who has to live out this role. You can marry Harry and have the society wedding of the year and all the baubles you could ever want. But every morning you're going to have to wake up and face yourself in the mirror – face who you really are before you put that mask back on for another day. Day after day for the rest of your life."

"No." Why was he resurrecting all this?

"Every day, you'll die a little bit more. And in the end, you'll have everything you could ever want and nothing."

Words struggled against Jasmine's choking breath. "How dare you? Who are you to come here and accuse me? You don't understand anything. You don't understand anything about me!"

"Tell me, then, Jasmine," Luke said. "Tell me everything about you. I want to understand."

Jasmine paused. His earnestness touched something in her. But where would she begin? How could she tell him about her shame and guilt? How to describe those long-ago images that still haunted her, still drove her now? She wasn't just living out the enchanted life her mother had dreamed for her. Nor was she afraid of stepping the path her mother had taken. She was trying to achieve something more than that. She was trying to make it all come out right in the end, on her own terms. It was her private atonement for her shame. Couldn't he see? She was trying to make right something that she'd made go wrong, balancing out the darkness of what had happened that terrible night long ago, with everything she could offer of herself. She hardly knew what it really meant, only that this urge drove her with a momentum she couldn't control. Harry and her new life, her success and achievement, they were what had risen from the ashes of her shame. The girl that Luke thought he'd known was dead to Jasmine. Only her life now had any reality. That was what she was searching for – a life without ghosts. She saw Luke waiting there and realised she did not have the words to tell him.

Instead, she took the offensive. "I belong here now. This is my world." She gestured to the whole of London stretching out around them. "This is my now and my future. Just who do you think you are? After ten years of nothing – nothing between us, nothing I owe you – you dare to come and make your speeches at me! What right have you?"

"Goddammit, Jasmine!" Luke exploded, moving away. Startled, she stared at him. He turned back in exasperation. "I love you. I've always loved you."

His words caught them both off-guard. In the silence, the noise of the traffic crowded out all thought. They were standing very close.

Jasmine shut her eyes. It was like hearing news of a disaster. But an overwhelming relief welled up like tears. Someone knew. He knew her struggle. He knew the chain she had put around her heart. He knew her.

She opened her eyes into the intensity of Luke's gaze. Leaning up towards him, she felt his kiss on her lips. Suddenly, she realised that she had always wanted this. That afternoon up in Firefly Clearing, she had wanted so much to hold him in such an embrace but she had made herself strong and cold. She kissed him now with the passion she had feared.

This was how it should have been all along, she thought. This was a happiness beyond all thought and striving. This was how it could be.

This, and a lifetime of guilt and self-loathing. A life trapped by the past, like a moth on the sticky tongue of a reptile.

She pulled away from Luke. "No. You're crazy."

She had to gather her thoughts. Seeing him again, it had stirred up so many feelings. But things were different now. She was different. Ten years had passed. A long time. She had moved on.

"Who do you think you are?" she began. "Turning up out of the blue and – and pulling this – this manipulative charade? I don't even know you any more. It's been ten years, damn you! You don't know me, you just assume you do. Just like you've always assumed everything!"

Luke did not seem surprised by her outburst. It infuriated her and propelled her into fiercer argument. "What do you think is going to happen? That I'll drop everything – my life here, my career, Harry and everything he means to me – just because you're acting out some romantic Hollywood dream? Wake up! You like to play

Big White Saviour to the poor of Asia, don't you? Still the little master to the core. Well, I don't need you to save me. I'm not the poor little servant girl any more. I don't need your damn pity! You always loved telling me what to do and how to live my life and what ideals I should have. How dare you? How dare you come here now?"

"Isn't that what Harry does? Tell you how to behave, what tastes to have, making you into his own Eliza Doolittle?"

"Who told you that?"

"Just a guess." Luke held her gaze. "Obviously a good one."

"Harry's been the one sure thing in my life all these years," Jasmine said. "When my mother didn't write, I knew she'd been deadly serious about everything she said before I left – that my past and everything in it would be dead, including her. I had to make a new life – a wonderful, happy new life – and she would live it if I lived it. If I failed, her whole life would have been wasted, can't you see? I was so frightened I would fail her. But Harry was there, this handsome, charming boy who loved me more than anyone or anything, who was ready to give me everything I could dream of. He makes me feel safe and protected and loved. He's been like a father to me."

She was breathing hard, shaking uncontrollably. "Harry … He's been so good to me. I owe him my happiness. And you, Luke, you and me, we were just kids. It's too late now for anything between us. It would never have worked back then – the little master and his servant girl! How can it work now? But the wedding – everything's ready …"

"Are you trying to convince me or yourself?" Luke's voice was gentle.

She did not notice the tears creeping down her face. "Don't you see? We've always been a golden couple, Harry and me. That's how it'll always be."

Luke was watching her. He did not try to touch her again. There was a sadness in his eyes. But he was smiling. "My poor Jasmine," he said.

Anger cut across her tears. "You're impossible!"

Jasmine moved away, searching the traffic, and saw a cab. She waved frantically. He was so patronising, so infuriatingly confident! As the taxi pulled up, she said, "I'll tell you what's a mistake. Your coming here. And my letting you talk nonsense to me."

Luke shook his head. "One day – maybe not now, but one day – I'm going to hear you talk about me like you talk about those baubles you love so much."

"I never want to see you again, Luke."

He shrugged and smiled as if he did not believe her. Then, he turned away and headed across the bridge towards Waterloo. Jasmine stood by the taxi.

"Where to, love?" the driver asked.

As Jasmine watched, Luke raised his hand without looking back and cocked a salute. He had known she would be watching!

She climbed into the cab and slammed the door in fury. "Chelsea," she said. "Don't call me 'love'."

The cabbie spun the taxi in a U-turn. "Sorry, love," he said absently.

* * *

The answering machine in the hallway of Harry's house clicked on as the call came in. Jasmine's voice floated tinnily through as she started to leave a message. "Hello, darling, I thought I'd catch you before you left for work. Are you there?"

She paused, waiting for him to pick up.

In the bedroom, Harry looked up from towelling his hair and listened. It was eight thirty in the morning, the Thursday before their wedding.

"No? You must've gone already," Jasmine went on. "Just calling to see how your client function went last night. I'll catch you later. All my love, darling."

She hung up. The machine clicked off and rewound itself Harry sauntered across to the bed. He was flushed and warm from his shower.

Sitting down on the edge of the bed, he stroked the naked body that lay entangled in the sheets.

"Mmm, that's nice. Who was that? Your wife-to-be?"

"I told her I was having cocktails with an old client last night." His hand slid up into the crevice of the buttocks.

"'Old', am I?" his companion laughed archly.

"We *have* known each other a long time."

"Good save ..." The teasing laugh was deep and throaty.

He nuzzled the familiar, long back. "What you and I have, it'll never change, will it?"

"No, silly. What a thing to say!" She rolled onto her side and he took in her full, supple body. She was blonde, with eyes as green as envy. She was almost forty and big-boned but her body was well toned. Her breasts and buttocks were still proud and high and she luxuriated in the heavy sensuousness of her curves. Marietta Asquith reached up and stroked Harry's cheek. "What's the matter, baby?"

Harry stood up and began to dress. "I thought that Jasmine was different from all the other women. She had an innocence you don't get in English girls. She seemed so pure and trusting. Like an exotic, delicate flower. But she's changed."

"Well, she's grown up, got more sophisticated. You groomed her well."

"I made her, yes. An innocent, adorable little kid with more money than sense when we first met – and now, look at her. Poised, gorgeous, sexy. And a bitch like the others." Harry turned, his face twisted in pain. "She's lying to me, I know it! She's having an affair."

Marietta laughed. "Jasmine? No, she's not the kind."

"She's often home late, away at weekends, off abroad. She says it's work, but I don't know what she's really up to."

"Like she doesn't know what you're up to?"

Harry glared at her. Marietta sat up in bed and scrabbled for her cigarettes. "Only joking, darling. God, you're touchy these days." She lit one and inhaled. "I know Jasmine. She's a dear, sweet girl.

Perhaps rather too serious about her work but absolutely devoted to you. I like her – she's been wonderfully good for you. Don't let your nasty suspicious mind go and ruin it all. We have a cosy little arrangement – she made you nice again and I like you better when you're nice. I know you've had your ups and downs. But ever since you proposed, things have got back on an even keel – thank God! Ugh, I couldn't bear all those endless dramas and suspicions when you were with those other English girls – you were so tiresome."

Harry sat down on the bed again, his shirt half buttoned. Trying to control his temper, he told Marietta about the disastrous evening at Bibendum and his suspicions about what Jordan had told him. "It doesn't seem to fit. Something's wrong and I don't know what it is."

"You humiliated her in public? Christ, Harry!"

Harry looked down, sullenly buttoning his shirt.

Marietta sighed. "Right, I'll humour you. Could Jordan be lying?"

"This is the strange part. I checked up on him through someone I know who knows Danesleigh, his junior director. Jordan was in London all the time Jasmine was away."

"Was she really abroad?"

"I thought of that. I looked through her things. I found a used airline ticket. There's a stewardess I know –"

"The one you had a thing with two years ago? You crafty boy."

"She looked up the records and a Jasmine Lian did travel to Kuala Lumpur using Jasmine's ticket."

"Well, she probably did go on business but Jordan didn't need to be there."

Marietta stubbed out her cigarette. "You *are* being ridiculous. If I were her, I wouldn't have stood your nonsense. You're damn lucky she's such a sweet-tempered little thing. Good Lord, interrogating her like you did and calling her a slut in public – Harry, really! You probably frightened her to death – no wonder she couldn't give you a straight answer! What did you expect?"

He stood up sulkily. "Maybe you're right. Maybe I am too

paranoid."

"Poor Harry, you have to learn to relax."

He tucked in his shirt-tails with angry determination. "Well, I'm not taking any more chances. After the wedding, she stops work."

"But you used to be so proud of her success. You liked her drive and energy."

"Must you always defend her against me, you of all people?" Harry struggled with his tie. "She's changed. It's different now. I adore her but, God, she's driving me crazy."

Marietta laughed. "Because you can't control her? Harry, relationships evolve. So, you two have been going through a bumpy patch. It happens once in a while – especially if you've been together as long as you have. Here – you're making a mess of that. Let me help you."

She slid out of bed and leaned against his back as she reached up to adjust his tie. They watched each other, for a moment, in the mirror. Harry seemed calmer, more hopeful. He let his hands drop to his side as she handled the knot. Her full lips curled into a smile. "The wedding is on Saturday. She'll be safely yours after that. Stop working yourself up over nothing."

Harry shifted sheepishly. "I suppose you're right."

"Besides, it's more fun if she's got a little spunk. Consider it a challenge, Harry, my gorgeous boy. The more headstrong the filly, the more satisfying the taming, surely. There – that looks better." Marietta patted his buttocks, her hand lingering for a long moment.

"Now, off you go or you'll be late."

10

Mrs Fung eased herself out of bed. It was past midnight. The pains in her stomach had flared up again. Perhaps it was the excitement – Jasmine would be married tomorrow. Every week reading Jasmine's letters about her new life and her wedding plans, Mrs Fung felt as if she would be there to see her daughter marry.

In the kitchen, she opened her cabinet of medicinal herbs, searching among the jars for the angelica root. Her *chi* – life-energy – had been sluggish and now amassed in turmoil. She felt it igniting with the overheating of her fire energy. She had brought up blood again, the colour and texture of coffee grains.

The angelica would disperse Mrs Fung's pent-up energy, release it through perspiration and wind, ease off the pain. She boiled stalks of the pungent root in a saucepan with green tea.

In the living room, she sipped the mixture and felt its heat soothe the pain. She sighed. In a while, it would be a dull ache again and she would be able to sleep. In the dark of the living room she remembered the darkness of a night twenty years ago. She had sat here weeping for the husband she had lost, weeping for all the wrong choices she had made. And for her daughter, who cowered in the other room.

He had started to brutalise Jasmine that night, knocking her to the floor. Mrs Fung had tried to stop him. "You do what you like to me! Leave her alone!" After he had gone, cursing her, she sat amid the debris of their struggle, the broken glass, upturned chairs, smashed ornaments.

Alone now in the dark, Mrs Fung said, "My pretty one, you are safe now, far away from here. I'm happy for you, so happy tonight ..."

Mrs Fung had been happy like this once before. It surprised her to remember it so clearly. The happiness of youthful hope. She had been sixteen – Lian Mei-Ling, the second daughter of the wealthy Lian family. Her father made his money in the import and export of wholesale goods. His company had offices across Malaya. He was planning to move his base to California in partnership with a cousin when Mei-Ling met Tommy Fung.

Tommy was dashing, handsome, and five years her senior. Mei-Ling loved the way his gaze owned her, she adored his sly smile. He smelt of aftershave and cigarettes. His touch was exciting, dangerous. They would have a life of travel, love and adventure, he told her.

"He's a gambler and womaniser!" Her father roared. It was a hot, still evening. They had waited dinner an hour for her and her father's irritation turned now to rage. "It's well known, you stupid girl. He's only after your money and position!"

"He loves me," she wailed.

They had had this confrontation many times before. Mr Lian had hastened his migration plans because of this. The sooner they left for America, he would say, the sooner his daughter would forget the scoundrel. Now he barked, "I'll send you and your mother on first. The boys can help me finish off here."

She stood tall and held his gaze. "It's too late, *Ah Teh* – Father."

"How dare you defy me!"

"I don't belong to you anymore."

He stared at her.

"I'm not coming home. I only came to tell you the news." She had married Tommy Fung that afternoon. They had spent the rest of the day drinking cheap champagne in a hotel bar. She had felt daring and grown-up. In those few hours, she had been so happy. She was Mrs Tommy Fung and what a wild time they were having. Their future together had looked so glorious. They had known each other six weeks. He waited outside in his fifth-hand MG.

Her father cursed her. Her mother cried as he cursed his

daughter, cursed her marriage, her future. "You are no daughter of mine. You will die before you see this family again. Get out and don't come back. Go and live in hell with that bastard. That will be justice."

In the car, Tommy drove like a demon. His face was hard in the glow of the dashboard. "You said he'd have to accept it if we presented it to him just like that – married. You said he loved you!"

"He does! He just needs time ..." She trailed off into silent tears.

She had never been to his house before. It was in a deprived neighbourhood of town beyond Night Soil Bridge. She stumbled after him down the unlit path to the bungalow in an empty compound. It was ugly and small and smelt of dirty clothes and liquor. "You said you had a big house and you lived with your mother."

"I said many things." He drank from a bottle of whisky. "I never knew my mother."

He pulled her into the bedroom and made her undress. She sat on the edge of the unmade bed and waited for him to turn his back. He took another swig. "I said, take your clothes off."

He possessed her with rage. That was all that he possessed, her body and her devotion. She had given up everything else for the love of him. "And I love you, too," he snarled.

After he had satisfied himself, he rolled onto his back. His snoring drowned out her weeping.

Her family set sail for San Francisco the following month. She never heard from them again.

"Your father loved me in his own way," she would tell Jasmine. "But he had hoped for so much. I was too in love to see that. Don't make my mistake."

Tommy had an old van, which he used for business. He bought plastic dolls in Thailand and sold them in Penang, he peddled Indonesian carvings to shops in KL. Sometimes he brought in pornographic materials packed in a cargo of children's toys, in crates of cigarettes. Girlie magazines, dildos, harnesses, porn movies, whatever his customers asked for. It made him a good living.

For special customers, he bought girls from Bangkok and shipped them through the old trading post of Port Weld, which had declined to a fishing village built on stilts. A pre-dawn passing of two fishing boats and the transfer of goods was made. Mrs Fung saw the girls when he brought them home to be deloused and prettified. They could have been no more than seven. "My cousin's daughter," he would explain. "I got her a job as a kitchen help." Mrs Fung did not believe him but she said nothing after the first time when he had beaten her almost unconscious. She would give them a newspaper parcel of dumplings. Slipping them what money she could spare, she whispered, "The gods will watch over you."

Tommy saw other women and spent her housekeeping money on prostitutes. He passed his time in bars, playing dice. Occasionally he would win but mostly he lost. He would come home ugly with liquor and spoiling for a fight. She never learned to live with the terror of his raging violence. Fear settled in the core of her, ran in her veins. Sleep scattered at the sound of his footsteps, coming in late at night, the smell of him. But she learned to protect her head with her arms when he hit her, curl into a ball when he kicked her, never fighting back.

She had seven pregnancies before Jasmine was born – three miscarriages, two stillbirths and two sickly boys, who were born alive but never saw their third birthdays. "Your rotten cunt cannot give life! The filthy blood of your family kills our sons!" her husband screamed. "I will never have sons to carry on my name because of you! There will be no sons to pray at my grave as is my right!"

Jasmine was the child of her old age and the hope she had never dared to have. "You must know how to look after yourself," she would say to her little girl. "Men cannot be depended on. My father gave me up when I didn't do what he wanted – that was his punishment for me. My husband beat me when I couldn't give him what he wanted – money, position, sons. Make a man love you more than you love him – then it is you who will make the conditions."

By the time Jasmine was born, Tommy would disappear for weeks, sometimes months. Mrs Fung never knew where he went or when he would be back. He had business and women in Bangkok, Jakarta, Manila. But he would turn up again when he had run out of money or had to lie low after another of his scams had failed.

He often left her without money. To survive, Mrs Fung worked as a cook, at wealthy homes along Swettenham Road, the millionaires' row where her father had once owned a house. Her first pay was one hundred and fifty ringgit a month.

Her husband's debts continued to mount, and soon even their house was secured by a creditor. To meet the interest payments, Mrs Fung took on additional duties as a servant. This earned her an extra fifty ringgit a month. Late at night, she made dumplings and snacks to sell at the morning market with a profit of thirty cents a piece. On her days off, she sold *laksa* – curried noodles – from a makeshift stall on the side of Market Road at a profit of a ringgit a bowl. She sewed buttons for a clothing manufacturer at three ringgit per five garments.

"Money, money, not having it, wanting it, counting every cent," she would sigh to Jasmine. "That has been my life. Everything I earned, your father took. I couldn't even pay off the house, only the interest. Every month was the same, I had to fight with him to keep money aside for the mortgage."

But once Tommy Fung had given her thousands of ringgit, though she wished he had not. She never spoke of it but the memory hovered like a ghost.

Jasmine was about six. Tommy came home late one night in a jubilant mood. "No one can say I don't provide for my family," he announced, making Mrs Fung pour him brandy and pulling Jasmine out of bed. He sat down at the kitchen table, the little girl squirming sleepily on his knee.

As Jasmine awoke uncertainly to his affection, Mrs Fung caught her anxious look but both knew better than to spoil Tommy's mood.

"Here!" he slapped a wad of thousand ringgit bills on the table. "Bet your precious Daddy Lian never brought home so much in a day! Take it, get something nice for my lovely girl." He kissed Jasmine wetly on her cheek and cuddled her in an overwhelming embrace. Jasmine struggled in alarm.

Mrs Fung started towards them. "Tommy."

In the past few months, the trail of young girls through their house had increased. Suddenly, Mrs Fung knew what trade had earned such amounts of money.

"Tommy!" It burst from her with terrified fury.

But as Tommy looked up, rage rising in his eyes, she felt afraid. Then he let Jasmine go and that was all that mattered. Jasmine slid to the floor and ran to her mother. Mrs Fung said, "Go to your room."

"You dare to raise your voice at me –" Tommy began.

"Where did you get this money?" Mrs Fung faced him as Jasmine hovered behind her, an arm around her mother's waist.

Pride seemed to struggle with anger for an instant. Pride won. Tommy laughed,

"My cousins have many daughters and I'm a fucking good businessman." He sighed, as if letting the dregs of his anger go. He poured more brandy. "Come, you've been a good wife. Don't think I don't know that. Here, take the money. It's yours. I look after my family when I can."

"I don't want your filthy earnings in this house," Mrs Fung said. She was trembling – with fear or rage, she did not know. She felt Jasmine clinging to her and the spread of notes on the table seemed an accusation from all the little girls that she had faced in this house. Mrs Fung turned and walked out of the kitchen, dragging Jasmine with her. "Go to your room," she whispered urgently. "Don't come out till I tell you. Go!"

Just as the door shut safely behind her daughter, Mrs Fung heard Tommy come for her. The scrape of the chair. Then his heavy footsteps. Terror raised the hairs on the back of her neck. But she carried on walking away. He kicked her first in the base of the spine. As she fell, she folded her mind into nothing as she had learned by then to do and succumbed to his will.

He never gave her any money again. But he stopped bringing the girls through the house – perhaps fearing that she might now betray him to the authorities. For that, she had made an offering of thanks to the gods. She and Jasmine never spoke of these incidents. Instead, she would talk about how life would be for her daughter in the future. Then, a few years later, Tommy was gone and the future was theirs. The future, always the future, for only the future might save Jasmine.

"Now your father has left, I'm paying off half the house already. Soon I'll be free of his debts. Don't get trapped like me. You have the brains to make money for yourself, free from any greedy, drunken fool. Don't give up your life for any man."

With her husband gone, every extra cent became Jasmine's future, free from Tommy's plundering. When Jasmine was ten, the little girl took on chores after school for a few extra ringgit – cleaning Mr McAllister's shoes every day, polishing Mrs McAllister's collection of silver from England once a week. Later, she ran errands for the other households along Swettenham Road, watered the two-acre garden of a wealthy Chinese family, dusted and swept for an Indian judge. The Chinese family wanted to hire Jasmine as a junior maid full-time. "No," Mrs Fung said, "my daughter will never be a servant." As a young teenager, Jasmine got a job in the evenings at Top Best Department Store off Taiping's Main Road. She would be a salesgirl in the ladieswear section. That was when the trouble began.

Jasmine was growing into a pretty girl, bright-eyed and spirited, with a dimpled smile that could melt any heart. Thirteen now, she had small firm breasts and an unconscious sexuality. She would become a striking young woman one day, Mrs Fung thought, and it made her proud and also afraid.

Jasmine set off for her first shift with excitement. "I'm going to be the best sales assistant they ever had! I'm going to earn so much money for us, *Ah Ma*!"

But after the first week, Jasmine seemed subdued, hunching into herself, her face a mask. She would not tell Mrs Fung what was wrong, shrugging off her mother's questions. Mrs Fung felt the old chill, the same unease that frightened her when men she had never seen before used to come asking for Tommy. She remembered how, sometimes, when they saw Jasmine – a beautiful child at five or six – a strange intensity seemed to brighten their lingering gaze.

Unsettled by dread, Mrs Fung went to the department store one evening. She stood behind the tall racks in the sports section and watched Jasmine at work on the far side of the floor. None of the other salesgirls talked to Jasmine, huddling together to chat and giggling as they glanced at her. Some customers walked away when Jasmine approached: a pair of middle-aged women seemed to come to the ladieswear section just to sneak a look at her, nudging each other and smirking when she looked towards them. But it was the men who froze Mrs Fung's blood.

A group of teenage boys trailed Jasmine, like flies round a honeypot, daring each other to approach her. Several older men went up to her on the pretext, Mrs Fung made out, of buying presents for their wives. They led Jasmine towards the lingerie racks, smiling too fondly and leaning too close. One tried to make her try on a bra. Another draped a slip against her, staring as the folds curved over her breasts. All of them touched her.

Mrs Fung watched, her heart aching, as Jasmine endured it all in a cold, robotic manner. Inching away where she could, twisting away from a touch, Jasmine held her features immobile to every comment and insult. When a thick-set man with a moustache reached up to touch Jasmine's hair, Mrs Fung pushed her way past the huddle of salesgirls, elbowed a young woman out of the way and sent a rack of underpants crashing to the floor. The man looked up at the noise behind him and in that moment, Mrs Fung slapped his face, grabbed Jasmine's arm and swept out of the store.

At home, sobbing in her mother's arms, Jasmine cried, "'You're Tommy Fung's daughter', they all say. 'I know your daddy. You've grown up so pretty. Come with Uncle, we'll have some fun.' And they always touch me. I hate it when they touch me, *Ah Ma*! But I didn't want you to know, you'd only worry and stop me working there. Pay is pay, and I can look after myself."

"No more working! I curse your father's name! Somehow, we'll make do."

But both of them knew that, without extra income, they would never have enough to make real her dream for Jasmine's future. Jasmine tried other sales positions in shops around Taiping but the advances did not stop. Gossip had built on gossip and her cold refusals seemed to add to the thrill of the deal. *You're a tease. You sure are Tommy's girl, trying to up the price all the time. But the old man himself would give me a fair price for you, we're old friends, he and I.*

Some seemed to think they could do business with Mrs Fung as they had with her husband. The thick-set man came to Mrs Fung to offer Jasmine a job in his coffee-shop. "I'm doing you all a favour, for Tommy's sake. I know you need the money. But you tell your daughter not to be such a bitch next time."

A friend of a friend of Tommy's sent an intermediary to Mrs Fung. "My client has a law office in KL. He wants her to be his filing clerk. She can stay with him and his family. He saw her last time he came to Taiping. He knows she's just the right girl for him – hard-working, clever and so pretty. If she's smart, she can maybe even rise up in the firm, you understand. My friend maybe will pay for her to go to night school in KL, to study law – if she's a sweet girl to him, you know."

Disgusted and horrified, Mrs Fung refused them all.

Finally, Mrs Bok, Mrs Fung's neighbour, gave Jasmine a position in the Boks' electrical goods store on Main Road. "Men are such pigs," she said. "Don't worry about your daughter. I'll make sure no pig touches her." In the air-conditioned shop, among the piles of VCRs, hi-fis and gadgets, Jasmine found the sanctuary she needed. Under the parental eyes of Mr and Mrs Bok, she turned to her advantage the new customers her presence brought – like a nanny dangling a toy before a squalling child, she diverted the men's attention to the shiny gadgets spilling across the floor. By the end of her first week, she'd sold a talking alarm clock, a stereo cassette radio with a dazzling display of lighted panels, a singing telephone and a hand-held mini TV. After the first month, she got Mr Bok to put her on a commission-related salary and doubled her earnings within weeks.

"You must go and never look back," Mrs Fung said to Jasmine, in the dark of early morning the day her daughter left for England. Her suitcase was packed by the front door and they sat for one last time together in the living room, Jasmine curled against her mother. "Forget who you are. Forget Tommy Fung and the men who've treated you like filth. You are better than all of them. Men will do anything to get what they want. Be like them to beat them. Make them show you they love you, but keep who you are safe from their evil and filth. Do you hear me?"

Now, sitting alone in the living room so many years later, Mrs Fung thought of all Jasmine had achieved. Through all the suffering and sacrifices, Jasmine had made it. They had both made the ambitious dream real. They could not go back now even if they wanted to. Mrs Fung finished her hot brew of tea and angelica. She was an old woman now and her life did not matter. But her daughter, she was still young and she had escaped. In the darkness, Mrs Fung smiled.

*   *   *

On a glorious July afternoon, in a Norman chapel near the village of Midhurst in Sussex, Harry waited with his best man. His mother and her third husband sat in the front. At the far end of the pew were Harry's father and his second wife. Harry's step-brothers and – sisters from his parents' various marriages ranged across the pews behind.

The wedding party was crowded with titles and wealth among the morning suits and expensive hats. From the legal world, there were Jasmine's colleagues, judges, QCs and the senior partners of major City firms. Harry's friends included bankers, substantial Lloyd's names and heads of multinationals.

In a copse across the water meadow, a shadow leaned against

a tree, watching.

Two black Rolls Royces swung into the courtyard. Marietta, the matron-of-honour, stepped out of one with the bridesmaids, checking their dresses and the flowers in their hair.

The shadow moved towards the edge of the copse for a better view. The sunlight washed over him. It was Luke.

Jasmine emerged from the car with Julian Masters, the senior partner of Carruthers.

She wore an Italian bridal gown with hand-sewn pearls. Her thick hair was interwoven with fresh flowers and pinned up. A veil floated around her face. She moved up onto the steps.

Amid the flurry of activity, as Marietta tucked and straightened Jasmine's flowers and veil and gown, plumped up her train, Jasmine glanced up over the neat church lawn towards the water meadow.

Their eyes met.

And Luke stepped back into the shade of the trees.

Julian Masters came up, "Ready?."

Jasmine started. She stared, uncomprehending, at him for a moment. He offered his arm. Mechanically, she took it and he began to lead her into the chapel.

The processional music began. The congregation clattered to their feet, looking backwards for the bride. A murmur of appreciation rippled over them.

Harry stood proudly erect before the altar. He glanced backwards and flushed with pleasure at the sight of Jasmine at the threshold of the chapel.

Jasmine flicked her gaze back. Out towards the copse. But her veil blurred the scene like cataracts. Marietta's blonde head obscured the view. Jasmine strained back. The bridesmaids scurried into position, blocking her vision. They all beamed at her.

Julian Masters led Jasmine down the aisle.

Had she really seen him?

Perhaps she had only hoped it.

The faces and colours of the congregation blurred by. The music churned in her ears. Her mother would have been so happy.

Jasmine almost felt her there in the front pew. Mrs Fung had been writing to Jasmine now since Jasmine's visit to Taiping, sending her letter to the American Express address. Her last letter, in Chinese script and unsigned as usual, embraced Jasmine still. "What double happiness I have this week," her mother had said. "My precious child to be married and the first blooming of my flame tree. The buds are small and only a few have opened – tiny specks of red like chilli powder over the tree! The gods have given us their blessing. Your future will be bright and full of joy, I know it."

As Harry turned to watch her, his handsome head bright in a shaft of light, Jasmine blinked back her tears. She wished with all her heart that things might have been different. She wished her mother could have been here.

She wished that Luke might have been here.

But he was there. She was sure of it. She had not imagined him out there by the trees.

As the vicar intoned the words of the marriage ceremony, Jasmine remembered the night on Waterloo Bridge. In the last few days, it had replayed itself time and again in her mind. The truth of his accusations gnawed at her still. With an effort, she tried to shut out the memory.

Would he come into the chapel now? she caught herself thinking. In spite of her bitter words that night, would he still come for her?

* * *

In the safety of the trees, Luke stared at the courtyard of the chapel. He had not meant for her to see him. He did not know why he had come. Perhaps he had hoped that she might still change her mind.

She would not come out alone, he knew that. But he still waited. He would see her married and then he would go. He laughed at the absurdity of the situation and sat down on a log.

* * *

Harry looked across at Jasmine and crinkled a proud grin. "I will," he said.

A childish fantasy. Luke beside her instead of Harry. Luke with Harry's qualities. Luke living in London, dashing and successful in suits with a lifestyle like Harry's. A charmed life together. An enviable couple. And so very much in love.

" ... for so long as you both shall live?" The vicar paused and looked up at Jasmine. She stared at him and then at the man at her side. Beneath the veil, she smiled but they could all hear tears in her voice as she answered, "I will."

A murmur of affection rippled over the congregation and Marietta dabbed her eyes again. Harry lifted her veil and brushed aside her tears. Softly, he kissed her.

11

After the reception in the grounds of Oaklands, Harry and Jasmine caught a flight to Rome from Gatwick. Harry had booked the honeymoon suite in an Edwardian-style hotel above the Spanish Steps known only to the *cognoscenti*. By midnight, they were having supper on the red-tiled terrace of the suite, the lights of Rome beyond a cascade of rooftops. The rooms behind them were old-world opulent, wood and rich furnishings tempered by modern pastel colours and halogen lighting.

"Happy honeymoon, wife," Harry murmured, clinking his champagne glass to hers.

In this setting, the anxieties and secrets of the last month seemed a lifetime away. Here, Jasmine felt as if she were living the fairy tale ending to all her yearnings. "Happy honeymoon, husband."

She focused on the present as they spent the summer days strolling through the city, stepping from medieval to classical Rome in the turn of a corner. Everywhere the splendour of the Renaissance filled her with awe. This was the mythic Europe she had learned about at school – the Pantheon, the Coliseum, the piazzas of Michelangelo, palazzos and churches every few paces. "It's all so ... so old!" she exclaimed, making Harry hoot with laughter.

He cuddled her. "You're so sweet, my love."

They were standing on the terrace of the Capitoline Museum late one night. Harry's embrace enveloped Jasmine. Seeing his pleasure, she played up her naivety. "It's so amazing that they just leave these old ruins everywhere – the Coliseum right there in the middle of a roundabout and the Circus Maximus almost like a public park. If this was Asia, we'd've cleared up all this mess in no time – fixed up the crumbling Coliseum into a snazzy shopping complex and how about Circus Maximus refurbished for the next Commonwealth Games?"

Harry's laugh soared out across the dark.

The Forum lay below them, and to the south the Palatine Hill brooded above the city lights. It was almost eleven and the museum guards were beginning to usher out the last of the visitors. Harry said something in Italian to one and he left them alone for a few more moments.

Harry drew Jasmine closer as they gazed out at the view. He was like a gentle bear, touching her with delicacy in spite of his muscular bulk. His voice was soft. "We could almost be lost in time. Is this what the emperors saw? Down there, the lights of Rome two thousand years ago and you and me forever here and happy ..."

Jasmine could almost believe the magic on that Mediterranean night. She felt Harry's enveloping presence against her and it conjured a welling up of emotion. She let it embrace her. She could almost believe his romantic fancy of their ageless, timeless love.

Harry knew Rome well and he delighted in showing her all that he loved about the city. They walked arm in arm, like all the Italian lovers around them. He insisted on being her guide everywhere, telling her stories about the Roman emperors and their murderous power struggles. His stories made that ancient society come alive for her among the ruins. He revelled in his role in a proud, paternal way and she let him take charge, happy that he was happy.

Jasmine felt again an intimacy with Harry as he relaxed into the romance of the city. Sitting in cafés in the piazzas and wandering along the banks of the Tiber, they talked about how they first met among friends in Christchurch meadow, how Harry pursued her with flowers and serenades beneath her window.

"That guy in the room next to mine emptied his carton of milk over you!" Jasmine grinned at the memory.

"It was off, too."

"You were singing 'One Fine Day' in that awful falsetto at

three in the morning!"

Late one afternoon, in the gardens of the Villa Borghese, Harry said, "We're going to be so happy together from now on, I just know it. I used to be cynical about marriage. Look at my parents – Mummy's on number three and who knows how long that's going to last? Dad's on number two – though he just might be happy with Monique. She absolutely adores him. I never thought I'd find the right girl but here you are. I promise you, we're going to last. We'll be old together and we'll still be happy."

Jasmine squeezed his hand. Her heart went out to him. She knew that his parents' marriage had been troubled throughout most of his childhood. As the eldest – and the eldest son – he seemed to have taken on every dip and swell of their rows and acrimonious truces. Nowadays, he tried to have as little to do with his parents as he could, visiting Oaklands only when his father and step-mother were away and having hardly any contact with his mother and half-brothers and – sisters on both sides. Seeing them all at the wedding seemed to have stirred up his memories.

Harry was silent a long time, lost in thought. Then, almost to himself, "You know Mummy had a string of affairs."

Jasmine nodded but said nothing. Harry seemed to have almost forgotten she was beside him. In the creeping dusk, he might have been a boy again, hurt and bewildered, trying to make sense of adults' tangled relationships.

"Dad knew, I'm sure, but he just looked away. He was more interested in his medieval French troubadours and their notions of courtly love. That's a joke, isn't it? He was the leading expert on courtly love, going off across Europe to lecture on the obscure academic circuit and right there at home ... He's the last of the great gentlemen scholars. I used to wish he was less of a gentleman, 'Do something, ask her about it, confront her!' but he never did and I never told him. They'd row about everything but that. The worst of it was that she made me a part of her guilty secret. I never told anyone this before. She'd have her love-letters and secret liaisons and she'd tell me about them, giggling like a school-girl. I was only six or seven. 'Don't tell Daddy,' she'd whisper. 'It's our little secret, just you and me.' I began to hate her after a while."

Jasmine felt an ache of pity for the little boy he had been. "I didn't know. My poor darling. To make you her confidant – how could she put such a burden on you?"

"Why did she have to tell me?" Harry turned to her plaintively. "Did she want my approval or something? To hear me say, 'It's okay, Mummy, go and have your little adventures, Daddy won't mind'? Christ, he was my father. I just couldn't bear it, seeing him pretend he didn't know, letting her run rings round him. I hated him for being a coward and a fool!"

Harry's fists balled on his knees, his old, angry pain pounding the veins in his forehead. His large frame was rigid with suppressed fury and hurt. Jasmine slipped her arms around him, soothing him as if he were a child. "We're going to be different, my darling, I promise. Your father's happy now, that's what's important. Your mother, too, in her own way. And you're here – we're both here, this is a new beginning and we're going to make our marriage bloody brilliant."

Her mimicry of his usual bravado made him smile. She felt his body relax and he laughed. He hugged her close. "You're right – as 'bloody' usual … "

They walked back towards their hotel. Jasmine felt their intimacy deepen for she realised that it was as his wife that she had been allowed to see his old hurt. Over the next few days Harry seemed to have a new affectionate energy with her, as if he, too, saw that he had forged a new bond between them. Jasmine luxuriated in this new closeness with burgeoning hope.

Harry took her down Via Condotti and bought her a whole new wardrobe for their stay – Armani slacks, Versace silk tops, Ferragamo shoes and handbag. It was excessive and Jasmine felt embarrassed, but she could not stop his insistence. She tried to buy him a jacket but he fought to pay for it and, in the end, he bought himself several casual suits to leave her nothing to buy him.

In the afternoons, they took long siestas, lying in the still heat drifting in and out of sleep or making love with slow languidity. One evening, while Harry showered and finished dressing, Jasmine went down to the Spanish Steps to wait for him. She watched the crowd and listened to the buskers. She found herself savouring these few moments alone without Harry. As if coming home to her own space for time out after a hectic week.

"Where were you?" Harry's voice startled her. He turned her round to look at her. "God, you gave me a fright. I didn't know where you'd gone. I was frantic! Are you all right?"

"Of course." Jasmine was surprised at his anxiety. But it touched her, too. "I'm a big girl, you know."

"I know, but wandering around on your own – it could be dangerous."

"Don't worry so, darling." She smiled at him and took his hand, leading him down the Steps.

'Just don't do it again, all right?" he said, as if to a child.

Jasmine glanced at him, bristling. But he was just worried for her, she told herself. "Alright. I'm sorry."

She hadn't meant to apologise but the words had just slipped out. She was annoyed with herself. She had done nothing wrong and he had merely overreacted. So why did she feel guilty, as if she had tried to run away from him and been caught in the act? She shook her head and pushed it from her mind.

Beautifully dressed, they strolled up and down Piazza Navona. Jasmine loved this flamboyant Italian ritual and wished she could speak the language. Everyone seemed to know everyone else as they stopped to chat and preen, their hands and faces animated.

They ate in an out of the way *trattoria* where Harry seemed to know the proprietors. Beneath a vine-covered bower in a little restaurant in Trastevere, they feasted on mussels and *ossobucco* as a group of Italian men competed with each other to sing soulful songs over the remains of their meal. Harry impressed them all with a bad imitation of Elvis's version of "It's Now or Never" while making her giggle as he gazed, lovesick, into her eyes.

"*Mia cara!*" She danced up happily to kiss him when he

finished, their embrace bringing applause of its own. She felt dizzy with laughter and delight.

Later, over coffee, she watched a family group across the courtyard. There were almost ten of them, three generations together. They were still eating and she noticed how the old man, who must have been the head of the family, was tenderly attentive to the young woman by his side. "He must be her father," Harry said, noticing Jasmine's focus. "Look, I think that's her husband, that young chap across from her."

He leaned across and spoke to one of the waiters. Then, he told her what he'd learned. "The young couple's been married three months. They've just told the family she's pregnant. I've sent across some Cognac to congratulate them all."

Jasmine took his hand. "That's so kind, darling."

When the bottle arrived for the family, the old man came across to thank Harry. On hearing that they were on their honeymoon, he called over Amaretto for them and soon they were pressed into joining the family table.

Sitting among these friendly people she did not know and could hardly speak to, Jasmine felt deeply happy for the first time in a long while. Seeing Harry so amiable, his blond looks stunning next to the dark Italians, she remembered again why she had fallen in love with him when they had first met. What was it Harry had said once? About the honeymoon never being over. Was this what it was like to fall in love all over again? Warmed by Chianti and Amaretto and Cognac, she didn't want it ever to end.

* * *

In the last week of their honeymoon, they visited the second-century ruins of Ostia Antica, once ancient Rome's main port. The heat was glaring and still that afternoon. Jasmine found shade by some pillars near a tree and sat down to wait for Harry as he poked around the temples and mosaics. She had not slept well that night, pursued again by her old nightmare. Waking in terror, she had watched the dark turn to dawn. In the morning, she had been subdued and withdrawn. She had not managed to shake the heaviness all day. She sighed and tried to relax. The bright sun and stifling temperature gave her a sense of being back home in Taiping, as if she had chanced on a mysterious civilization on the edge of the forest. Only, the vegetation was European and the air lacked the thick density of tropical humidity.

Jasmine leaned back against a pillar and wished she could share all her memories of her childhood with Harry. She envied the intimacy he had shared with her that evening at the Villa Borghese. She remembered his anger and suspicion when she had come back from Malaysia and knew she did not have the strength to tell him the truth now. Not when she saw how happy they could be. She had to focus on the future now, not the past. Always the future, as her mother had taught her.

She thought suddenly of her father. Where was he now? Somewhere in Bangkok still? Twenty years on. She tried to picture him older, frailer perhaps, with white hair thinning to nothing. But she could not. He would always be robust, towering above her, charged with a reckless energy. He could terrify her with a glare or a grunt. And sometimes, he could make her feel more special than a princess.

The memory startled her. In its midst was the image of the old Italian man tenderly smiling at his daughter that night at the trattoria. She knew it was childish but she wished herself in that young woman's place. Jasmine closed her eyes. She had wanted so much to believe her mother's experience of her father. For so long now, it had been easier to remember him as the hard-drinking, vicious bully that he was. Her mother did not regret his leaving. Neither could she. Their lives had been better without him. Her mother believed so much in that, reminded her so much of it. She knew it was true. But for a time, she had secretly longed for her father.

When he turned up after months of absence he used to bring her wonderful presents – a blonde bikini'd Barbie once, a garishly coloured mini-keyboard that played "Top of the World" at the press of a button. He told ridiculous jokes and made her laugh with impersonations of Bruce Lee. She was his "lovely girl", his "little princess". "Chinese Barbie!" he would cry and she would stand on tiptoe, a snooty look on her face, hands outstretched.

Would he be proud of her now? Jasmine had a fantasy that he would hear news of her from time to time, and saw him in a coffeeshop in Bangkok, looking at pictures of her wedding that she had somehow managed to send to him. She pictured him chuckling to himself, tenderly placing a finger to her photograph.

It used to make her feel so bad, those good moods he was sometimes in, when he would treat her with such fatherly love. Their intimacy excluded her mother deliberately. He played on it – perhaps, Jasmine realised when she was older, to spin the illusion of a bond between them that was more than momentary. "Your mother doesn't understand how it is between father and daughter," he would say, winking. "She's just jealous of my special girl, eh?" There were times when Jasmine took up the game and felt ashamed in her betrayal of her mother even as she recited the script, "You're going to take me on your adventures, aren't you, *Ah Ba*? Just the two of us alone!"

And in the end, he had left and she had never said goodbye. Jasmine stood up suddenly. She did not want to remember that night, that last violent argument her parents had had. What had happened between her and her father? She rubbed her hands across her eyes as if trying to block out the past. But the shouting and falling fists spun again in her memory.

Jasmine had tried to stop him hurting her mother again. She wanted them so much to love each other like she loved *Ah Ma* and like she loved *Ah Ba*. He could love her, Jasmine – why couldn't he love *Ah Ma*? Why couldn't he be kind and loving to *Ah Ma* as he was to her? She had screamed at him, pummelled him with her childish fists. Thrown at him her entangled love and fury. She had provoked him. Made him do what he did. Her mother had fought him, drawing blood. And in the next tumbling, violent moments, he was out of the house, shouting obscenities at her mother and he was gone. He never spoke to Jasmine in those last moments, never said goodbye. Never told her when he was coming back. She felt a terrible shame at what had happened. At what she had made him do.

What had happened with her father hovered like a ghoul between her and her mother. Jasmine felt as if she'd seen it in her mother's eyes every time *Ah Ma* had looked at her. *Ah Ma* had blamed *Ah Ba*, thanked the gods for his departure. She cast her hate upon the man who had gone, and saved her love for the daughter who had remained. Jasmine had made herself believe in the roles her mother had cast for them. But in the depths of her heart, she carried the burden of a guilt she could not forget. Jasmine was yoked still to the weight of that love and that hatred that had finally exploded them all apart that night.

When her father didn't come back after a few months, Jasmine had felt the guilt of betrayal hook into her heart. She had tried to make peace between her parents and, too late, she had realised that only a choice between them could finally stop the horror. She'd taken her mother's side against *Ah Ba*, fought her mother's battle with him. She felt shame seep over her again. He'd gone for good – left them with only the guilty memory of what had happened. Over the years, her mother's memories of how her father had been began to filter out those other memories of her own. *It's better that he's gone. Don't be sorry.* Jasmine remembered his temper and his mean, bullying violence, his drinking and how he always tried to get money out of her mother. She made herself remember nothing else. The violent drunkard – that was the truth of how he was most of the time, but she came to remember only those things to the exclusion of the charmer he had sometimes been with her. And, thankfully, it deadened the pain of her shame.

But a guilty horror still hovered at the edge of her mind. Her mother had wanted her to escape to a new life, for her education, for a better future. The terror lurked that her mother had really driven her away as her father had been driven away, this time cloaking her banishment in words of hope. But this new life was an exile from her home and all that she held close to her heart, from Luke, from who she really was. It felt sometimes like an iron mask of lies and make-believe. Long ago she had put it on gladly even as the terror of banishment had gripped her. She'd made her father leave them. The accusation of her own mind weighed her down. She wore it still to make right for her mother what she had made wrong. In a heart that felt bruised still with old wounds, she saw no path but obedience to her mother. This new life was her penance and her salvation, it seemed to Jasmine, and whatever pain it brought, she would bear it as if it were due to her. Whatever happiness that came, she clung to with the gratitude of the child she used to be.

Jasmine leaned against a tree, looking up at the Mediterranean sky through the leaves. A light breeze brushed her face. In her adult mind, she knew she couldn't have stopped her father leaving. And she knew he had only played at the devoted father whenever it suited him. She saw, too, that the violence into which she had been born had grown large and bloated long before her. And yet, a childish part of her still wished he had stayed and it had all worked out. That she might have somehow saved them all. That they might've been happy together like the Italian family she'd seen the other night. The wish made her feel guilty as if she were betraying her mother once again. In spite of herself, a hot shame flushed her.

She thought of Harry talking about his father and how he seemed so determined to make their new life together last for ever. She smiled wistfully. She wanted it as much as he. She would do anything to make it work, she knew. She had escaped the past. It had no grip on her now, she told herself. She had succeeded in changing her life and she had succeeded in reaching the top of her profession. Harry had been the one solid, loving presence through it all. She had given her whole self to him with the devotion of a child. The love she had for Harry was not tainted with shame. Loving him made her free. It exorcised the ghoul that trailed her memory. And now she was Harry's wife and the realisation filled her with pride. In the ancient custom of the Chinese part of herself, a woman can never be a fully adult woman unless she is married, and until then, she remains her father's child. Jasmine had taken the final passage out of her parents' house now. She was no longer their child but a wife, and thus, a woman. In her rational, modern mind, she knew that such a path to freedom was no more than a corridor in the dark labyrinth of an old prison. But it was a tradition as old as the generations and, in spite of herself, it still bound her heart.

Through her proper devotion to her husband, she would make up for all the wrongs of her past. It would wipe her slate clean. She would succeed in this new role as she had succeeded in all the others. She had staked everything on this – reconciliation with her mother through her old promise, her deep feelings for Luke, maybe even her career. The promise she had murmured to Harry came back to her. *We're going to be different. This is a new beginning and we're going to make our marriage bloody brilliant.*

Later that day, on the train back to Rome, she was still distracted and vague in spite of her efforts to stay with the light mood of their day's outing. The after-haze of her memories dampened her spirits. She was faced again with the secrets the last happy week had pushed from her mind. Harry sat opposite her, sun-burned and tired, chatting about the ruins with increasing lack of enthusiasm. She tried to focus on what he was saying, regaling herself with her promise to him but it seemed that the harder she tried, the more forced and unnatural her manner became.

"… you're not listening to a word, are you?" Harry said at last.

"Yes, I was," she said, a little too quickly. " 'The Roman apartment blocks were sometimes five storeys high and had sanitation and running water.' "

Harry sat forward and took her hand. "What's the matter? You've been tense all afternoon."

"I'm just tired."

"I haven't been able to get through to you all day. Like you've withdrawn into some secret place I can't get to." He squeezed both her hands in his. "I don't like it when you're like this. I feel you've cut me out. As if you don't want me to get close."

"No, Harry, don't think that."

"Is something on your mind? You've had that faraway look for a while. As if you're thinking about someone."

"Someone?" She was sounding guilty, she knew it. But she couldn't help herself.

Harry paused, scrutinising her. It made her nervous, as if he was invading into her thoughts, trying to plunder her secrets. She tried for a neutral tone. "I was thinking about my parents. I wish they were still alive to share our happiness."

He nodded, composing his face into serious concern. But she wasn't sure he believed her. Ever since their argument over her trip to Malaysia, he seemed to be watching her for any slightest change in mood or constancy. And when he wasn't sure of her, it was as if he sifted everything she said, played back in his mind every nuance.

Jasmine changed seats so she sat next to Harry. She entwined her arms in his and cuddled up to him. "Thank you for a lovely day, darling. I'm sorry to be so sombre."

He stroked her hair and she could feel his shoulders relax beneath her cheek. But her mood seemed to have infected him and neither spoke again for the rest of the journey.

By the time they'd showered and changed back at the hotel, it was late. All their favourite *trattorie* were full. "Never mind, darling, let's be adventurous," Jasmine said with a brightness she did not feel. She was tired and hungry, and she could see Harry's mood darkening. They walked on, but each restaurant Jasmine thought they might try Harry didn't like – it was too crowded, too ugly, too empty, too touristy. Finally, over an hour later, they settled on one near Santa Maria Maggiore at Jasmine's urging. It seemed to have some local ambience and Harry grudgingly agreed. When they'd sat down, Jasmine realised in horror that they were surrounded by English tourists in panamas and floral sundresses. The waiter handed them a "tourist menu" in English. Harry's mood had lifted but now a scowl began to twist his mouth.

Jasmine put her hand on his. "It doesn't matter, my love. Let's eat since we're here. The food might be okay."

But the pasta was soggy and the main courses were rubbery and tasteless. Jasmine watched Harry anxiously. Her appetite was slipping away as anxiety knotted her stomach. Harry prodded at his food in a temper, chewing and swallowing with a violent distaste. He glared at her and at their surroundings. She flashed on their public scene at Bibendum. Please don't spoil it all, she pleaded inside, please don't hate me, please, it's just a meal, we'll get it right tomorrow, please, I'll make it up to you, my moodiness, this restaurant, our silence, I'll make it right ... But she was afraid. His silence frayed her nerves and she couldn't face an outburst, another crazy quarrel. She was frightened to provoke him so she said nothing.

But with the meal eaten at last, they seemed to rediscover a buoyancy that had deflated. It was after eleven, but as they headed back to the hotel Harry took a detour to buy them *gelati* cones. Busy with the melting ice-cream, they came upon the Trevi fountain like a vision out of the narrow streets. Jasmine tugged hesitantly at Harry and they sat by its edge, spray cooling them. The rush of water and the happy mood of the crowd dispersed their tension. Harry slid an arm around Jasmine's shoulders and she looked up in relief. He wore a smile and a sorry look. He took a breath to speak but she touched her fingers to his lips and shook her head. As she leaned up to kiss him, she thought, curiously, of how, often, at the end of a contretemps between them, it was Harry who was the supplicant in apology.

Her mobile phone bleeped in her handbag. Harry frowned. "Who the hell is that?"

Jasmine shrugged and reached to answer it. "Hello?"

Harry hissed, "Switch it off."

It was a Hong Kong client calling from Sydney. Jasmine began, "I'm on holiday ... my honeymoon ... Why don't you call my assistant?"

"Hey, congratulations, sorry to disturb you," the casino tycoon said, "but, since I got you on the line, it won't take long."

Harry sliced his hand across his throat. Jasmine nodded but her client was already reeling off his problem. It was a straightforward tax point she knew the answer to instantly. Without thinking, she whispered to Harry, "It won't take a minute," and turned away as he made a move to grab the phone. The client had not been confident of her assistant's advice and had wanted her personal reassurance. She stood up, momentarily absorbed, and paced a few steps away, her back to Harry as she talked into the phone.

He gesticulated as he tried to make her face him, his anger growing. His expression startled her. Suddenly realising her mistake, she pushed the call to an end. "Any more queries, speak to my assistant, he's a good lawyer, yes, I trust him ... 'bye."

When she turned to him, Harry was very close to her. Jasmine knew she'd been stupid to take the call. She'd have to make it up to him, apologise with all her energy. But then she saw his anger and froze. He seemed possessed by a rage that madly exceeded the range of her offence. His furious scowl was beyond reason and the hatred in his eyes frightened her. Her voice was thin when she managed to speak. "Some clients are like children ... panic when Mummy isn't there."

"How the hell did he get your personal number?"

"He said my assistant's temp gave it out – obviously by mistake," Jasmine began, in dismay.

"What's the matter with you, leaving your phone on while we're on honeymoon?"

"Darling, we've been using it – you called to check train times to Ostia this morning."

Harry grabbed the phone. "Switch it off now!" He jabbed at the buttons. Groups of people within earshot glanced at them.

"Darling, the call didn't take long. Let's not spoil –"

"Damn you, who's spoiling it all? Who gave me the silent treatment all afternoon?"

"It wasn't 'silent treatment'." Jasmine felt her frustration and panic rising into tears.

"Whose fucking office is her lord and master? Christ, we're on our bloody honeymoon and they can't leave you alone. More to the point, you act like you don't want them to leave you alone. What the hell's the matter with you?"

Jasmine reached out blindly through her hot tears. "It was a mistake. I'll talk to the practice manager when I get back. Harry, please."

He jerked the phone away from her. "Look, I've tried to be patient. All day, I let you alone, I said to myself, 'Nothing's wrong, sometimes it's okay to be quiet together.' God knows how hard I try to make allowances for you. And you just carry on with your own bloody agenda, your little secretive ways!"

Jasmine shook her head desperately. How did they suddenly get here? She had tried so hard to salvage the evening. The phone call was just a stupid mistake, why couldn't he see that? She pleaded, "Stop, Harry, please, don't."

A flash of real fury. "Don't fucking tell me what to do!"

A choking pain in her throat. She stood terrified, pinned down by his glare.

There was laughter nearby. An Italian couple, the girl in the boy's embrace, leaning against a wall, watching them. The boy called out, "*Basta!*"

Enough.

Jasmine looked at Harry. He was being ridiculous, she thought defiantly, waving the phone around. The young couple could see that. She mustered her composure. "Give me the phone, darling. Let's go back to the hotel. We're both tired."

"You want the phone?" Harry fumbled with the battery. He pulled it out. "Here – I've made it safe now."

He threw the battery into the fountain. As Jasmine cried out, the momentum of his anger made him hurl the phone itself towards the stone horses rising from the water. It bounced off the marble and splashed into the pool.

"For God's sake!" She was angry now. His childishness, his sulking all night, his oppressive attention all the time, never leaving her alone, making her justify every action and word and nuance, her own anxiety and guilt all blurred into defiant fury. A fighting energy impelled her to deny him his victory. She climbed over the balustrade into the water.

"Leave the bloody phone, it's dead!" Harry shouted. He paused, chagrined. "I'll buy you another. Jasmine! Come back here!"

There was shouting now from the crowd and more laughter as they watched the spectacle. When Jasmine ignored him, Harry leaped into the water and splashed after her. "Fucking stupid bitch!" he cursed, through clenched teeth. He grabbed her arm and jerked her round, making her stumble. Pain shot through her and she cried out. Angry, humiliated, defiant, she struggled in tears against his strength.

He hauled her bodily from the fountain. Water streamed from them, their clothes heavy and wet against their tangled limbs. She pulled away with furious strength. "Let me go!"

He slapped her. A vicious back-handed cuff across the mouth. It snapped her head back and sprawled her to the ground. She slumped on the wet stones, stunned and winded. Her jaw felt numb as a hot ache began to spread across her lips and one side of her face. She could taste blood where her teeth had cut into her cheek.

Harry was bending over her. She felt his arms circling her, heard his tearful shame. "Oh God, Jasmine, I'm sorry, I don't know what came over me, it was an accident, I'm sorry."

She pushed him away. "Leave me alone."

People were gathering around them. With an effort, she struggled to her feet. Harry hovered beside her. Not looking at him, eyes averted from the crowd, she walked unsteadily away. They parted to let her through, Harry a few paces behind. She could hear him crying as he pleaded with her. She began to tremble but made herself walk on, doggedly aiming for their hotel. Harry's grief trailed her. "I'm sorry, Jasmine, I'm so sorry."

*   *   *

Somehow, they managed to get through the next few days. Harry was a picture of misery, doing anything he could to try to please Jasmine. "Anything you want, I'll do it. I promise you, it won't happen again, my love. I love you so much, you must believe me."

He shepherded her everywhere like a gallant puppy, solicitous to her every need, desperately charming. Jasmine found she could not stay angry with him in the face of his penitent devotion. She knew, with shame, that she had provoked a large part of what had happened with her distracted manner and the secret she was afraid to share with him. They had both been tired from the long day's outing. The evening had not gone well. Stupidly, she had answered the phone instead of switching it off as Harry had wanted. She had turned her back on him. She had taken a business call on their honeymoon! He was right, she hadn't put him first. And like an idiot, she'd escalated the row by wading into the fountain. Her own guilt shamed her. All he wanted was a wife who loved him and showed it, a partner in life with whom he could share everything. She'd failed him. And she had lied to him about her whole life. He had lashed out in frustration – how could she blame him for that?

She managed to cover up the bruise with heavy foundation and artful use of makeup, sunglasses and a Hermes scarf Harry bought her. As the pain and the welt subsided, the memory of the row took on an air of unreality as if it had all happened in a terrible dream. The real Harry was the one she was with in the present, loving and concerned, ready to carry out her smallest whim. This was the Harry she loved.

"My darling," she murmured, letting him kiss her at last. He fastened a bracelet round her wrist. It was three-coloured gold and studded with diamonds. They stood on the terrace of their honeymoon suite on their last night in Rome. Jasmine knew they looked a beautiful couple, so close and tender together. She gazed at the gold and glittering gems. He must have bought it that afternoon as she slept.

"I know this can never make up for what happened," he said haltingly. "But I just wanted you to know how much I love you."

She put her palm on his cheek. "I know."

His grateful look of relief touched her heart.

12

The Kampung Tanah Business Development Committee had been formed with Wong as its Chairman. Its eight other members were the men that Tan had contacted – including Lingam, the lawyer, and Lee, of Lee Hotel. It received funds from the International Business Development Foundation. The businessmen knew Tan as Mr Dunstan Khee, the Foundation's Vice-President. The funds were redistributed to the nine members as consultancy fees and expenses.

In early July, they attended a "conference" at a five-star international hotel in Kuala Lumpur, all expenses paid. Charming escorts with names like Sherry, Honey and Alexis took them on a tour of the city in chauffeur-driven limousines. The girls went shopping with them, showed them what to buy – Gucci belts, Ralph Lauren shirts, Italian crocodile-skin shoes. They ate at expensive restaurants, drank Cognac, talked business prospects with Mr Khee.

Tan smoked a cigar and wore black tie to the inauguration dinner. He exuded power and glamour and meant them to know that they were still merely guests in his world. The men wore lounge suits bought that morning.

"But you, gentlemen, are the key to this prestigious project." Tan stood at the place of honour at the table. The businessmen listened, enthralled.

"What we want from you is commitment to whoever wins the development project. We are a group of non-political business interests. We do not care who wins the tender but once the development is under way, we want your full support. Why?

Because we believe that the local community and international business interests can build a successful local economy if we all work together." Tan smiled. "What's the catch? What does the Foundation get from all this?"

Wong and his colleagues exchanged glances. Doubts had been voiced on their journey to Kuala Lumpur. Now they would get their answer.

"I'll be honest," their host continued. "We want to make money. Lots of money. And if *you* make money, *we* make money. If the project proceeds smoothly, we all win. There are no losers. *You* are part of our investment. We invest in people because people are the future."

His words rang out. He watched his audience digest his flattery, buying into his picture of the future.

He raised his glass. "To commitment, friendship and the future!"

The businessmen downed their drinks in one and broke into exuberant applause. Back in Kampung Tanah, the Committee members networked throughout the town. They talked about the rewards of progress, forecast rich prospects. "Development can only bring jobs and good living. There can be no losers."

In the coffee-shops, in their offices, at home, in the market, Wong and his colleagues worked hard for their fees.

"You want to get left behind? The country bumpkin who didn't know gold when he saw it?"

But anxiety about relocation dogged the Committee.

"Dr Chan says we should make submissions to the planners against it."

"I'm a farmer, I can't live in an apartment."

Wong was reassuring. "If we move, I'm sure it will be to a modern New Town – all mod cons."

"We won't give up our properties for nothing," Lingam gave the lawyer's perspective. "If we stand together, we can lever a good deal for everyone."

Lee said, "Relocation is a small price to pay for a slice of the larger action."

Their persuasion rippled through the town in soothing waves.

Their opinions became received knowledge as more and more people repeated them. Farmers who were once doubtful began to picture the profits from selling their land. Market traders planned to move to retail space. Everywhere else in Asia, it was boom-time. Why not for them, too?

Dr Chan's influence waned. The town's anxiety had rallied to his warning against unknown outsiders. Now, soothed by the confidence of their leading businessmen, they began to see him as naive and out of touch.

Lee's son was in Ibrahim's school. Lee invited the headmaster and his wife to dinner at his hotel. They talked about the future and what it held for their children.

"You're a professor," Lee said. "How can you stick with Dr Chan's backward-looking ideas?"

"He's not anti-development," Ibrahim said.

"The Committee believes in people. People are the future. Think of it! Your school in the same town as our own Harvard. With the right input, your school could prepare our children for entrance there – parents from other states might even send their kids to you for that."

Ibrahim looked thoughtful. Lee told him that the Committee wanted to donate computers to his Science Department. The equipment was already on order. Six computers on-line to the information superhighway, loaded with the latest educational software. By the time the university opened, the school would have IT-skilled students, ready for the entrance exam. "The future of this town's children is in your hands, Professor," Lee said.

Ibrahim could not find a reason to refuse the gift.

Lingam, whose practice had been established in Kampung Tanah for thirty years and who had a staff of twenty, invited Sarojaya to his office. He said, "Dear boy, we'll all make money out of the development – I can afford to be generous. I've recommended you to the Committee as their new legal adviser." He then set out the terms of a generous retainer.

Sarojaya could not believe his good fortune. The retainer covered his overheads and allowed him to buy equipment for his sparse office. Lingam and Co. fed him small commercial cases and introduced him to potential clients in the region. This was the break that could secure his foothold in Kampung Tanah.

The new caseload and networking opportunities filled the young lawyer's empty hours and he threw himself into his work. He had less time and interest for his *pro bono* work with Dr Chan.

* * *

The pre-tender enquiries and negotiations took place in Kuala Lumpur during August at Consortium 2000's downtown offices. Jasmine flew out after her honeymoon, with Jordan, Danesleigh and the design-and-build team. There was also a site visit to Kampung Tanah.

It was a relief to throw herself into the logic and coldness of the law again. Jasmine was up early in the mornings, preparing for the meetings, and worked late into the night with the other lawyers and the survey team, drafting and debriefing after each day's negotiations. She channelled her concentration into fierce advocacy for her client. Buzzing with brittle energy, she forced the pace, working her legal team hard. Keeping her emotions in tight control, she was determined not to make allowances for the bruises that dogged her. "I fell down the stairs when we got back from Rome," she laughed, wanting to believe her lie. "Running for the phone."

Harry telephoned her every night. Sometimes he called twice a day. She would stiffen at the first sound of his voice, but as they started to speak, his tones always so concerned, so full of love for her, she would allow herself to relax into their old closeness. It had touched her that a huge bouquet of roses from him had awaited her arrival from London. The flowers had pride of place in her hotel room and as they chatted on the phone, her gaze would come to rest on the lavish blooms. On her return from the site visit, a magnum of champagne was chilling on ice in her room. The note with it said, "My darling – I can't live without you. From your devoted husband." She knew he meant it. She slipped the note into her wallet and sometimes, when she was alone, she would take it out to read again as if it were a ticket to their future.

Her colleagues were all men. They joshed her as they drank the champagne and worked on the contracts. She felt a blush of pride mingled with hope. Her husband loved her and he did everything right to show it. Things were back the way they should be. She thought only of the future now. Once this Malaysia deal was settled, she would be able to plan how she would juggle her commitments to her career and to Harry. She owed him that and she promised herself she would not fail him again.

"My wife better not hear about all this loving attention you're getting!" Scott, the architect, laughed. "She'll want me to do the same for her every time *I* go away."

Jasmine smiled, but a residual twinge of pain in her jaw turned it into a wince.

* * *

Ibrahim and Sarojaya, at the prompting of the Committee, tried to talk Dr Chan out of making trouble over the development.

"I'm not making trouble. I hired the consultant to improve our bargaining position against the developers."

Ibrahim said, "We don't need to be 'against' them."

"Who's looking after the town's interests?"

"The Committee."

Dr Chan snorted. "The Committee! They're looking after their own pockets. And everyone's kow-towing to them." He jabbed a finger at the two men. "Why? Because suddenly they see dollar signs. The Committee's bought you. They bought the town."

"Are you accusing us of taking bribes?"

"The computers, what are they?"

"They are for the whole community, you fool! For the benefit of all our children." Ibrahim trembled with rage.

Dr Chan realised that Ibrahim genuinely believed that he was acting in the best interest of the children in his school. He sighed.

"The consultant's contract will be cancelled," Sarojaya said.

"No!"

"This town won't pay the fees."

The doctor said, "I'll fund it myself."

"Then you're more of a fool than we thought," Sarojaya said.

The next day, the young lawyer reported back to Wong. They sat in Wong's spacious office. The refurbishment had only just been completed and the room smelt of paint and new carpets.

"He can't fund the investigations himself," Sarojaya concluded. "With fee plus expenses – equipment, data and assorted experts – he can only afford it if he hocks everything he has. And his surgery and house are already mortgaged."

"He might have cash-flow problems that a donation might ease. Say, equipment for his surgery, larger premises?"

"He has an ugly word for that – and it's not 'charity'. He's a man of principle." Sarojaya looked away. "Whatever that means."

Wong said, "He's just a stubborn old man. He'll come round. Let him stew on it and then try again."

* * *

In late August, Consortium 2000 received the six bids. A public display was mounted in the lobby of their prestigious headquarters in downtown Kuala Lumpur. Press releases and brochures were distributed. Journalists arrived in Kampung Tanah by the coachload. *The Far Eastern Economic Review* published a profile on the chairman of the Consortium, Dickson Loh. *Businessweek* reviewed the six companies tendering for the project. The *New Straits Times* and other Malaysian papers summarised the different proposals and pundits made their guesses as to which would win. The national media of each of the tenderers championed their own candidate and *The Times* in London profiled Bill Jordan as the new hope for British enterprise.

Consortium 2000 was on its way to being known across the world.

The human-interest angle was carried in the Malaysian press. The inhabitants of Kampung Tanah, dazzled like mouse-deer caught in headlights, became the focus of the feature pages.

And then Dr Chan launched his attack.

He had already been quoted as strongly opposed to any development. Now, he leaked a section of Luke's draft report to the press. On the front page of *The Malay Mail* was his picture and a banner headline, "Dr C: Jordan Relocation No Benefit to Locals". The computer representation of the relocated town was also pictured, inset with a photograph of Luke. Luke was unavailable for comment but the leaked passages of his draft were quoted at length. He had highlighted two factors discrediting Jordan's proposal.

First, Kampung Tanah Baru – New Kampung Tanah – would be located ten miles away from the university town and accessible only by a circuitous detour from the new highway. The local people would not be involved in the economy of the main town and the isolated position would discourage business flow to the community. Luke stated, "Contrary to what the law provides, Jordan's relocation does not benefit the people of Kampung Tanah."

Secondly, he criticised the design of the university town and infrastructure as damaging to the environment. He recommended changes which would reduce pollution and land degradation. He wanted to retain tracts of forest for soil protection and air quality. He criticised the height and style of the buildings as unsuitable for the slopes and incompatible with the natural environment.

Jordan Cardale's design was not the only one to include relocation – the Korean bid also proposed a new local town. But Jordan's design was bold and futuristic, intended to grab attention. It was thrusting with confidence and power. It had the mark of success and it took the full heat of public scrutiny.

In the same article, Horatio Sarojaya was asked for his reactions to the report. The young lawyer's continued attempts to influence the doctor had had no effect. But he had done his best, he felt. Short of physically restraining him, Sarojaya could not stop Dr Chan exercising his rights under the law. Sarojaya meant to be neutral in replying to the journalist but, unpractised in handling the media, he made a few too many "off-the-record" remarks while the tape-recorders were still running.

"We have a right to voice our opinions on the winning design," the newspaper quoted him, "and we will ask for modifications if the development doesn't benefit us. We are the small pawns among the big players of government and private developers – we will stand up for our rights."

Pressed to predict whether his community would participate in the planning review procedure, he was quoted as saying, "We'll vote for what's good for us, not what people push us towards."

*   *   *

Tan, reading the papers by the pool at his country club, slammed his palm against the table. "Dammit!"

"What's the problem?" Kidd asked without opening his eyes. He lay on a deck-chair while a girl with big hair and ample breasts massaged his shoulders.

"Wong promised they'd put the lid on the doctor. Get the consultant sacked." Tan threw the paper across to his brother. "Those two are still free and vocal. And the bastard lawyer sounds like he's still the doctor's pal!"

"Shit." Kidd sat up and pushed the girl roughly away.

"Wong wanted computers for the head teacher, cash for the lawyer. They got it."

"And they fucking crap on their side of the deal." Kidd prowled the sun deck.

Tan laughed suddenly. "They actually believe that shit I fed them. Their balls have got so big, they've forgotten we own the fucking lot of them."

"Cut them down to size." Kidd sliced the air by his crotch with an imaginary blade. "Zzt-zzt for the lawyer and he won't forget again!"

Tan nodded. "And the teacher."

"Ibrahim? He didn't shoot his mouth off."

"He didn't stop the lawyer either. One in, all in. That's what our 'friendship' means. If they don't know that by now, it's time we gave them a tough lesson."

"So, Wong as well?" Kidd's eyes glinted. "We made him Chairman, like commanding officer. Fucking no-neck and greedy – he takes the money and doesn't keep the line of control."

Tan nodded. "But just put the frighteners on him and Ibrahim. The punishment must fit the crime, that is only right."

Kidd rolled his eyes at his brother's code of morals. "You want absolute control of these buggers, they gotta be shit-terrified of you!"

"There is a right way of power and a wrong way."

Kidd decided not to argue. He said, "And the doctor?"

Tan paused. Chan was different. His opposition had been there from the start. He was the darkness entwined with the light of the Tao. He presented a necessary task to be resolved on the road to enlightenment. He was the specialist work that guaranteed a high bonus fee.

"He won't accept gifts of friendship."

"Let me deal with him – he'll be licking our arses by the time I'm through."

"No," Tan said. "He'll squeal to the authorities or the press. Any whiff of scandal would threaten our client's scheme."

"Not if I tip him so close to the edge one breath will puff him out – pfft!" Kidd flicked a finger as if at a fly.

"No." Tan fixed his stern gaze on his brother. "Be subtle so your enemy does not expect it when you strike, and be as light as air so you leave no trace. That is our way."

Kidd rolled his eyes again. "Mencius, Confucius, ridiculous," he thought. But he said nothing. His brother was the head of the family and the business.

Tan said, "We see to Wong and his friends, and the town will see to the doctor."

13

Jasmine plumped up the cushions on the sofa for the third time in ten minutes. She had flown home early from Kuala Lumpur once Jordan's bid had been submitted to the Consortium. She stood back and anxiously surveyed the drawing room. Now that she had moved into Harry's house, the signs of her presence tempered the uncompromising masculinity of his decor – a pastel armchair from her flat and matching cushions, flowers everywhere, a bright rug as the centrepiece of this room. Everything looked perfect. Crossing to the patio door, she slid it open and the freshness of the late August evening rippled through. Harry had wanted her to sell her Chelsea flat but she had argued for letting it. *Only till the market improved*, she had promised him. She had bought the flat with money *she* had earned. It was her property. She could never sell it, she knew. How could she explain to him what that meant to her?

She heard Harry's key in the door and a nervous anticipation stiffened her. Before she had left on this recent trip to Malaysia, they had quarrelled. He had not wanted her to go. *It's just after our honeymoon. You give too much to your work. Have you thought about what I said – you taking time out, travelling with me?* She had soothed him with a promise: after Jordan's deal was wrapped up, she'd look at giving up work. She was afraid to mean it and afraid not to, but she'd said it. It had stopped his angry words, taken away the scowl on his face. It had stopped him before he could hit her a second time. He was Harry once more, trusting and happy. She hadn't lied to him, she told herself. She'd just said she would look at giving up. Secretly, she hoped she might come to an arrangement with the firm to work freelance as a consultant or, at least, reduce her caseload, and that she might persuade Harry to be happy with such a compromise. His loving concern while she'd been away – the flowers, the touching phone calls – gave her confidence that he might be open to that option.

She checked her makeup in the mirror as she heard him come into the hall. She was wearing the silk Max Mara dress that she knew he liked. Everything was just right.

Harry looked up in surprise when she stepped into the hall. "You weren't due back till tomorrow."

"I wanted to make you happy," she said, as she reached up to kiss him. She took his keys and briefcase and slipped him out of his jacket. She ran her fingers across his broad back. He gazed at her as if seeing her for the first time. She felt him relax under her touch, letting himself be seduced by her. She smiled with delight and stroked his hair, loosened his tie.

"You look beautiful." His voice was hoarse. She could see his desire in his face. She let him run his hands over her body, his touch possessive. She opened herself to his lips as they searched out her throat and shoulders and cleavage. Pleasure and relief washed over her. Everything would be all right, she was sure now.

Harry could not take his eyes off Jasmine. Her dress shimmered around her as she moved, clinging to the curves of her body. When she turned to lead him through to the drawing room, Harry let his gaze linger on her creamy bare back. This was the woman that he had loved, a beautiful woman whose feminine charms beguiled him. He had lost her in recent years to an ambitious ball-breaker of a bitch. He felt love well up again. It pushed aside for now what he had found out about her lies while she was away. All that didn't seem to matter in this moment. Seeing Jasmine tonight, so loving and beautiful, he wanted to believe in her guilelessness. She loved him, he could see that tonight, and that was all that mattered. Things could be how he had always dreamed they would be.

Their vicious row about her trip lay between them but they sidestepped it with delicacy. Jasmine served Harry champagne. He could smell the aromas of dinner warming in the kitchen. She asked solicitously after him and listened attentively to everything he said. He could see she was anxious to please him and it touched him. She seemed like a little girl, hovering around him, her dark eyes so earnest. There was a shy uncertainty in her manner he had not seen in a long time. He found it as charming as he remembered it to be. When he remarked on how happy it made him to come home to such a wonderful wife, she beamed and clasped her hands to his.

For a while, they were the golden couple again.

After dinner, Jasmine sat curled against Harry on the sofa. The evening had turned out so well. Harry was relaxed, a docile giant beside her as he stroked her hair. She had one more surprise for him, something she was sure would show him her devotion to him. "I got you something," she said.

She brought out a small gift-wrapped box from the side table. It was from Asprey's. Smiling happily, she offered it to him with both hands, a Chinese sign of respect. He looked at her for a moment, his face hard suddenly. He reached up one hand for the gift. He said nothing, watching her through narrow eyes.

"I wanted to make it up to you," Jasmine said. "I've been so distracted with my work, what with business trips. Go on, open it."

It was a Patek Phillipe watch, platinum interlaced with gold. Harry held it in his hands.

"Put it on."

Harry did not move.

"What's wrong?"

He looked up at her. His face was twisted with angry pain. "Why did you buy me this?"

"I wanted to show –"

"This is a present that a husband buys his little wife after a business trip. How much did this cost you, darling?"

"What does it matter?"

Harry shouted suddenly. "Tell me, damn you. You tell me fuck all as it is."

Jasmine flinched. What had she done wrong? She stared at him in confusion. She tried to speak but her voice failed her. With an effort, she managed to whisper, "Almost three thousand pounds. What's wrong, Har –"

Harry rolled his eyes. "Well, fuck me, Ms Megabucks. You have that kind of money to throw away on a miserable watch?"

"It's not your money, Harry. Let's not quarrel. I was only trying to –"

"Fucking right it's not my money – and don't you make sure I know it." Suddenly, he grabbed her, his voice pleading. "Is this how guilty you feel? Three thousand pounds' worth of guilt?"

"What – what are you talking about?"

"Don't lie to me!"

Her mouth went dry. He had found her out.

"Fuck you, I know you're having an affair."

Jasmine felt as if she couldn't breathe. She thought of Luke. The night on Waterloo Bridge. She shook her head. The colour rose to her cheek.

Harry was strangling his rage with an effort. He did not want to hurt this woman he loved. What had happened after Italy had frightened him. They had argued about her coming trip to Malaysia. The flat of his hand thwacking into her head. It was as if a demon had possessed him. He had had nothing on her then, only a suspicion. If only she had given up the trip. If she had done that for him, it would have been a sign of her love. The look she had given him of horror and pleading. It had cut him to the core. Afterwards, he had sworn that he would never hurt her again. Now he saw the blush on Jasmine's face.

"I was right." Harry's voice was a wail of anger. "You're having an affair with Jordan!"

Jasmine almost laughed with relief "No!"

"You lied to me about your trip to Malaysia in June. Jordan told me that there was no meeting in KL then."

"Jordan? How do you know him?"

"I got an introduction. Client development, expanding my portfolio. We've been best pals since July."

"How dare you go behind my back?"

"How dare *I*? That's the only way I can keep you under control, you sneaky bitch." Harry worked to tether his anger. He rasped, "I didn't want to believe it. I thought maybe he was lying."

Jasmine floundered. "I did go to KL for a meeting."

"I got the confirmation I needed when you were away. I spoke to your secretary. She said you'd taken those days as leave – to make wedding plans with my family." Harry shook her. "You lied to the office! You lied to me! What're you trying to hide? I wanted to believe you. I twisted all credibility and possibility so that I could fit the truth into your story. But I kept coming back to the one unchangeable fact – you lied to me! I thought we had something good between us. I love you. I thought you loved me. Why are you doing this to us?"

His glare frightened her. His hands gripped her arms with furious strength. Her mind raced. How to answer him? Panic thudded in her chest. In spite of herself, she began to cry.

"Fucking bitch, stop crying! You always do this. I hate it when you do this!"

Jasmine gulped desperately but, in her fear, she could not stop.

He dragged her to her feet with a violence that made her head snap back. He shook her before pushing her away. She fell to the floor.

Harry sat down again, his features twisted in despair. Crouching towards her, he implored her, with his large, muscular hands. "Look what you made me do. I didn't want to hurt you. Why do you do this to me each time? Stop crying, damn it!"

With a supreme effort of will, Jasmine mastered her panic and stared up at him. Strands of hair clung to the sweat on her face. She was breathing hard. Her voice was harsh when she spoke. "I'm not having an affair with Jordan. Or anyone else. I told you I went to a meeting in KL and it's the truth. The reasons were confidential."

"I'm your husband!"

Jasmine scrabbled for time. "You don't go blurting your business confidences to me. Or sensitive financial information."

"Don't fuck with me, Jasmine."

"All right, I'll tell you. But first, you tell me something. Are you doing business with Jordan?"

Harry shook his head and looked away. "He doesn't need any of the funding opportunities we can offer."

Jasmine thought, that was because *she* had stitched up the funding for Jordan long before. But she said nothing.

Harry went on defensively, "But we get on pretty well. I'll clinch a deal with him yet."

Jasmine took a breath and said, "I went out to KL to meet privately with our associate firm there. Our department is looking to expand and, at that time, it was not appropriate for too many people in the firm to know where I was or what I was doing. Our 'wedding plans' were a convenient front. I'm sorry that you had to find out about my little white lie."

"And Jordan?"

"Since I was out there anyway, I checked out the site and gathered background information. He didn't know about my trip. None of my time or expenses were charged to him. Sometimes the best lawyers get their edge from fact-finding missions like that. Only the second-rate lawyers charge their clients for everything they do."

There was a sneer and a challenge in Jasmine's voice. She was telling him that she was the best in her field. That she was above trivial squabblings over money. Her gaze locked on his. It was almost as if she dared him to rise to the bait.

Jasmine felt exhilaration sweep away her powerless fear. She watched him twist himself into a knot of agonised fury. He was falling for it. She had thought that he had found her out, but in all his attempts at clandestine investigations he had come nowhere near the truth.

She recognised suddenly her power over him. He loved her with a desperation. He needed her. He needed to feel as if he were in control. And she had the power either to give him that prize or tear it from him. It had been the same in their recent row, and in their fight in Rome, and at Bibendum. It had always been so, for as long as she had known him. And he always came back. He was in her thrall, devoted to her, miserable without her, his happiness at her mercy. He would never leave her, she saw it now. He would always be there, always come back, no matter how much she hurt him. She knew, in that moment, how much she needed that in him.

She said, "Even if Jordan had known about my secret trip, why should he tell you? To him, you're still just a tout – you don't have any valid business with him –"

She did not finish what she was saying because Harry lunged at her. He pounded three punches into her chest and abdomen. As she lay there gasping, he kicked her high up in the thigh for good measure. "I made you who you are," he snarled. "I can break you just as easily."

The watch landed on the carpet by her face. His heavy Oxfords took a step and its face shattered as he ground his heel into it.

He left her gasping and retching where she lay. The front door slammed and she was alone.

In a strange way, the physical pain was a release. She let it fill her body and mind in the hope that she could think of nothing else. She felt a hate for what she had said to Harry, and a disgust at what she had realised about their bond. It made her sick that she had protected the truth again with another lie. So many lies in her life. They tumbled through her pain – siding with her father against her mother in their little games, letting her mother take her memories of her father from her, making Luke hate her up in Firefly Clearing so many years ago, pushing him away that night on Waterloo Bridge. Choosing always the hope of a better future. On that terrible night long ago, she had felt with her father what it was to love whom you should hate and hate whom you needed to love. She had tried to choose one over the other but the tangle was too tight to unravel. She'd chosen her mother, and *Ah Ba* had gone, and never come back. Now, she had chosen her husband over everything else that had ever mattered to her, and Harry didn't even know it. It felt as if whatever choice she made, she would never make the right one. If this pain was a punishment, perhaps she deserved it after all.

She rolled onto all fours and tried to get up. At least, she thought grimly, this time he had hit her where it would not show.

* * *

The man in the metallic-blue Mercedes watched the Kampung Tanah Primary School. At twelve thirty, the bell rang. The children streamed from the buildings. It was a week after Jordan's bid had been submitted to the Consortium.

The boy was about seven and wore glasses. He carried a Power Rangers backpack over one shoulder.

As he passed the Mercedes, the man stepped out into his path.

"Jimmy Wong," Kidd said, spreading his mean lips into a grin.

When Jimmy did not arrive home, Mrs Wong did not worry at first. But as the afternoon passed and she could not find him, she went to her husband. "Jimmy's not back from school yet. He's never this late."

Wong looked up and saw her silhouette in the frame of the door. His memory flashed to another silhouette framed there – his early-morning visitor from months before. A chill gripped his heart.

Mrs Wong wanted to call the police. She was verging on hysteria.

Wong grabbed her. "No police. It's just a joke." He emphasised each word. "I will handle it. No police and he'll be home tonight."

Wong had read the newspapers. Sarojaya had promised Wong that the doctor would be kept quiet. Wong had promised Dunstan Khee. But they had both underestimated Chan. Wong had tried to contact Mr Khee over the last few days. He wanted to explain – they had made a mistake about the doctor, it wouldn't happen again, he would sort it out. But he had not been able to get through.

Wong had expected something. Another visit under cover of darkness, perhaps. Even a roughing up. But not this.

The phone rang.

Wong picked up. His face turned ashen as he listened to the caller.

"Done. Smooth as a young girl's tit." Kidd was high on the adrenaline of that afternoon. He sat at the hawker's stall at the night market with Tan. "Any time you want a job done, you can count on me, big brother."

It was after ten in the evening. Petaling Street, Kuala Lumpur's old Chinese quarter. The market heaved with crowds milling at the stalls of pirated watches, clothes and cheap cassettes. The food stalls bustled with customers wolfing satay, noodles and barbecued ribs.

"I've been in contact with Wong. He's screaming down the highway now!" Kidd guffawed.

Tan motioned to him to keep quiet. At a satay stall further down, Ibrahim and Sarojaya sat at a table with their families. They had come to the capital to view the display mounted by the Consortium and had made a holiday break of the trip. Tan had been trailing them all evening.

"You always worry too much," Kidd snorted. "Man, I wish I could be there to see him when he finds the boy. Whoa, when he opens the box and finds the heart!"

He mimed opening a lid and shrieking, eyes mad with terror. He laughed with manic glee.

* * *

At the time that Wong's car approached the outskirts of Kuala Lumpur, Ibrahim and Sarojaya moved through the crowd. Their families followed. They paused every few steps to browse at the stalls. Two men in tinted motorcycle helmets inched after them. Although it was a dry night, they wore long rain macs.

Wong sped along in panic. A pounding agitation coiled about his chest. He stared wildly at the green highway signs as he entered the capital. They pointed to destinations he did not know. Before he could think, his car was swooped into the freeways and oneway systems that tangled through Kuala Lumpur.

The two helmeted men jostled the crowd into turmoil. A woman tripped, a stall collapsed, people shouted and pushed. The men blocked Ibrahim and Sarojaya. In the chaos, they were torn from their families.

Wong went through an underpass. Where was he? Cars screamed past. Round a roundabout, up onto a flyover. The lights of neon advertisements dazed him. The steering-wheel was clammy with sweat.

In an empty alleyway, stinking of decay, Ibrahim fell to the ground. A boot swung into his chest. The helmeted man pulled him up. Fists pistoned punches into his body.

Sarojaya curled on the ground, moaning from his broken ribs. The second man kicked him in the spine. Sarojaya arched back. The man smashed a boot into his head.

"You wan' money?" Ibrahim rasped. He twitched a hand towards his pocket.

One of the men laughed. A manic cackle. He kicked the teacher.

Sarojaya hissed, through the blood in his mouth, "Goddammit! That's enough!"

The man who had laughed seized Sarojaya and slammed him against a wall. "We'll say what's enough, you fucking shit!"

Sarojaya screamed without breath, blood from a punctured lung catching him in the throat. The man flicked open a switch blade and cut open Sarojaya's trousers at the groin. Sarojaya whimpered.

"Remember this, you little fuck. You take our friendship, you do what we tell you. No more second chances." The man sliced off Sarojaya's right testicle. Beyond his wretched wail and before he blacked out, Sarojaya heard the man laugh again.

Wong pulled up at the Yaohan Plaza shopping complex. It loomed dark and deserted. The voice on the telephone had said he would find Jimmy here. Wong got out of his car and looked fearfully around. He had been travelling non-stop for over six hours. He felt weak, his nerves shredded. His bladder throbbed. He walked towards the main doors. Overhead spotlights cast pools of light into the eerie blackness. Then a sound. Wong froze.

On the far side of the steps, a pillar. Behind the pillar – he was afraid to think what he might find.

Across town, the quieter of the two men hissed in Ibrahim's ear. "You're paid to do what you're told. We expect you to obey." He shoved his helmeted face forward and Ibrahim shrank away. "Ask Mr Wong."

Tan and Kidd slipped out into the crowd. They removed their protective macs and rolled them up, dumping them into bins behind a coffee-shop. Through a maze of side streets, they came to a powerful Yamaha motorcycle with false plates. They climbed on, with the air of brothers who had had a good night out, and sped away.

Jimmy huddled in the shadows behind the pillar. He clutched his backpack and a box to his chest. Earlier that evening the man in the car had brought him to the amusement arcade at this shopping mall. Jimmy had played on the machines with money the man had given him. He had been waiting for his father for six hours, the last two alone after the shopping complex had closed.

When Wong found him, they both wept in each other's arms.

"Why did he leave me, Daddy?" Jimmy gulped.

"It's OK now, I'm here."

"He was nice."

"Ssh, ssh."

"He gave me this for you." Jimmy pulled out the box.

Wong took the Cellophane-wrapped box of Davidoff cigars. His mind was spinning. His son was safe. It had just been a joke, after all. He laughed a little. He would call his wife on the mobile to tell her the good news.

Wong stood up and moved into a pool of white under a spotlight. He unwrapped the Cellophane and opened the box.

In the shadowless glare, a pig's heart glistened dark and foul, arteries and ventricles trailing on a plastic sheet. A smell of putrefaction burst into his face. With a cry – animal fear and wailing despair – Wong dropped the box. Blood stained his clothes as the heart and its ooze tumbled against him.

He dropped to his knees. A bloodstained piece of paper caught his eye. Wong picked it up. It was limp and warm. He could just make out the Chinese characters. The note said:

FRIENDSHIP UNTIL DEATH

Wong lost control of his bladder.

14

Jordan sat at the head of the table, Jasmine tensely beside him. Nick Roberts was on his other side, opposite her. She had never seen Jordan so angry. Danesleigh was taking notes, a little apart from them.

The meeting room in the offices of Messrs Carruthers looked onto New Square. To ease her discomfort, Jasmine glanced through the windows. Outside, a diffuse September light brushed over the quad. Barristers in wigs and robes hurried past on their way to court, their clerks close behind trundling barrows of documents.

Jasmine made herself turn back to the meeting. International newspapers and magazines were spread out on the table. Roberts was saying, "To sum up, the doctor is viewed as a lone maverick. Mr Sarojaya, who appeared to support Chan's anti-relocation views, has since distanced himself. Dickson Loh, Chairman of the Consortium, has made light of Chan's rhetoric – I quote, 'an old man out of touch with the world today'."

Jordan interrupted, "I'm not worried about Chan's hot air. It's the consultant. People take facts and figures seriously. His report is damaging us."

The regional press had launched Asia's green debate on the back of the Kampung Tanah story. In the booming economies of South East Asia, property development had been a free-for-all. Unchecked building fever raged for decades. Cement and tarmac ravaged once fertile lands. Litter, pollution and resource degradation were the consequences. But an educated generation was now awakening to green politics. The time had been ripe in Asia for re-evalution when Luke's report broke in the news.

Luke gazed out from the pages of *Asiaweek*. Jasmine closed the magazine. His blue stare unnerved her. She had not known of his involvement in this project until she had read it in the papers. She wished she did not have to be in this meeting. They were talking about him like an enemy. She did not know if she had the strength to do the same.

It had been a month since the tenders were submitted. In another few weeks, the Consortium would come to its decision. Jordan said, "The Consortium may not choose our design with all this controversy. And if they do, there are the planners to contend with. I want this bad publicity stopped."

Roberts said, "McAllister's report is not about facts and figures. His charts and forecasts are based on conjecture – like economic forecasts. It may all be expert opinion but it's just opinion."

"What's your point?"

"We have to discredit him. Like you discredit an expert witness in court. If the jury don't trust him, they don't trust what he says."

"I like it." Jordan smiled for the first time. "Jasmine?"

Jasmine roused herself as if clawing her way out of sleep. Roberts felt sorry for her. Since her honeymoon two months before, she had been beset by bad luck and ill health. She had fallen down the stairs at home. Migraines and back pain had also kept her from the office. Now, she wore tinted Dior glasses – because of an eye infection, she said.

As a result, Roberts had taken control of this new issue in the Jordan Cardale portfolio. He liked to think that he offered Jordan a hard-edged approach which Jasmine, for all her attempts at masculine posturing, lacked. The two men shared a competitive streak and a taste in high-stakes risk. It was only a matter of time, Roberts thought smugly, before this prize client would belong to him.

Before Jasmine could speak, he said, "I've researched his background."

"His background?" Jasmine was startled. What did Roberts know about her and Luke?

"Chan got McAllister's name through Green Action Direct, the radical environmental campaign group. The locals think he represents Green Action."

Jasmine said, "Is he a signed up member? I always thought Lu – McAllister is an independent consultant."

"He is an independent. Green Action haven't confirmed that he's been retained by them."

"Then how can you say –"

"They haven't denied it either." Roberts was enjoying her confusion. "Look, personally, from what my sources say, I think he's acting independently. My guess is Green Action are waiting to see how it all turns out before they decide whether he's a good thing to latch on to for their global cause."

"Most campaign groups have public directories of consultants. If they give out a name, it doesn't mean there's any link," Jasmine said. She tried to keep her tone businesslike. It felt strange referring to Luke so impersonally. "Presumably this is how Chan got McAllister's name. How can you twist that into anything to use against McAllister?"

"There's enough of a link for the inference to be drawn – as the locals have done. It's enough to undermine his standing by pointing to his hidden agenda."

Jasmine felt a chill as it dawned on her what Roberts was planning to do. "Where did you get all this information?"

Roberts was patronising. "Ever heard of resourcefulness – and private investigators?" Jordan was impatient. "Go on."

"If McAllister is seen as a leftie green campaigner with his own agenda – hijacking a local issue, even using the good doctor as part of a larger anti-development plot to keep Asians in their paddy fields – then the slant of his report will speak for itself. The Asians have always been deeply suspicious of whites with 'we know what's good for you' attitudes. Tar the man with that brush and public opinion will feather him."

Luke's work in other parts of Asia – for the UN and independently – had made him enemies. Roberts read from a sheaf of papers. A number of Asia's progressive enterprises were being curtailed because of Luke's consultancies: logging prohibited, dams scaled down, factory production interrupted. Businesses stung by his work had been eager to spill their resentment to Roberts's investigator.

"But his job is to find environmentally sustainable solutions to these businesses, and there's a cost to that," Jasmine began.

Roberts said, "If I didn't know better, I would've thought you were defending the man."

Jasmine's laugh sounded hollow to her ears.

Roberts went on, "Jasmine is to go to KL with Viscount Danesleigh. The press will pester you for comment. You dismiss his report in the light of the evidence which you will present to them. Assert all confidence in our design and Luke McAllister will never work in Asia again."

Jasmine was speechless.

Jordan grinned. "It's rough and ready, Nick, but I like it. Of course Jasmine! She's one of them. Coming from her, it'll hit just the right note."

"We'll fine-tune the script for her." The scheme was typical of Roberts's high-risk, high-gain tactics and he was enjoying himself.

The men spoke as if she were not there. Jasmine found her voice. "No. I can't do it."

Jordan looked surprised.

"I won't be part of a smear campaign. This is all half-truths and manipulation of facts."

"It's an interpretation of the truth." Roberts smiled condescendingly. "Within the libel laws, of course. It's what we lawyers do best."

Jordan was assessing her through narrowed eyes. Jasmine could not control her rising voice. "This is a sensitive time in Asia's environmental history." The words tumbled out. "Once these accusations are circulated – and blown up – in the media, it would take Luke the rest of his career to re-establish his reputation."

Jordan raised his eyebrows. "Luke? Do you know this man?"

"No. No, I don't."

"Isn't it just like a woman to feel sorry for a good-looking bloke?" Roberts gave the other men a knowing wink. To Jasmine: "It's him or us, my girl. Time to play hard-ball."

Jordan said, "If you're not a hundred percent behind me, then you're against me."

"She's been off sick a lot lately." Roberts's tone was patronising again. "Don't be too hard on her. Perhaps a rep from your KL office has the media skills."

The two men turned back to their discussion. The dull pain in Jasmine's eye that had persisted over the last week intensified. She had shown too much of her feelings.

Jordan had picked up on her connection with Luke. The moment had passed, but would he forget it?

Roberts was drafting out the details of their strategy on his notepad, conferring with Jordan. He was consolidating his advantage. Jasmine realised that her most prestigious client portfolio was slipping from her control. Her mouth went dry and panic startled her. She was losing everything she had worked for. At home. Now this.

Danesleigh touched her arm. "Are you all right?"

Roberts glanced up, mid-sentence. He said, "You don't look very well, my girl. Take a break. I'll tie things up here."

Jordan said testily, "Edward, take Jasmine out to lunch. I'll see you back at the office."

Jasmine let Danesleigh tidy her papers, pull back her chair, help her on with her jacket. His solicitous care was comforting. She felt relieved to escape the conflict that this meeting had thrown at her. She would not have to stand up to Roberts and Jordan. And she would not have to be the public embodiment of Luke's humiliation.

Harry's explosive temper had succeeded in wearing her down. She was shying away from confrontations. Anything to avoid his anger. And the violence.

As she walked from the table, she turned and saw the two men deep in discussion. She had let them intimidate her, she thought.

As if they had been Harry. Jordan's terse accusations. Roberts's contempt. Their big masculine frames dominating her. She felt the fear coursing through her blood.

Jordan was nodding, his clenched strain of recent weeks calmed by the solution the lawyer was planning. Roberts was almost flamboyant. He was revelling in his coup, ignoring Jasmine as she retreated.

Danesleigh held the door for her. She did not move.

At this moment in her life, when every hope she had had for her marriage tasted as ashes, she watched as her career trickled away into Roberts's clutching hands. If she walked out of the meeting now, she would lose Jordan. She would lose the position and respect in the firm it had taken her so much hard work and determination to earn. She would be just another female lawyer who had cracked under the pressure. And, in spite of what she had said to Harry about giving up her career for him, she realised more than ever how much her work meant to her. It anchored her and gave her a sanctuary. It was an independence from Harry to which now, most of all, she needed to cling. She could not let him tether her at home, hobble her to his domination – not now, not when she'd felt on her body what he was capable of. At least, if she still controlled this one part of her life, she might have the strength of self to endure through the worst moments of their embattled relationship.

As for her scruples about Luke, she owed nothing to him, she told herself. Not after all these years. Harassment and risks came with his job. He knew the score. That was where his much flaunted integrity took him. It was not up to her to protect him. Her job was to do what was best for her client, regardless of her personal feelings. That was what *her* professional integrity required.

At home, the humiliations she had endured in the last months had battered her until she hardly knew her own mind. These men were not Harry, she thought. He might stampede over her with his physical strength but she had a strength he could not touch – an identity that threatened him: she was a successful lawyer in her own right. If she walked away now, she would lose the one thing that she had left. The one certainty that had always defined her dignity – her work, regardless of Harry or Roberts or Luke. Or any man.

She walked to the table and placed her briefcase upright between the two men. "There's nothing wrong with me, Nick," she said. "I'll do it."

*   *   *

Jasmine crossed the campus of the university where Luke taught in Penang. She wore linen Versace slacks and a silk top. Her sunglasses did not look out of place in the glare. She had arrived in Malaysia a day early, without Danesleigh, on the pretext that she had other client business to attend to at Seng & Mustafa in Kuala Lumpur. She would meet him at the Regent Hotel in time for the press conference tomorrow. In fact, however, she had stopped in Kuala Lumpur only long enough to change planes straight for Penang. The night before her flight, she had quarrelled with Harry again. She had barricaded herself into her study until she heard the front door slam and it was safe. At dawn, he was still out when she left for Heathrow. She felt irrationally euphoric – this time, she had escaped.

The bougainvillaea on the lawns were bright with colour in the hot afternoon. A cool sea breeze crinkled through the palm trees.

In the Development Research block, Jasmine came to the open door of a book-lined office. She kept her tinted glasses on. A ceiling fan circled and large windows overlooked the glittering sea. Luke sat engrossed in statistics on a computer screen, surrounded by textbooks.

Jasmine had come to explain. She had rehearsed what she would say. Whatever lay ahead, she was only doing her job, it had nothing to do with how she felt about him. She respected him, admired his courage, envied his integrity. It was just business, nothing personal.

She could not let him hear the words Roberts had prepared for her without telling him in person first. She owed him that, at least.

He was concentrated on his work. It was the same expression she used to catch when, years ago on picnics, she would glance up from her book to see him engrossed in his. Then, as if she had called his name, he used to look up straight into her eyes. And they would both smile.

Luke looked up into her gaze.

A smile of pleasure creased across his face. He said her name as if he had seen her in a dream and he was half-way across the room towards her. Then he stopped. They stood awkwardly a moment.

She stepped forward and held out her hands. She felt his hands in hers and a soft breath escaped her. "Hey," she said.

"Hey." He stared at her as at a vision made flesh. "What are you doing here?"

"I have a meeting in KL. The ticket included a stopover so ... You look busy ..."

They were still holding hands. He let go and moved away. "Come on in."

Luke went over to the computer and started closing down the applications, tidying the books. "I'm finishing off the Kampung Tanah report. I guess you've seen the hoo-ha in the press."

"I, um, thought the town didn't agree with the doctor. Didn't they terminate your contract?"

"This is the report on all six proposals for the doctor. After the contract is awarded, he wants the full report on the winning design submitted to the planners no matter what. He paid me in advance and won't take any of it back. He's like a man possessed – the more they pillory him, the more entrenched his views have got. There's trouble ahead."

"Oh?"

"There's a lot of money at stake. They're not going to let one old man stop them. And the way he's going about it – like a fanatic – it's not making him any friends."

"Why don't you get out before this 'trouble' you're predicting?"

"I'm used to trouble. I make it all the time. It's my job. Besides, one of the designs has a serious flaw – a potentially dangerous one. No doubt, the Consortium have their own expert team assessing the bids. But I can't walk away from this till I know that the problem is properly addressed – if the flawed scheme wins."

"A design flaw?"

"Yeah." Then he laughed suddenly. "I'm sorry, you didn't fly all this way to listen to me bore you with my work! How long have I got you for?"

"Till tomorrow morning," Jasmine said, realising that Luke did not know she acted for one of the tenderers.

*　　*　　*

They drove out towards Batu Ferringhi – Foreigner's Mile. Before they reached the sprawl of seaside resorts, Luke turned down a track to a coffee-shop on the beach. In the shade of palm trees, Jasmine sipped iced juice from a plump green coconut and watched a fisherman reeling in his net.

They had slipped into their old familiar friendship. After the tensions that had become the norm with Harry, Jasmine felt an ease with Luke as she had not since childhood. He was warm and familiar with her, in spite of her angry words thrown in his face that night on Waterloo Bridge.

They talked about inconsequentials for a while. She told him about her life in London, her circle of friends and her work. She did not brag as she had before. His jibe about her "baubles" still stung her.

She did not know why, but she avoided mentioning her involvement with the Jordan Cardale tender.

Luke's warm gaze discomfited her. He did not tease her this time but listened as if absorbed by the pleasure of being with her. She watched him watching her, and realised how happy she was to be with him again. The anecdote she was telling trailed to a pause and she forgot to continue.

Luke grinned and took a gulp of Tiger beer. He said, "How's married life?"

"Great," she said brightly. "Harry's wonderful. Doing well. He's putting together an Asian portfolio. We hope to manage a trip together next year – business spiced with pleasure ..."

It was practised patter. She beamed. Luke nodded. She said, "You? Are you involved?"

"Not right now." He was watching her.

His eyes seemed to read her every thought, invade her heart. She felt a burning creep into her cheeks. He could not see her eyes behind her sunglasses yet seemed to hold her gaze. She looked away. It was just an illusion, she told herself firmly, he couldn't see through her facade.

She said, "This mountain development is a big boost for Malaysia's international reputation. From what I've seen in the news, you and the doctor are stirring up a hornet's nest."

"My client shouldn't have leaked my report. It was a confidential, technical document meant for his eyes only. I never get involved in local politics – it compromises my independent standing. The leak makes it look like I'm stirring up the locals."

"It'll blow over, won't it?"

They spoke about the development, Jasmine playing the role of curious bystander. Luke had no reason to suspect her interest might have been more than casual. All the data, specifications and plans he had reviewed had originated from the Consortium, the tenderers or their technical team of architects, surveyors and engineers. The legal documents – where her firm's name would have been mentioned – had not been available to him. In the general media, neither her name nor her firm's had been mentioned. Yet.

"What's this design flaw you talked about just now?" Jasmine said.

"It's Jordan's tower. They've positioned it on the outcrop to the south. It's futuristic, powerful and I can see why they want it on that precipice – the sheer cliff emphasises the tower's height and makes it an awesome citadel. But ..." Luke hesitated. He squinted at Jasmine, assessing her. He seemed to come to a decision. He went on, "Boreholes have revealed the presence of limestone several layers under the outcrop. The height of the tower means that the foundations will have to be very deep – so deep that they will penetrate into the limestone at one corner."

"So?"

"Limestone is notoriously unstable. Add the mountain gradients, plus the wind velocity at that height above sea level and there's a serious risk of structural damage."

"What kind of damage?"

"At best, a few cracks, a little movement in the foundations. Tilting of the tower. At worst, subsidence. Given the tonne upon tonne of steel and granite making up the tower, you can translate that into a major landslide of colossal proportions."

"Are you sure?"

Luke nodded. "They've located the new local town at the base of the outcrop. The new town hall is right under the tower. Any landslide would wipe out the town."

Jasmine stared at him. "That's unbelievable."

"That's why I have to see this thing through. Jordan's is the only design that requires foundations so deep. None of the others even come close to the limestone layer – and that's reflected in their designs. If you're looking for a status edifice theirs are definitely more timid and unimpressive. But some of them, especially one of the Malaysian designs, are more environmentally appropriate and technically innovative. I think it would be crazy if the Consortium gave the project to Jordan – but his design captures their 'world-first, history-in-the-making' ambitions. And he's ahead of the others on costs and timescale. That's why he'll probably win. If he does, the planners must insist these risks are properly made safe."

Jasmine felt suddenly cold and afraid. The CD-ROM images of the tower flashed, huge and magnificent, before her. Then, crumbling, giving way in a cloud of rocks and rubble. Tumbling down to engulf the pretty all-mod-cons town below. Bone and flesh grotesquely distorted, crushed. Thousands dead.

Luke was saying, "He'd have to move the tower back, away from the unstable outcrop. Or lower its height."

"You can't be right." She had hardly any breath to speak.

"The risk is there."

"But how big a risk? Maybe you're being alarmist."

"Thirty per cent chance. Big enough to scare me. But for gung-ho developers – winning the contract, making money, those are the things that drive them. To the exclusion of all other issues. Jordan's design stands out above all the other bids. He wants to win, it's obvious."

"I can't believe Jordan would be blind to the dangers."

"I don't know how his mind works. But I know what the facts and figures tell me," Luke said. "If Jordan's design wins without change, there's going to be a disaster."

15

" There's something I have to tell you," Jasmine said to Luke. They walked barefoot along the white sands of the bay. A stiff breeze dispelled the afternoon heat. Cottonball clouds drifted across the sky.

"What is it?"

Luke was grinning as he glanced at her. Jasmine had to tell him why she was here. But she was afraid. Being with Luke again, spending the day as they used to, she remembered a happiness she had not felt in a long time. The day was passing so quickly and she wanted it to last forever. If she told him now, the spell would be broken.

She said at last, "I saw you. At the wedding. But when I looked back, you were gone."

She would tell him later.

"I had to see you."

Jasmine took his hand. They walked on.

"Your mother made me tell her every detail," Luke said. "At first, she pretended to be angry that I'd gone against her wishes. But she was so excited." Luke did not take his hand away.

Jasmine watched a ship on the horizon. "Thank you."

"What for?"

"For coming in spite of everything. For being so kind to my mother. For this, today, seeing me."

Luke stopped and they stood very close. Jasmine laughed awkwardly. She let go of his hand and began to walk back the way they had come.

* * *

That evening, they ate at an open air food court on Gurney Drive, the sea just beyond. Couples strolled along the narrow esplanade. Scooters and cars cruised by at walking pace. They ordered noodles, satay, fresh oysters fried with egg.

It had been a long day but the tastes and smells of home energized Jasmine. The warm night and the buzz of Asia, being with Luke. She felt comfortable here. She belonged. But, although it was dark, she did not remove her sunglasses.

"I'm going back to Taiping tomorrow night," Luke was saying. "Why don't you come? Your mother would love to see you."

"I have a meeting. I'm due back in London the day after."

"Fly back via here. I'll meet you, drive you down. It's only an hour or so."

"No, I won't have time."

Luke said, evenly, "You're ashamed of who you are."

"That's not true!"

"You're ashamed of your mother." The words snapped out before he could think.

"My mother's none of your business."

Luke felt angry. "She's still a servant in your eyes, isn't she? Can't Mrs Harry Taunton be seen hobnobbing with the servants?"

"That's enough!"

"Why does it matter? Her work was hard but honest."

"You can't understand."

"She slaved all day. Why? For you. So you could have a better life. How can you just abandon her?"

"Stop," Jasmine faltered.

"There's no shame in what she did. She's never been ashamed."

"She hated it!" It was a wail of pain. The families at nearby tables stared. Jasmine rushed on, startling Luke with her intensity. "*Ah Ma* was humiliated by it all. Fetching and carrying for all those rich wives. Cleaning up after their brats. Shouted at by their husbands. Begging for extra work anywhere she could. Selling her pitiful little cakes behind her market stall. Sewing buttons, taking in washing. Her eyes failed and her hands were raw, and still she worked on late into the night. You never saw all this. You were just another rich kid she had to pamper. Don't you tell me what shame is because I've lived it all my life."

She had started to cry, her sobs raw as if from a pain she still lived.

Luke flushed. He had not been able to control his old anger at Jasmine. He wished he had not spoken. But he had seen Mrs Fung the week before. She had looked haggard, smudges of pain around her eyes. She was losing weight. "I'm sorry." He reached towards Jasmine. "It's just that – your mother misses you. She's been –" But he remembered his promise to Mrs Fung. "She's – getting old," he finished lamely.

Jasmine felt his words reach into the childish longing for her mother she had buried long ago. She struggled to contain her emotion. "Don't you think I know how old and frail she is?" The defences she had single-mindedly constructed over the years were crumbling. She took off her sunglasses and hid her face in her hands, giving in to her grief

She was aware of Luke's sudden silence. She knew then that he had seen it – the bruise under her left eye, naked without the shading glasses. Shifting a hand, she tried to conceal it as she sensed him ducking down to look closer. She did not want him to see. But a part of her longed for someone to know. She had hidden the reality of her marriage for what had seemed a lifetime. It had exhausted her – the practised patter, the facade, the unacknowledged terror. She could not keep it up.

She lifted her head. The bruise was two weeks old, aching still. She saw the shock and anger on Luke's face.

"Who did this to you?" Luke's voice was quiet but his eyes flashed.

Jasmine did not look at him.

"It's Harry, isn't it?"

She said nothing but she saw that her sharp intake of breath told him all he needed to know.

Luke's face was hard, the muscles in his jaw clenched in fury.

His fists coiled instinctively. But when he spoke, his voice was gentle. "Let's take a walk."

In the cool dark, they strolled along the esplanade. Jasmine felt relief overwhelm her. She began to cry again, but this time, the tears were like a cleansing release. Jasmine curled into the protective calm of Luke's chest. She felt him stroke her hair. Her sobs eased as the breeze and the sound of the waves lulled her.

Sitting on stone steps down to the beach, the high tide lapping below, Jasmine began to tell Luke everything her heart had hidden. Harry had taken her wealth and status for granted from the start. He had been charmed by her freedom from the social constraints that bound his class of friends. It was Harry who had taught her everything. At dinner parties if she said something gauche or laughable, he used to kick her under the table. But he had adored her for not being stuffy, snobbish and English. Whenever they argued, they always used to make up with tender passion. "He always looked so pathetic when we'd had a row. I felt awful for never telling him the truth." Jasmine felt as if she were in a dream, speaking so freely now and feeling no fear. "But Harry would never be able to understand. And his family – their friends are lords and dukes, how would they be happy with a servant girl and the daughter of a – a whore-master?"

Since the honeymoon, she told Luke, Harry had started to beat her again. There was a ferocity she had never seen before. She could hardly bring herself to repeat the names he called her. "But it's my fault. He feels something's wrong so it makes him angry, that's natural, don't you think? He made me who I am. He's my husband now, he has a right to know everything about me and I'm cheating him of that. And my work. It takes me away for days. I work late. After he suspected that I'd lied to him, he pounced on anything to start a fight. He wants me to give up. But it's my lifeline. It's who I am. We don't make up anymore like we used to. We put on happy faces and we're the golden couple again. He wants children. He thinks it'll help give a focus to the marriage. He thinks I've stopped taking the pill – but I haven't."

"Leave him," Luke said, with controlled fury.

Jasmine felt drained but she made herself go on "I can't fail. I swore I'd never live my mother's life. My mother sacrificed everything for me, how can I fail her now? Harry's a decent man underneath, I know it. I just need to make him feel secure again. He looked after me, he was everything to me. Like a father."

Luke remembered the smug, barrel-chested man coming out of the church. He had led Jasmine on his arm as if on a leash. He had pulled her, directed her, told her where to go and where to stand. The loving groom, or the policing bully. "He may put you in hospital one day!" Luke gripped her shoulders. She was like a rag doll. "He may kill you!"

She said, mechanically, "He wouldn't do that. He loves me."

"Goddammit!" The surrender in her tone enraged Luke. "How can you think that love excuses everything? Look at you! What's happened to you? What has 'love' done to you?" He stood up. He wanted to hurt the man who had abused Jasmine. The man who had reduced her to this tormented puppet. But Harry was not here and Jasmine slumped at his feet.

Luke crouched down. "You must make plans. Just in case. A friend you can stay with. Promise me."

"A friend. I don't know anyone. Marietta, maybe – but, no, she's his oldest friend." Jasmine stared at Luke as a realisation seemed to numb her. "All my friends are his friends."

"Then leave now. Before it's too late." His helplessness enraged Luke.

"I can't. I've told you."

"If he tries anything again, call me. Any time. Wherever you are. I'll come for you." He took her hands in his.

"Thank you," she said.

Luke touched her cheek. She was not in a state for any more talk tonight. They could finish this in the morning and perhaps, then, she might listen to reason. "Where are you staying?"

"I – my bags are at the airport – I hadn't thought –"

Luke could not bring himself to leave her alone in the impersonal emptiness of a hotel room. They drove back to his one-bedroomed apartment on campus. It was stark and functional, adequate for the short periods he was at the university. Luke felt awkward suddenly and busied himself showing Jasmine the kitchenette, the shower, the bedroom. "Here's a towel and a T-shirt. You take the bed. I'll be out here on the couch." He closed the door between them. Throwing a light blanket over the sofa, he unbuttoned his shirt and slipped off his shoes.

When he looked through later, she was already curled up on the covers. Her clothes lay on the floor. She had managed to pull on the T-shirt but must have fallen asleep almost immediately. He padded in and folded her clothes on the chair. Leaning over, he spread the flannel sheet over her. Sleep had softened her taut features. He brushed his lips against her temple. She smelt of sweat and the salt of the sea. She stirred. He lingered, watching her. Her skin was caramel soft. He reached over to the bedside lamp.

"Don't leave me." Her voice was warm with sleep. "Please. Hold me. Just for a while."

Luke switched off the light. In the darkness, he lay beside her and cradled her in his arms. He could feel her breath slowing as she fell asleep again. Her body was warm against him. He buried his face in the soft web of her hair. He lay awake for a long time, aching with sadness and desire. Sadness for them both that the ambitions of their youth had driven aside a love that they had hardly begun to understand. And desire for her that longed to kiss her, taste her, free her, caress her and lose itself in the embrace of her love. He curled against her and listened to the distant waves.

He did not know when he fell asleep but when he woke, it was already dawn. Jasmine was gone.

*   *   *

The drought had choked Kuala Lumpur with dust, and waves of heat shimmered above the growling traffic. The limousine snaked downtown from the Regent Hotel. In the air-conditioned interior,

Jasmine and Danesleigh were sealed from the heat. The window to the chauffeur was closed. Jasmine had caught an early flight from Penang and had had just time to check in to her room and change before meeting Danesleigh in the lobby for the limousine. She now sat immaculate in a Chanel suit, shielded behind tinted glasses.

Cool and elegant in a grey bespoke suit, Danesleigh sat beside her. "This is the first I've heard of it," he was saying. "Such a scenario would be disastrous. Our prestige development subsiding, risking millions and injuring heaven knows how many people – it's unthinkable! Bill would never allow a faulty design to go through. Who told you all this?"

"There've been rumours. I heard it from someone." Jasmine looked away.

She had approached the question of the tower obliquely, afraid that what she revealed would betray Luke. But she needed reassurance from her client that Luke was wrong. A confusion in her will sapped her of certainty. She was tired of the conflicts in her life, the contradictions that divided her. Her mother. Harry. Her career. Jordan. Her marriage. Luke. Luke, always Luke, persisting, embodying all the choices that she could have made.

Danesleigh was saying, " ...quite outrageous! We can sue them for libel, can't we?"

"We don't know how serious this talk is. A court action could attract unwarranted publicity. But, as the company's lawyer, I need to know about any potential faults or weaknesses, particularly at this crucial stage."

"Bill has the technical knowledge to vet what the architect and design team come up with. He would only go with the very best. This project could propel him into the premier league."

Jasmine felt relieved. Danesleigh was right. It was inconceivable that Jordan would risk the company's reputation and hundreds of lives. Luke had to be mistaken.

"Could this come up at the press conference?" Danesleigh flicked through his calfskin notebook. "We don't have Bill's instructions."

"There's no time," Jasmine said. "If it's raised, we'll go with what you've told me. In fact, I'd rather you didn't bring this up with him just yet. I suspect it's just malicious gossip."

"But he must be told."

"Of course," Jasmine improvised. "But I want to get more information, so I can give him a full report. If there's anything to report. It was just a throwaway line over a drink, it may not amount to much more."

The press conference was held in the glass-and-marble atrium of Jordan Cardale's offices. Journalists and television crews crowded the landscaped indoor garden. A waterfall tumbled over *faux*-wilderness rocks. CD-ROM images of the Jordan Cardale design for the university town played on a giant screen. A model of the town spread across the central display cabinet. Jasmine and Danesleigh exuded confident enthusiasm for the design and dismissed Luke's report.

It was Jasmine who was the central mouthpiece, an icon of the modern Asian – beautiful, sophisticated, educated, the perfect synthesis of the ancient Orient and new vibrant energy.

The story was on the *Nine o'Clock News* that evening. The piece was intercut with additional research material from sources hinted at during the conference. Jasmine watched it alone in her hotel room as she packed to catch the midnight flight back to London.

She remembered then that she had not managed to tell Luke why she had gone to see him.

* * *

The television was on in the living room of Raymond Goh's house. The older men were waiting for the financial news. The buffet dinner was in full swing. It was the celebration of the third wedding anniversary of Raymond and Jeanette.

Mrs Fung had contributed several dishes and now sat with the women, catching up on gossip. She was frailer than she had been, her complexion chalky against her dark eyes. She picked at her plate but ate nothing. She spoke little. She was easily tired these days.

Children played in the hall. Raymond and the younger men were in the spotlit yard, intent on a fighting-top contest. Luke had mastered the game while on a project among the farmers of Kelantan and had introduced it to his friends in Taiping. A chalk circle had been etched roughly on the ground. Within it, heavy discus-shaped tops from two competing teams battled to knock their opponent out of the ring.

Luke coiled a thick rope round the seven-kilo hardwood top. His T-shirt was drenched with sweat, his muscles rigid from the strain of the last hour's contest. It was a game of strength and skill. Success depended on the power and accuracy of a throw. The month before a new player had torn the ligaments in his shoulder from a careless one.

Raymond was a sergeant in the Taiping Region police. Luke had known him since boyhood. He catcalled with the others, gulping Tiger beer. "You got no chance, man!"

Raymond's top already spun in the circle. Luke curved his disc behind him and did not pause to aim. He threw with a powerful motion, lashing the rope like a whip and grunting with an angry effort. The top skidded into its opponent and ricocheted out. The men scattered out of its path with a yell. It swept into plant pots, shattering them.

The taunts rang out.

"Lousy shot!"

"No concentration!"

"You play like you're in love!" Raymond clapped Luke on the back.

The party hooted. Luke's laugh was strained. "How'd you like a throw in your big mouth?"

Jasmine's crisp voice cut through the noise. Luke snapped round.

He reached the patio doors in a few strides. From the far side of the room, Mrs Fung stared in astonishment at the television.

Jasmine might have been a movie star giving an interview. She projected power and glamour. She held herself with poise and her delivery was polished. She was saying, "New Kampung Tanah offers local residents new houses with modern facilities. Each family may choose from these five prototypes. The natural setting of the old market town will be retained in the new location. The community will also have a town hall, which the current town lacks."

Cut to the LCD screen. The Titiwangsa Tower soared above the valley where the new town nestled. The escarpment swooped upwards from the town hall as if part of the civic building.

Back to Jasmine – a close up. "This new university will be Asia's centre of learning. The best in modern design has been incorporated with the highest standards of civic planning. New Kampung Tanah will be only a short drive from this mini-city for the twenty-first century. It will benefit through increased employment and business opportunities. It would be sheer prejudice for anyone to suggest that New Kampung Tanah offers no benefit to the local people."

"Are you referring to Dr Kenneth Chan's strong anti-development views?"

"My client has no quarrel with Dr Chan and, indeed, respects the passion with which he holds his beliefs. However, there are certain radical campaigners who might take advantage of him for their own ends."

This provoked a barrage of questions.

When the clamour ceased, Jasmine began to speak. "What is Luke McAllister's link with Green Action Direct? What is his secret agenda in aiding the local community in Kampung Tanah? He claims he is an independent consultant. He claims he works within the law 'for the benefit of the community'. But what is the work of Green Action Direct?"

Luke stared at the screen in confusion and stirring fury. What was she talking about? He had no connection with the radical group. They were based in Germany and their recent provocative campaign missions in South East Asia had earned them more antagonism than favour in the region.

Jasmine was saying, "All Asians will recall that, in London last year, Green Action protested outside the Malaysian High Commission against a dam project here. They bombed staff with eggs and flour. Recently, in Frankfurt, they ambushed an Indonesian delegation with burning rubber tyres to protest against fire-clearing of forests in Sumatra."

Luke was breathing hard. Jasmine was tapping into the knee-jerk disgust and indignation that those two incidents had inflamed across Asia. It struck him with horror what she was trying to do. It was all insinuation and suggestion but, blow by blow, she was going to ruin him.

"Dr Chan contacted McAllister through Green Action Direct. Why has McAllister not declared his interest? What is his secret agenda?"

The reporters off-screen broke into uproar. Luke was rigid with anger, blood pounding in his head. He took a step towards the television, fists balled. Jasmine's face filling the screen was beautiful, luminous – but also cold and hard. It was a look he had never seen before. It shocked him. Hatred and contempt for her flashed into the rage coiled inside him. But a part of him could not believe in this Jasmine. Surely it was an act. Surely she could not do this to him and truly mean it. He searched for straws but they vanished even as he tried to clutch at them.

Her face on the screen was talking about the dam in Sri Lanka and how his involvement had diminished it. She listed all the development projects he had *hampered, curtailed, destroyed, brought down* across Asia – logging, new factories, casino and tourism complexes, airports. She was so good with emotive jargon, so casual in her damning hints, so earnest and sincere. It made Luke sick with disgust. There was enough factual truth in everything she said to give credence to all the false accusations tangled in it. He might still unravel truth from falsehood but no one would care by then. Like drops of poison in a fresh stream, the damage was done and the taint would infect everything he did or said.

He was dimly aware of a cry from Mrs Fung. Someone had been translating for her what the woman lawyer had been saying. He turned to see her staring at him in horror and confusion, tears of distress brightening her eyes. As if wading through a swamp, he made his way over to her and took her outstretched hand. Her voice trembling, she kept repeating, "I'm sorry, so sorry. I'm sorry, my good boy."

Luke did not know whether she was sharing his pain or apologising for what her daughter had done. He put an arm around her.

PART TWO

YIN

Yin

The feminine principle. It is the nurturing spirit that allows us to love and guides us to wisdom. It is the intuitive emotion that, in yielding, holds us against the storm and, in endurance, roots us to life.

16

Ten days afterwards, the newspapers reported that Dr Kenneth Chan had died in a car accident in the early hours of the morning. His car had plunged off the road while manoeuvring a bend in the hills outside Kampung Tanah. "Initial reports suggest that he had been drinking. Heavy rain throughout the night was likely to have reduced visibility and worsened driving conditions along the narrow mountain route."

Local people interviewed portrayed the doctor as a bitter and disillusioned man. As the town's support for his anti-development campaign diminished, he had taken to disrupting community meetings to highlight his cause. He seized every opportunity to force his views on all and sundry. Most people felt that his criticism of the developers was jeopardising their future of partnership and enterprise with their new benefactors. When they failed to reason with him, his friends shunned him and soon the patients at his clinic dwindled. His growing isolation made him depressed and prone to bouts of uncontrolled anger.

"I didn't know he drank," one neighbour said, "but I'm not surprised. He was far gone. Something like this was bound to happen, the way he was carrying on."

*   *   *

Farul Zain, Jordan's project manager, leaned back. He said, "The word here in KL is that the consultant fellow got the old man drunk. You know what you whites are like with your alcohol and wild living."

Jordan snorted, but the mood in the room was light-hearted. It was three weeks after Jasmine's appearance on the news. They sat in a private reception suite in the offices of Consortium 2000 with the Jordan Cardale tender team – Danesleigh, Scott the architect, Jasmine and the local lawyer, Benson Lee, of Seng & Mustafa. The night before, the Consortium had decided to award the tender to Jordan Cardale and they had held a private dinner to celebrate with Jordan and his team. Today, the public announcement would be made. In the conference room next door, they could hear Dickson Loh, the chairman of the Consortium, starting the proceedings.

"There's talk of a conspiracy by greenies," Benson interjected. He was a studious, wiry man in his thirties. He had handled the legal aspects of Jordan's project where they had come under Malaysian jurisdiction – the construction contract, elements of the joint venture and the setting up of a Malaysian corporate vehicle for the English company.

Jasmine stood by the window. She said nothing.

Benson went on, "There's talk that McAllister's working for more than one radical green group. At best, he was using the doctor to discredit this major development and by proxy, all progressive projects. At worst, they were aiming to manipulate the outcome of the tender process and planning review, to send a warning to developers across Asia. The rumour is that the doctor was about to backtrack and switch sides." Benson snapped his fingers. "So he had to go."

Jasmine turned round. "That's outrageous!"

Benson shrugged. "It's what they're saying. Dr Chan panicked after you pushed the link with Green Action. The whole of Kampung Tanah was turning against him and his family. He was going to break from the consultant."

"But – how do you know all this?"

Benson spun a hand in the air. "People talk – who knows what's true or not? Dr Chan died without telling anyone what he was about to do – it's a free-for-all for the conspiracy theorists. And the bets are on that it's McAllister who killed Chan. Whatever he says or does from now on will be tainted by that rumour, whether it's true or not. That press conference you carried painted the background nicely!"

"I always knew I could rely on Jasmine to do a thorough job." Jordan was watching her.

From next door they heard the final words of Dickson Loh's speech, booming out of the sound system. "And so we are delighted to announce the winner of the tender for the design and construction of Titiwangsa University, the Asian university of the future. Jordan Cardale PLC."

*   *   *

An aide of the Chairman ushered them onto the stage in the packed conference room. The applause from the delegates and dignitaries was deafening as the audience rose to greet them. Banks of television cameras and spotlights faced them. Cameras popped and flashed like fireworks.

Jordan strode up to Loh, a distinguished elderly man with the jowly look of wealth.

The two men shook hands, posing for the photographers. Together they unveiled the model of the Jordan Cardale design. Jasmine stood with the rest of the team at the Consortium's main table on the stage, an array of microphones ranging across its length. They shook hands with the Consortium team, all the while playing to the cameras. Kampung Tanah was represented by Wong and the town councillor, Mokhtar Kamaruddin. They stood to one side in their best suits, overwhelmed by the noise and crowd.

There were speeches of mutual gratitude, respect and admiration. Jordan began his with a few words in Malay, drawing murmurs of appreciation. He talked about Asian values and global partnership, the harmonies of East and West, how privileged he felt to be a part of the Asian century to come. "Who will be the leader in this Asian millennium? That's what everyone is asking." Jordan adopted a challenging tone. "The Chinese are building a new industrial town north of Shanghai, to be completed by Chinese New Year in the spring of 2005. China is the largest country in Asia, with the largest workforce and the greatest natural resources. Biggest is best, some people might say." He paused. "But – we all here know that 'Small is beautiful.' Malaysia has a special, unique animal – the mouse-deer. He is small and swift but, most of all, he has brains. He is the king of the forest even though he is smaller than the tiger and the elephant.

"Jordan Cardale is proud to work here in Malaysia with Consortium 2000 to show who will be the leader of the Asian century. We will complete the Titiwangsa Tower, the tallest tower on the highest site in the world, by New Year's Eve 2004. When 2005 dawns, the world will see that the mouse-deer will have beaten the old lumbering dragon – with the speed of the present for the brains of the future!"

A cheer of laughter and appreciation raced up over the applause. The speech had been written for Jordan by Danesleigh and Jasmine. He sat down and nodded to them, grinning. The schedule he predicted was just feasible, allowing ice-thin margins for delay and error. Zain and Scott had worked furiously in the previous months to shave time off the excavation and construction of the tower, sacrificing periods that might otherwise have been set aside for in-progress monitoring, adjustment and correction. It had been one of the factors for the success of the bid.

A question was shouted from the floor. It was a journalist from an international environmental monthly. "Did Dr Chan's death help speed your timetable along?"

A startled hush fell.

Jordan signalled to Danesleigh, who leaned towards his microphone. "I don't see the relevance of –"

"Since Dr Chan's death, you have no opponents to your design. That should help speed up the planning review, wouldn't you say?"

With the raising of an eyebrow, Danesleigh indicated that the question was in bad taste. He said, "Our thoughts are with Dr Chan's widow and his three children at this time. We offer our deepest condolences to his family – as I am sure all of you here would wish to do."

But the journalist persisted. There was a murmur of disapproval among the invited audience.

Danesleigh said, "Jordan Cardale will, of course, follow the proper planning review procedure. But it is a matter for the residents of Kampung Tanah whether they wish to bring any submissions to the planners. *Encik* Kamaruddin? Mr Wong? Perhaps you're in a better position to answer this question."

Wong cleared his throat. The town councillor nodded and Wong declared, "We are all sad for Dr Chan's family. But he was not in touch with how the rest of us feel about this project. We support this development. We look forward to working together with all you people here for the benefit of our area. Where we all work as a team, everyone wins."

"So Kampung Tanah will not be submitting to the planners against the design?"

"No, no, we all approve of it. We like the relocation package. The funding's fair and the legal side of things looks very good for us."

Applause exploded from the audience. Jasmine enjoyed this moment – her manipulation of the relocation aspects had helped to win these people over. Jordan smiled in triumph.

There were raised voices from outside the conference room. As heads turned, figures burst in through the door, security guards pursuing a man. Loh's personal bodyguards stepped in front of their employer.

The intruder struggled away from the guards. He strode with furious energy and determination towards the stage.

Jasmine started out of her seat.

"The Jordan Cardale tower will collapse because of its defective design!" the man shouted. "What does Bill Jordan have to say about that?"

It was Luke.

* * *

The news crews scrambled towards Luke as the security guards rushed to grab him. He stood on the floor below the stage, unshaven and dishevelled, his eyes alight with anger. "How did Jordan Cardale win?" he shouted. "Their design is flawed and dangerous! The tower must be moved back! You must know it's too tall for the location."

The security staff began to bundle him back up the aisle. Jasmine stared in horror. Luke seemed on the edge of sanity. His wild-eyed zeal frightened her. Why was he doing this? What had he turned into?

"Let him go!" It was an order. Dickson Loh was back in control. "Consortium 2000 has nothing to hide."

As calm returned to the room, Luke wrested himself from the guards. He strode forward again and stopped at the foot of the stage, braced for the verbal fight to come. He ignored Jasmine.

"Mr McAllister," Loh said, "we know who you are from all the commotion you've been causing in the news. We also know your personal and ideological agenda —"

"I have no agenda but the truth," Luke said, struggling to rein back his rage. "Others may put out lies about me for their own gain. I'm not interested in gain. Only the truth."

"Jordan Cardale won," Loh continued as if he had not heard, "because its design captured our vision for Asia's university of the future. It's bold, innovative and unforgettable. It also won on costing and its package to the residents of Kampung Tanah for relocation. Further, its post-completion management experience is faultless.

Our independent team of surveyors, architects and engineers assessed Jordan Cardale's design thoroughly. Our own geophysicist prepared the geological survey and report. Our team analysed the construction materials and the design and phased plans. We are quite satisfied that the Jordan Cardale design is safe and without flaw."

Jasmine was barely listening to Loh. She was aware only of Luke standing below the stage. She could not look at him. Jordan startled her when he leaned across, covering her microphone with his hand. He hissed, "The bastard'll have a go at us next. You take it."

Jasmine nodded, in a daze. She whispered, "What – what do you want me to say?"

"I want him finished."

She glanced up into his dangerous eyes. With an effort, she made herself sit up tall and straight, pushing her mind into gear. She said, with an attempt at steely resolve, "No problem."

Jordan sat back, his face expressionless. Jasmine forced herself to look at Luke. Her hands felt cold and damp. Her pulse was racing. Did she have the courage to confront him face to face? She felt nausea rising.

Loh went on, "Be very careful, Mr McAllister. When you accuse Jordan Cardale, you also accuse Consortium 2000. We have not failed in our duty to judge the tender bids fairly and with the utmost concern for safety. And you will see that our choice will be vindicated at the planning review."

Luke let out a laugh. "I don't know what you or Jordan Cardale have done but someone's made sure that the planning review will be a farce."

An uproar surged among the audience and the reporters. Jordan nodded to Jasmine and she stood up. She hesitated. Seeing Luke right there in front of her, she could not bring herself to hurt him again. His agitation and edgy intensity disturbed her. She wanted to reach out to him, explain, see him again as she had always known him. But they were enemies now, she thought, and it was she who had made them so. They could not go back to what they had been. She had destroyed that. She sensed Jordan shifting impatiently beside her. Jasmine cleared her throat. She had no choice but to go on. She picked up the microphone. She said, "It is the responsibility of the winning tenderer to satisfy the planners. If you have anything to say, you had better be sure of your evidence before you start making accusations against Jordan Cardale."

Luke turned to her. His face was a mask of enmity. "I have no evidence but this. The people of Kampung Tanah, led by Dr Chan, had a fighting spirit a few months ago. They wanted to defend their homes and their lifestyle from blind progress. The planning review gave them that chance. But something happened. Something – someone – frightened them. Or bought them. And now the doctor is dead and there is no single resident of Kampung Tanah willing to go to the planners to ask for what is their due under the law ..."

Infusing his words was his anger at Jasmine, and she sensed it like a blow. She worked to keep her voice professional. "Your accusations come very close to defamation, Mr McAllister. It is my client's policy to prosecute any libellous attacks to the fullest extent available. As you have clearly stated, you have no evidence. I suggest you keep your speculation to yourself."

They stared at each other. They had not spoken since those few hours in Penang. There was a bitterness in Luke's tone although his face was hard and cold. "You can play big-time lawyer games all you like. But the fact is that the tower is unsafe in the current design and, if it is built as it is, there will be a disaster. I aim to stop it."

"We're all tired of your empty accusations." Jasmine appealed to their audience in mock-weariness. Then crisply, "Where is your evidence?"

"I have no evidence." For the first time, Luke faltered. "I had reports and analyses, all the work from my investigations, but they've been destroyed. Or stolen. There was a fire – arson – at my office on campus. I'll have to recompile the data. It'll take months."

Jasmine laughed. Its hollowness underlined her caustic words. "You expect us to believe your ridiculous stories on the basis of evidence that, in fact, does not exist? That probably never existed. Do you take us for fools?"

Luke's features softened for a moment. The fire in him seemed to wane. There was pain in his eyes. His voice was quiet when he spoke at last. "No, I know you're not a fool." Jasmine looked away. He went on, "I wish you'd met Dr Chan. You'd have liked him.

Few people know what's worth fighting for. He believed in what *he* was fighting for. He wanted to make a difference. He would have taken it to the planners and to appeal beyond that. I aim to carry on his fight."

Jasmine gathered her senses. With an effort, she made herself meet his gaze. He was trying to make their confrontation personal but she reminded herself that this was business. Whatever she felt about him she had to disregard. She was not going to be manipulated. "Your arrogance astounds me, Mr McAllister," she rounded on him with sudden energy. "The planning procedure is available only to residents of Kampung Tanah. You are not a resident. You have no right under the law to make submissions to the planners. If any residents wish to make submissions that is a matter for them. Otherwise, it's none of your business. Now, please, stop making a fool of yourself and go home." She paused. Then used her final weapon against him: his race. "Go home to your own country."

Loh signalled his staff. The security guards seized Luke and began to bundle him out. The news crews swarmed, shouting questions at Luke and up to the stage. Flashes fired. The invited guests argued in confusion.

Luke shook off the arms that grappled at him. Jostled by the crowds, he stared up at Jasmine. "Don't you have a conscience?"

His words were almost drowned by the noise, but she heard them. She watched him turn and stride out of the room. She felt sick.

* * *

That night at the champagne reception in the ballroom of the Istana Hotel, the news came. The Western guests wore black tie, Jasmine was in a cream Christian Lacroix evening dress. The Malaysians were elegant and poised in formal long-sleeved batik. Jasmine sat with Jordan and Danesleigh at Loh's table. The altercation that morning had not dampened the success of the day.

"Jasmine dispatched that greenie damn well!" Loh said. "You've got a fine lawyer there, Bill."

An aide hurried up to the chairman, bending down to whisper urgent news. Loh looked surprised, then a slow smile of vindication spread across his face.

"What's up?" Jordan asked.

Loh said, "McAllister's been arrested."

"What?" Jasmine gasped. "What for?"

Benson leaned towards Jasmine. "See, I told you so."

"What do you mean?"

"McAllister killed Dr Chan."

17

It had begun with a telephone conversation three weeks before.

"You were right to tell me, Edward," Jordan said into his mobile. It was the day after Jasmine had spoken to Danesleigh about the tower. "Instruct her to pursue her enquiries. I want to know who's spreading these rumours ... Yes, of course the design is safe ... I'll see what I can find out through my contacts ... You've done well."

Jordan rang off. He looked out of the limousine at the gaudy Jeepneys clamouring to overtake on the inside lane. The limousine was heading inland from Ninoy Aquino International Airport towards Makati, Manila's commercial district. He had come here for exploratory discussions with an Australian hotel chain that was expanding into the Philippines. With its Titiwangsa tender under consideration, Jordan Cardale was now attracting blue-chip clients with major construction contracts. And now this talk of faulty design and dangerous construction. Jordan scowled.

Jasmine had not named names. Jordan cast his mind over the possibilities. Closest to home was his own team. The architect and surveyor. He had depended on them to produce the winning design. And the Consortium geophysicist. Jordan cursed. Had he been too dependent on the loyalty and silence of these men?

The tender bid submitted by Jordan to the Consortium showed that the tower foundations would rest safely in the granite – above the limestone substratum and without piercing into it. This had been possible only through manipulation of the geophysical data to obscure the fact that the foundations entered the limestone layer at one corner of the tower. Jordan had made sure of it through the geophysicist employed by the Consortium who provided the graphic logs – the logs showing cross-sections of the different layers of soil and rock below the surface of a site.

On a scheme as big as this, Jordan had had to depend on many professionals and experts who knew the extent of his illicit manipulations. He disliked such dependency for it exposed him on too many flanks. But he needed their skills. And, he reflected, he paid damn well for their collusion. Scott, the architect, had balked initially at the risk and had tried to minimise the height of the tower. But he and Jordan went back a long way and he had too much to lose to refuse Jordan anything – a prestigious reputation and growing international client base, which Jordan's contacts had brought him, and a bulk of undeclared wealth from the favours he did for Jordan. Jordan relaxed. He always made sure that his people depended on him as much, if not more, than he depended on them. If Scott grassed on Jordan, he'd be shooting himself in the balls. Jordan checked the architect mentally off his list.

Tsui, the geophysicist, had been Jordan's greatest coup. A man from inside the Consortium technical team. The source of all the geological data on which the tenderers and the Consortium itself would rely. Tsui had assured him that, once he had manipulated that data, no one would know unless they physically carried out another geological survey involving expensive heavy machinery and bore-holes. Jordan liked Tsui, a mainland Chinese, who had no morals and no god but money. Jordan had paid him extravagantly and did not doubt his loyalty. As for Zain, the project manager and surveyor, Jordan thought him a weak, cowardly man, who'd grown accustomed to the wealth and status that working for Jordan had brought him. Zain would never have the gumption to stand up against Jordan nor the inclination to lose his easy riches. Besides, these men knew that if they bit the hand that fed them – as Sarojaya and Ibrahim had inadvertently done – they would have to face the consequences. His team were professionals and he was sure of them – at least, for now.

Jordan considered the other five tenderers. Any of them would gain from elimination of its competitors. But his reliable sources had revealed that they were plodders who played by the rules. He had always been confident that he had nothing to fear from them. So far, he had heard nothing of substance to change his mind. The only campaign he knew of against Jordan Cardale, and against the development as a whole, had always been waged by Dr Chan.

From the start Dr Chan had been an uncompromising enemy. He could neither be bought nor out-manoeuvred. Jordan frowned. He preferred to avoid extreme tactics, but time was running out. He had three weeks before the Consortium came to their decision. Any hint of his design being dangerous could lose him the whole project. Whoever had deduced the fault in the design had to have had a detailed knowledge of construction engineering and technology, as well as land development and geophysical substrata analysis. The doctor had access to an independent technical review of both the site and the design plans through the environmental consultant.

Jordan could not be certain that the consultant was the one who had identified the issue. But it was a place to start.

*   *   *

A few days later, Jordan had the confirmation he needed.

He sat at the desk in his executive suite at the Inter-Continental Hotel in Makati district, reviewing a box of discs on his laptop computer and assessing several thick dossiers. They had been delivered to him wrapped in brown paper. They belonged to Luke. On Jordan's instructions, Tan had arranged for Luke's house and office to be searched. Kidd found nothing at the house. At the office on campus in Penang, however, a locked filing cabinet produced Luke's entire Kampung Tanah documentation and data, all neatly labelled. Kidd removed this hard-copy set. He then took the micro-chips from the computer, the common target of high-tech thieves, and smashed the hardware. For good measure, he emptied the remaining contents of the cabinet onto the floor and set fire to the room.

As Jordan scrolled through Luke's report, his anger and panic intensified. Luke had deduced a discrepancy in the project data. Luke set out at length the bases of his deduction. He concluded that there was either an error in the graphic logs or in the design of the tower – but from the information he had, he could not exactly identify which was at fault. Jordan had been confident that the manipulated data would pass not only the Consortium but also the planning review. Even his own team had overlooked the discrepancy, which might easily have been insignificant had McAllister not been so extensive in his analysis. Jordan noted that he had applied a number of comparative ratio tests and cross-checking formulae of his own devising and it had been these that had thrown up the discrepancy.

Luke's conclusion was that the tower's foundations would enter the limestone substratum, the instability of which would lead to an unacceptable risk of subsidence. Jordan cursed. Tsui had assured him that the falsified data had been watertight. Jordan had had to trust Tsui on that for he himself lacked the expertise to cross-check everything his team did. But McAllister had been too meticulous and tenacious, following through every figure and calculation to expose the discrepancy where most other consultants might have taken the broad view.

Jordan knew the risks of building into limestone. But he had estimated that in this case the risk would be minimal – not the thirty per cent chance assessed by Luke. He had manipulated the data merely to avoid any hint that his design might be less than perfect. As far as he had been concerned, minimal risk was zero risk.

Jordan stood up with such fury that he overturned the chair. In the current climate of controversy focused on his design, any debate over safety risks would lose him the tender – and the world-class prestige he had fought for.

* * *

Tan had delivered the package to Jordan and, as instructed, met his client that night in Ringo's, a dark smoke-laden bar off Burgos Street.

"Tsui. Where is he now?" Jordan said.

"Seattle. We fixed him up with the hotel development there as you instructed. He's making good money."

"I don't pay for fuck-ups. Remind him of that." Jordan briefed Tan on Tsui's failure.

"My contacts in America will get it done."

"Just enough to let him know who owns him."

Tan nodded. He swivelled his eyes to check the tables around them. No one was paying them any attention. Tan said, "I've been in contact with Wong. He has some bad news."

Jordan said nothing but his face hardened.

"The doctor's threatening to go to the police."

"Shit! What does he know?"

"Not much. But he suspects. The attack on the teacher and lawyer – he thinks it's the reason the town changed its mind. The two never reported the attack to the police but everyone knows about it. Chan doesn't know who's behind it but he's talking about a conspiracy. So far, our people have managed to keep him from going to the police – or to reporters. But they won't be able to hold him off much longer."

"Goddammit!"

The bar was air-conditioned but Jordan was sweating. He had never needed to come so far down the line before. In previous projects, money and fancy perks had been good currency to get what he wanted. On occasion, he had had to resort to physical violence – but usually the mere threat of it had been sufficient.

He gave his instructions to Tan. "... and I want you to take care of it personally. Kidd talks too much – I've heard he's been bragging about the lawyer's balls."

Tan was pale. "Is there no other way?"

"You'll be well paid for it."

"It's not the money."

"What then?"

"No killing." There was a strange intensity in Tan's voice. "I told you when we first worked together."

Jordan leaned forward. "We had a deal. You're being paid to secure Kampung Tanah to my bidding. I've paid you and all I see are your fuck-ups."

"I can make them right."

"We've come too far. There's only one way now."

"No. If I take a life, *I* pay with a life. It is the harmony of things."

Jordan downed his whisky. "I don't have time for this."

Tan's face was taut with conflict. This enterprise had not proceeded as he had promised. His Kampung Tanah network had taken money and benefited from his patronage but given only trouble in return. And they had failed to win over the doctor. They had caused him, Tan, to fail *his* patron. It was a dislocation of order that boded ill. He owed it now to Jordan – and to his own harmony – to redress the balance. But he balked at murder. Tan said, "Give me another chance."

"There are no second chances in this game." Jordan softened his tone. "I don't like this either. But if Chan goes to the police, or if the consultant's report gets out, it's over. Not just for now but the whole game – Jordan Cardale, Tan Securities, the lot. Wiped off the board. I've got the consultant's report. All you have to do is make sure of Chan. McAllister is just his employee – without the doctor and without his report, he's nothing. It's easy. Eliminate one player and the game is ours."

Tan's mind flashed blank with terror. If you take life, you will pay for it with your own. The principle of harmony dictated it. That was why he had never sanctioned killing. But he knew that Jordan was right. There was no leaving off with the journey unfinished. And there was only one safe way forward.

Tan made himself focus. They were bringing progress and enlightenment to people who would otherwise have no future, he had told Wong. Did he himself not believe that? The doctor's ignorant pride was endangering their objective. He had been given opportunities to bend from his arrogance and he had shunned them. In the path of the onrushing water, those who do not bend will break.

More than that, the doctor was now a force of danger to Jordan and himself. Tan saw his justification then. The balance of this enterprise had always been out of kilter because of the doctor. The darkness was seeking to swamp the light. If they did not defend their own territory, its deadening gloom would win.

Tan nodded slowly. "It's not murder," he said. "It will be justice."

*   *   *

The interview room stank of urine and bleach. Luke sat at the battered table. Raymond, in full sergeant's uniform, had intercepted him as he had driven into Taiping late that night from Kuala Lumpur after the Consortium 2000 conference. In his squad car, Raymond had escorted Luke's Land Rover to the police station. Now, sternly professional, Raymond sat against the wall with a clear view of his prisoner. His standard-issue pistol hung in the holster by his side.

The wire cage door was shut. Through the bars high up on the wall, a grey dawn lightened the sky.

"Am I under arrest?" Luke said for the third time. He looked tired and drawn, his face roughened by day-old stubble.

The senior detective sat across from him. He was Chinese, in his late fifties, grey haired but still lean. He had a spartan severity, as if he had channelled the poverty of his youth into discipline and rectitude. His name was Lam Meng-Ho. There were two dossiers on the table in front of him, one open on top of the other. "Tell me again what happened."

"If I'm under suspicion, arrest me," Luke barked. "If not, let me go. I know my rights!"

There was a curl of dislike on Lam's face. "You are not in an American movie, Mr McAllister."

"You don't have a thing on me, do you? Kenneth was murdered.

But not by me."

"By who then?"

"I told you – find the guy I saw with him!"

Lam said, "You whites like to give orders, ha? Did you tell the doctor how to run his campaign?"

"Jesus! How many times do I have to tell you?"

"Tell me again. I'm just a stupid Chinaman."

Luke ignored the sarcasm. "Kenneth contracted me to report on the tender bids and to submit an application to the planners. My report is objective and technical. Somewhere along the way, Kenneth got over-zealous and antagonised a lot of people. It wasn't a campaign."

Lam said, "Let me be clear. I don't like you whites. Your kind sucked Asia dry in the past and you're still trying get what you can out of us. You people are proud and weak. None of your tricks are going to fool me. So just answer my questions without this American movie-talk, okay?"

Luke assessed the contemptuous mask opposite him. He sighed. "I arrived late that night at the doctor's house. It'd been raining all day."

"What time?"

"Around eleven. Kenneth let me in and we talked. I told him about the burglary and fire at my office – all my papers gone, everything else destroyed." Luke ran his fingers through his hair. "Look, there must be a connection. First, they took my report and now, Kenneth's dead."

"Who are 'they'?"

"Whoever that man was – him and the people he works for. I have an idea who they might be."

"A conspiracy?"

"Yes."

"Like the one the doctor shouted about?"

"Yes."

"And who's behind it?"

"Jordan Cardale. Maybe the Consortium's in on it, too."

"What evidence have you got?"

Luke could not reply.

Lam laughed, "You're a loony, paranoid – or you're an extremist greenie."

"Jordan stood to lose the most from our submission to the planners. He was getting all that bad publicity already."

"And your proof that the developers stole your papers, burned your office and killed Chan?"

"I don't have any."

Lam snapped, "Then stick to the facts. What happened next?"

Luke began to argue, then thought better of it. He told the story again.

"Kenneth got manic. 'A bloody conspiracy!' he shouted. 'They can't scare us! I'm not giving up, I tell you!' His patients had stopped coming to him. His friends wouldn't see him. His kids were bullied in school. No one was talking to his wife when she went into town. There'd been threats against him, vandals at the surgery."

"'But I know what's right!' he said. 'And I have to do it. Our Lord didn't let all the abuse and hate stop Him. This is the cross *I* have to bear. What we believe in makes us who we are. We have to be true to that. No matter what. That is what makes us truly alive.' He quoted the Bible. 'Whoever wants to save his life will lose it, but whoever loses his life for the truth will save it – for what good is it to gain the whole world and yet lose your very self?'"

"The call came about one thirty. An emergency call-out from Lee's Hotel. A man. In a panic – his wife was ill. They were from out of town. Kenneth told me this as he got his medical things together. He looked exhausted. It was raining heavily again. 'They're not your patients,' I said. 'Why not send them down to the hospital in Ranjing?'"

"He said, 'These people need me. I've been idle for months because of this trouble.'"

"I got a bad feeling about it. The arson attack, the threats and vandalism. But Kenneth laughed. I had to get back to Penang for the next morning so I left with him. At the trunk road junction, I turned towards the highway and he went the other way. In the dark, with the rain clattering down, that bad feeling spooked me. So I headed back to Lee's Hotel. I turned the blind corner by the hotel, aiming to go into the forecourt. But Kenneth's car was there in the road. I slammed on the brakes and my headlights caught the men full on. Kenneth was out in the rain with this guy, right there inches away from my bonnet. The guy stared straight at me, startled. Chinese. A perm and moustache – maybe fake, thinking back on it. A split second and the face hardened again, eyes set. He ducked his head down and scuttled over into Kenneth's car, passenger side."

"Kenneth came over. He said, 'It's okay, I've seen him with Lee before. His wife's not here. Their car broke down about five miles up. He'll show me where.'"

"'You want me to come?'"

"He laughed. 'Don't be so paranoid. I'll be fine.'"

"He got in his car and they drive off, heading uphill out of town."

Luke said, "I'll know that face anywhere. You've got to find that guy."

Lam flicked a glance at Raymond. "Sergeant?"

Raymond took out his notebook and referred to it. "Officers at Kampung Tanah talked to everyone at Lee Hotel, including Mr Lee. Also they interviewed the locals. No one knows anything about this man with a perm. No calls from the hotel, no one answering that description seen that night."

Luke interjected, "I did a photo-fit with the police artist right after they found Kenneth."

"No one recognised the face," Raymond said. He added, "I'm sorry."

Lam was watching Luke closely. He grimaced at Raymond's apology. "That's enough, Sergeant."

Luke stared at Raymond. His friend looked away. Luke turned to Lam. "I saw him!"

"Are you saying that all those people the police talked to were lying?" Lam said.

"Or too afraid to tell the truth."

"Aah, the conspiracy," Lam sneered. "Supposing I believe you. Supposing this man exists and he went off with the doctor. How did he kill Chan? It looks like a straight drunk-driving accident."

Luke said, "The doctor doesn't drink. Never did. He wasn't drunk the last time I saw him."

"The top people of Kampung Tanah say he had a drink problem." Lam read from his dossier. "Wong Keng-Wi, businessman. Lingam, lawyer. 'Disappointed because of his lost cause, bitter and hated everyone.' 'Abusive to wife and those who tried to help him.' Even his wife says so."

"What? Maria?"

"She says Chan was drunk the night of the accident."

"She'd gone to bed."

"She says that you made him a drunkard. You two always drank when you came to visit."

"What?"

"Is she lying, too?"

Luke stared blankly. Why *was* Maria lying? He began, "Maybe they're forcing her to lie. Or paying her ... but, no, Maria wouldn't take money – nor would she do such a thing –"

"'They' again! Who are 'they'?"

"Damn it!" Luke stood up suddenly in frustration.

At once, Lam was on his feet. Raymond shot up, legs spread, his gun drawn and aimed at Luke. Luke froze, startled.

Raymond came forward. His voice was hoarse. "Sit down, Mr McAllister."

Lam's hand was half-way to his shoulder holster. He let it drop, hooking his thumb into his belt, his head cocked back. His eyes never left Luke. There was a challenge in them, almost as if he dared Luke to make a move. Breathing hard, Luke glanced at Raymond. His friend's face was set but a bead of sweat trickled down his cheek. Raymond's gaze was intense. He shook his head imperceptibly. Luke sat down.

The detective eased himself back onto his chair and leaned

back as Raymond bolstered his pistol. Raymond moved back to the wall but remained standing. Lam seemed to be enjoying the shock that Luke had involuntarily shown. Luke said with a sigh, "Find the guy who was with him – he's the key. Either he saw something or knows something. Or he killed Kenneth."

"*You* were the last to see the doctor, isn't it?" Lam said

"Are you accusing me of Kenneth's murder?"

"No one's talking about murder except you. Why are you pushing the murder story?"

"Why are you disregarding it?"

Lam said, "We have no evidence for murder except rumours and scaremongering. No mystery man, nothing saying there was anyone else there but Chan. Forensics can prove his high alcohol level. We have witnesses who say he was depressed and had no more hope. Your story is the one that doesn't fit. It would make me happy to arrest you for manslaughter if your drinking with him led to the accident – but it won't stick in court. Everything looks like accidental death."

"But the man I saw –"

"Maybe a genuine traveller, passing through."

"You're going to close the investigation."

Lam ignored Luke. "Maybe someone you made up. Or someone you're working with."

"I'm not working with anyone."

Lam opened the second dossier and laid it on top of the first. "This is my file on you, Mr McAllister. All your connections and activities from press reports since Dr Chan hired you. Plus my own investigations."

"I have nothing to hide."

"It looks like that. But you're a guest in this country and, for a foreigner, you have many noisy opinions. I don't like smart-mouthed whites like you. You're a troublemaker."

"I've done nothing against the law."

"Ever since you got involved in the Kampung Tanah project, there's been trouble. Foreign reporters poking their noses into this country's affairs. Foreign experts telling us what we should or shouldn't do. Rumours about conspiracies and corruption – all coming from you and the doctor."

"Kenneth was inclined to get over-excited –"

Lam slammed his fist on the table. "What is the secret agenda of your campaign? Who else are you working for in addition to Green Action Direct?"

"I don't work for Green Action – how many times do I have to say it? I have no connections with any campaigning or political organisation. Your investigations should support that."

"So why are you spreading lies about murder and conspiracy? What do you want to stir up?"

"Why are you investigating me for sedition when there's a murder that you're calling accidental death?"

Lam was white with fury. "The investigation of Chan's death will be closed. But *I'm* not finished yet. I watched you for months. If you have proof about murder, give it to me. Don't spread lies and speculations about conspiracies. We're a civilised country. We stand by justice, and justice means hard evidence."

Lam signalled to Raymond to escort Luke out. "So far, all you've got is *kacau*. You whites like to make trouble where you don't belong. That may work in the West but not here. I'm letting you go. For now. I'll find out your agenda, you can be sure of that."

Luke stood up. He said, "I'll get you your hard evidence."

18

Raymond walked with Luke out of the station. It was a glaring white morning and though it was still early, the damp heat was heavy and close. They walked across to where Luke's Land Rover was parked on the street.

Raymond said, "Lam's got nothing on you that's going to stick."

They stood by a row of shop-houses. At this time in the morning, the street was almost empty. Luke searched for his keys. In the shade of some trees across the road, a black BMW was parked, the figure inside watching the two men. Luke squinted but could not see the face through the tinted windows.

To Raymond, he said, "Am I under investigation?"

Raymond hesitated. He said, "I shouldn't tell you anything."

Luke nodded. But he didn't move, staring at the BMW. The number plates did not have the 'A' of Perak plates, the state of which Taiping was a part. They were 'W' plates, a Kuala Lumpur registration. He remembered the charred remains of his office at the university and the debris after they had ransacked his house.

Raymond followed the line of Luke's gaze. He frowned. "Know the car?"

"No."

"You think it's something?"

Luke leaned against the door, turning away from the car. He was tense despite his casual posture. "Maybe. But they're not going to make a move outside a police station. Probably just keeping tabs. We'll see what happens when I leave."

Raymond squinted across the street again. "I don't like it."

Luke was determined not to show his concern to whoever was in the car. He would not be intimidated. He moved round to check the tyres, his tone deliberately light. "I'm not worried. You're pretty quick on the draw – you'll get them before they get me."

"Dammit, man," Raymond said, but he grinned. "Don't pull that again the next time you're in police custody. I'd hate to take you out in the line of duty."

"Thanks for the tip."

Raymond kept the BMW in sight as he leaned on the bonnet. He seemed to debate with himself about something. Crouching down by a tyre, Luke waited. When Raymond finally spoke, he kept his voice low. "It's a bloody mess-up. We've been friends since we were kids. You were my best man." He paused, chewing something over. At last, he said, "Lam's on a mission of his own. CID. Central haven't authorised an official investigation of your activities."

Luke busied himself checking the front tyre. Out of the corner of his eye, he watched the BMW. What the hell did they want? To Raymond, he said, "Look, you don't have to tell me anything."

Raymond looked away. "We're friends. I believe your story but it's not up to me. Lam heads the investigation into the doctor's death. He got his orders through to us here in Taiping to hold you till he got here. I took it – I reckoned I could watch out for you or something. He got me liaising with the team at Kampung Tanah and doing his legwork this end. I'd heard about him – shit, now I know why no one likes him. He behaves like a big *tuan*, the king boss over everyone.

"My guess is Lam's out to make a name for himself He's got a good reputation as a solid detective but his service record is unremarkable. He's been on the force thirty years or so now. I think he's after a trophy case before it's too late. He cares more for that than finding out the truth."

Luke snorted, "Bag a guy who's been in the news and, hey, you get your name in the paper. Jesus, he can't even find the guy I saw!"

"Don't underestimate him. All he needs is hard, legitimate evidence and he'll have all the authority he needs to make a case against you."

Luke stood up. He looked at his friend. He knew how much pride Raymond had in his badge, and what a professional betrayal it was to him to reveal police matters in this way. But they had grown up with a strong affection and loyalty, almost as if they had been brothers. Luke knew that, in the same way, he would help Raymond if the time came. He thought of Jasmine and the friendship that they, too, had once had. He said, "Ray, thanks."

Raymond made a dismissive sound. "You watch yourself."

"Sure."

Raymond indicated the car. "You want me to check it out?"

Luke stared across at the BMW. There was no movement from inside but he was sure whoever it was was staring back. Anger broke through his uncertainty. He had been threatened and intimidated on projects in the past but he had never fled from a confrontation with his tail between his legs. Lam's bull-headed antagonism goaded him still. Luke had promised him the hard evidence he wanted. If whoever was watching him had had anything to do with the doctor's death, now was Luke's opening. He would not wait for them to make the first move. "If it's me they want, I'll go. You watch my back."

Luke began to stride across the street, his walk relaxed, but he was tense, ready for whatever might happen. Out of the corner of his eye, he saw Raymond moving to a clear position, one hand covering his pistol.

The door of the BMW opened. Jasmine stepped out of the driver's seat. A jolt of anger stopped Luke in his tracks.

She stood behind the door as if behind a shield. She was wearing an old T-shirt and jeans. Her hair was tied hastily in a short bunch away from her face. She wore no makeup. She looked as if she hadn't slept.

Luke turned on his heel and strode back to the Land Rover.

She started towards him. "Luke!"

To Raymond, he said, "It's no one." He climbed up into the Land Rover and started the engine. He swung out in reverse and paused to change gear. She was standing in the middle of the street staring at him plaintively. He shifted his gaze away.

The Land Rover roared past her. "Luke!" She stared after it, watching till it rounded the corner out of sight.

"I came to say I'm sorry," she said to the quiet street. Raymond watched her curiously. Then she saw him and turned away, hurrying back to the BMW

*   *   *

"I must see him. I have to explain," Jasmine said to her mother.

After she had tried to speak to Luke, Jasmine had parked the car inconspicuously in a car park in Taiping and walked to Mrs Fung's house. Making her way through the streets of Taiping, she felt she'd become Malaysian again. No one turned to stare at her as they would have done if she'd been in her designer outfits and immaculate makeup. Without her disguise, she was just the Taiping girl she'd always been. Only the confidence of her Westerner's stride hinted at something other.

Jasmine had felt highly strung all day, anxiously hurrying to help her mother with her work. Now they crouched in the seclusion of the garden, a plastic pail behind them, digging weeds from the flower-beds. It was after four and the light was weakening into amber. Jasmine could not control her agitation. She worked the soil furiously, hacking at the coiling roots.

"You have a good heart." Mrs Fung looked up from her patch. "I know you didn't mean all those things you said on TV about Luke. I told him you would make it right to him."

"It wasn't wrong what I did," Jasmine said, but the words felt like a prayer without faith. "I had to – it wasn't anything personal. I'm a lawyer. My client has to come first."

She looked away. She was glad for the tasks that had filled the day, for their need of her energy. She talked on, desperately giving slack at last to her turmoil of guilt. "I was going to tell him before. Now, he doesn't want to see me. But it's because he doesn't understand. If only I could explain to him. I want to make things right with him. Even if that puts me against everything law school taught me about professional ethics. It's not easy for me, you know. I shouldn't see him. Luke is my client's enemy. My association with him is a conflict of interest that could cost me my career. If I declare it, I'll have to step down from the case, hand over to that Roberts. If I don't and someone finds out …"

Her voice trailed off. These words had spun in her brain for weeks, silenced only by her desperate schedule of work. The panic suffocated her. It was all going wrong, everything she touched. At home she hardly saw her husband: Harry came back late and, sometimes, only to pick up some fresh clothes. She had been relieved at first but the guilt of her failed marriage gnawed like poison. On the nights he stayed away, he told her he was staying at the company flat round the corner from the office or that he was away on business. She did not question him, afraid to catch him in a lie. At least, for as long as he was not having an affair, she told herself, they might have the chance of working it out. She twisted the questions over and over in her mind. How could she make Harry love her again? How could she make them find their way back to their lost hope? If only she could reach beyond his hurt and suspicion. Sometimes he tried, too, she knew. She recognised the conciliatory tone in his attempt at a joke or a polite question about her week. She clutched at the tokens of peace he offered and, for a time, they might get along almost too well. And then, something would go wrong. She was never quite sure what it was she said or did that might start it all over again. But they would be fighting again – about a dinner date, a stray remark misinterpreted, the perfume she was wearing: things that had no meaning but somehow, in that moment, had become the very definition of their beings. And Harry would be gone again, storming out to nurse his hurt and anger.

At work, Roberts hovered like a vulture, secretive since his introduction to Jordan, working to usurp her, she was sure of it. She drove herself with a desperate energy. She worked to diversify her client base, her pride refusing to allow Roberts to beat her. In her office, she was in control and respected. It satisfied her, she told herself, it empowered her. But she felt as if she was skidding on the edge of collapse: any moment now, a flicker of unevenness and it would all be over, spinning into a headlong crash.

Even in sleep, she found no respite, the old nightmare tearing her awake. It was fragmenting into more and more surreal mutations – Harry exploding from inside her gut, her mother shrivelling before her eyes. She hardly slept now, staring night after night at the ceiling.

On hearing of Luke's questioning by the police, she had left the banquet as early as she dared: she had to avoid arousing curiosity. She had paced in her hotel room for an hour in an anguish of indecision, half out of her evening clothes and wiping the makeup off her face. Finally, she had driven the three and a half hours up to Taiping in the dead of the night. She headed straight for the police station and, seeing his Land Rover parked outside, she had stopped. She had not known what she would do – go in and try to help him or wait for him to emerge, if they let him go, or turn around and drive away, not get involved, not try to make amends. She had sat there all night. She knew only one thing for certain. She had to see him. Whatever happened.

The skid was about to flip into a crash. She knew it. But she had to hold on. She had to try to hold down the chaos, make things right again. Through the long night in the car, she had it fixed in her mind, somehow, that in settling matters with Luke, she would be starting the process of rebuilding the shattered unity of her life.

Jasmine looked at her mother. "I have to see him. It's the right thing to do. Isn't it?"

The scarlet bloodstains of the flame tree seeped across the afternoon sky above them. Mrs Fung took her daughter's hand. The soil was gritty between their skins. Mrs Fung said, "I don't understand about what's right and wrong in business. All I know is that you are my precious child I would do anything for. And Luke, he is my sweet, good boy. I wanted you to be so happy, my darling girl, and I thought that a new life would give you that. Luke, he is strong and I didn't worry for him like I worried for you. But to see you two now, as if like strangers and enemies ..."

Jasmine listened to her mother's familiar voice. Sitting here so close, the smell of the earth like a balm, it seemed as if the years had never passed. She felt like a child again, proud to be given a duty in her mother's beloved garden, the work and the soil on her hands rooting her to their common bond. For a moment, it gave her relief from her panic. She realised, for the first time, how old and gaunt her mother looked. There were shadows of pain around her eyes and age had begun to fray the firmness of her voice.

Mrs Fung searched her daughter's face. She had watched Jasmine all day, seeing in her unkempt appearance and strained features the tumult of her heart. But Mrs Fung sensed there was something more that Jasmine was not telling her. Her daughter's sudden return, her almost manic concern for Luke, had a deeper root. Mrs Fung understood why Jasmine had spoken out against Luke. Jasmine drove herself onwards towards a better future, clung with all tenacity to her fragile new life – that was what Mrs Fung had taught her. Don't look back, no matter what. Escape, that is your destiny and your duty. She had channelled her daughter's will well, Mrs Fung thought, but she felt no triumph.

A fear chilled her. Mrs Fung stared deep into Jasmine's eyes. There, in their dark, liquid heart, she saw something. The shadows of a night twenty years ago shifted through her memory. Blows and curses. A man raging against a woman, hitting her across the face, in the belly.

Mrs Fung let out a cry.

"*Ah Ma*, what is it?"

Mrs Fung could hardly speak. "He's a jealous man."

"What?"

"Your husband."

Jasmine looked away. She tried to pull her hand from her mother's but Mrs Fung would not let go. Her mother said, "He hurts you."

"No." Jasmine tried to control her trembling. She forced a laugh. "No, of course not."

Mrs Fung paused, confused. Her mind was in turmoil. Was Jasmine lying? Or perhaps it was a warning of the future, what she had seen. Luke. And her daughter. If Jasmine's husband found out! "You must leave," Mrs Fung cried. "Go back to your husband. You have a chance to escape the past. Go home. Forget Luke, forget me."

Mrs Fung was cold with fear. The spirit had not been appeased, after all. She had not been its proper guardian. It would visit the past upon her daughter, shape the hope of her marriage into a hideous parody of what her own had been. Mrs Fung was close to tears. "I was foolish! I thought that, in our lives, we can change the path we travel and start a new journey. But each step leads on to the next. So the journey may change – but the path is made up of all our footsteps, from the very first to the very last."

Mrs Fung gasped as if she had seen a ghoul.

"*Ah Ma*, what is it?"

The old woman's voice was trembling when she spoke again. "Our past belongs forever to the journey we are now on. We cannot shake it off like the dust from our feet. That is what frightens me."

"I don't understand."

Mrs Fung relaxed her grasp. She steadied her will. She looked intently at Jasmine and came to a decision. Her daughter would not rest till she had made peace with Luke. But, after that, there had to be no more contact. She said, "You must not let anything pull you back from your new life. You will see Luke tonight and you will say to him what you have to say. Then you must leave."

"How?"

"Go to him. His house is up in Firefly Clearing."

"Firefly Clearing?"

"No one else must see you. Before tomorrow breaks, you must go." Mrs Fung pulled Jasmine into an embrace. "Promise me you will go. Leave him be. Promise."

"Yes." Jasmine did not understand but the intensity of her

mother's command held her.

A warm breeze rippled the hot afternoon. Sprinklings of red from the flame tree floated across the garden. Jasmine looked up at powder-puff clouds. Firefly Clearing. Their old place shimmered in her mind.

"He meant it, then," she murmured.

"What, my dear?"

"About building our house up there."

*   *   *

There was a new moon that night. Through the dark lattice of the trees, its sly sleepy wink followed Jasmine's progress up the forest trail to Firefly Clearing. With only a torch to light her way, she had at first been uncertain, hesitant. She was not sure she could still recognise the vague definition of the shortcut they had always used. The forest closed in on all sides. To stray from the paths could mean she might never find her way back, each disoriented step taking her further into the thickening, trackless depths. But as she climbed, first along the Jeep track and then finding the familiar path through the dense trees, she found that she remembered the trail after all. She had taken these paths so many times with Luke at night. The darkness felt like an old friend here, the looming shapes and living hum of the forest like the texture and sounds of home.

She came upon the clearing suddenly, over the crest of a steep incline, the flat sea below at her back. Weaving trails of light tangled round the clustered rocks. Jasmine switched off her torch and watched the magical dance of the fireflies with untainted wonder. Beyond, the shape of the house stretched across the clearing, wedges of light from the open windows softly illuminating the grounds.

Jasmine crossed the natural yard towards the low verandah. As she approached the steps, a voice said, "I wondered if you'd try again."

She could not see him at first. Then the creaking of a swing drew her gaze aside. He sat in the shadows on the verandah, his feet up on the rail. "How did you know it was me?" she asked.

"No one else would come by that path."

She stepped up onto the verandah. She could see him better now. He looked fresh and rested, a bottle of Budweiser in his hand. Chopsticks and the remainder of a plate of noodles sat on the low table beside him.

He said, with an edge, "What do you want?"

"I came to explain."

Luke waited.

"To apologise. I tried to tell you in Penang but – well, things got confused. I'm sorry you didn't know I act for Jordan Cardale."

Still nothing.

"I'm sorry I had to say the things I said about you. At the TV conference. And yesterday. It was nothing personal, I want you to know that. That was just business. You know what it's like."

Luke's tone was harsh. "There's no such thing as 'just business'. Everything's personal."

"What I do in my work has no bearing on my personal feelings."

"What you do makes you who you are."

"Life's not so simple."

"Why did you bother to come?" Luke stood up. There was disgust on his face. "You are the public face of Jordan's dirty work. You twist the truth about my work by innuendo, you manipulate the law to exploit the people of Kampung Tanah, you hide behind it to push through a faulty and dangerous construction. And all for what? For the money you never had and for the status you always longed for. Everything *is* personal."

Jasmine pushed on desperately. "I had to do what I did. But I feel as bad about it as you."

"Lame sentiment is easy."

Suddenly, Jasmine felt angry. "Look, I said I'm sorry. I have to act in the best interests of my client, that's my job."

Luke said, "The ruthless commercial lawyer with the heart that cares. I'm touched."

Before she could reply, he rounded on her, the force of his fury like a blow to her face. "Do you know what you've done? My work, my reputation – they're destroyed! How long will it take me to get those back? Through the libel courts? I don't have the money for that. Even if I did, it would take years and who would care at the end of it? The damage sticks, no matter what a judge might say, you know that. You may like playing powerful lawyer and winning your little points but what you do has consequences far beyond your legal games. You've knocked me down and it may take me blood and sweat to get up again, but you can be damn sure that I'm not beaten. You might live with that, but what about the tower? People will die because of what you're fighting for. Can you live with that?"

"Stop!" Jasmine lashed out. She knocked the bottle out of his hand. Beer splattered them both as the bottle smashed to the floor. A sob convulsed her but she fought it down. She let her anger take the momentum. How dare he accuse her, imply she was a murderer? He was twisting everything she was trying to do, reading her every impulse through his self-righteousness. She cried, "I came when I heard the news of your arrest. I wanted to help in whatever way I could. Make things right. I don't believe you could have killed the doctor – whatever people say about you. I took a risk coming to see you. How dare *you* judge *me*?"

Luke seemed drained suddenly. His tone was quieter when he spoke again. But the hard edge remained. "I'm not under arrest. The police are closing the investigation. Accidental death."

"What?"

"Sorry you came all this way for nothing."

Jasmine was confused, the impetus of her anger derailed. Luke came up to her. He studied her for a long moment. The lines on his face were hard. Jasmine felt a spinning fear. He had never turned on her before with the disgust he had shown in the last two days. His fury at her shook her. Now it hit her for the first time that she might not be able to make things right. The bravado she had felt at the press conference was gone. She and Luke were enemies, and that knowledge was like a gash in her heart.

Luke was watching her. After a moment, he said, "You really meant what you said."

Jasmine found herself pleading. "Why shouldn't I? Do you think I came here for other reasons?"

"Don't you always act for the best interests of your client?"

"My being here has nothing to do with that. This is a personal visit." She felt on the verge of tears. She had to convince him of her sincerity. She couldn't give up, not now. Not ever. It startled her – the realisation that losing Luke mattered to her so deeply.

Luke said, "In Penang, you told Jordan, didn't you, about my report? Was that a personal visit?"

"No – yes – I mean ..." She didn't want them to go this way. She wanted to talk about them, about her and Luke, about what was personal. She floundered, trying to find a way back but he pushed on.

"Now the report's stolen. Or destroyed. Interesting coincidence, don't you think?"

"These allegations –"

"Are unfounded and your client will sue. Yes, yes, we covered all that yesterday," Luke interrupted. "Stop playing legal word-games. Kenneth has already died because of this project. Many more could be killed if the tower goes ahead unchallenged. You can hide behind well-chosen words but the truth will always be there."

Jasmine was confused. Why was he talking about the tower again? Had he heard nothing from the start of what she'd tried to say? Her mind began to work, her tears and distress pushed to the background. "You said the doctor's death was an accident."

Luke hesitated. He seemed to debate something with himself. Jasmine frowned. Finally, he led her to the far side of the verandah. They sat down in cane chairs. The light from inside did not reach them here. The sliver of moon was setting and the stars sparkled across the deep sky. Luke told Jasmine his suspicions about the murder of the doctor, the arson at his office and Jordan's involvement. But he did not give details of the grilling by Detective Lam.

"I've been digging around," Luke said. "There's talk in construction circles about Jordan's unethical methods in other projects – bribery, fraudulent invoicing, to name but two. But nothing has ever been proven. There are many companies who play fast and loose, and so long as you keep the right people happy, no one's going to rat on you."

"But murder and arson?" Jasmine was trying to take it all in, sorting the mass of information he had given her. But she kept asking herself, what his motive was in drawing her into these speculations.

"You don't have to believe me. As you well know, *I* have no concrete evidence."

Jasmine peered at Luke through the darkness. It didn't make sense. He had been antagonistic, hostile at first. Now he seemed to be trying to bring her alongside his cause. What was he trying to do? Was this some scheme to destroy her as she had damaged him? Startled, she drew back, her guard up. She said, "Why have you told me all this?"

Luke paused. Could he make her understand? Had he been right in trusting her with what he knew? If Jordan was behind all this, what was Jasmine's part in it? Luke still wanted to believe that she had nothing to do with it. He wanted to believe that he could trust her.

Seeing her again tonight, trying so hard to do what was right, he had caught a glimpse of the girl he had lost. In spite of his anger, he realised that he needed her to be the same passionate person he had fallen in love with all those years ago. In the last weeks, a crusading fury had consumed him. Ever since Jasmine's accusations had been broadcast across the world, he had worked like a demon on the report that would vindicate Kenneth's crusade and his own name. Then his months of work had been destroyed in the arson attack but it had only intensified his determination to get to the truth. Dr Chan's death made it all the more personal that he should not fail. But he realised tonight that the intensity that drove him was not just about the death of his employer and friend. Nor was it just a crusade to stop the tower being built.

He saw that now. It was a need entangled in his love for Jasmine. He needed to believe in her. If he were right about Jordan's involvement in Kenneth's death, it had been a risk to detail his suspicions to Jasmine. But something he had not been able to control had impelled him to face the risk. At last, he said, "You're the woman I love. In *your* language, it's personal – not business."

Jasmine couldn't believe what she had just heard. She felt light-headed all of a sudden. As if he'd said the words she'd longed to hear. But instinctively, her guard closed ranks again. She wanted so much to believe him, but could she trust him? She forced herself into her professional persona. "I'm Jordan's lawyer. We know your play now – you're just making it easier for us to put up barriers against your enquiries."

"What you do with what I've told you is up to you. That's the risk I have to take," Luke said. "But, as his lawyer, you are best placed to find out for yourself. Ask the questions I've asked. Open your eyes to all there is to see. Look for the truth. You can smokescreen outsiders – and maybe even the police – but behind all that someone knows the truth. If there's nothing to find you won't find it, and you'll know for certain that I'm wrong, that I'm just a loony leftie radical. And you can fight me with the full power of that conviction." Luke took her hands. "But if the truth is more sinister – well, I can't tell you what to do then. You have your professional ethics, your conscience. It'll be up to you what you do with the knowledge you have." His voice was low and intense now, his pale eyes seeming to glow in the light from the sky. "Whatever you choose to do, that will be who you are for the rest of your life. This is not a game. This is not just about your client or my report or the development. This is also about you. You can't run away from the truth forever. Not just the truth about Jordan. The truth about your past. About your life with Harry. About you and me. The truth about who you really are."

The urgency of his tone held Jasmine. His intensity had stilled her objections. In spite of her resistance, he had reached beyond to the bond they shared. What he had told her undermined everything she had worked for. If what he said was true, her role as Jordan's lawyer was farcical, the victories she won for him with such energy were contaminated with crime. She did not want to hear any more. She grabbed at the weapon he had inadvertently offered her. She said, "There's no 'you and me'. There never was. I don't owe you anything just because you love me. I know what you're trying to do. You're not getting any confidential information on Jordan out of me."

Luke stared at her. She had not understood at all, he thought. Perhaps she had not even heard him.

Jasmine saw the pain in his eyes before he mastered it. She felt a flush of shame but what could she say? They had gone too far beyond apologies. She wanted to erase it all, the professional stand-offs that had been forced between them, the ambitions that had torn them apart all those years ago. But how? She remembered his arms around her that night in Penang. She felt again the passion in their embrace on Waterloo Bridge, the desire in that feverish kiss. What had happened to the love that had once been so easy? The question repeated itself endlessly in her mind. What had happened that they were here again in Firefly Clearing, facing each other in anger as they had done that afternoon long ago when they had first said goodbye?

"You should go," Luke said. "I'll drive you down."

19

Mrs Fung stood at the shrine beneath the flame tree. The setting moon was yellow as a dead man's eye. The *tok-tok* bird counted out the moments between the silences of the night. Mrs Fung knelt and, with trembling hands, lit the night-lights in front of the wooden tablet. The scent of the burning oil mingled with the yeasty sweetness of the night-jasmine. She counted out sheaves of joss-sticks, anxiously bringing them to smoke from the night-lights. The canopy of the flame tree dropped red tears into the makeshift temple below. Mrs Fung shook a clutch of incense sticks with praying hands, her head bowed to the unseen spirit. "See how my child has grown," she pleaded. "So strong, so proud. There is hope for her. She can escape still. If it's justice you want, take me."

She planted the sticks into the soil before the shrine and lowered her face to the ground three times. The effort twisted the ache in her stomach and a cold sweat dampened her. The pain made her dizzy but she had to finish the ritual. From Jasmine's visit, she had understood only that their hope for the future was at stake. She had never seen her daughter so distracted and uncertain. Jasmine's rush of words and explanations clumsily hid fear and despair.

"Don't break her," Mrs Fung pleaded with her secret demon. "She is not to blame. She was never to blame. It was I. And I will take the punishment for what I have done. Do what you like with me, but leave her to her future."

Jagged shapes in her stomach ground tight, forcing a cry of pain to choke with the bile that oozed up. Mrs Fung spat the taste of rust. The flickering light caught the grits of old blood in the vomit on the ground. She had hidden all this from Jasmine, numbing herself with herbal medicines. Amethyst orchid to quench the blood, meeting-happiness flower for the pain, sealwort to draw out the yin energy of her heart. "I'm just weak from the flu sickness going round," she had said to her daughter.

The few hours of iron-willed control over her ailing body had left her buffeted by its terrors and anguish. The secret inside her burrowed to the surface like maggots from a corpse. She had disturbed the order of life, wronged her father, her husband. All her life, she had struggled to restore the rightness of things. But the scales had not been balanced and chaos was returning to claim its justice.

Everything she had done, she had done for Jasmine. In her loveless marriage, she might have surrendered day after day to despair, losing the shreds of her will to Tommy's hatred. But Jasmine had given her a hope. Jasmine, precious and beautiful, like the flame tree Mrs Fung had nurtured with such passion – hers was a new life taking root in a future that might have been different. Mrs Fung had done it for Jasmine, but how could she expect the gods to understand? All they said still was that the rightness of their world had been disturbed. She had given up everything to make it right, couldn't they see that? She had given up Jasmine and her own chance for a new life to stay here for the rest of her days, in penance for the balance she had shattered. Despair and helplessness seized her in painful spasms. She had done all she could. She had done it all with the only motive that had any meaning, her love for her daughter. Why was that not enough for them?

"But Jasmine is not to blame!" The old woman's voice cracked. "Let her go free. I am yours already, look at me. It will not be long and you will have what you want from me. Isn't that enough? When I am gone, all things will be right again. What more do you need?"

The sadness of a lifetime racked her with weeping. Through her sobbing, she railed against the secret that enslaved her. "What more do you need? What more?"

* * *

"Darling boy," Marietta said. "Can we just pick up the dress shirts and go?"

Harry stood in the hallway of his Fulham house, angrily going through the week's unopened post. Anything addressed to Jasmine, he scrutinised, tearing open personal letters only to throw them aside. "Harriet in New York ... Charlie and Lavinia's wedding ... another bloody christening ..."

"We'll be late, Harry."

He ignored her and clicked on the answering machine, fidgeting on his feet as it rewound and played back the week's messages. All from people he recognised. He began on the post again. "She's having an affair, I know it," he said, as he said every time he went through this ritual.

Marietta looked stunning in a new lime Kenzo outfit and Harry was still obsessing on his wife. She tried to keep her humour. "If she's with her lover now as you suspect, he's hardly going to be writing letters and calling, is he?"

Harry glared at her and headed into the living room for a drink. Rolling her eyes, Marietta followed. "God." She exhaled as he handed her a gin and tonic, the glass clumsily splashed. "I'm glad I never married you."

He knocked back a neat whisky and poured himself another. "Dammit, I should've forced you. We'd've been good together, hey?"

"Nobody forces me to do anything," Marietta said, icily. "Besides, *we* are good together. Precisely because I don't belong to you."

"She's making a fool of me."

"Why don't you wake up, sweet angel?" Marietta flopped onto the sofa. "Jonathan and I are perfectly happy – he has his own little domain and I have mine. We have what you might call a mutually beneficial arrangement. He came along with the capital to invest in my design venture so it's thanks to him I've now got the two shops in London and one about to open in Paris. As for my part of the deal – well, let's say that I have my gorgeous boy," she smiled smugly at Harry, "and he has his. In fact, he has rather a few. But so long as we play our parts to the world and keep our family accounts in order, what we each do – and with whom – is our own business. The best marriages are made on such understandings."

Harry wasn't listening. "If she's having an affair ..."

"Well, you are, too, so you're even. Now, please, get the shirts."

They were to have cocktails back at her Knightsbridge flat where Harry had been spending most nights this month. Jonathan kept a wardrobe and toiletries there for the sake of appearances but he was usually away on diplomatic missions abroad. When he was in London, he lived in the flat she had decorated for him in lavish style in Mayfair, not far from Whitehall in the daytime and close to the Soho clubs at night. Marietta glanced at her watch. Her guests were due in an hour. She had not even begun to put her evening outfit together. And she had left the caterers unsupervised. She sighed. "I'd never have encouraged you to marry her if I'd known you'd get like this."

"She was different. I wanted her because of that." A plaintive note softened his voice. "She was so innocent, so vulnerable. I thought she wasn't like other women. That she wouldn't have secrets. But you women all have secrets, don't you? Playing your little intrigues, never caring who you hurt. All my life I've seen it – even in Mummy. Especially in her. And all those other girls – English roses rotten at the heart."

"Come now ..."

"I'm no woman's fool! I've got my secrets, hey?" Harry began to stalk the room, eyes darting in search of his wife's infidelity. The old fury had consumed the moment of softness. "I've too many secrets, no one woman will get a hold on me. But her secrets? I'll find her out."

He stormed out into the hallway, bursting into the dining room. He opened the sideboard, scanned the empty table, peered behind the framed paintings. The adrenaline began to carry him. He would find her out. Yes. The momentum threw him into the kitchen, the conservatory. For a big man, he moved quickly on his feet. He flung open cupboards, scattered papers, scanned the appointments calendar, scraps of notes.

"Harry!" Marietta followed him in dismay.

Pounding upstairs, he started on the bedroom. Marietta strolled after him, anger hardening her red lips. She leaned against the door frame, swilling her drink. "For God's sake, Harry."

"I gave her all my energy. All my love." Harry wrenched the bedsheets up to his face. He drew in a long breath. No smell but Jasmine's. "She was going to be my creation, my pure woman. A child of the East, uncorrupted by our English hypocrisy." He flung the contents of the laundry basket to the floor, rummaging on hands and knees. "She had everything. She's throwing it all away. For what? For a quick fuck behind my back – is that such a thrill for her?"

He charged past Marietta onto the landing. Jasmine's study. He tried the door. It was locked.

His eyes were beads of glass. Seeing only a vision in his mind, he began to ram the door with his shoulder. Hot fury flushed his face. The veins on his neck and temple stood rigid.

"Harry, that's enough."

A kick and the door flew open with a splintering crash. "Lock me out, huh?" Harry panted, his rant picking up momentum again. He had not been into Jasmine's study for some months. It had been a guest room, which he had given up for her, his own den being up on the second floor. "You can make this the baby's room when you give up work," he had said.

The walls were lined with books interspersed with modern European *objets d'arts*. A filing cabinet stood in one corner. Harry began at the Scandinavian-designed oak desk by the window, rummaging through the drawers, forcing the lock on one of them. "Fucking nothing!"

"What the hell are you hoping to find, Harry?"

"I don't know, but I'll find it!"

Marietta's face was cold with disgust. "Stop it."

He did not hear her. He worked furiously through the desktop accessories, flicking open books, scattering pens.

"You're being ridiculous." Marietta put her glass down. "I've put up with your tantrums over Jasmine for too long. You can't spend a moment with me without thinking of her. It's got to stop, Harry. Please. You're ruining it for us."

Harry grappled with the leather jotter, peering through the seams.

"Harry, do you hear me?"

He pulled at the edges. Something – a piece of paper – had been tucked into a fold at the side of the leather casing.

Marietta seemed to make up her mind. "I'm going now, Harry. Are you coming?"

"I've got you now, fucking bitch."

"Damn you! If you don't walk out of here with me – now." Marietta's voice was trembling. A look of distress emerged through her cold anger. She said, without conviction, "I'm warning you, Harry …"

The jotter came apart in his hands. A piece of card flipped to the floor. Harry fell on his knees, hunching over his find. He turned it over in his hands. It was a photograph.

"I fucking knew it! Look at that! I've got you now, you lying whore!"

Harry recognised the boy's face in the picture. It had been splashed across the pages of all the international magazines in the last few months, older and more serious, but the same face that was in this old photograph. He twisted round, holding his prize aloft, his face bright with triumph. "Just look at that!"

But Marietta was gone, the echo of the front door shuddering through the house.

* * *

Harry caught Jordan coming out of his private Chelsea health club.

A sandy-haired man was with him, toting a racket and a Head gym bag. He hung back as soon as he saw Harry, slipping away to his red Porsche with a brief nod to Jordan. Harry was sure he knew him but could not place him.

The January dawn was grey and weak. Jordan's Jaguar pulled up. He handed his squash racket and sports bag to the uniformed chauffeur. To Harry, he said, "Bit early for a social call."

"I have something that might interest you."

"Get in."

In the luxurious warmth of the leather and wood interior, Harry showed Jordan the photograph. The chauffeur sped along the narrow streets towards King's Road, then headed east along the river to the City. The photograph was well worn but in good condition, as if it had been handled many times with great care. Jordan held it up to the light. A girlish Jasmine screamed with laughter, her hair blown across her face. She sat on a rock, the sky behind. A young man wrestled with her, grinning with pleasure. Jordan recognised Luke. He flicked the picture over. On the back was a scrawled message – "Pax? All my love always, Luke" – and a date. Eleven years before.

"Well, well."

Harry barked, "She's having an affair with him!"

Jordan remembered Jasmine's initial hesitance to take on the TV conference. But she had done so and her performance had shown no mercy for the consultant. He flashed on her confrontation with McAllister at the awarding of the contract. She had been fiercely uncompromising. Jordan recalled that the information about McAllister's damaging report had come from Jasmine. She must have got it from the consultant himself. He said to Harry, "Her affair might not be such a bad thing."

"What?"

"She hasn't let her personal connection with him get in the way of my business. In fact, the opposite. She's used him to get some very valuable information for me." Jordan filled in the background outline for Harry but he glossed over the detail she had given him and what he had done with it. "She's a smart bitch – you should be proud, mate."

Harry grunted. This was not turning out as he had hoped.

"Why did you show me the photo?"

"That consultant's working against you, isn't he?"

Jordan took in Harry's bulk, his combative posture. He had never believed Jasmine's recent bad luck with accidents and eye infections. The proof now scowled beside him. Jordan said, "You don't want your wife to have a career, do you? These incriminations could do her some damage, you're thinking."

Harry did not answer.

Jordan said, "Jasmine's quite a woman. I can see why you want to keep her all for yourself."

"I'm mad about her." A grin crept up on Harry in spite of himself.

"Nothing like a beautiful, intelligent woman, hey, to get the blood flowing?" Jordan laughed. "They can drive you to distraction. Drain you of all your worth. No woman's ever got her hook into me. They take too much energy, know what I mean? No empire's been built by a bloke that's hung up on a woman. But plenty have been ruined by 'em. I'll get a wife one day – a man needs sons to carry on his work, right? For now, I got all the comforts I need from women who know their place."

Harry jerked his chin. "I know how to get more than I need."

"Sure you do. Look, I sympathise with you, mate, but Jasmine's the best lawyer on my team. She's been a real fighter for me on this Malaysia project. I need her to follow through. Do you know for a fact that she's seeing the consultant? This photo's pretty old."

"Not for a fact. But ..." Harry told Jordan of Jasmine's first lie about her visit to Kuala Lumpur. "She covered up with another cock-and-bull story but I don't believe her."

Jordan was thoughtful. Jasmine was still in Malaysia to put in place the post-contractual elements. So far, he had no reason to doubt her loyalty but he had learned by now that there could never be any certainty other than self-interest. It served her now to put his position above her private affairs, but would there come a time when she would choose otherwise – especially where that most typical of female motives, love, was involved? He said, thinking out loud, "I have other good lawyers … Maybe I *have* relied on Jasmine too heavily up till now. Got to spread your risks, and all that."

Harry suddenly remembered where he had seen the sandy-haired man before. "That chap outside the Harbour Club. Robertson, isn't it? I met him at one of those partners' functions at Carruthers."

"Roberts. Good bloke."

"He wasn't on your team then."

"No. I've got some new work that he's just right for." Jordan looked out at the traffic as they passed Tower Bridge. Divide and rule, he thought. Jasmine was clever and hardworking, but she played by the rules. Roberts had an edge to him. He was ambitious and not afraid to do what was necessary to get what he wanted. "You have to know enough about the law to know how not to get caught," Roberts had said once. And, best of all, Jordan knew he could get a stranglehold on Roberts. His sources had pinned Roberts's weakness for gambling: all it took was a downturn in the man's luck and Roberts was his.

"I need Jasmine to follow through on Titiwangsa," Jordan said aloud. Jasmine's connection with the consultant might still yield useful information. But he would have to play it carefully, treading the tightrope of her trust. "In the future, she could be doing less of my other work. If you want her at home – who knows? – she might be useful to me on a consultancy basis. You know, part-time or on project work."

Jordan Cardale was moving into a new arena. The blue-chip law firm of Carruthers had given the company respectability and Jasmine had played a part in legitimising its activities. Her belief in her client had given credence to all her public statements and negotiations. But she could not be kept in the dark for much longer. Now that the strands of Jordan's networks were becoming more complex, Jordan needed a lawyer who would not be shy of unorthodox methods. With Roberts keen to offer a pragmatism of a kind that Jasmine could not – and probably would not – this would be an opportunity to wind her down.

"You got to play it right," Jordan went on. "Women need to be massaged round to your way of thinking. The 'heavy-handed' approach – if you get my meaning – just gets them all waily and uncooperative."

Harry nodded, taking it in.

"I know it's hard going. Just work with me and you'll get what you want. For now, don't let on that I know about her little affair. I'll get my people to have a dig around. See what more we can find out, hey?"

Harry chewed his lip. He wasn't sure that he wanted firm proof of Jasmine's adultery. The possibility of it enraged him with indignation. But the reality? The thought gouged tatters in his stomach. He just wanted the old Jasmine back. He had tried everything he knew but his confrontations had only made her fear and hate him. Coming to Jordan like this, he suddenly felt like a sneak and coward. But what else was left to him?

"All I want is a perfect married life together – you know? – just like how I always imagined it would be," Harry said. "Is that so bad?"

*   *   *

"You're all whores," Harry said to her. It was several days after he'd seen Jordan. He sat in an armchair in the Soho hotel room. The girl knelt at his feet. She said nothing, her eyes downcast. Harry felt his anger rising like a physical tide.

Since his conversation with Jordan, Harry had gone over everything Jasmine had told him about that trip to Malaysia before the wedding, about her work on the Titiwangsa project. In the last few months, he had found himself quizzing her over and over about her parents and her life, her friends, her colleagues and clients, whom she saw or spoke to, what she did when he wasn't with her. He hadn't been able to stop himself. A desperation he did not understand had driven him on and on. And now, he had got the answer he had been looking for. She had lied to him and he had proof.

He shouted at the girl, "You're all fucking whores!"

The girl had a taut body with pert young breasts. Her shiny dress hardly covered her pudenda. Chinese, maybe Vietnamese. No older than nineteen. Harry smirked. "Well, Marietta has better taste in whores than in bloody hotel rooms."

He staggered to his feet. She did not raise her demure gaze. He slapped her. Her head snapped up. Fear in her eyes. Harry relaxed. He was in control. He liked seeing her pain. Somehow, it justified the one that churned inside him. That pain had always been there, it seemed to him, chafing at the reins he tried so hard to hold taut.

He coiled his body into his next punch and hit her again. She thudded to the floor with a yelp. Tried to scramble away. Blood dripped from her lips where teeth had caught flesh. Harry felt a rush of relief. The bursting tension that had swollen every part of him was easing, dissipating into each blow. A dizzying exhilaration swept through him. The thought struck him that she deserved it. A feeling almost like joy leaped in his throat.

He gave himself to the rush. It was a freedom he had not dared to seize before. With Jasmine, whenever he hit her, guilt clamped into his gut. He hated himself for what he did to her and detested her for provoking him into it. Afterwards, an agony of remorse would overcome him, reduce him to a tortured prisoner of their love. But this! This was different. This sad little slut deserved it. They all did. Every single wretched bitch. Jasmine deserved it.

He felt it like a revelation. Every woman he had known. Every one of them who had hurt him and betrayed him. They deserved what he did to them. He felt a new vigour. To strike without guilt. That was freedom beyond anything he had known. The power of it thrust its adrenaline into him.

"Good, very good." Harry's voice was hoarse with excitement. "That's what I like."

He grabbed her and shook her. She winced, shrank away. Every inch the fucking victim, he thought. The exhilaration choked inside him, as if caught in a kink.

"Christ, can't you do this right? Resist me, bitch. Fight me, goddamn you!"

She stared in terror. He twisted his face into a grin. "She paid you for anything I want, isn't that right?"

She nodded.

"Well, this is fucking it. Now do as I say."

She tried to pull away. He grabbed her. Yes. This was it. There was a roaring in his head. A rush of laughter and desire caught him up in its wake. He let the demon take him. He forgot everything. He had no past and no future. There was only the present moment, the aching thrill of each breath. He was no one and nothing, there was only flesh and muscle, exerting in the moment to explode in boundless, terrifying energy. The girl's arms flailed. He lifted her. Dropped her onto the floor, front down. The crash and reverberations felt strangely satisfying. He was bursting with fury and lust. He unzipped his fly, fumbled with his shorts. He was so hard the agony was unbearable.

"Fucking bitch, I'll show you who's in charge. Whore, fucking cunt, I'll show you what you deserve!" He jerked her head back by her hair. Tore at her dress till it fell away. He was aware dimly that he had crossed over into the darkness he had always feared. He could not stop now even if he wanted to. Once started like this, he might never stop again. It frightened him but a fascination gripped him. He could smell her fear. Harry gasped to breathe. His heart felt as if it would explode. "You like it, don't you, being taken by force? You women all fucking like it. Filthy fucking whores."

He pulled her arm back in a half-Nelson – high – making her whimper. Straddling her, he entered her from behind with such force that she cried out in pain.

Forty minutes later, a car pulled up outside and hooted. Harry peered out of the window as he dressed and saw Marietta's canary yellow Porsche. She waved.

The girl sprawled across the carpet, her naked body marked

with cuts and welts. Her dark hair covered her swollen face. She was sobbing quietly. A condom smeared with semen and blood lay beside her. There was semen on her face. Harry felt strangely relaxed. It was like the first time he'd had sex for real. He forgot the hurt and the suspicions. He stopped picking through the debris of the past. For the first time in a while, he felt alive in the present. And a whole evening with Marietta lay ahead.

But horror lurked in his gut. He tried not to look at the girl. After this first time, he could so easily give himself over again to the freedom – and then, he knew, nothing would ever hold him back, not love, not will-power, not even fear of the consequences. Nor would there be remorse. He felt as if he was coming to after a drug-induced hallucination. This was what he was capable of – the broken bruised body was hypnotic in its painful heaving and he found his gaze drawn to it in spite of himself.

He could kill her, he thought with horror and certainty. He could kill Jasmine and feel no remorse afterwards. An icy chill shafted through him. He felt as if he had seen into the pit of his soul. If he gave in to the rush of this uncontrollable madness in the thick of a row with Jasmine … Harry screwed his eyes shut but the horrific image blasted across his lids. His fists pounding into her. His hands round her throat, squeezing till her neck snapped. Kicking. Beating. Breaking every inch of skin. Snapping every bone. A whimper escaped him.

It must never happen again. He must never raise a finger against her again. Never be drawn into an argument. Never touch the wound inside him again. He would shut in the darkness once more, close it up where it belonged behind the scarred remains of his heart. But now that it had tasted freedom, he could not ram it all back into its vault. Like a murderer with a stinking body in the cellar, Harry turned away from the bolted door of his thoughts. He would never come down here again. Never come close. Never even catch a whiff of the decay within.

Peeling two hundred pounds out of his wallet, he threw the notes at the girl. With a show of bravado, he said, "Clean yourself up, bitch."

Out in the neon-lit evening, he clambered into Marietta's car. She was dressed in a green Vivienne Westwood two-piece. She liked green. It matched her eyes. She revved and pulled away. "Had a good time?"

"Just what I needed." Harry attempted exuberance but there was a deadness in his voice.

Marietta shot him an irritated glance. "I thought that this would've brought back the old Harry again. What's happened to you, my gorgeous boy?"

20

When Jasmine returned to London, Harry was waiting for her at home. The housekeeper had straightened the disorder and arranged for the repair of the broken door and furniture. Harry sat in her study, unshaven, his big frame slumped in the chair. He held up the photograph to her.

"What's this?" He had a sad, lost look. But there was an alertness in his eyes he could not hide.

Jasmine felt exhausted. She did not have the energy to confront his invasion into her study. She had been working long hours and the flight back from Kuala Lumpur had worn her out. But, most exhausting of all, had been the struggle to contain the turmoil of her emotions. She knelt down beside Harry's chair. "We were kids." She managed to keep her voice calm in spite of the lie. "He was an exchange student. A gang of us went for a picnic."

"You're still seeing him, aren't you?" Harry was still slumped where he sat. The leash he held on his temper curled his fist.

"Only since this Titiwangsa project. In the course of my work."

"Are you having an affair?" His voice was strained as if he was afraid of what might happen when she answered. A vein throbbed in his forehead.

Jasmine shook her head.

Harry blinked. He hardly breathed. "I so want to believe you, my love."

"I'm not having an affair." Her eyes did not leave his. It was a statement of fact and the confidence in her voice was real.

Harry did not move. She waited. She was too tired to feel any fear. Would he believe her? She felt too drained even to begin to try to convince him if he didn't. She would ride it out as she had endured all the other rows. It was the fear that was the worst. Strangely, without it, she almost did not care about the pain of the blows. She began to close in on herself, waiting for whatever came.

Harry shifted in his chair. He looked pale. The anger was evaporating from him. It was as if he had glimpsed a horror only he could understand and he had decided not to doubt her. He said, with desperation, "Promise me you're not having an affair. Promise me? I don't know what I would do if I found out you were having an affair."

"I promise, my darling." Relief flooded her. Jasmine found herself trembling. He had not struck her. He had not shouted at her. She stared at his familiar little boy's face.

His effort to overcome his anger and suspicion had not escaped her and she felt moved. She thought of what they had once been – and what they might yet fulfil. He still loved her, she thought, loved her enough to put that above all his doubts and pain. Perhaps this was the turning point. Perhaps all her endurance had paid off. He had battled himself out and the real Harry was back, the Harry with whom she had fallen in love. She had been right to ride out all the pain and abuse. Relief flooded her as if she had atoned for a terrible guilt. The shame she had carried with her all these years might yet be washed clean. In spite of herself, an image of her father loomed in her mind. It was of the last time she'd seen him, on the night he had walked out.

He had moved on with his life, wherever he was, in Bangkok or Saigon, living the life that made him happiest. Perhaps now she could move on, too. She had endured through Harry's violence as her mother had endured her father. But this time it was different. Harry was here and he was ready to change. The ghoul was gone. Harry was not her father. There was no shame in their love and its rightness had endured through all the difficulties. Harry was here and he would always be here. Gratitude and devotion overwhelmed her. She said, "What's happened to us, Harry? How did it all fall apart? We had such hopes ..."

Harry leaned forward and clasped her hands. He searched her eyes and saw her relief and hope. He had not slept in four days and his emotions were straining beneath the surface. Marietta had cooled after his rampage through Jasmine's study. Although they had reached a truce that night she had bought him the Vietnamese girl, their relationship had changed. He had not regained the fuck-you easiness she used to love. Her desire to remake him into the boy she'd once owned had become the drone of a nagging wife. They were becoming like combatants in a marriage gone sour. Marietta had demanded back the key to her flat and they would meet now only when she said so. Jasmine was right: what had happened to them all? Because of Jasmine, his long affair with Marietta was in trouble. Because of her, he had lost control of his senses, dragged crazily in the wake of jealousy and fury and maddening desire for her. And, he knew, because of Jasmine, he had once been happy. Maybe they had a chance still. There was only one way forward now, he thought. The other way, he had seen, and it had horrified him. The flash of blood and her broken body dimmed into the darkness of his mind. He had seen it again in that moment as he had asked her about the photograph. It had frightened him for he knew he could easily do it. And yet, it tantalized, like a forbidden intoxicant he had tasted only once and wanted again. And so there was only one way for them to go now. He *had* to believe her. He *had* to trust her with all he was worth. Tears welled and his face crumpled with the conflict of his emotions.

Harry met Jasmine's embrace with desperation. He clung to her as she began to weep. He felt her kisses on his face and responded with eagerness. The sound of her sobbing touched him. He felt his old urge to protect her well up. Seeing her distress, he was sorry that he had ever doubted her. All that had passed between them in the last few months had been madness. He would let it all fade into the darkness, he swore it. "We can work it out, my love," Harry murmured, and they both believed it.

* * *

The planning review passed the winning tender with only minor adjustments. No submissions were made on behalf of the local residents.

Luke had worked feverishly to re-collate his data. He hoped that, in spite of his lack of legal standing to make a submission, he might still prove the reality of the tower's danger. But Jordan Cardale and the Consortium denied him site access. The independent tests and analyses he needed could not be gathered again without substantial finance. In the past, he could have relied on the goodwill of other scientists and professionals for analytical input as well as data; now, many were unwilling to link their reputations to his.

Luke was unable to meet the planning review deadline.

He tried to speak to Dr Chan's widow but did not succeed. There was always someone with her, members of the Development Committee and their families – Wong's wife, Wong himself, Lee who owned Lee Hotel, his sister – or neighbours hovering like bodyguards.

Luke asked questions all over Kampung Tanah about the man he had seen with the doctor, bringing out a copy of the photofit. But, to the local people, Luke was the white trouble-maker, the man who had talked Dr Chan into his campaign. "Leave it alone, man!" a market trader shouted. "You're the bastard that wants to stop our new development!"

"The police already came with this stupid picture. Nobody seen the guy before! Piss off!" A store owner shoved Luke into the street.

Civil injunctions against Luke were issued by Jordan Cardale, Consortium 2000, a geophysicist, a site surveyor and also by Wong on behalf of Mrs Chan. Over the months Lam dogged him. Luke was bound over by the local magistrates court to be of good behaviour, because of a scuffle outside the Consortium's offices, a shouting match with Zain, the project manager, at the tower construction site and a confrontation with locals at Dr Chan's funeral. If he broke the order, he would forfeit a hefty bond.

"One more," Detective Lam warned, "and it's a prosecution, McAllister."

Confrontation was getting Luke nowhere. He changed tactic and tried to pursue his investigations more covertly.

Meanwhile, the publicity had harmed his professional future and he urgently needed to limit the damage already done. Potential clients had cancelled consultation contracts in Indonesia and Vietnam. The Science University in Penang had postponed indefinitely a lecture series he had been scheduled to give on Private Developers and the Environment. He was asked to step down from the panels of environmental delegations.

Working furiously on all fronts, Luke forced himself to put Jasmine out of his mind but it was an almost impossible struggle. He swung from anger to frustration to a longing he could not deny. He had tried to contact her after their confrontation that night, but in his strained exhaustion, he did not know what he wanted from her or how speaking with her might help either of them. But she wanted nothing to do with him. He did not exist for her, she had said in their one telephone conversation. It was early evening in London and he had managed to get her direct line at the office. She had nothing to say to him, now or ever, she kept repeating. She asked him not to call again and hung up. *Please*, she had begged, the desperation of the word hanging on the dead line. He did not bother her again. He struggled through the year focusing on his work like a driven man.

Phase I works began. A long snake of land was cleared with blasting and bulldozers, levelled over the months into the outline of the highway up into the hills. The marshy land below the precipice was shorn and infilled in preparation for New Kampung Tanah. Its town hall and a batch of modern homes would be the first structures ready for occupation. Foundation works for the tower began high above. The uproar of blasting, piledriving and the endless scraping of mechanical diggers exploded across the once quiet hills.

In addition to the troops of workers recruited from outside, there were jobs for the local people on the construction sites. Business boomed for noodle stalls and goods stores. Along the roadsides, hawkers brought their wares to the construction workers.

Smallholding farmers leased out their land to accommodate cabins housing the workers. Bars opened offering karaoke and pool. Wong's transport and freight service expanded to meet the new activities in the region. Lee's Hotel and Restaurant doubled its income.

The walk-through prototypes of the new homes in the relocated town, complete with furniture and fitted kitchens, captivated them all. This excitement played to Jasmine's advantage in the negotiations for the household transfers. As she had predicted, she out-manoeuvred the Kampung Tanah lawyers on the legal and financial implications to the extent that they walked from the table believing *they* had won the better deal. Sarojaya worked with Lingam's office on the negotiations, and later in processing the paperwork for each household. The lawyers' businesses thrived as each transfer introduced them to new clients.

Everyone in Kampung Tanah was making money out of the development, getting something as if for nothing. The talk everywhere praised the foresight of their community leaders and the buzz of success obliterated the memory of the doctor and his campaign.

The preparation for the planning submission had cost Dr Chan his personal fortune. The day after the doctor's death, Wong had used his influence with the bank to delay foreclosure on the doctor's home and practice. While the controversy over Luke's involvement in the car crash had circulated in the aftermath, the Business Development Committee offered to set up a trust fund for the education of Dr Chan's two children. "They can remember their father as a good man," Wong had said to the doctor's widow when he came to tell her the good news two days after the crash.

"You've been so kind." Maria Chan was a small, vivacious woman, now grown timid from the months of conflict and isolation. The church committee and the Women's Society had been central to her good spirits and their loss to her had been desolating.

"Kenneth is at peace now. But you all have your lives ahead of you. This police investigation is so unnecessary. Asking all these questions around town. Everyone with any grudge against the doctor can just badmouth him and it will go on the case report."

Maria Chan had been grateful for the sympathies of Wong and his family. Through their goodwill some of her friends were beginning to call again. "We have to live our lives," she said.

"A man can have a few drinks when he's stressed and depressed – goodness, we all do it, you ask the husbands." Wong laughed sheepishly. "A tragic accident, that was what it was. The police just need confirmation of the truth – that it was accidental death – and they can close the case."

Maria Chan understood the bargain.

Wong touched Maria Chan's arm. "He was drinking that tragic night, wasn't he?"

Maria Chan looked away. "Yes," she said.

The doctor's funeral was paid for by the Business Development Committee. The speakers emphasised the doctor's skill as a physician and his devotion to his family. A plaque was put up in his church, paid for by the Committee, commemorating his "hard work and contributions to society". How easily money bought history, Wong thought.

After the investigation into her husband's death was closed, Maria Chan and her children moved away to live with her parents in Johor. With careful investment of the trust-fund money, she would have enough to put one of the boys through medical school.

*　*　*

The morning after Dr Chan's accident, Tan had flown out to Vancouver with Kidd, on business for Tan Securities Limited. They stayed in North America for three months, travelling across the continent to New York via San Francisco, Dallas, Chicago, Toronto and Orlando. They were exploring the home-security market for their front company while putting out feelers for their unofficial business network. The trip also served to remove Tan from Malaysia during the investigation into the doctor's death.

Tan was back in his clean-shaven appearance with short sleek hair, spectacles and business suits. His wife and children joined him for part of the tour to visit Disney World and Key West.

"We're free in the Land of the Free, man!" Kidd slapped his brother on the shoulder. They were cruising down from Seattle, heading through the sleet towards San Francisco. Kidd had got word earlier that day that their instruction to their Seattle contact had been executed. Tsui, the geophysicist, had been visited by an intruder. In a struggle, Tsui's left arm had been broken in several places in such a way that healing would be a long and excruciating process. He was left in no doubt that he had failed Jordan in not having tied up all the kinks in the manipulated geological data. He was also assured of what more would come to him if he broke ranks now. He had not reported the incident to the police. Kidd was in high spirits, but Tan had been subdued since they had left Kuala Lumpur the week before. "Everything's going as planned," Kidd said. "They won't ever find you. You did a perfect job. Relax."

But Tan could never relax again. Peering out into the bad winter light, he watched the freeway skid by under them. Cars slicked past on the four lanes around them. On the wrong side of the road, banks of headlights flew towards them. Kidd yakking away, taking his eyes off the road to look at him. They were going to die.

A cold sweat shook him in spite of the vents blasting heat. He couldn't breathe. His heart was pistoning so hard he knew something would snap. Frantic, he wound down the window and gulped in the damp air. He had killed a man and it had been easy. Pouring whisky into his gullet, the man pleading and choking. Two bottles and the doctor was out of his head. Tan had pushed the doctor into the car, reached in to rev the engine and then let the man go. Speed and the whisky did the rest. The flash of the exploding car at the bottom of the ravine had felt cleansing. There in the rain, the darkness alight with fire, it had been a moment of liberation. He hadn't killed the doctor, not with his own hands, no direct link. He had let him go, hadn't he?

But the moment had not lasted.

A few days after, Tan's wife was driving the children home from school when a goods lorry careered across the lanes ahead of her. There was a multi-vehicle pile-up and her Volvo was a wreck. Miraculously, she escaped with whiplash and the boys with minor cuts and bruises. It was the justice of the gods, Tan knew it. Only his daily prayers and sacrifices had diffused its fatal impact. At a Buddhist temple in San Francisco, Tan made a five-thousand-dollar donation to the shrine of Kuan Yin, the goddess of mercy. Whenever they stopped at a city with a temple after that, he would make a donation and pay his respects to the gods. Every morning and every night, he would find somewhere outdoors, compulsively clear a space and burn joss-sticks at a makeshift shrine. If something prevented him from this ritual, he would be jittery, distraught.

When they heard that the police had closed the case, Kidd tried again to distract him. "You can sleep easy now. They'll never know it was you."

"But *I'll* know." Tan stared at nothing. "The gods also. They're just waiting for the right chance again."

*   *   *

Later that year the flame tree blossomed again, its arching foliage green against the abundant scarlet. Smooth limbs were maturing into the grace of their prime, hardening sinews gaining the character of age. The firecracker red of its flowers blazed above the house, a beacon across the neighbourhood.

That year Mrs Fung closed her business. Her weakening body and the pain had made it impossible to continue. She missed the daily trip to the market and the creativity of her work. But her old customers still called to pass the time of day over a cup of tea, often finding friends and neighbours already there. And the money Jasmine had sent her over the years enabled her to live her dream: she devoted herself to her garden, channelling her ebbing energy into this one indulgence.

The recent years had been unusually dry. The monsoon

seasons brought threatening storms and static winds, but rainfall was irregular and timid. *Padi* and crops suffered, and the price of fresh produce soared. The sun bleached Mrs Fung's garden of its colour, withering the delicate plants. Every afternoon, watering had become a ritual, no matter how much pain she was in or how weak she felt. She progressed across the flower beds and shrubs with the hose, her wide-brimmed hat and long sleeves sheltering her from the heat. Water was a life-force to her garden and as its cool washed the soil, it would revive her for another day.

* * *

In the aridity of the cities, traffic and dust baked in the stifling air. Heat shimmered off tarmac and cement across the network of highways and towns. Pavements and roads cracked as the parched earth beneath them shrank and flaked. On construction sites, red dust hung like clouds above the open scars.

Up in the hills, near Kampung Tanah, the wind whipped off soil exposed from cleared jungle. The local infrastructure could not expand fast enough to meet the tumult of new settlers. Waste and sanitation facilities cooked their organic deposits into reeking disease-ridden stews. The sites, the workers' accommodation units, the streets of Kampung Tanah, the trunk road and their peripheries collected the litter and waste of progress – plastic bags, cans, wrappers, rubber tyres, scrap metal.

The young people who had stayed for the jobs spent their wages at the new bars and shops. There was a disco and two new cinemas. Speculative entrepreneurs had joined the influx of labourers and the bandwagon of opportunities was looking good. Crime increased in Kampung Tanah – brawls and burglaries, muggings and rapes. Deaths on the road from speeding and drunk driving were common. First Safe Limited, a subsidiary of Tan Securities run by Tan's cousins, set up a shop offering security services for individuals, households and small businesses.

On their first anniversary, Harry took Jasmine to Paris. They seemed at last the happy couple as they strolled through the flea-markets by the Seine and in Le Mouffetard, kicked up autumn leaves in the Jardin du Luxembourg. They stayed in an ornate guesthouse, set back in its own fountained courtyard, not far from Café Flor.

Jasmine's business trips abroad had dwindled that year since Jordan had won the Malaysian tender. Nick Roberts was handling Jordan's venture in the Philippines and Jordan's new work was being channelled through his department. He had got close to Jordan himself, taking fishing trips with him on his yacht off the coast of Thailand and accompanying him on business trips to Hong Kong and Darwin. Often, Roberts's wife flew to join them and Jordan's chauffeur was at her disposal to take her shopping and sightseeing while the men were working. In the cities, their nights often ended in casinos and private gambling suites where Roberts, egged on by Jordan and applauded by his wife, indulged his taste for risk on a grand scale. Roberts was on a roll and Jasmine knew he was enjoying the decline of her career. She was grateful that, at least, he refrained from gloating openly.

Jasmine was left with the in-progress work for the Titiwangsa project and a few of Jordan's continuing corporate and taxation matters. Her other clients still produced major work – company restructurings, European joint ventures – but for the first time her fees income did not reach her previous year's level. She was beginning to spend more time on unbillable but hopeful client development than on fee-producing work.

Since her reconciliation with Harry, crouched on her study floor, she had felt a new hopefulness for her marriage. She was home earlier in the evenings because of the slack in her workload and she found Harry following. They spent several nights a week at home alone together over a meal she would cook. Afterwards, they would watch a rented movie, snugly in each other's arms on the sofa, or take a bath together. They were making love again, at first with the awkwardness of new lovers but soon their old familiarity returned. Jasmine felt a contentment she had not experienced before. When they went out with his friends, she enjoyed the true front they presented. They were indeed the golden couple again and she felt exhilaration and hope lift her spirits. She gave more of herself to the role she realised Harry longed her to fill, radiantly by his side at his client parties, rearranging her meagre work schedule to follow him on business trips to Zurich, New York and Jakarta. She embarked on a project to redecorate his Fulham house and make it into *their* place, softening the bedroom first with pastel and lighter fabrics. He talked again about transforming her study into a bedroom for their child but she always sidestepped that line of conversation. A reluctance she preferred not to analyse dogged her. A child with Harry would tie her down, commit her to this role of wife and mother, and she wasn't ready for that yet, she told herself. Without a child, she might still escape. But that was a thought that caught her only in the flash of an unguarded moment.

She followed Harry on the itinerary he had planned for their romantic weekend, listening to his expositions. It touched her that he took so much care to make sure she was pampered. She let him buy her designer outfits in old-fashioned boutiques where he sat like a king selecting concubines. She laughed happily for him, enjoyed the best of French cuisine gratefully and gave herself to him appreciatively. They had not yet argued about having a child and he seemed determined not to let it become an issue. She was grateful for that and anxious to show how much his new sensitivity meant to her.

Harry had become a Senior Vice-President of De Witte Cootes. His Asian portfolio had been growing since an introduction Jordan had given him to a young construction company in Manila. His commission-based income would soon be bringing him half a million a year and this knowledge gave him a generosity of spirit. With Marietta keeping her distance, he spent more time with Jasmine, his tenderness towards his wife seeming to bring back the vulnerable qualities he had first loved in her. Jordan had been right about using the soft touch on women, Harry thought.

"Here's to us." He raised a flute of champagne. They sprawled on the antique four-poster in their hotel room.

"Happy anniversary, my darling," Jasmine said.

The shift in her standing with Jordan had disturbed her, but she had not dared to confront it. She told herself that this lull in her career freed her to devote herself to Harry. Perhaps she might even warm to the idea of having a child, the champagne and languid evening softening her. Harry could be so loving. She wondered if fatherhood might bring out the best in him. As for her, she thought, it might be, after all, the most fulfilling path into which to channel her energies. She belonged at last in Harry's world so why not seal it with their flesh and blood? But panic rose in her gut. Memories of his violent rage, the words he would shout at her, vicious and obscene. Memories also of her father's temper, *Ah Ma* stepping between him and Jasmine, hiding her bruises and stifling her cries so that her daughter would not know.

But they were just memories, she told herself. In the past. They were not the future. Seeing his golden features by candlelight, Jasmine wanted to believe that Harry was everything to her. She was grateful that he had stopped beating her. Her devotion to him and their marriage seemed to have mellowed him. She wanted so much to believe she'd made the right decision in surrendering herself to him. To believe that she had no past and no thoughts other than for him. Not even for Luke. Luke was a shadow, immaterial and powerless, she told herself. All he had accused her of, warned her of, she had tried to leave behind in the dark of that night at his house. In Firefly Clearing – their special place.

Jordan had won the tender, the construction was a reality. What good would it do to rock the boat? Besides, it was her marriage that was important, her love for Harry and his for her, their devotion to each other. That night, she responded to Harry's love-making with intense feeling, and afterwards fell into sleep in his arms.

But as dawn seeped across the sky, the nightmare came again. Stumbling through the familiar devastation, she came upon herself seated in the dark, weeping as if her heart would break. Blood soaked her tunic and hands, smeared her face. In fear and pity, Jasmine reached towards the seated figure but stumbled.

On the floor lay a body, emaciated and twisted-limbed, unnaturally pale. The throat was slit, blood pulsating like a fountain, drenching the clothes and hair. Breath wheezed and bubbled. The eyes flicked open.

The scream tore silently out of Jasmine. She tried to run but could not move. Silence and stillness and a terror that writhed like a thousand maggots.

She was the living corpse. She knelt and gathered the broken body into her arms. It was strangely without substance.

The stained knife gleamed in the hands of the seated figure.

A crowd materialised as if at a road accident. Harry pushed through and started to mop up the blood with a white towel. He pulled the body from her in panic. The cloth caught at the airpipe, his rough hands snapping back the head. In his anxiety, he crouched on top of the limbs, cracking them, tearing a hand with his boot. Jasmine tried to stop him and they scrapped absurdly over the disintegrating body.

Luke walked past, his face averted. Jasmine hurried after him, the remnants of the corpse in her arms. Her heart lifted – he would know what to do, they could be friends again like they used to be. She called his name, shrieked it, but no sound came. He turned and spoke to her but she could not hear him. And then he walked on, disappearing into the crowd.

Jasmine sat up weeping, tearing the sheets from her in panic.

Startled awake, Harry grasped her in his arms. He wiped the hair from her face, kissed her, soothed her. The strength of him frightened her. His smell suffocated her.

"I'm here, my darling," he whispered, "I'll take care of you, hush now …"

21

In October and November, a year after construction had begun, the monsoon, sweeping in early, unleashed its violence over Malaysia. After the aridity of previous years, electrical storms battled like giants over the cities, shorting circuits on office blocks, flashing flames into badly wired buildings. Thunder shook foundations, shocking as the bombardment of heavy mortar. Rain fell in sheets, cold and grey like corrugated iron, unrelenting and furious. It tore fronds from palm trees, loosened slates off roofs. The shrunken earth, baked hard in the dry years, had lost its elasticity and water flowed unblotted into the cracks. Rising up from the ground, welling up in the rivers, the floods that came ruined acres of crops and engulfed whole communities in mud and debris.

The wet weather delayed work on the Titiwangsa construction. Blasting in the foundations of the tower could only be done in the short spells between the rains. Cement poured into one corner of the site to stabilise marginal entry into the limestone stratum was not binding the fault as projected. The rising water-table liquefied the earth into swamp and additional pumps working to full capacity struggled against the floods. A large workforce with bulldozers and cement had to be reallocated to bulwark the bursting banks of the watercourse south of the foundations. In the marshy land below, emergency drainage had to be dug to ease the pressure from the thundering waterfall plummeting from the precipice. Work on the town hall and new housing pushed on.

At the turning of the year, the rains did not ease as they should have with the coming dry season. Pundits speculated on the causes of these unpredictable weather cycles that were increasingly extreme, citing the greenhouse effect, the depleting ozone layer and the loss of the rainforests. Completion of Phase I was delayed for a month, then another. Visiting the site on his way to Manila, Jordan met with Zain, the project manager. He said, "No more postponements. I expect you to stick to the January deadline."

"It depends on the weather, Bill. They can't make us pay liquidated damages in such cases –"

"That's not the point," Jordan shouted, above the noise of the pile-driver. The two men stood in hard hats on a platform overlooking the foundation quarry. "We have a reputation to keep and a promise to deliver on. If we lose more time, the tower won't beat China's industrial town to final completion. Jordan Cardale does not let a bit of weather hold them up."

"But –"

"The Phase I completion ceremony will take place fifteenth January. Pomp and circumstance, no holds barred. CNN, the BBC, they'll all be here. No excuses, Farul, just do it."

Zain ground his objections into silence. He had already crossed Jordan once on this project and he would never risk it again. In the pre-tender design stage, Zain had questioned the safety of the tower's height. It was only then that he had understood the reality of his personal bond to Jordan and what he would lose if he broke it.

Zain increased blasting and excavation activities, pushing each stage of the works to the extreme. To maximise all resources, work continued non-stop through the night. The monsoon did not cease after New Year, easing only to fluctuate between drizzle and normal rainfall. Layers of exposed soil from the denuded rainforest washed down the slopes as if the red earth bled. Water seeping into hard-pressed waste facilities round the construction sites dispersed the stink and foul matter across the landscape, flowing it into the gullies and streams. The rivers churned with silt and debris, ravaged stumps of trees and the litter of the new populace in the region.

Some evenings, light-headed from exhaustion, Zain would look out beyond the site over the hills and valleys, and in the brief twilight, it seemed to him as if the earth groaned and shifted in the agony of violation. The howl of machinery was its cry of pain, the soil bleeding like unhealed scars. Its clothing of vegetation torn away, his own work pillaging its flesh, it wept rain for tears.

The squawk of his radio startled him. I need some sleep, he thought.

*　　*　　*

Jordan looked up from the dossier he was reading. He sat in Kidd Tan's glass and chrome office in Kuala Lumpur, the air-conditioning too cold for the overcast day. Kidd was watching him from across the smoked-glass desk, beaming.

"Excellent work," Jordan said.

"Of course."

The file was the final product of a long investigation. Clipped to the inside cover was a copy of the photograph of Jasmine and Luke taken on Bukit Larut. The dossier included copies of Jasmine's birth certificate, Malaysian identity papers and those of her parents. There was a recent picture of Mrs Fung taken in a Taiping street with a telephoto lens. There were others showing Luke with Mrs Fung. From school records and casual information provided by Taiping locals, it was clear that Jasmine and Luke had been at the same school and that Mrs Fung had worked for many years as the McAllisters' servant. There was an unconfirmed report that Luke had recently broken off a three-year relationship because of Jasmine.

"She hasn't visited her mother since she left eleven, twelve years ago?" Jordan asked.

"Difficult to tell. But apparently not since we began the investigation." Kidd leaned back in the leather chair. He had been overseeing the Tans' Malaysian business since their return from the States and there was a new authority in his manner.

"And the consultant?"

"As with the mother."

Jordan tapped his fingers, thinking out loud. "She'll be out here in January for the Phase I ceremonies. I want to know what she gets up to."

"No problem. We have security people up on the construction site anyway," Kidd said. The legitimate face of Jordan Cardale bought genuine security services from Tan Securities for its many construction sites around Asia.

"I mean, *every* move."

"Well, you assign her a car with chauffeur cum personal assistant – one of my people – and you'll know every time she pisses."

Jordan snorted at the thought. "Do it."

"Are you expecting something to happen?"

Jordan shrugged. "She's got more of an edge than I gave her credit for. Such people are either very useful or very dangerous. Whichever way, I want a handle on her."

* * *

"*I* will do it." Tan leaned into his brother's face and jabbed his cigarette at him. He had come straight to the office from the airport on his return from Manila. "Why didn't you tell me that Jordan was here this afternoon?"

Kidd raised his palms in helplessness. "He was in and out, man. You weren't here. The dossier was ready …"

"And why wasn't I told about this investigation on the lawyer?" Tan began to pace again, sucking on his cigarette. He had lost weight, his gauntness jagged with restless energy. His hair was severe in a close-crop, greying at the temples.

"You were busy on the Philippines project." Kidd exchanged glances with their cousin Pang, a young, beefy man, who sat in one of the two chairs opposite him. After the brothers' return from the States, Tan had eased off his schedule for seven months, "to follow up on their American breakthrough". In fact, he had been prescribed time out by the family's doctor for overwork and nervous exhaustion. After his family's car accident, he had been racked by terrible visions of what could happen to them. If his boys were late home from school or his wife was out for a long period, he would work himself into panic. At home, he upgraded the security system and fire alarms. He worried constantly about his children's health, alarmed by all the childhood illnesses that came and went.

Tan had only been able to resume his usual activities in the last two months. Kidd went on, "Pang did a good job on it."

Tan punched his cigarette at Kidd as if wielding a gun. "You think I'm not up to the job any more. I see it in your every move."

"*Tai Koh* – Elder Brother ..."

"*I* gave you your first job and *I* gave you this big boy's job. *I* am the head of this family and head of all our operations."

"I haven't forgotten, *Tai Koh*. It's just that with your – ah – health problems this year, I didn't want to burden you."

"I don't have any 'health' problems!"

Kidd signalled Pang with his eyes.

Tan saw the look pass and a desperation hooked into him. He watched Pang leave the room. It was not Kidd's new authority that riled him, he knew. It was the control Tan himself had lost – suddenly, inexplicably, that year – the control over his mind and rational behaviour.

His mother had just been diagnosed with Alzheimer's disease. A mudslide at the Chinese cemetery where his father was buried had destroyed headstones and dislodged some coffins. "These are signs," Tan had screamed one day. "Warnings from the spirit world!"

Kidd had rolled his eyes. "There've been floods and landslips everywhere with this monsoon. And *Ah Ma*'s old – sickness happens."

It was Kidd who now liaised with the Kampung Tanah Committee – as "Dunstan Khee's associate". He was also gradually taking over their network of unofficial business. Kidd was transforming himself from wild boy into the *taipan* of the family. Meanwhile, Tan's own work in Manila for Jordan was easy, but it was taking him all he had to maintain his concentration and endurance on the job.

Tan held his brother's gaze. He was not going to be beaten by the doctor's ghost. He had lived through a year. His family was healthy, happier than ever. Harmony had prevailed, he had made sure of it. Tan said, "Kampung Tanah is my project. I'm going to see it through to the end."

"You can't go as the driver. The locals know you as Vice-President of the International Business Development Foundation. Pang can –"

"Don't lecture me. No one will know me." Tan stared Kidd down as if eyeballing a demon. He would regain control. The fear that had emasculated him would be subdued. Tan made a promise. "I will see this job through. The doctor's not going to stop me. He's gone. I won't let you – him – or anyone – sideline me out of the work *I* have left to do."

He sat down and leaned back as if in perfect control. But a flush of sweat broke under his jacket and he was trembling.

* * *

"The architect has signed off Phase I completion," Zain said into his mobile phone. He stood in the muddy battlefield by the watercourse as bulldozers and cranes roared. Teams of workers toiled with scaffolding, concrete and sandbags. It was the day before the ceremony. A steady rain was falling.

"Excellent." Jordan's voice crackled from London.

"But there's a problem. Additional works to the south wall are required where the foundations bank the watercourse levee. We've had mudslides and the ballasting needs to be reinforced before the Phase II sub-structure work can go ahead. We're working on that now." Zain hesitated, then went on. "We'll have to move the ceremony scheduled for tomorrow."

"No more postponements."

"But with the site unstable and the remedial works, I can't have visiting dignitaries in here. Anyway, they'd see all the works going on and questions will be asked."

"Hold off the works."

"The risk of a further slide is high. The rains aren't easing up. It could be a bad one. We have to secure the bank now."

"Dammit!" Jordan looked out at the clear winter sky over the Docklands.

"The intensive work of the last months has increased the stress on the land. Particularly the additional blasting. You need to come out on-site, Bill – see what we're up against." Zain watched as a bulldozer stood churning mud in spite of its caterpillar tracks.

"No. Danesleigh is doing the PR tomorrow. I'll be in Bonn speaking at a construction conference. If I come rushing out to you, it's going to stir up speculation." Jordan hunched into his mouthpiece as if going for Zain's jugular. "Just fix it. Do what you have to. Do you understand me?"

Zain had worked for Jordan for eight years. Eight years, inextricably entangled in numerous developments with too many things to hide. But Jordan had made it worth his while. In Kuala Lumpur, he now had a large house in Damansara, the hilly residential area of the wealthy elite. His two daughters were at public schools in England. His son had just started at London University studying medicine – at foreign students' fees. Jordan had once sent a chauffeur-driven limousine unexpectedly to the boy's lodgings with free tickets to a Madonna concert. The boy and his friends had gone, trusting as children.

"No need to thank me," Jordan had said to Zain. "I can find your children any time, anywhere they are. Right now you have a good life and a happy family. But what I give I can also take away. Don't forget."

In the noise and rain, Zain knew that he would never escape the secret of his success. He said into the mobile, "I'll see to it, Bill."

* * *

The fifteenth of January dawned pale and watery. The drizzle had eased a little by mid morning, but an overcast sombreness remained. The lowland tranche of the highway had been completed with the tower foundations and part of the relocated town. A VIP convoy of four-wheel-drive vehicles, trailed by press coaches, drove the five hours from Kuala Lumpur. They progressed off the new road onto the old narrow trunk road and rumbled over the unmade base of the upper section of highway.

The ceremony was held at an observation point about a mile west of the tower foundations. It would be followed by festivities in New Kampung Tanah – a parade and funfair – culminating with the opening of the town hall there. A hundred families had already moved into their new homes, and shops were opening in the main street. The local people made their way down to their new town throughout the morning, preparing for the festivities and visiting their friends' finished homes.

The observation point was a terraced overhang, which offered a panoramic view east across to the escarpment on which the tower would stand and into the new town valley below. Curving along the frontage was the shell of a multi-storey building, soon to be a covered market for coffee-shops, restaurants and hawker stalls. On the ground level terrace, Dickson Loh nominally laid the final stone of the building before invited dignitaries and the international press. The crowds trailed damp and mud from the unmade road onto the concrete floor. Golf umbrellas hovered against a spitting drizzle.

Jasmine and Danesleigh sat on a platform with the other VIPs. The assistant that Jordan's Kuala Lumpur office had assigned to them, who went by the name of Kaw, was ranked against a side wall with the other VIP aides. The press shuffled on the wet ground, extending recording equipment and cameras like bait.

The President of the Planning Committee, Ismail Mohammed, had the place of honour. Mohammed was a tall, distinguished man in his late fifties. Previously a senior prosecutor in the Public Prosecutor's Office, he had come to believe that education and good housing were the keys to community and responsible citizenship. Now retired from law, he devoted his energies to public service through the Planning Committee, governorships on education boards and charitable foundations. His presence today transformed a private ceremony into a moment of national pride.

The celebratory speeches were made, Dickson Loh for Consortium 2000 followed by Mohammed and, finally, Danesleigh for Jordan Cardale PLC.

Suddenly, a South African voice from the floor cut through the clapping. "I have a question for the Viscount." It was a tall, well-groomed journalist with a dark beard and short-cropped hair. Heavy-rimmed sunglasses obscured his eyes.

"Questions at the end." Loh signalled to Danesleigh to continue.

"Pieter Lund, *Construction Monthly*, Johannesburg," the clipped twang persisted. "Why is this ceremony being held down here? Mr Loh was meant to lay the final stone to the Titiwangsa Tower foundation, wasn't he? Is the foundation not ready?"

"The foundation has been completed," Danesleigh replied smoothly. He smiled as if at a child. "The recent rains have made the construction site – well, rather like a mud bath. As a courtesy to our distinguished visitors, we considered this a more appropriate venue."

"We all know of the rumour about the defective foundation design of the tower. You're not trying to stop us from seeing the foundation works, then?"

"Mr Lund," Danesleigh laughed, "it's the rains that make the mud. If you want to sling it, aim at the sky, not at us."

Amid the laugher, the ceremonials moved on and the South African was forced to take his seat again.

Soon, the convoy of vehicles was reassembling its passengers for the drive down to New Kampung Tanah. Loh walked with Mohammed and Danesleigh, their assistants trailing them. Loh was saying, "These reporter fellows are out to get a scoop even if there's no big story."

"Our project manager warned us about the mud yesterday. It's pretty bad even down here on a completed building." Danesleigh turned to Kaw, a gaunt silver-haired man in heavy glasses. "I'll be travelling with Mr Loh and *Encik* Mohammed. Bring Ms Lian in our car when she's ready."

"Yes, sir." Kaw handed Danesleigh his briefcase, respectfully not meeting his eyes. Jasmine stared out over the valley, alone on the terrace. In the distance the visitors dispersed and vehicles began to jolt their way down the hill. She was slim and elegant in a dark Yves St Laurent pantsuit. Her stylish but sturdy Gucci shoes were already stained with mud. Her hair was damp from the drizzle but she was relieved to find a few moments of quiet.

The South African's questions had disturbed her. For the last year she had been able to ignore the doubts that Luke had posed. She had succeeded in closing him out of her life, aborting any contact he tried to make with her, stifling any thought of him. This visit back to Malaysia had made her uneasy. It had stirred Harry's antagonism and propelled her back into the old arena of conflict.

Harry had tried to make her cancel the trip, at turns jokey, pathetic and, finally, exploding in anger. He accused her of manipulating him: she'd had no intention of giving up her job as she had led him to hope. They had not had such an argument in almost a year and its ferocity startled her. But this time something had changed. She was not so afraid of him as she had been. Anger formed in her gut and also, a new disgust. She watched him with a strange objectivity and his range of tactics seemed to take on the quality of a vaudeville act. She saw the brutality in his face as if looking on a stranger. And, suddenly, she wondered why she loved him. Why she had ever loved him. It was as if she recognised Harry for the first time – not the charming Englishman, not the lost little boy but who he really was behind those faces he played so well. Staring at him in that moment, she felt a spinning vertigo.

In its dizzying wake, she had come back to Malaysia and to the conflict of loyalties that haunted her. All the confrontations she'd had with Luke pursued her with renewed intensity. A bright windy day by the sea. *If Jordan's design wins without change, there's going to be a disaster.* A long walk through the jungle night up to Firefly Clearing. *You are the public face of Jordan's dirty work.* Luke's voice echoing over and over in her mind. *I love you, I've always loved you … You don't love Harry, you love all those baubles he can give you.* Jasmine closed her eyes. She had braced herself to face Luke that day but, to her surprise, he had not been there.

A figure appeared at the far end of the terrace.

It was the journalist. The last thing she needed now was to face prying questions. She moved away from the balustrade where she had been leaning and, as she did so, she saw Kaw coming across the VIP platform. She did not like the aide that Jordan had pressed on her. He was everywhere she turned, persistently helpful, relentlessly watchful. But now she was relieved to see him. She headed towards him.

The journalist picked up his pace.

As Jasmine glanced back, she recognized Luke's walk.

"Damn you." It was almost a plea under her breath. She recognized his features now under the sunglasses and tinted beard.

"Jasmine," Luke called. And then he saw Kaw.

Jasmine saw the older man take in the scene, glancing at Luke and back to her before averting his gaze.

She could not deal now with a confrontation with Luke. Her instinct was to escape, to lose Luke – Kaw, too – and double back to the car.

She switched directions and walked away from both men.

*   *   *

From the site office, Zain watched the continuing work on the watercourse bank. Across the vista, he could see the VIP convoy snaking its way down the hill, its head disappearing behind a jutting spur. His suggestion to the KL office for the change of venue had been accepted without question. But the vice coiling round his temples and stomach remained. The work on ballasting the mud bank would be comical in another context. No sooner would they finish one section and move on to the next when the bank would burst again along the first segment.

The foundations were waterlogged and the reinforced steel frame at sub-structure level held back the earth like a fish-net against sludge. At design stage, they had factored in rain and water drainage but not this extreme of deluge. Jordan's obsession with his vision of achievement had blinded him. In recent weeks, the more Zain faced Jordan with the dangers of pushing the pace of the works, the more Jordan pressed for solutions – as if by the sheer force of their will they could control and subdue the rain and the earth.

The shouts of the workers from the riverbank whirred like crickets across the site. Zain stared in horror as his radio shrieked to life.

"It's going! Move! Move!" The foreman's voice, shrill with panic. "Boss! Boss! It's not holding!"

Tiny figures of men scattered from the bank far away. Bulldozers and cranes tilted like toys and shifted with the moving soil, tumbling, sinking. Churning curtains of water, more mud than liquid, billowed out from the crumbling embankment. Above the noise of machinery, the growl was as of distant thunder. The ridge of the wall began to collapse, the force of the water and debris accumulating power and momentum in this sudden unleashing.

Zain pelted down the steps into the mud, running towards the slide.

*   *   *

As the silver-haired man turned away, Luke hurried after Jasmine. He followed her up a staircase, to the first floor, then the second. She realised she could not escape when she reached the third floor. Backed into a corner of the terrace, she turned to face Luke. "What do you want?" She grasped the offensive. Indicating his disguise, she added, "What are you doing in this – this get-up?"

He had taken off his glasses and his eyes were unnaturally blue against his darkened hair and beard. "Don't you like it? *Wella*'s home treatment – brown-black."

Jasmine rolled her eyes and turned away. The scar of the escarpment gaped across the valley. Steel pylons stabbed into the earth, interlaced with the rotating cranes into an alien forest above the trees.

Luke came up to her but she shrank from him. Serious now, he said, "There are injunctions against my coming up here. This was an opportunity I couldn't pass up." He put on the slack-jawed South African accent. "You can buy any identity you want in Bangkok – if you have the right contacts."

Jasmine tried to slide past him but he stepped in front of her. He said, "Please – I need to talk to you."

"We have nothing to say to each other. Stop trying to see me. Stop calling. Stop everything." She ducked past him, but he grabbed her arm and swung her round. "Damn you, let me go!"

He shook her. "Listen to me, there's something wrong on the site. I was up there. I couldn't see much, they wouldn't let me in, but there's some mad activity up there." Jasmine struggled against his grip.

Luke said, "I have to get into the construction site. They're hiding something. I need to know what."

"Let me go!"

"I need your help." He spoke urgently now. "The place is crawling with security. They're not letting any journalists pass – I've already tried. But you're their lawyer, they'll let you through."

"You're crazy!"

There was a movement by the stairs. Luke whipped round and Jasmine pulled free, rushing past him. Kaw hovered like a shadow by the doorway.

Jasmine stopped in her tracks and stared. How much had Kaw heard?

That was when the rumbling earth caught them.

22

The walls of the foundation quarry caved in with the weight of the mudflow from the watercourse. Steel shafts and pylons buckled. Cranes teetered and crashed into the sliding earth. Bulldozers, diggers, trucks slithered in nose-dives as the ground gave way. Men tore at sinking slopes, grappling for hold, scrambling, falling. Rock and earth and twisting metal crushed down to silence their screaming. The completed foundation began to crack.

The years of dry weather had crumbled sinkholes and cavities into the limestone substratum. Ceaseless rain had liquefied large tracts of the bedding layer. Cement poured down boreholes in one corner of the site was like a Band-aid on a suppurating wound. The moving mass of earth and mud above tore implacably against the fragile structures of metal and concrete with growing momentum of weight and speed. The thin layer of granite between the surface soil and limestone bed fractured. The weakened corner of the site buckled. The full weight of all that churned above sank down into it.

The fracture splintered into many. The limestone bed collapsed. The escarpment jolted, tilted. A shaft at the weakest corner appeared. Earth and rock separated along the racing fault across the promontory.

The sound was like engulfing thunder. Across the length of the ridge, reverberations shuddered loose earth into a series of sympathetic slides.

The jutting escarpment slumped, as if in exhaustion, sliding down against the slopes like a crumpled, decaying tramp into his doorway. Its full weight slammed into the town hall below, folding the upper floors into the ones below. Councillor Kamaruddin was being shown the meeting hall by a junior Consortium 2000 director. They were crushed in an instant. Wong and the other eight Committee members were strolling through the polished corridors when the mass of concrete and rock ground their bodies to pulp.

The momentum of the slide skidded and flowed down the full length of the slope, taking with it the new town, tracts of forest, cleared ground and any car, float, surprised resident and costumed child in its path. Churning debris rolled and crushed flesh and metal. Sliding rocks severed limbs from torsos, crunched into snapping bones. Mud and earth suffocated those who did not die instantly. Those whose mangled bodies still lived when the ground stood still again could wish only that they had died.

Jasmine stared in horrified fascination as the escarpment collapsed. Luke stood in her line of vision, head twisted round at the grinding roar. Behind her, she heard Kaw let out a low-pitched moan of terror. The building trembled from the shockwaves along the ridge shelf.

The floor slipped from under them. Jasmine pitched forward. Kaw threw himself backwards, grappling frantically at a pillar. Luke fell hard against the latticed balustrade. His upper body tipped out into empty space, his legs swinging up off the ground. Above him, suddenly, treetops and earth. Below, the sky.

The building slid several metres down the slope. Its upper storeys tipped down towards the valley.

Luke's flailing arm caught ironwork. He hooked it. The momentum of his fall yanked into his shoulder and arm. His body slammed round into the concrete ridge of the terrace. The weight of the upper storeys crunched the ground floor into the moving earth.

Jasmine slid down the smooth floor. There was nothing between her and the valley below but the balustrade. She saw Luke swinging below her.

With a jolt, the third-floor terrace snapped off from the main floor.

Jasmine thudded against the balustrade and pitched out into

air. She slammed into Luke, his one arm reaching out, grasping, grabbing. He held her across the shoulderblades, his hand clawing into her armpit. She circled her arms round his waist, her face rammed into his back, her legs jerking against emptiness.

The terrace hung vertically downwards, held only by the iron cables that reinforced the now shattered concrete.

They swung midway between sky and trees. Jasmine felt Luke's arm shaking with the strain, holding her with an impossible rigidity. They were both breathing hard, unable to speak or think.

Looking up, Luke saw the roof and gaping walls, perched as if about to tip over onto them. The main floor was pitched at a sixty-degree angle above the broken cliff of concrete. There was a pillar to the side, rammed still unbroken between the floor and ceiling.

"I'm going to lift you," he gasped. "Reach the balustrade. Then the pillar."

She whimpered but twisted up to see. Luke strained to pull her up, a guttural cry of pain tearing from him. Jasmine let go of his body and stretched out tentatively towards the balustrade.

Her jacket slipped between his hand and her skin. She felt herself falling, his hand scraping against her arm.

His fist tightened around her wrist. Her weight jolted her shoulder. Luke yelled with pain as the pull of her breaking fall tore at his anchoring arm, ripped into the muscles that strained to hold on to her.

She swung far below him now, dangling at the mercy of his strength.

*　*　*

"Pass her to me." Luke squinted up. It was the silver-haired man. He had anchored his legs against the pillar and stretched out his arms. He blinked wildly with terror but a fierce will set his jaw. Up close like this, he did not seem as old as his hair belied. His arms were smooth and strong.

Luke hissed to Jasmine, "Pull yourself up. Grab my arm."

"I – I can't!" Jasmine's breath came in gulping sobs. She glanced down at the swaying earth far below. A wail began in her.

"Look at me!" Luke gasped. "Look up here! Reach up your other hand!"

Jasmine looked up at Luke so far above her. His eyes held her, willed her to stretch out her hand towards him. In the safety of his gaze, she strained upwards, fingers twitching to bridge the distance. The sinews of his hand that clutched her wrist locked white and sharp. Her fingers reaching out, brushed the back of his hand, groped towards his wrist. Hooked, grabbed his trembling forearm.

A cry of immense effort and Luke wrenched her up to the balustrade. She snatched at the latticework. His arm left her, swung down to her waist, propelled her up again and as she let go strong hands seized her arms and jerked her upwards. She crumpled, weeping, onto the sloping floor.

"Go up, move," Kaw said.

Jasmine inched away from the precipice, clutching the floor with her body.

The silver head appeared again over the concrete cliff. Luke looked up and reached out his free arm as he prepared to lever himself up with the other. The man's face was wet with sweat and smeared with grime. He stretched down and locked his fist over Luke's arm. Their eyes met in the instant before the effort. Suddenly Luke knew the face. The man saw the flicker of recognition. His eyes widened in panic. Luke stared up at the man who had been with Dr Chan that rainy night long ago. There was no perm, no moustache, but the face was unmistakable. Dangling half-way out of his anchored position, held only by the wrist, Luke was entirely at his mercy.

Tan was breathing hard, sweat trickling across his face. After the earthslide had stilled, without thinking, he had scrabbled to the edge and reached out for the woman. He could have left them, climbed out to safety. Why hadn't he? The accusation howled in Tan's mind. He blinked wildly. He had recognised the white man earlier. Yet he had not stopped to think and, now, he was betrayed.

It could be so easy. Just to loosen his grip. Just to let go.

Tan wrenched upwards and Luke fell against the floor. Tan scrambled upwards, to the windows behind. Clambering out of the empty frames, he landed in the loose earth. Without looking back, he clawed up the weak slope, half sinking into the soil, his breath rasping. He made it across the crevasses and debris onto the remains of the road and began to run down the hill.

*   *   *

Jasmine felt Luke's arms around her shoulders, drawing her up from the floor. She groped out for him and clung to him. He buried his face in her hair, kissed her temples, her cheeks, her eyes.

Then, with a firm assurance, he brought her to her feet. He said, "We've got to get out of here."

They clambered through the back windows, half sliding down the wall to the mess of earth. Following Tan's path, they scrabbled up onto the ledge and began to hurry down the road.

It was then that the enormity of what had happened opened out before them like an abyss.

Parts of the road had caved in all along the slope. The car waiting for Jasmine had tumbled off the gravel down into the trees. Rock falls scattered fans of debris across the remains of the road.

Jasmine and Luke stood still.

Across the valley, the tower escarpment had vanished. Beneath the emptiness where it used to stand, a contortion of rubble, rock, twisted pylons and mutilated trees slumped down the hillside over a vast expanse. There was a quiet and stillness in the air as if the surrounding forests were deathly afraid. Only a mournful breeze moved, weeping with drizzle.

Far down the road, a man was picking his way hastily through the chaos. "Who was that man?" Luke squinted at the moving figure.

"His name is Kaw. From Jordan's KL office."

"Jordan?"

Their narrow escape began to sink in. Jasmine murmured, "He saved our lives."

"He was the man I saw with the doctor – the night that Kenneth was killed."

"What?"

"Come on!" Luke started running. "I have to talk to him!"

The crumbling road led them to the tip of the massive blockade, which stretched for miles down the slopes. Here, the force of the slide had broken up the road and shunted the vehicles at the head of the VIP convoy down into the valley. Limousines lay up-ended, crushed and twisted amid the earth and trees. A coach of journalists lay on its side. There were signs of movement among bloody bodies, a news crew struggling to rescue equipment from the hold, a reporter pointing his video camera erratically at everything and shouting a running commentary. Men in suits hovered around their wrecked vehicles barking into mobile phones.

Dickson Loh's Mercedes had been near the back of the convoy. It stood in the frozen black tail of untouched vehicles. Loh was rooted to the road, staring in disbelief at the disaster before him. Mohammed and Danesleigh, pale with shock and stripped to their shirtsleeves, but patrician to the last, were already organising rescue teams from the uninjured around them.

"Edward!" Jasmine shouted to Danesleigh. He was making his way down the embankment with three other men towards an upturned vehicle.

"Jasmine! Thank God!"

"I'm all right! You?"

He gave her the thumbs up. "We've called the emergency services on the mobile. But it'll be a while before they get through – it looks like the road further down the valley is blocked."

* * *

Hundreds of people ran towards the site of the slide impact, weaving the distant figure of Kaw into their crowd. They were the residents of Old Kampung Tanah who had not yet come down to the festivities in the new town. Old Kampung Tanah was some miles away along the ridge of the next hill and had been untouched by the slide. Among the horrified crowds heading towards the devastation were construction workers whose shift had not begun. The hundreds slowed to a crawling mass as earth and boulders mounted in a fanning expanse over the impact site.

Luke pushed his way through them, Jasmine struggling to keep close. People scrambled and fell over rubble and debris, sobbing and screaming the names of their families and friends. A few had managed to climb high overhead. Loose rocks bounced from under every moving foot down towards people below.

A shower of mud and rocks scattered above Luke and Jasmine, forcing them to dive out of the way.

Broken bodies lay everywhere, contorted into impossible positions, half buried in earth, rivulets of blood mingling with the muddy run-offs. Limbs torn off by the impact of the rubble protruded from crevices between boulders. A man below Luke was pulling at debris and shouting to someone trapped beneath the mound of earth.

A child's body dressed up in national costume for the celebration parade lay like a rag by a crushed car. Where the head should have been was blood and brain matter.

Jasmine could not stifle the sobbing moan that escaped her. Her hand clutched the wail of pity and horror rising within her, forcing it back, forcing her shuddering panic to stillness.

Tan was pacing a tight jittery pendulum not far from them. Tears were streaming down his face, his hands gesticulating in terror. His flight to safety had been cut off. In the destruction all around, there was nowhere for him to go. Death and blood blocked every direction.

Luke grabbed his shoulders and faced him. "Hey! What's your name?"

In that moment, the man scrabbling in the earth below them dislodged a spray of rocks, triggering a rubble slide onto people further downhill. The mound he was working on collapsed into itself, crushing him and the victim he had been trying to rescue. After the sliding rocks stilled, five more were dead.

Luke and Tan lost their foothold and skidded several feet down the slope.

Scrambling up, Luke shouted above the clamouring panic, demanding calm. "I want teams of six people!" The authority in his voice commanded attention. "Search slowly. Don't try to move any heavy loads. The whole area is unstable, anything could trigger more slides. Help the walking wounded first. Then anyone injured who can be carried. Anyone you find alive and can't move, stay with them, mark the place. Rescue services are on their way, they will help those who we can't help." He repeated his words in Malay and Cantonese. And again in English. He climbed to a vantage-point, focusing the people around him with a confident certainty. Tan shivered nearby, his face buried in his arms.

Luke singled out a number of construction workers. "You. And you. You there. Take a team, spread out. Organize those others there into teams. Move carefully."

The men nodded and moved off with small groups. Luke's simple words reined in the rising panic. Men and women scrabbling about aimlessly in personal anguish were given a focus. Luke had simplified it for them, narrowed the possibilities into clear instructions. His specific objectives – the numbers on each team, the order of rescue priorities – pre-empted the uncertainty that threatened to engulf them in hysteria.

"You there!" Luke pointed to a reporter and his cameraman scurrying towards them, video equipment aimed at him. "Put that down. Get your team together and search over in that section."

The news crew ignored him.

Luke moved nimbly towards them, shoving the camera into the cameraman's face with the force of his momentum.

"Hey!" The reporter stepped up to Luke. "We're just doing our job!"

"People are dying here. Your job now is to help them."

The cameraman was still shooting from the ground where he had stumbled. Luke towered over the reporter. He said, "I don't have time for this. Are you going to help these people?" He turned away and called to a sturdy woman, speaking to her in Chinese. "You. Get four people together. We need a base for the people we find."

The reporter said to his cameraman, "Keep shooting. I'll work with the rescue."

Luke went on, "We need blankets, water, bandages – get another group, four more people, to fetch those from Kampung Tanah." Luke turned to Jasmine. "I want you to help her."

"No, let me stay with you –"

"Don't argue."

Jasmine looked in distress at Luke. What if she never saw him again? What if, in the instability of the slide debris, he was caught in a rock fall, a land collapse?

"Get some men to help you. That space there, " he went on, indicating shallow ground uphill on the road they had come, "clear it for the support base. It's out of the rock-fall zone."

Luke took her hand, his voice softening. "Now, go. I'll be all right."

*   *   *

Luke grabbed Tan again and shook him. "You! What's your name?"

The man stared stupidly at him. He held up his hands, caked with blood from a body he had fallen on. "I didn't do this, not me. Life for a life. Two lives I give back for the one. It's enough, isn't it? Enough?"

"What's your name?"

"I paid already. Donations at Kuan Yin temple. I didn't do it myself, he drove the car, he crashed it. Why this now?"

Luke shook him. "Your name!"

The man frowned. He said, "Tan."

"Tan what?"

"Ronnie."

"Right, Ronnie Tan, you work with me." Luke held him with his gaze. He groped for a connection through the man's disturbance. "Ronnie, you saved my life. And Jasmine's. You gave back two lives."

Tan's eyes juddered away to the corpses.

"Ronnie, look at me. That's right, look at me. You can give back more lives, stay here with me. Help me."

"Give back more …"

"Yes. Don't be afraid. Work with me."

Tan nodded weakly. But he did not try to move away.

*   *   *

The rescue work continued through the afternoon. A heavy drizzle began again, adding to the treacherous run-offs pouring down the slopes. The animal cries of the immediate aftermath grew dim and scattered as life and energy ebbed. With each person found alive, there were six dead. The teams of able-bodied worked with subdued desperation, speech conserved to barked phrases.

The military helicopters arrived in the early afternoon. Unable to land, they winched down handfuls of military and civilian rescue workers and Red Crescent medical staff. The severely injured that could be moved were winched up to be flown to the nearest hospital in Kuala Terengganu on the East Coast. The squawk of walkie-talkies and bull-horns joined the clamour on the slopes. Further downhill, army units began work to clear the road. Heavy equipment for large-scale rescue, emergency and medical supplies and the bulk of additional rescue workers would not get through for another day.

Television crews, straggling from their upturned vehicles, roamed the disaster site. Pursuing a lead on Luke's real identity, they surrounded him, tearing him away from his *ad hoc* rescue teams.

"McAllister, who do you think is responsible for the disaster?"

"You posed with a false identity as a journalist earlier. Why was that?"

"What's your reaction to this terrible tragedy?"

Luke cut across the questions. "Dr Chan was working to prevent this type of disaster when he was killed. My report warned of the design fault in the tower foundations. This terrible disaster could have been prevented. A full and proper planning review would have revealed the instability of the tower."

"Are you saying due process was not followed at the review?"

"If the planners had had all the right information before them about the tower design and the topography of the site, I'm convinced they would have come to only one conclusion – that Jordan's design should not have been constructed. This disaster could have been prevented. Why was it not prevented? There must be a full public inquiry and all those responsible must be brought to account."

Luke looked strained. His clothes were muddy and torn. He was wet from the rain. But there was a determination in his features that projected through the cold lens of the camera. "Now, please, let me pass. There's work to be done."

Of the five men working with Luke, three were construction workers. Their strength and technical knowledge gave him what he needed to extricate a number of victims who had been trapped by earth and rubble. A news crew filmed Luke and his men painstakingly bring out a woman from under a collapsed wall. Working with levers and struts fashioned from branches and twisted iron, the five men managed to inch enough leeway for Tan to drag her out, her legs broken and bloody.

Two men took their turn to carry her to the base on a makeshift stretcher of jackets and timber from door frames. A third followed to steady the stretcher on the slippery inclines. The news crew tried to speak to Luke again but he pushed them away. They disappeared after the stretcher like a royal entourage, trying to get an interview with the woman.

Luke and Tan slumped against an uprooted tree, some way

from the other man on their team. It was the first breather they had had in several hours.

"It'll be dark soon," Luke said. His voice was quiet.

Tan had worked doggedly in the team like a man possessed. He had said little, his hysteria clamped down into robotic severity, each corpse they unearthed driving him deeper into his mask.

Tan stared out at the devastated landscape.

"Tell me about the night you were with Dr Chan."

Tan took a breath, almost in relief. As if he'd been expecting this. But he said nothing.

"You know I saw you that night," Luke persisted. "You recognised me up there on the terrace."

"Luke McAllister." Tan's voice was shaky "I've heard of you. You've been trying to pin the doctor's murder on someone."

"So you agree that it was murder?"

Tan attempted an edgy bravado. "You playing 'Police Interrogation' now?"

For a moment, Luke said nothing. Then, he turned and watched Tan. He said, "Kaw. Ronnie Tan. Which is it? Employed by Jordan. Whoever you are – why did you save me? You could've just let go."

Tan snapped him a blinking glance. He raked his memory in terror. What had he said to McAllister? Had he given his own name? When? He saw the blood and mud on the *ang mo*'s clothes, the cuts on the white man's arms and face. Looking down at himself, Tan saw, as if for the first time, the blood of the bodies he had touched staining him. The old panic clawed at his chest. His veneer of bravado was coming apart. He gasped, "I don't know why –"

"'Two lives for one'," the *ang mo* pressed. "What did you mean?"

"Shut up!" Tan shouted, trying to scrabble to his feet. "I don't know what you're talking about!"

McAllister grabbed him and forced him over. Crouching over Tan, pinning him to the ground, McAllister leaned close. His voice was hoarse with fury. "You know how the doctor died, don't you? Tell me what happened."

Tan struggled. McAllister punched him in the face. He hissed, "This disaster was what the doctor was trying to prevent. If he hadn't died, we might've stopped this. All these people are now dead but they could've been saved!"

"No!"

"They died because the foundation works above collapsed. The doctor knew this could happen – that's why we were trying to stop Jordan."

Tan grappled with the *ang mo*, the blood from his smashed nose blinding him. The white man slammed him against the rocks, winding him, then hunched over him. "Listen to me! Thousands are dead because of Jordan. This could have been stopped. But the doctor was killed, my data destroyed. Whoever did that just as surely did this. Just as surely as if they had killed these people with their own hands."

A cry gutted out of Tan.

"Tell me what you know!"

Tan's arms flew up to hide his sobs. His body heaved as he whooped for breath. McAllister slackened his hold. He said softly, "It's killing you, isn't it, whatever you know? Why are you protecting Jordan? He's the one who paid for the doctor to be killed, for my office to be destroyed. Am I right? He's the one behind it all, isn't he? Tell me what you know. Give his life for all these lives that were taken."

Tan's fists sledge-hammered into McAllister's stomach, then groin. McAllister crumpled. Tan reached for a rock and smashed it into the side of the white man's head. As McAllister fell, Tan levered himself up and began to run.

23

By late afternoon, a crude base camp had been cleared in the safe zone Luke had indicated. A handful of men set up a relay of flat-bed trucks to ferry provisions from the old town of Kampung Tanah, seven miles away from the disaster area and untouched by the slide. Progress was slow along the subsiding road and the blankets, water, bandages and medicines had to be hauled on foot the last half-mile to the camp.

Mohammed co-ordinated the rescue operations from the camp, working with the army captain who led the teams brought in by helicopter. Mobile phones were commandeered to boost communications across the vast site. Mohammed knew the area layout from memory, having reviewed the planning applications, and sketched outlines in the mud for the captain.

Around the rescue base, a semi-habitable centre began to emerge. Plastic sheering hung over trees and salvaged hardboard and canvas from destroyed parade-floats gave some shelter from the drizzle. Bedding and dry clothes were piling up in a corner, ferried down from Kampung Tanah in gunny sacks. Hawker stoves were somehow trundled in and were brewing vats of thick tea and broth.

Jasmine toiled with the dozens of others in the drizzle, clearing undergrowth, passing boxes and blankets over rough ground. She could not stop thinking of Luke and glanced anxiously towards the jagged scar of the slide. It was early, she told herself, he would still be searching the debris with his team, he would not come yet. He would return later, when it got dark, she should not worry now. But she could not stop watching for him. As the rescue workers began to bring in the injured, she found herself co-ordinating a growing hospital camp.

The hours blurred into sequences of blood and horror – reaching out to receive injured bodies from those who were themselves hardly able to stand, staunching wounds that flowed red and warm over her hands, helpless in the face of torn flesh and shattered bone. She dreaded to come across Luke among these broken bodies. Several construction workers trying to rescue a child had been brought in, their chests and legs a mass of blood. Relief tangled with fear when she did not see him among the injured, for it meant that he was still out there. Perhaps he *was* hurt but lay undiscovered in a rock fall, or they were even now trying to move him. Or perhaps ... the worst ... She shied away from the horror of that. She made herself focus on each present moment. She did not know, she told herself, that was all. It did not mean anything had happened to him. She clung to that hope. But in the dark shadows of her heart, guilt lurked. She was a part of Jordan's team, the lawyer who had run rings round these people to entice them to the relocation package, the team player who had brought Luke down. She was to blame for all this. She could have stopped it but she hadn't. She hadn't listened to Luke, hadn't wanted to believe him. And now, if anything happened to him ... A terrible despair threatened to swamp her. She stared at all these people, covered in blood, wailing in agony. They had come to the site of the slide like sheep herded by what she had done for Jordan. Their blood tainted her heart even as it stained her hands and clothes.

She forced herself to focus. She could not change what had happened but she would do what she could to help them now. With desperation, she moved among the victims, fashioning bandages and tourniquets from whatever she could find, helping a woman to sip hot tea, comforting an old man as he sobbed in pain. She held a woman as she died, the death throes long and violent. Jasmine sat by the body, sobbing. But then she roused herself again, numbly arranging for the corpse to be moved. Within moments, another injured was brought to fill the place. Jasmine worked on. There were others who needed help. She hardly noticed the tears that dampened her face, making her gulp for breath, blurred her vision. The cries of the injured were inhuman, a chaos of moaning and shrieking, whimpers and sobs. The fresh air of the hills grew tinny and sweet with the smell of blood. Survivors around her searched the mass of shifting pain for son or daughter, parent or lover, afraid to find them, afraid not to.

As the day drew on, Jasmine longed for Luke to come. Where was he? Was he all right? Would he make it back uninjured? Alive? She could not lose him now. She began to shake as it hit her. She had almost died that day. But Luke had been there. As he had always been. The realisation gripped her like a fever. Even through those long years in England, she had never let go of him in her heart. She had always loved him. No matter how hard she had fought against it, it had always been him. Even now. There was no one but him. It hit her like a physical blow. If she had died, she would never have known this exhilarating, terrifying certainty. And now, knowing it, what if she never saw him alive again? Jasmine could not control the cry that wrenched itself from her.

There was a commotion by the entry to the hospital base. Men bearing makeshift stretchers. One of them shouting, "We found them near the top – where all the construction work was this morning. There are more hurt up there! Send more teams up there!"

Jasmine started towards the group. Luke was not among the rescuers. Her heart hurt in her chest. Please, don't let it be him in the stretchers.

She came up alongside the injured men. They were dark. Asians. Not Luke. She felt dizzy with relief. And then she recognised Zain, the project manager. He was with two construction workers who had survived the collapse at the tower site. One of the men was babbling, going over and over again what had happened. She made out that, running to the aid of their co-workers, Zain and the two men had not reached the splitting seam when the ground under their feet began to crumble. Tumbling with the minor slide, they had been lucky enough to have stayed near the surface. Zain's pelvis and legs were broken in several places and he was unconscious.

Many hours later, as the light began to fade, Jasmine saw him. She looked up as she finished bandaging a gash on a woman's arm. Luke was picking his way over the rows of bodies. Blood matted his hair around an ugly gash by his temple. He was drenched, his feet stumbling woodenly. In a moment, she had encircled him in her arms. She clutched the shape of him, ran her hands over his arms and chest and face, as if making sure of him. "Luke! I was so afraid you might've been – So many of the rescue teams brought in injured – I kept thinking, what if …?"

Luke managed a laugh over his fatigue. "So you do care after all."

"Damn you." But she was smiling, leaning up to silence him with a kiss, tasting his saltiness and the warmth of his lips. He drew her close against him, enfolding her into all of him. The noise and devastation around them fell away. Nothing else existed in that moment but the homecoming of their embrace. They were conscious only of each other, acknowledging without thought the love that had always bound them.

When she drew away, Jasmine reached light fingers up to the gash on Luke's face, unaware of the smile brushing her lips. "We'd better see to this. What happened?"

Luke stared at Jasmine. Her face was streaked with grime and tears. She looked pale and exhausted. He had never seen anyone more beautiful.

Jasmine caressed his cheek. "Luke?"

Luke said, "Kaw. Tan. He got away. He was badly affected by all the death around him, you saw that. He knows something. I hoped maybe he might talk, tell me what happened with Kenneth. But I pushed him too hard. We tangled, he ran –" Luke jerked his head and winced.

"Gently …"

"I tried to follow. But he's gone. He could be anywhere in this chaos. Most likely trying to get off the slopes."

In minutes it would be dark. Jasmine looked into the gloom where the valleys would be. "Will he manage it?"

"I need him to," Luke said. "And then I aim to find him."

* * *

"No one expected this to happen," said Mohammed, the President of the Planning Committee. "Except you, Mr McAllister. Tell me what you know."

They sat on boxes on the edge of the encampment by the weak light of a kerosene lamp. Mohammed looked exhausted, his fine features bearing the shock and grief of all he had seen that day. He had heard that the controversial environmental consultant was on the site and had now found him. Luke sat stiffly while Jasmine cleaned the gash on his temple, the skin around it already bruising.

"My warnings were carried in the media at the time," Luke said. "Because of the piercing into the limestone substratum, the risk of subsidence would be high. Surely your planning board realises the risks of building into limestone."

"Of course! The risks are considered so serious that the planning regulations governing this area specifically disallow it. But there was nothing in the reports and data that came before us that supported your allegations."

"You mean all the information you got didn't reveal that the foundation would be partly built into the limestone?"

Mohammed nodded.

"Even the geological survey provided by the Consortium geophysicist?"

"You can be sure that if we had had any data that confirmed your allegations, we would have required modification of the tower. Without that, your statements to the media were just hot air – the destabilising tactics of a radical green activist with an agenda to prevent Asian progress."

Luke gestured to encompass the devastation around them. His voice was harsh. "Is this what it had to take for you to believe me?"

Mohammed hunched over, resting his elbows on his knees. He rubbed the bridge of his nose. "I don't know what to believe. There's talk of sabotage, acts of God, the revenge of the aboriginal forest spirits ..." He straightened and sighed. "There'll be an official investigation and, if they find evidence of foul play or criminal negligence, a criminal investigation will follow. I have no role in any of that – my prosecuting days are over. In fact, as President of the Planning Committee, I myself will probably have to answer to the investigators. I personally have nothing to hide and I know there's been no misconduct among my colleagues. Our integrity will be proven."

Luke said, "What do you want from me?"

"Why did you come here in disguise?"

Luke told him what he had told Jasmine on the terrace.

Mohammed nodded thoughtfully. After a pause, he said, "You did good work on the slopes today. Many people owe their lives to you. I saw you organise the people, channel their panic and distress. I've heard about your skill and courage in the rescues you led."

"I did what I could."

"You're not what I expected of a hysterical greenie capable of sabotage."

Luke snorted. "Is that what they're trying to pin on me?"

"I'm taking a risk on you," Mohammed said, "but sabotage is for cowards and I don't believe you're that kind of man."

Luke waited.

Mohammed said, "I want to see your analysis and data. I don't know what weight the investigators will give to it, if any at all. But I need to know for myself whether we were wrong because we were deceived or because of a mistake or misjudgement."

"What I have is incomplete."

"Let me see whatever you have. If your analysis merits further review, I'll do what I can to ensure the official investigation takes due note of it. Then, if appropriate, the official channels will get the information needed to complete it."

Mohammed turned to Jasmine. "In the present circumstances,

I don't believe you have any legal grounds to object to my obtaining Mr McAllister's perspective on the landslide."

For a moment, Jasmine could not understand why he was addressing her. "Object?"

"I expect that you will advise your client of my discussion with Mr McAllister. I have nothing to hide. Indeed, I'll be informing the investigators of our talk. Let's be clear that I'm not taking Mr McAllister's side. I just think he deserves someone, at least, to consider his views seriously."

"My client ..." Jasmine floundered. How could she justify her client's role and her own involvement in the disaster? She could find no use for legalism after the horrifying scenes of that day. If Jordan had known about the risk of collapse and gone ahead with the tower anyway, he was responsible for the deaths and injuries of all these people. And she had protected him, fought for him. She had devised the legal package to move them right under the path of disaster. What could she say to make any of that right? What words could she use to smokescreen it all? She felt as if she were free-falling into chaos. But she was still Jordan's lawyer and Mohammed was waiting for her reply. She groped for words. At last, she said mechanically, "I have no objections."

Mohammed stood up, stretching his back. He said to Luke, "Your being here in disguise – it won't look good to the investigators whatever your story. I don't know if I'm doing the right thing in trusting you. I hope for both of us they don't find any hint of sabotage."

He picked up the kerosene lamp and moved slowly away.

* * *

A cameraman from an Australian network had been the only one to have caught the slide from start to the final settling dust. Television stations around the world were already negotiating with the network for the purchase of the transmission rights of those pictures.

It was the scoop of the decade. The news crews straggled into the bar at Lee's Hotel in Kampung Tanah as night fell, taking the last of the rooms in the hotel and de-briefing the day's events over rounds of drinks. Without live transmission facilities, they were sending sequences of moving stills back to their stations using mobile phones interfaced with laptop PC modems. Other journalists had sent audio reports via mobile phones, playing back their interviews into the mouthpiece. One stills photographer had even fought his way onto a winch to ride a helicopter back to civilisation in order to courier his film to the labs.

VIP visitors who had not been injured also made their way up to Kampung Tanah to spend the night. Dickson Loh's staff, armed with cash and cheque-books, arranged accommodation for their guests at hotels, lodging a few at the homes of local residents. Tan's distant cousin, the director of First Safe Limited, and his family had not gone down to the opening festivities. He hired out his house to Dickson Loh and Danesleigh, the overnight rates he asked including the use of his fax machine, telephone and Suzuki Jeepnik.

The old town was macabrely deserted of its own people. Its streets and public spaces shuffled with exhausted visitors and journalists. Construction workers sat in coffee-shops and dormitories, drained and in late shock. The local people who had survived thronged together in each other's houses as if in vigil for their dead and missing.

Out on the slopes, rescue work continued through the night. The professional teams had grown over the afternoon, winched down over numerous helicopter trips. With their head-lamps and reflective overalls, they combed the twisted landscape like strange glowworms. Mohammed and scores of local volunteers stayed at base camp, sleeping where they could and working in shifts among the injured.

In the early hours of morning, Jasmine sat with Luke by a spluttering fire at the far end of the encampment. The wood was sodden and the fire smoked. The drizzle had stopped and, through the tattered clouds, they could see the stars. They were alone now, taking their out-shift while the handful of volunteers who had rested by the fire moved across the hospital camp. Luke wrapped a blanket around them both. The night air was cold and they drew close on the log that made their bench. Jasmine snuggled into Luke's embrace, entwining both her hands in his.

They talked in quiet tones, recounting the day they had lived through. Jasmine spoke of the children who now slept fitfully in a section of the camp – how she had held them to her, their eyes wide with terror, some scanning faces for their parents, one whimpering for her mother over and over again. Luke told her about the courage of one member of his team who had crawled into a crumbling mound of debris to pull out an old man.

Eventually, their voices trailed away and they watched the flames of the fire in quiet stillness.

After a while, Jasmine said, as if from sleep, "When we get down from here, I'm going to take a long hot bath."

"When we get down from here," Luke smiled, "I'm going to take a long hot bath – and sleep for a week."

"Mmm." Jasmine wriggled against him, picking up the memory game. "When we get down from here, I'm going to take a long hot bath and sleep for a week – and … and ask you to do them with me."

"Do the rules allow that?" Luke teased her fingers under the blanket.

"Damn the rules," Jasmine said mildly. "I've lived my life by too many rules. And they're all the wrong ones."

Luke leaned down and kissed the side of her throat. She arched her head back, luxuriating in the touch of his lips. There was nothing beyond the firelight but the cloaking night. It concealed for her the past and the future and all the ambitions that had hewn out her life in London. Sitting here with Luke, touching him, kissing him, it seemed as if they had always been thus entwined in their hearts. Nothing else mattered. There was only the present and the commanding intensity of her emotions. Nothing else was real.

"When we get down from here," she said, her voice low, "take me back to our special place, Luke. Where we used to watch the fireflies and where we were the happiest. To before we said goodbye that awful afternoon so long ago. Take me back so I can do it right this time around."

"You did it right then. You were right to leave."

"But not how I left. I wanted that afternoon to be special, so we would always remember it. But I had to spoil it all, don't you see? And so we argued and we were lost to each other."

"I'll always remember that afternoon."

"Yes, but for all the wrong things."

Luke did not seem to hear her. "We hiked up through the old track, past the three rocks, cut through the slimy bog – like we always used to do. It was mid-afternoon and really muggy."

Jasmine laughed at the old landmarks they had named together. She picked up the narrative. "We took the photo on the boulder. I've still got the copy you sent me, you know. You tickled me like crazy, mean thing, tried to make me look silly in the picture."

The fire conjured the scene again, its sparks like magic dust.

"We climbed down again and that was when it really sank in." Jasmine's voice was a murmur. "I was going to England and I'd never see you again. All I had left with you was that afternoon. I felt afraid, like time was slipping from us, like something was going to happen and I wouldn't be able to stop it. I wanted to hold on to it for ever, but if I did, I knew I'd never leave."

Luke spoke softly, his cheek against Jasmine's. "There was so much I wanted to say to you. I just didn't know how. I was afraid to lose you. I didn't want us – what good fun we had, what adventures we went on – I didn't want it all to change. I didn't want you to change. I didn't know how to say what I really wanted to say so I told you not to leave."

They were there again, facing each other across the distance of the clearing. Jasmine said, in a small voice, "I was terrified but I didn't want you to see. I was going to a strange country thousands of miles away where I knew no one. The English were people who'd always been masters to servants like my mother and it scared me –

how would they treat me in England? But it was my one chance to change. To get away from my memories of that terrible night when my father walked out. I've never talked to anyone about it. He beat my mother again. Really badly this time."

"I didn't know," Luke murmured.

"They were quarrelling. But it was my fault. I made it worse. I … Then he …" Jasmine faltered. She could not tell him. "*Ah Ma* rushed at him. Then he turned on her. He walked out after that. He never came back."

Luke held her hand tightly. "It wasn't your fault. You mustn't blame yourself for him leaving."

Jasmine wished she could believe him. But Luke had not been there. And she could not bring herself to say out loud what had really happened. She did not know the words to tell him of her shame. What good would it do now? Luke did not have the power to absolve her. She said, "I had to leave, don't you see? My mother wanted me to escape – everything, the past, the life we'd be trapped in because of my father's reputation. I did whatever she wanted of me. I felt guilty, don't you see? It was my duty to live the new life my mother longed for. I wanted to tell you everything back then but how could I? I didn't even really understand it all myself. All I knew was that I had to go. And then you said out loud the secret words that I'd guarded so hard – 'Stay, why don't you stay?' you threw at me. You had everything – money, class, education, freedom to choose. All these things meant so little to you and all the world to me."

"I wanted to stay. I wanted to be a daughter to my mother. I wanted my future in yours. I wanted it all. But I was afraid to love you. Because to love you meant to give it all up, to give up my hopes, my life, my dreams, my chance to be free from the past, everything because of love. And I couldn't do it. And I didn't know the words to tell you. And so I shouted and ranted at you and blamed you for everything that I envied of you. I lost myself in it. I made myself hate you and I wanted you to hate me. It was the only thing I could do, the only way I could leave you."

Luke's voice was husky in her ear. "I was an idiot. I told you to stay with your mother, I lectured you about ideals and principles and what's important in life. I didn't see you, only my fear at losing you. The more you said, the more I wanted to win you round. So I talked and talked about abstractions and what's right and wrong. And all the while, I should've been telling you how much I loved you – how precious you are to me, how much I love the way you make me laugh, your temper, your determination, your beautiful eyes, how I love everything about you."

Tears glistened in Jasmine's eyes but Luke could not see them. She said, "I love you, Luke. I loved you back then in Firefly Clearing. I love you now. It's always been you. Only you. All these years, I've tried to deny it. I got my 'new life', just what I wanted, but it's never been real. With you, there's only the truth. It's the only rule that matters. All these years, there's never been a day that I've not thought about you. I don't know what to do any more, Luke. All I know is that I love you, with all my heart."

Luke slipped both his arms around her, lifting her so that he cradled her from behind, wrapping his body around her like a cloak. She folded her arms over his, stroking his cheek with hers, her hair falling against his face. They stayed this way for a long time, silent and wearily content.

24

Harry drained his fourth Carlsberg that morning. He sat under the fan in Ling Ho coffee-shop on the main street of Ranjing. The chair was too low for him and the table creaked as he leaned against it. He had arrived in Kuala Lumpur from London the night before and driven up to the crossroads town in a hired Mercedes.

Ranjing was crowded with relatives of the landslide victims, reporters and curiosity hounds. They waited in coffee-shops, gathered at the police checkpoint set up at the foot of the route up to Kampung Tanah. The earth and debris blocking the road near the destroyed town had been cleared earlier that morning. Convoys of army trucks, rescue workers and first-aid crews had rattled up the slopes four hours ago.

The midday sun seared through the clouds. Steam began to rise off the roads and pavements. The sound of a return convoy snaking down the hill ended the waiting. Harry paid for his drinks and made his way to the checkpoint in the wake of the excited crowd. His cotton Paul Smith shirt was drenched with sweat and clung to his back. The suffocating heat flushed over his face and neck, dampened every pore. He had seen Jasmine on the news, too distressed to speak into the camera, but alive and uninjured. He imagined her coming through the checkpoint and falling into his embrace, calling his name with love and relief. There would be gratitude in her voice and he would kiss her. "My darling, I'm here now," he would say.

In the last year, he had felt his love for her deepen. The troubles they had experienced in the first months of their marriage had faded with Jasmine's ambition. "You have everything that would make your parents proud now, my love," he had said to her. He had won her round with this argument, he thought with satisfaction. He had said, "They would be proud to know that your marriage is a success and that they would be grandparents soon," and she had listened to him. Her loyalty to her parents' memory was charming. He smiled fondly.

He had almost lost her, he thought. He had had a bad feeling about her trip here. But he had not tried hard enough to stop her. He had been weak. It frightened him how close he had come to losing his one precious love. He could not let it happen again.

Police kept the crowds back while medical crew hurried to greet the returning trucks. The injured were carried into ambulances. The whine of sirens sped through the town to the local hospital and to the hospital in Kuantan on the East Coast. The other survivors – VIPs, journalists, visitors and construction workers – stumbled out into the crowd, faces shifting with delayed shock and relief. A policeman collected the clipboards of names and addresses from the escorting officer, to be followed up in the investigation to come.

Harry towered over the crowd. He could not see Jasmine in the mass of Asian faces. Perhaps she would be in the next convoy. And then a movement far behind the wall of trucks caught his eye. He tracked along the edge of the crowd, glimpsing the progress of the moving figures between the obstacles of trucks and ambulances.

It was the consultant, McAllister. Jasmine was with him. They ducked into a copse of trees, hurrying towards an alley behind a row of shop-houses. Harry followed them at a distance. They walked quickly through the alley into a side street, weaving among the rows of scooters and up onto the covered "five-foot walkway". Harry trailed them, obscuring himself where he could behind pillars, a news-stand, stacks of bins outside a hardware store. He saw the consultant take Jasmine's hand to lead her quickly on. Later, McAllister guided her with a hand round her shoulders. They both looked surreptitious. Guilty.

Harry's lips were a thin gash of anger. A muscle worked furiously in his jaw.

* * *

Luke and Jasmine turned down an unmade road, long grass and muddy puddles scattering ahead of them. A cluster of *atap* houses stood at the end, across the coconut grove where a few yellow cows grazed. Partly obscured by a bottle-brush bush was Luke's Land Rover. He had parked it there the day before when he had caught a ride on the journalist coach up to Kampung Tanah.

Harry crunched out into the centre of the path from behind a cluster of metal bins, his shoulders hunched forward belligerently. "Jasmine!" His hands balled into fists by his side.

Harry's voice hurled at Jasmine as if from another life. She snapped round. What was he doing here? How had he got here? He loomed like a bull before the charge and she felt terror clench her guts.

She had thought that she would have a few days to gather her senses before facing Harry and the reality of her English life. After the cool of the highlands, the midday heat down here was suffocating. Her head spun and she could hardly breathe. Harry was here and she would have to tell him ... tell him what? She was gripped by panic. Luke stood beside her. If Harry had followed them from the checkpoint, how much had he seen? How much did he know? She had promised him that she wasn't having an affair. He would think she'd lied to him all along. What would he do to her now?

"Jasmine! Come here!" Harry shouted. "You, McAllister! Get away from her!"

Luke did not move. Harry's tone was like a slap in Jasmine's face. But he couldn't do anything to her now, she thought. Her marriage was over. Her golden marriage, the golden life she had tried to believe in for so long, for her mother's sake. It was over. But, then, it had never really been. Her panic subsided. She thought of the last time she had seen Harry – he'd had that same ugly look in his face as he'd tried to stop her coming out to Malaysia. Seeing him now, red-faced in the bright sun, she felt again that revulsion that had shaken her. In the last year of apparent happiness, a part of her had shrivelled, she saw now. She had closed it off, starved it of vitality. She had played out her role as Harry had wanted and their marriage had survived. She had taken that for happiness. But her shrivelled heart had festered and when they had quarrelled again a few days before, its poison had awakened her like an antidote. She saw it more clearly than she'd ever realised before. She had never really known Harry. She had never really loved him or been loved by him. Everything he had made her and given her had no reality beyond the script they had both played out. Baubles. Nothing but baubles.

"Jasmine! Do you hear me?"

Jasmine stared at him. He had no hold on her, she thought curiously. Not any more. He never had, only *she* let him. It was as if shackles fell from her. She felt light all of a sudden. *Only she let him*. Her mind reeled at this knowledge. She had the sensation that she could do anything, overcome anyone.

Luke took a step towards Harry. Jasmine reached out a restraining hand. She said, "Let me speak to him alone." She could not control the tremor in her voice.

Luke nodded. But he did not take his eyes off Harry.

Jasmine walked towards her husband. She felt herself trembling – not from fear but a strange intoxication. She attempted a lightness of tone. "Harry. What are you doing here?"

"I came for you. What the hell are you doing with him?"

"He was at the ceremony."

Harry scooped her into his arms. "I'm here, my love," he said. "I came across the world for you. As soon as I heard the news. I dropped everything."

Jasmine did not struggle. She felt as if he was holding someone else's body. Her voice seemed to her to speak from a long way away. "Thank you for coming."

"Christ! You sound like a bloody hostess!" Harry pulled away but mastered himself. "I'm your husband. Of course I would come.

My darling, let's go home. Everything's fine now – you're safe and we're together again."

He took her arm.

The pain of his tightening grasp made her angry. No more – she would not let it happen any more. She stood her ground. "Harry."

"Darling?" Harry smiled, with strained patience. His eyes flicked to Luke, watching from a distance. "Let's go."

Jasmine took a breath. She held on to her anger, stoked it till it hurt. It was time to end the masquerade. "I – I don't want – I'm not coming with you," she said.

Harry's laugh was jittery. "Of course you are. You don't know what you're saying." He tugged her.

With a sudden force, she snatched her arm away. "I said no. I – I need some time alone – away from you. Give me time."

"I don't understand!" Harry lunged in panic at her, held her by both arms. "I came for you. I'm your husband. I love you. What's going on? We've sorted out our difficulties now. We had a wonderful time in Paris, didn't we? We've made up, haven't we?"

He was so close, she could smell the beer on his breath. His body pleaded with her. But his arms held her with crushing power.

"Let me go, Harry."

"When was the last time we had a scrap? When? I've not touched you in anger for months now! What's going on? Tell me! I saw you holding hands, I saw him touch you like he owned you."

"Harry." An old defiance goaded her. She felt a strength she had almost forgotten. Standing here in the heat, knowing how closely she had escaped death in the hills, she knew she would never be afraid of her husband again.

Harry was breathing hard. His eyes stared at her. He let her go with a suddenness that made her stagger.

Jasmine said in a low, clear voice, "It's over, Harry."

"What the fuck –"

Her mouth was dry, her breathing so shallow she could hardly speak. But she made herself continue. "It's over. Our marriage. You and me. I'm sorry."

"You've been screwing that bastard all along, haven't you? Bitch, tell me the truth!"

"No."

"Fucking whore!" Harry stalked an invisible cage, ever decreasing in on him. His arms and fists bulged with hardly repressed violence, the air around him a substitute for her body. It was as if he knew that if he started on her now, he would not stop until she was dead. "*I* made you everything you are! *I* gave you everything! *I* own you! And still you wanted more. So I tried. I tried so hard. I've been understanding and romantic with you – I've tried to be perfect for you. I gave up Marietta for you!"

"Marietta?"

Harry shouted in her face. "You didn't know that, did you? Your dearest friend, your matron-of-honour – I've been screwing her for years! When you went on your business trips. When you thought I was entertaining clients. Even before you and I ever met."

Jasmine felt her chest constrict. She tried to speak but could make no sound.

"And I fucked her the week of our wedding. You know what present she gave me once when you were away? A whore! Just like you. I've had plenty of whores just like you. You have no hold on me, you damn bitch! No fucking hold. You're nothing to me. I made you – I can break you again."

A crystal-clear fury shot through Jasmine. She had been duped all along. All the time he'd demanded her faithfulness, threatened her with his possessive rage, he'd been sleeping with Marietta. And with prostitutes! How many? What did they do? The questions started but she forced them aside. Marietta, who had made herself Jasmine's best friend. From the start, Marietta and Harry had been lovers, even while he and Jasmine had seemed so in love in Oxford. Jasmine felt sick. She thought of Marietta talking girl-talk with her, advising her about men, about Harry, decorating her Chelsea flat *just as Harry would like it,* organising the wedding, the wedding list, the guest list. And playing Harry's pimp.

"Why?" she cried. "Why?"

Harry coursed on, unstoppable now, "Because she and I are good together. We're a pair, we've always been – ever since we were kids. She's the only one who understands me. But she never wanted a cosy little marriage. She's too wild. That's what I adore about her."

"She got herself that poofter, Jonathan, for the sake of appearances and for his cash. And I found you. But not in the calculating way she got Jonathan. I cared for you. You gave me something special, believe me. I thought you'd be different from all the English girls. I was happy with you. And because I had you, I didn't need Marietta and so she and I could be great together. I could be her match, you know? But I fell in love with you. That wasn't supposed to happen. I needed you and it changed things. It changed things for Marietta and me, too, but that doesn't matter any more. It's you I want with me always. It's you I love. You belong to me. No one can touch you. You're mine, you're safe with me. I'll make sure of it."

Harry swung from anger to self-pity to exuberance to desperation. Jasmine could hardly take it all in. His monstrous pact with Marietta revolted her. It frightened her that he did not seem to see the hideousness of the game they'd been playing with her. That he still believed that she'd go home with him. Did he really think they could go on with the masquerade after this? A deeper horror and disgust shook her. Harry was no different, after all. With his prostitutes and drinking and violence, Jasmine saw it with terrifying clarity. She had found her father in Harry and she had clung to him. She had never escaped. The ghoul reared its leering mask. It had been there all along, tainting her marriage with the old shame. Nausea wrenched her gut, convulsed her throat. She fought it down, the bile bitter in the back of her mouth. "It's over, Harry," she said, her voice hoarse. "I want a divorce."

From a distance, Luke saw Jasmine brace herself against Harry's rage, her determination carrying her quiet voice above the shouting. "Goodbye, Harry," she said, and turned away.

Even as Harry wound his arm back, the flat of his hand open to slam into Jasmine, his fury screaming from his gut, Luke propelled himself towards them. Jasmine registered his shout of warning too late and the blow caught her between the shoulder-blades, thudding her to the ground, throwing the breath from her.

Harry hauled her up and drew his fist back to pound her in the face.

Luke launched himself at Harry, hurling him from Jasmine, who crumpled to the ground, retching for breath. He jabbed a swift short blow at Harry's windpipe. The bulkier man fell to one knee, gasping for air. He threw himself at Luke, trying to bring him down. Luke pulled back and Harry crashed onto the dirt.

Luke stood out of reach, his relaxed posture masking his fighting skill. He said quietly, "That's enough. You touch Jasmine again and I'll kill you."

Harry crawled upright, massaging his throat. Luke glanced towards Jasmine. She was beginning to sit up, painfully mastering her breath. Seeing his moment, Harry rushed him.

Luke wrenched a step to the side, and without the expected impact, Harry stumbled off-balance. Luke shot a blow into his kidneys and an elbow into his falling chin. Turning, he punched Harry's face, feeling the nose collapse under his knuckles.

Spasms of pain and nausea held Harry to the dirt. Luke walked away from his heehawing gasps.

Jasmine felt Luke's arms around her shoulders. He said gently, "Are you all right?"

She nodded, averting her eyes from where Harry writhed. She looked up at Luke as he drew her to her feet. She said, "Take me home."

* * *

Mrs Fung's joy wavered over the static. "My precious one, you're safe! I saw you on the TV. I was so worried. But the gods have been good to us! I'm so happy! And my boy Luke, is he safe?"

"*Ah Ma*, he's here, he's not hurt." Jasmine laughed with

pleasure to hear her mother's voice. They were speaking on the mobile phone in Luke's Land Rover. Jasmine sat beside him as they now sped to pick up the north-south highway to Taiping. It would be a long drive, two hours from Ranjing to the intersection for Taiping, and two hours after that. Jasmine said, "He's bringing me home to you now."

"No –"

"We'll be there in about four hours."

Mrs Fung said, more forcefully, "No. Don't come."

"What? Why? I want to see you."

Luke glanced across and then back at the road again.

"People have been asking questions. Trying to find out about you …" Mrs Fung's tight voice said over the phone.

"What people?"

"I don't know. Someone asking a lot of questions. Last few months. The grocer in town, he told me this man was showing an old picture of you and Luke and asking about you all. Your old Form Six teacher, she still comes to see me even after I stop my meal service, she said that someone also was asking at the school. And the neighbours, they've seen strangers looking around this area, at this house."

"Do they know who this man – these people – are?"

"No. Everyone knows my daughter went overseas and never came back, I never have news. They pity me, they say you are unfilial, but that's how I wanted it. Why ask questions now, after all these years?"

"A White man?"

"No – one of us." Chinese.

Jasmine's mind reeled. The anxiety of the old secret gripped her again. It was a knee-jerk panic. No one must know her past – that had been the chant that had driven her for so long. Perhaps the man was a detective, hired by someone in London. Harry. Jordan. Marietta. Perhaps her mother's family in San Francisco. Perhaps. Perhaps. The scenarios raced in her tired thoughts.

"Perhaps …" Jasmine began, "*Ah Ba*, after all this time –"

Mrs Fung's bark cut her off. "No!"

"Maybe it's him. Or people he's sent."

"You father will never come back." The old woman's voice was shaking with emotion. "I won't let him destroy your life. Like he destroyed mine. I promise you that."

"*Ah Ma*, I want to come home."

Mrs Fung's voice shook but she insisted, "No. Don't come. Not yet. Do this for me. You mustn't come."

"*Ah Ma* –"

"No. Daughter, listen to me. I don't want you to come. I love you, my little one. I'm happy you are safe. But don't come."

The line went dead. Mrs Fung had hung up on her.

Jasmine switched off the phone and stared out at the rubber plantations rushing by. Her panic was beginning to fade. What did she really have to fear from her past, she thought, with a curious detachment. Her past was who she was. She would face the shame, and what would come of that? Suddenly she saw the choice she had. She could live with it or let it destroy her. She did not have to let it break her, she realised. The new strength she had found in facing Harry began to take root. It was as if in rousing herself from Harry's thrall she had discovered her own sense of who she was. *Ah Ma*, she wanted to say, I don't care if the whole world knows where I come from, it doesn't matter any more. It never had. She reached out for Luke's hand.

* * *

In her empty house, Mrs Fung sat listening to her own laboured breath. The news of the strangers had disturbed her at first but today, she had been glad for the excuse to keep Jasmine away. Outside, against a darkening afternoon sky, the flame tree burned a deep red. The smell of rain sifted through the windows. It would be over soon, she thought. Her secret would die with her and Jasmine would be free.

Mrs Fung's face was gaunt and pale, the skin flaccid against the corners of her skull. Her clothes hung from her like moss from a tree, her skeletal arms resting on her lap, the jade bangle pitifully loose against her knuckles. The agony in her stomach was growing worse over the long minutes of each day and night.

She had not wanted Jasmine to see her like this.

PART THREE

TAO

Tao

The way of harmony. Only in the intertwined balance of yin and yang can we walk the path of life with true courage to illuminate the chaos with our inner light.

25

Luke turned the Land Rover onto the interchange with the north-south highway. Jasmine was asleep stretched out on the back seat. Now that the mobile was on, it rang with call after call from his friends. Susan –"Thank God you're safe, Luke." Raymond –"Good to hear you, man. Saw you on the news – shit hair job! What colour d'you call that?" and Luke, grinning, "What are you, the fashion police?"

He switched off the phone. They drove under the canopy of clouds darkening over Ipoh and rain splashed down in walls of water. By the time the Land Rover pulled up Bukit Larut two hours later, the rain had stopped but fat drops still dripped through the forest.

Raymond had alerted Luke's housekeeper and the fires in each room had been lit. A platter of fried noodles had been left in the kitchen under a wicker food cosy. Luke stoked up the fires till they roared. After the chill damp of the last two days, Jasmine felt her body unfurl in the heat.

But when Luke turned to glance at her, they both felt a strange awkwardness. Looking away, Jasmine became aware for the first time of the house. Luke's house. Built in Firefly Clearing. Everything in it – the sofas and armchairs, the soft rugs on the polished floors, the Asian and African art and pictures, books and journals scattered everywhere – everything seemed charged with an intense intimacy. These were his things. She had come inside his most personal space.

"Why don't you take a shower?" Luke said. "I'll – um – I'll get dinner together."

He gave her a fresh towel and his robe. They did not look at each other.

In the bathroom, she stood for a while, studying his simple array of soap, aftershave – Dunhill – and toiletries. After the steaming shower, she wrapped herself in his robe. It smelt intoxicatingly of him.

While Luke showered and shaved, she sat on the rug by the fire, drying her hair with the towel. The noodles steamed in the wok. He had opened a bottle of Californian Chardonnay.

He came through in a *sarong*, his chest bare. In spite of their exhaustion, they seemed to draw energy from the warmth of the evening. As they served up and brought their plates and glasses through to the low table by the fire, they did not speak. They watched each other shyly.

They sat close but not touching on the rug by the fire.

"This is delicious," Jasmine sighed, waving her chopsticks. Luke's robe was enormous on her. Her shoulder nudged upwards, soft as cream. As she spoke, her throat played in shadow and light. He was entranced.

She caught his gaze at last. Her slow smile flushed across her face. The firelight seemed to forge his torso in shapes of gold and granite. His smile laid before her his desire.

In the moment that he reached out to her, she drew towards him. Chopsticks and wine spun to the floor.

*   *   *

The next morning, Jasmine did not wake till midday. A mist had settled over the hills. Wisps of its trailing cloak curled in over the verandah and crept through the windows. Luke was already up. He had lit the fire at the foot of the bed. The aroma of fresh coffee wafted through. She heard the ping of the microwave in the kitchen.

Luke came through with a breakfast tray, his bathrobe carelessly slung on. He had shaved and apart from the dark colour in his hair, looked as she had always seen him in her memories. As he set the tray down on the bed, she reached up to touch his smooth jawline, inhaling the spicy smell of Dunhill. "That's better." She smiled, caressing his face with her lips.

He laughed. "And good morning to you, too." As he pulled her into his embrace, they almost upset the tray of coffee and hot buns.

"Look out!"

"Whoa!" Luke steadied the tray. He poured hot coffee and distributed the crusty chicken buns. Jasmine rolled her eyes with pleasure as the taste of the meat melted into her mouth.

Luke grinned. "Your mother insists on stocking my freezer every few months."

He walked over to the windows and unbolted the lower half-doors leading out to the verandah. Under the covers, they sprawled on the bed, munching their breakfast and looking out at the mist while the fire crackled and roared. Jasmine remembered the promise she had made to herself as a girl to come back to Firefly Clearing once a year no matter where she was.

"We're invisible up here," she said. "Like a magic mantle is cloaking us. No one can find us. Nothing can touch us."

But she should call her office. She should call Jordan. She should consider the legal implications of the landslide. This was a critical time for her client. A crucial moment for her career. She should consider the legal implications of her being here with Luke.

Jasmine looked out at the shimmering cloud that encased them on these hills. There was nothing beyond, nothing behind. She let its tendrils, creeping up onto the verandah, roll in towards her. It was so easy, just for this long moment, to let it obscure everything but the present. So easy to believe in its magic.

Luke was watching her and, as she turned to him, she saw on his face the accumulation of all that lay between them. Her anger, his furious idealism, her ambition and ultimately, her betrayal of their love.

"Everything that's come between us –" she began, her voice a whisper. Luke reached out a hand to her lips. He shook his head.

"I'm sorry, Luke."

"Ssh." He drew her towards him, cloaking her in his embrace.

"Let's believe in the magic."

There was so much Jasmine wanted to say but the mist seemed to steal away words, dispersing them into its formless whole. She reached up to Luke's face with both hands, drinking in their kiss. She slipped his robe from him, flowing her hands over the muscles on his back, burrowing in the down of his arms and chest. They fell together in the tangled sheets, her black hair tumbling into his face, her dark eyes melting into the light of his. They made love with soft intensity, at once teasing and alert with quiet passion.

In the diffuse light of the afternoon, their bodies brushed luminous as phosphorous on the sea, then golden with the flames of the firelight. Shadows wove among them, binding his strength to her gentle breath, her steadfast power to his suppleness. It seemed as if they had always been here in this place, entwined within each other, she the *yin* within him, he the *yang* of her spirit, the coming together of sunset and the rising dawn, here in this place of their childhood and their ancient souls. For the first time in her life, Jasmine felt the wholeness of coming home, a completeness of heart and spirit without words or thought.

*   *   *

Jordan slammed his fist onto the desk.

"Fuck the Environmental Safety Commission!" he barked at his secretary. "Tell them I'm not making any statements until my lawyers get here. And I'm not answering any questions until the formal inquiry."

"Yes, sir." Miss Yip retreated backwards out of the room, her Chinese features sallow with fright.

"And fuck the reporters, fuck the police and fuck the Consortium! You got that?"

Miss Yip nodded, unable to speak, and hastily shut herself out of Jordan's office.

Jordan turned back scowling to Kidd, who sat in one of the armchairs on the far side of the office suite. A telephone on the desk rang for the tenth time that hour.

Jordan swept his arm across the desk. The bank of telephones and intercoms crashed to the floor.

Jordan pulled himself straight with satisfaction. "Now we've got some bloody peace." He strode over to Kidd but he did not sit down. He paced.

Jordan's Kuala Lumpur offices were small but power-dressed in marble and steel, the corporate logo splashed like a designer label on the walls. They represented Jordan Cardale PLC in Asia, an upstart with big ambitions. Jordan had come straight from the airport eighteen hours ago and had not left. His eyes were red and dry from his long flight from Bonn where he had first heard news of the landslide.

For the last forty-eight hours, the Kuala Lumpur office had been like an outpost under siege. Jordan's staff fielded the rapid fire of phones and faxes and clamouring reporters at the door. Nerves were raw. Stress and tension crackled through the air-conditioned rooms. Beyond the oak doors of Jordan's suite, the muffled sound of battle still raged.

Since his arrival, Jordan had spent long hours marshalling his key troops – Danesleigh on a mobile out in the field, Nick Roberts in London, and Scott, the architect. But he still could not reach Tan. Or Zain. Or Jasmine. His mind raced with alternative scenarios and strategies, panic and fury jostling at his concentration. He had not slept for two days now. Stubble traced the hollows of his cheeks. Nick Roberts would be arriving from London within the hour. David Scott was flying in from Manila where he had been showing his preliminary hotel designs to Jordan's new Australian client. Danesleigh had flown back to town with Dickson Loh in the Consortium's helicopter and was now working hard at damage limitation with Loh and other Consortium players.

"Loh is threatening a law suit!" Jordan cried. "Christ! He's in with us on a bloody joint venture and he wants to sue!" He wheeled round and paced back towards Kidd. His head was pounding. He couldn't think straight. He snapped, "Jasmine. Where the fuck is she? What did you find?"

Kidd looked at his notebook. "She came down in the first convoy. Then, we don't know. I've got Pang checking out her mother's house."

Jordan swore. He had met with his lawyers from the local firm of Seng & Mustafa the night before. Without his London team, they were useless old women. He didn't need to be told what he couldn't do, he paid his lawyers to find solutions – no matter what. No fucking balls, the lot of them. Now Jasmine. He hadn't wanted to peg her for a deserter. But perhaps he had been right, after all, to guard his flank with Roberts.

And Tan?

Jordan barked, "Your brother?"

Kidd said, "He'll be keeping a low profile."

"You've heard from him?"

"Not yet. But I'm sure –"

"Where is he?"

"I don't know. But –"

"Goddammit! He was right there on international television! Working on the bloody consultant's team! Now he's disappeared. What the fuck is he playing at? What the hell was he doing up there at the ceremony?"

Kidd said, with a confidence he did not feel, "He was keeping tabs on the consultant and the Lian woman. It was a calculated risk that he would not be recognised. That still holds. It was a flash of his face, behind the consultant's shoulder. A blur. Unrecognisable."

"*I* recognised him."

"Look, we've worked with you on many projects. Give us credit, man, we know our job. Ronnie's gone underground till all this dies down. He'll resurface in a few days with information you can work with. That's doing the job right. Don't lose your head over it." Kidd returned Jordan's glare with a steady gaze.

Jordan blew out a breath. "I want to speak to him as soon as you hear from him."

"First thing he'll do, man."

Jordan sat down. He massaged his temples. It could all unravel. He had come so close to success. But he had relied on too many people to get him there. Tan, the other "contractors". Would they stand up to the pressure of the investigations to come? There would be the Environmental Safety Commission inquiry; the law suits – questioning and cross-questioning in trials brought by the Consortium and those seeking compensation; the criminal investigation – police crawling over everything and everyone. Jordan's reputation and hard work shot to hell. But he couldn't let them take it all away now. Not after those long, hard years. He had to stop them. He had to salvage what he could. Turn the battle around. Snatch victory, somehow. He said, "What's the security status on our contractors?"

Kidd ticked them off on his fingers. "First off, Zain. Kuantan Hospital, multiple injuries. One of our London contacts is getting 'friendly' with his son, to be with him 'in his family's time of need'. Mrs Zain is very grateful for this kindness. Zain will remember who he owes everything to."

"Excellent."

"Scott, the architect. He has as much to lose as anyone. He knows the score. He's secure. But I'm meeting his planc for a little chat just to be sure."

"Good."

"Nick Roberts. He's up to his neck. His gambling debts are now huge."

"Three hundred and forty five thousand pounds, to be exact. Plus interest at three per cent a day. But I'm giving him a period of grace. So long as he can pay me back in kind, our loan arrangement will work."

"He knows what will happen if he doesn't. He'll toe the line."

"Exactly."

"Tsui, the geophysicist who faked the sub-stratum data report. That Seattle contract we fixed him up with is big money. Since my people's visit to him, his arm's healing – slowly and painfully. He won't forget who owns him. He'll keep his head down, gobble from his golden rice bowl and do what we tell him."

Jordan laughed. This was what he wanted to hear. The battle might yet be won.

"Wong and his Kampung Tanah cronies," Kidd went on. "All dead. Or, at least, still missing. From what we could find out, they were in the community hall when the slide hit. No one could've survived the impact."

Jordan's laughter pitched wilder. 'A hundred percent secure, then."

"Looks like it. We'll know for sure when they get down to the bodies."

"If they can move a mountain." Jordan grinned savagely. 'And then if any of them can be recognised."

Kidd stared at him.

"Excellent, excellent." Jordan was enjoying the image in his mind. "What are you going to do about the consultant?" Kidd asked.

Jordan's laughter stopped. When he looked up, his eyes were hard. Kidd continued, "There's talk that the Kampung Tanah people are going to rehire him to work on their compensation claim against you. Some Western news teams are making a story out of the arson and missing report – they're speculating about what could've been in it, concocting conspiracy theories."

Jordan snorted. He'd seen the satellite and cable newscasts. There was a pile of faxed headlines on his desk from journalists worldwide, trying to provoke a reaction from him.

"We've got information that the prosecutor's office are going to ask McAllister to prepare a duplicate report for the formal investigations – and get him all the access he needs."

"What the fuck –"Jordan shot to his feet. He began to pace again. "They can't do that. What the hell was he doing up there in disguise? Trying to access the secure site under a false identity?"

"We've got records of that – statements from the guards, CCTV pictures. We could push the sabotage theory –"

"What evidence do we have of that?"

"We could rig something."

Jordan shook his head. "Too difficult. Too many people on the site – police, rescue workers. Too little time to do it properly. Then there's the problem of linking him direct to the hardware. All we can do is smear him with the suspicion. That won't be enough."

Kidd's eyes followed his client's tense circling. "His report was damaging to you before construction so we got rid of it for you. It wasn't my job to know what was in it but I'd guess that he predicted what's just happened. Am I right?"

Jordan stopped and glared at him. Kidd went on, "I'll take that as a 'yes'. Well, after the fact, I'd say that if his report were produced right now, he might as well be handing your head to the police on a plate."

Jordan spun round and tipped the coffee table into the air with one swoop. "Goddamn fucking hell!"

The table crashed down. Magazines, ashtray and lamp clattered over the floor. Kidd said smoothly, "If they pin this slide on you –"

"*What?*" Jordan shouted.

"Thousands dead because you put up an unsafe building. Which you knew was unsafe – didn't you?"

Jordan was breathing hard, but he did not speak.

Kidd's voice was matter-of-fact. "We have the death penalty in this country."

*　　*　　*

Kidd renegotiated the Tans' fees for the special services they did for Jordan. Through their network of "cousins" and "good friends", the Tans still secured Jordan's business interests across Asia.

"Double the previous fees per item. Paid in advance."

Jordan swore.

Kidd said, "Take it or leave it."

Jordan seemed leaner suddenly. His body was taut as if a tensile stress held him rigid. He had never thought beyond winning the game. By any means available. Bill Jordan never loses. It was his mission statement. He had never thought that his life would be a stake in the game. And now the full horror of what had happened sank in.

He had gambled and lost. He no longer controlled his hand. His life had become a chip that others could barter with. It wasn't about winning anymore. It was about staying one step ahead – and alive.

He looked at Kidd with the stare of a cornered tiger. Against his instinct to win every confrontation, he nodded. He needed to keep his allies close to him now, more than ever before.

For four times the usual fee, paid in advance, they agreed what had to be done with Luke. Kidd would handle it himself

Kidd smiled and shook Jordan's hand. "Thank you for your custom."

As he opened the door of the suite, Kidd turned and within earshot of Jordan's legitimate staff, gave them the public face of Tan Securities Limited. He said, "It'll be done, Mr Jordan. And we'll put extra security guards on the site as well."

* * *

"The bitch is leaving me!" Harry cried. He stood before Jordan's desk like a supplicant to an oracle. "I don't know what to do any more. I want her back. Help me."

He had driven to Jordan's from the outpatient's unit at Ranjing hospital. A blotch of plaster held together his broken nose, giving his voice a petulant whine. Purple swellings spread across his cheek and left eye. Under his stained shirt, a corset of bandage strapped in two fractured ribs. A jab of pain triggered another tirade. "Oofff-fuck! I'll kill her. This whole year I've goddamn tried so hard and she's just been laughing. I should've strapped her till she bled, bloody bitch."

Jordan cradled a phone between shoulder and ear, talking aggressively into the mouthpiece. He was hardly listening to Harry. The idiot's domestic problems were the least of his concerns. Jordan broke off and barked at Harry, "So where the hell is she?"

"I don't know. She went off. After *she* told *me* it was over – she has the damn gall to tell me it's over."

Jordan was saying into the phone, "As I've already made clear, all health and safety procedures were implemented, no, that is all I have to say." To Harry, "Where did she go?" Back to the phone, "No, you listen ..."

"She went with him, fuck knows where. I've got to find her, help me, Bill. I don't know who else I can turn to in this shit-hole of a country."

"She went with who?" Into the phone, "Our safety record has been impeccable ..."

"The consultant, she's bloody having an affair with him, I saw how they were together. He attacked me when I tried to stop them. I'll kill him!"

Harry had Jordan's attention for the first time that evening. The phone came away from his ear. He said, "McAllister?"

"Yah, goddamn bastard."

Jordan hung up the phone and took it off the hook. He stood up and began to pace. Harry trailed his eyes after him, his pleas pitching faster.

Jordan spun round. "Fucking shut up!"

Harry froze. Jordan turned and paced and turned again, glaring at the floor. "McAllister, hmm?"

Harry watched tensely but hope calmed him. Jordan had taken charge. He would know how to make it right. Jordan had command of every situation. He was ruthless and without fear. Harry respected that in a man. Admired it in a friend.

Jordan looked up at him and grinned. "Harry, old mate, you're a good bloke."

Harry looked uncertain. Jordan came up and clapped his arm round Harry's shoulder. "Don't worry about a thing, mate, I've got it all in hand."

"Jasmine?"

"I'll get her home to you." Jordan tightened his grip across

Harry's shoulders. His voice was a snarl. "You're a good friend to me, Harry, and your pain is my pain. She is – was – my best lawyer, right at the heart of my business. Fuck, the bitch screwed us both over! You've done good, mate. I'll find her. I need to know what's the deal between her and the consultant. Now, you go on home. Take good care of yourself. I'll take care of everything else. I'll find her and I'll get the truth out of her. And then the bitch will pay."

"What about the consultant?" '

'You'll see justice done."

Harry's long look was a question.

Jordan said nothing, his face cryptically confident.

26

Kidd slipped into one of the many alleyways in the run-down part of Klang, the port town an hour's drive west of Kuala Lumpur. It was almost eleven p.m. A straggly cat screeched and ran from underfoot. The path was rutted and littered with decaying rubbish. He unlocked a ramshackle door and disappeared inside. The converted store-room was behind a brothel. Music and jabbering voices hammered constantly. A low-wattage light glowed on a wall. The stench of incense from a makeshift shrine by the door made him gag.

In the cramped space beneath the corrugated iron roof were a bed, a sink and toilet and a gas barrel for cooking. Dirty bowls, six-packs of Carlsberg, empty cans and magazines lay across the cement floor. Tan was sitting up in bed, tensely alert. Seeing his brother, he relaxed.

"This should see you through." Kidd threw a package onto the bed. It contained cash, a change of clothes, makeup and new identity papers.

Tan examined his new persona. "Rashid Mokhtar, import-export. Goatee beard, glasses. Malay – tanning cream colour factor six."

He had made it down the hill after running from Luke. It had taken him ten hours of stumbling over rough ground and painstakingly following the unmade road. Outside Ranjing, he had hitched a lift with a lorry and after several interchanges by bus and taxi and another lift, he had arrived at their safe-house here, one of many scattered across the region of their operations.

Kidd said, "Jordan's getting spooked. You're going to have to reassure him soon, *Tai Koh*."

"Not yet," Tan said, too quickly. Then, more calmly, "It's not safe."

"Elder Brother, when?"

"Tell me about your meeting."

Kidd assessed Tan for a beat. Then he recounted what had happened with Jordan and his renegotiation of their payment. He popped a beer can and took a slug, pleased with himself "Cool or what, *Tai Koh*?"

Tan seized him by the lapels. The can clanked to the floor, fizzing. "No more killing! It must stop now!"

Kidd swiped his brother's hands off him. A push sent Tan onto the bed. Kidd pulled back suddenly, fraternal respect an old habit still. Breathing hard, he said, "It's part of the same contract, man, the doctor and the consultant. Jordan was too stupid to see that first time round. Now we make on his loss."

"No!" It was a strangled cry. Tan buried his head in his hands.

"I'm in charge now," Kidd snarled. "You're my *Tai Koh* and I still respect you. But you can't handle things any more. I'm running the business now. For all of us. For the family."

Tan looked up. "How's my boy? What did the doctor say?"

The first night at the safe-house, Kidd had brought news that Tan's younger son had fallen ill with fever. Tan had been distraught, weeping and praying at his little shrine. Kidd now said, "It's only measles. He must've picked it up at school. He'll be fine."

Tan grabbed Kidd's arm, his eyes unfocused. "You don't know. The spirits want justice. I took a life. Thousands are dead now. Justice is coming to me. To us all."

"Stop with this fucking bullshit!"

Tan tightened his hold. "*Ah Teh* has been coming to me."

"Father's been dead for eight years."

"He comes to me every night. Like how he used to be when we were boys. Serious, hunched a little. He's sad. 'That's not business, what you're doing, boy,' he said one time. 'I used to be proud of you. Now you're just no-good scum.'"

Kidd snorted. "The old man was a damn fool! He paid up every month to that protection gang, the White Monkey, bowed and scraped to their low-life collectors. It was you who fought back. Now they're off our turf and we play our own racket damn well."

"He was a good man!"

"Whatever. Look –"

"I wanted to make him proud. Give him everything money can buy. You know?" Tan began to sob. "I couldn't bear to see him treated like dirt. He was a good man. He deserved respect. I got it for him. We fought for it, you and me. But we're just like the filth that defiled him."

Kidd made an impatient gesture. "Bullshit! Just – just take it easy, man."

"I saw the bodies. Children mangled in the dirt. People with heads crushed. Legs and arms snapped at crazy angles. Blood, the smell of it everywhere. Because I killed a man. I might as well have killed them all. My sons, who have they hurt? They're going to die because of me ..." Tan pulled Kidd down, staring into his eyes. "Father said last night, 'Brother against brother, blood for blood.' You're so ready to kill, Kidd, is that how it will end? You'll kill me, won't you? For the business. For the family."

A growl of irritation burst from Kidd. He'd had enough. His brother had been carrying on like a woman ever since he'd got to the safe-house. Kidd scowled in disgust. He pulled free of Tan and stood up. "I'm going home. I'll be back in a few days."

At the door, he turned. Tan sat on the bed, staring into his own darkness. Kidd sneered, "There's no law of harmony or the spirits or what the fuck. The only law is the one you make for yourself."

* * *

Mrs Fung sat with Jasmine and Luke at the table away from the windows. The only light came from flickering candles set among the supper she had prepared. "Like this, no one can see inside from the road," she said.

Earlier that afternoon, as the mist had lifted from Firefly Clearing, Jasmine had called her mother. "*Ah Ma*, I have to see you. I can't leave without seeing you. We'll come after dark. That way it'll be safe."

Mrs Fung had tried to protest but her own desire to see her daughter had been too strong. "All right, when it's dark," she had said. "But you mustn't stay long."

Luke had parked his Land Rover a few roads away and he and Jasmine had walked to the house, keeping in the shadows. They had passed a man hurrying by, talking loudly into a mobile phone. They did not see him pause round the corner and double back, slipping the inactive phone into his pocket.

Mrs Fung had made Szechuan pork and broccoli stir-fried with prawns. She watched with pleasure as Luke and Jasmine ate hungrily. Jasmine could not see her face clearly in the candlelight. After she had caught up her mother in her arms, Mrs Fung had moved away, retreating into the shadows. *Ah Ma* had felt so fragile in her embrace. Jasmine wanted to touch her again, talk to her intimately. She wanted to hear from her mother how she was, see for herself how she looked. Mrs Fung refused to let them switch on the electric lights. "They may be watching us, no one must know you are here."

It was almost as if *Ah Ma* sought out the darkness. Jasmine could not get her to talk about herself, could not get close to her. Mrs Fung wanted to know everything about their experience in the landslide. She asked a stream of questions, teasing out the details, exclaiming at each turn of events. Jasmine found herself taking turns with Luke to tell the story of what had happened. Her mother insisted that they tell again and again how Luke rescued Jasmine from her fall – moment by moment, blow by blow. From the shadows beyond the candle flames Mrs Fung's voice, weak as it was, communicated her whole presence – her relief at their safe return, her horror at what they had lived through, her pity for those others who had not been so lucky. But in spite of her mother's attempts to hide it, Jasmine noticed that Mrs Fung did not eat much herself, toying with the same few morsels all evening. Beneath her chatter, Jasmine felt dread chilling her.

Luke was distracted all evening. The outside world that he and Jasmine had been trying to hold at bay was looming. His fax machine had been receiving communications ceaselessly. There were e-mail messages flashing on his computer screen, and when he had called his voicemail service, the electronic voice had alerted him to scores of messages. In the morning, he and Jasmine would both have to inhabit their professional lives again. They would have to decide then how to resolve the conflicts that awaited them beyond the night. He tried to enjoy their last moments of magic. But he could not push from his mind the disaster that had brought them together and which now lay unresolved between them.

Mrs Fung was asking, "But how can something like this have happened?"

The cicadas whirred in the silence.

Luke said, "What do you think, Jasmine?"

"There'll be an official inquiry," Jasmine began. It was easier, slipping into her rational, legal self. "Whether it was an accident, an act of God, sabotage or human error – well, that will be known at the outcome of the formal investigation."

"That's your answer as Jordan's lawyer. Now what do you really think?"

Jasmine faltered. Why did he have to bring up their lives outside – now, here, after all that happened up in his house? She said, "Until I'm no longer Jordan's lawyer, I have no personal opinion."

"Bullshit," Luke snapped in English. He was angry in spite of himself. He took a steadying breath.

"Don't let's start this again." Jasmine switched to English too, softening the command with her eyes.

Mrs Fung looked uncertainly from Luke to Jasmine.

Luke's tone was gentle when he spoke again, still in English. "You've been his lawyer for years. You worked closely with him on this project. You must have seen specifications, memos – I don't know, communications that must have indicated something was not quite right. I mean, he can't have pulled the wool over the eyes of the Planning Committee single-handedly – it's a legal procedure, lawyers would've been involved as well as the technical team. If you know your client's broken the law, how can you act for him?"

"I don't know that he's broken any law!" Jasmine didn't want the evening to go down this route. Couldn't he let it rest for just a little while longer? She stared, helpless, as Luke went on.

"Who was that man? Your 'personal assistant' – Kaw, a.k.a Ronnie Tan. Seen with Dr Chan on the night he was killed. What do you know about that?"

"Nothing! Why are you being like this?" Jasmine turned aside.

Luke grabbed her arm. "Why am I doing this? Because I love you. And I know you love me. I don't want to believe that you're mixed up in Jordan's schemes."

Mrs Fung tapped on the table. With quiet authority, she said, "Please – speak in Chinese. '*I love you. You love me.*' I understand that. What's going on? Why are you quarrelling?"

Jasmine did not know how to answer. Where would she begin? How could she tell her mother that the marriage she had been so proud of had been a sham? How could she tell her that the career they had both sacrificed so much for was now threatened by all that Luke was fighting for? In front of her mother that night, she had tried to behave as of old with Luke and, till now, she might have succeeded. She might have put off for just a while longer the reality she knew she had to face.

"Tell *Ah Ma*." Her mother's hands on Jasmine's were cool and dry.

For the first time that night, Jasmine saw her mother's face in the candlelight. She looked old, very old. Her skin was like frail tissues lingering over her sunken features. But her eyes were still bright and clear. It was only a moment and then she drew back into the shadows.

The dread twisted Jasmine's stomach tighter. Her mother was seriously ill. Jasmine was afraid to deepen the pain she had seen on her face. But the crack in her endurance had begun to widen. She could not contain the lies and secrets any more. For so long now, she had had no one to share her true self with, no one she dared to trust. Now, being with Luke, both of them here with her mother, Jasmine felt a yearning to be free at last. She held tight to her mother's hand. In Chinese, Jasmine said, "I'm leaving my husband."

A painful breath from the dark. Then, as if Mrs Fung had always known, "He has not been a good husband to you."

Jasmine shook her head miserably.

"He doesn't love you."

"I thought he did, once. But no, not any more."

"You don't love him."

"No."

"Tell *Ah Ma*."

In a quiet voice, Jasmine told her mother about Harry, about the violence, the abuse and threats, the adulteries. Her mother's old advice echoed in it all: "Make your husband love you more than you love him." Harry's jealous love of her had proved that, hadn't it? So why had it all gone so wrong?

Jasmine felt her mother trembling. "My poor little one ..." Mrs Fung's voice was cracked with tears. "I thought you had escaped ... but the past tortures us still."

"*Ah Ma*."

"You love Luke?"

Jasmine nodded, emotion suddenly choking her.

"Yes." Mrs Fung spoke with sorrow and tenderness. "I have always known. Ever since you were children. But I sent you away. I wanted you to escape. You're a good girl. For me, you made Luke hate you that day you said those terrible things to him. I know the sacrifice you made because you loved me. I was happy when you married the English boy. I thought maybe you will find happiness and success, just like we dreamed for you, and it will make up for what you gave up. But in your letters, I knew something was wrong. You were too happy, it was too perfect, you kept telling me how wonderful your life with him was. I wanted it as much as you. And then I saw how you were the last time you were here. I wanted you to save your marriage because I was frightened ... of what might happen if you did not go back to your husband. But you have found Luke again. You will love whom you love and the past will always try to drag us back."

Tears of anger and confusion burned behind Jasmine's eyes. "Why do you always speak about the past like this? Why?"

Mrs Fung said to Luke, "You've always loved my Jasmine."

"Always. And with all my heart."

Jasmine had been honest for the first time about her marriage but she felt no relief. It might have been a release in other circumstances, but she stared at her mother's dark shape in tumult. Her mother had known the strength of the feelings Jasmine and Luke had felt for each other all those years ago. And she had forced them apart. Fed Jasmine with her own ambition. Wished her into a life lived on another's dream. Her mother had driven her away. The ghoul shrieked its accusations still between them both. *Ah Ma* had always blamed her for what had happened with her father, just as Jasmine had feared. Jasmine felt as if she'd been trying all her life to make right the past by doing whatever her mother wanted of her and it would never be enough. Her mother still yoked her to the shame, dragging her back in spite of anything she might do. Jasmine felt the room shift strangely. Perhaps she would never atone, perhaps her mother had never wanted her to at all. What if Jasmine suffered the burden of the past as her mother was doing, all her life punished for one final hideous confrontation with her father as *Ah Ma* lived each day under *her* father's curse? Mrs Fung had guessed at Jasmine's unhappiness in the marriage, and yet she had sent her back to her husband as if her life depended on it. Was this love or punishment? Jasmine felt as if she could not breathe. Mrs Fung had loved them both, Jasmine and Luke. But she had shared only with Luke the ten years past that she had withheld from Jasmine – keeping her daughter away with a command she had made sacred from the start, all that time as silent to Jasmine as the dead.

Jasmine had believed in her mother's myth of transformation and escape. It was transcendence and redemption and paradise that could be gained here in this life. It had been the only faith she had had. And now ... She faced the truth she had always known. The trappings of wealth and status and independence had been nothing but baubles. Baubles crumbling to dust. She felt duped. Betrayed. As if she had been manipulated all her life to crush the only truths that had had any meaning – who she really was, and her love for Luke.

She did not know how to go on, caught in the crossfire of her inner conflict.

Luke turned to her, "What are you going to do?"

"Do?" She groped for sense. "I don't know. Go back to London. Organise my things. Divorce."

"Will you have somewhere to stay? Somewhere safe?"

"To stay?" Jasmine rested her head in her hands. "What? I don't know." All her friends were Harry's friends. That had been the way he had wanted it. She had dropped her own friends to make him happy. To make a success of their relationship. Now, who could she turn to?

"There's Sam," she said, almost to herself. "I know her from law school. We've lost touch but maybe ..."

"You'll stay with her, then."

Jasmine nodded vaguely. She was tired. She didn't want to think any more. All this talk was like crushed glass in the pit of her stomach. Her mother – sacrificing, betraying, loving, manipulating – hiding her frailty and illness in the shadows. Luke, expecting so much of her with his love, so certain of everything, so committed to his principles. The past. The truth. Honesty. Integrity. All the fragments grinding, shattering against each other.

Leaning into the candlelight, Luke said to Jasmine, "What are you going to do about Jordan?"

"Jordan?" She was confused. But irritation cleared her head. "I'll do my job."

"Doesn't anything that's happened in the last three days mean anything to you?" Luke could not stop himself. Once started, the words hit out at her. "All the things you've seen – all those people dead. What we've both been through. What we have now, you and me. Stop kidding yourself! How can you protect Jordan's interests now?"

"This is not the time –"

"This is *exactly* the time. This is real. For a moment, last night, this morning, we pretended that it was just you and me. Like it used to be. No issues, no history, no conflict. But it's real now. You love me –"

"Isn't that enough? I'm leaving Harry. I'm yours. That's what you want, isn't it?"

Luke tried to take her hand. She pulled it away. He wasn't getting through to her. He tried a new angle. "Look, I know you can't be directly involved in Jordan's schemes. I know you. I'm not asking you to give up your career. All I'm trying to say is, you're right there, he trusts you, you can find out the truth. You can get access to the project papers and plans, private memos, confidential information – anything that could lead us to the truth. About the tower collapse. Dr Chan's death. The planning review process."

"That's what you really want! Isn't it?" Jasmine felt her head spinning. "All this 'I love you, you love me' – like it's some magic charm you keep chanting – but it's all bullshit, isn't it?"

"What?"

Jasmine stood up, knocking over her chair. "Love! You! *Ah Ma*! Both of you throwing that word at me all the time. 'You're my daughter, I love you more than my own life' – do you, *Ah Ma*? And Luke – 'I love you, you love me.' What you want is what I know about Jordan! The oldest damn trick in the book and I fell for it!"

"Jasmine!" Mrs Fung stared in shocked incomprehension.

Jasmine rounded on her. The girl who had been stifled to silence in all the intervening years had found her voice. It was as if the tumult of the last few days had cracked the defences that had once walled her in. Raw emotion exposed for the first time screamed in rage and pleading. All her loneliness and fear, all her bitterness and pent-up fury erupted in words she had never dared to face. "You wanted me to 'escape'. You wanted me to live out your fantasy of success. What about what *I* wanted? Did you ever think about that? Maybe that's why *Ah Ba* hated you. Why Father beat you. He was never good enough for you, was he? Poor Tommy Fung – how could he live up to the expectations of a rich Lian? Is that why he left us and never came back?"

A moan shuddered from Mrs Fung. She tried to stand but fell back into her chair.

"Jasmine!" Luke slammed to his feet.

They faced each other across the table, hunched like ancient combatants. She would not be stopped. She said, "You! Personal and business – it's all the same to you. The funny thing is, I think you really do love me. But you're so caught up in your principles, you don't know whether it's *me* you love or what I can do for your cause!"

"That's not what I –"

"I'm not listening to you any more. Go back to loving rainforests and clean air and the ozone layer! It suits you better. They need your crusading fire and brimstone. I don't!"

Her words deflated Luke's anger. She was right. He had handled it all wrong, entangled between his driving objective and his feelings for her. The echo of his bulldozing words shamed him. He did not know what to say, how to piece together the trust he had shattered.

Jasmine pivoted between the two of them, Luke and her mother. "I can't do this anymore! *Ah Ma* telling me who I should be, what I should want. You telling me what I should do, what I should believe in. I don't know myself any more. We can't go back, Luke. We were fools to try. Life's taken us where it's taken us. This is what I am now. You are who you are. We can't change things. It's too late."

"No, don't – I'm sorry. I didn't mean … " Luke tried to reach out but she withdrew. "You're right. I was blind, talking like that. I know how it must've sounded. But that's not the truth. I love you.

You. I know we can work it out."

Jasmine shook her head. "Please. Just go. Before we say anything else we regret."

She turned away and masked her face with her hand. Tears burned into her cheeks. Luke and Mrs Fung drew close and spoke in quiet tones. The old woman said shakily, "It's all right. Go. Don't be anxious."

Luke said to Jasmine, "You know where I'll be."

She did not move. He turned away and slipped out into the night.

Outside, in a black Mercedes parked by the side of the road, the man who had passed Jasmine and Luke sat low in the driver's seat. It was Pang. He had reported his sighting to Kidd Tan over the cellphone network. He waited patiently now, having located Jasmine for their client.

As the Land Rover left Mrs Fung's house, Pang called Kidd to report that the consultant had left on his own. He listened as Kidd relayed new instructions from their client.

"Any trouble, let her speak to Nick Roberts" – and gave him the contact number.

* * *

Later, when Mrs Fung had made Jasmine go to bed, a truce of politeness between them, the old woman sat for a while on the verandah. She stared at the shape of the flame tree against the velvet sky. The violent pain she had tried to contain all evening washed over her. Its physicality pleased her strangely. It distracted her from the pain of her guilt.

When Jasmine had spoken of her failed marriage and her love for Luke, Mrs Fung had felt the terror of disaster. Everything she had done and sacrificed, everything she had made her daughter give up, it would have been for nothing. She had thought her daughter was safe. But Jasmine would return here for love, and the past would never let her leave again. The secret she had been hiding from her daughter would find a way of destroying them all.

Jasmine's bitter recriminations gouged into her. She wished she could tell her daughter the truth. But she had sworn that she would never burden Jasmine with that hideous knowledge.

So, perhaps her daughter would leave her now in anger. Unforgiving, purifying anger. And Jasmine would be free at last. From the past. And the secret. Free at last from her mother.

27

It was still dark when Jasmine slipped out of the house. She wore the cotton shirt and jeans Luke had lent her the day before, an old belt tightened round her waist. She had left a note for her mother. "I'm going back to KL. I have work to do. Please tell Luke I don't want to hear from him."

She strode down the path and into the road. The train station was about an hour's walk away. A deep silence lay across the neighbourhood.

Turning a corner, dazzling brightness pinned her against the darkness. Jasmine froze, shielding her eyes.

Headlights.

"Miss Lian." A man's voice.

"Who – ?"

The figure of a man came out of the blackness, streams of light pouring behind him. "Don't be afraid."

"What do you want?" Jasmine backed away, heart pounding.

"Mr Roberts wanted me to pick you up."

"Roberts? How did you find me?" She could not see his face. Suddenly he grabbed her arm. "Please come with me."

"Let me go!"

"Mr Roberts wanted me to take you to the airport."

Jasmine struggled against his grip

"Please come."

"No!"

He hit her across the face. "Don't scream." Pulled her against him, choking off her breath. With his free hand, he made a call on his mobile and then placed it to Jasmine's ear.

Nick Roberts's strained voice crackled at her. Jasmine stopped struggling in astonishment.

"Go with this man," Roberts said. "You'll be safe."

The man gave Jasmine the phone, letting her go. She moved away from him, eyes never leaving him. She said, "Nick, what the hell's all this about? Who's this thug? He hit me, dammit!"

"His name is Pang. He's one of Jordan's security people."

"He hit me!"

"Jordan sent him to pick you up."

"Did Roberts send him to slap me around too? I'm not going anywhere with this thug!"

"You'll do what Jordan wants." Roberts paused and tried to soften his tone. "Look, Jordan wouldn't authorise a security operative to hit you. I'll tell Jordan and I'm sure he'll deal with his man accordingly."

Jasmine said nothing.

Roberts went on, his voice quiet but firm, "Go with Pang. It'll be all right. At the airport a ticket to London will be waiting for you. Your passport and things from the hotel will also be there. Get on the plane. Go home."

"What?" Jasmine couldn't believe what she'd just heard. "What the hell is going on?"

"I'm acting on Jordan's instructions. He doesn't want you working on this. After your terrible experiences up on the hills, you need a rest. You're too emotionally involved."

"Cut the bullshit!" Jasmine was trembling but outrage spoke for her. "What's really going on? How did you find me?"

"You're screwing the enemy. We can't trust you – conflict of interest and all that." Roberts sighed. "Look, he wanted you brought to him. He wanted a confrontation. But I talked him out of it – I told him you hadn't sold him out to the consultant. You're not that kind of a girl, I know you. Whatever our differences, I don't want you getting caught up in this fucking mess. You don't know Jordan like I do. Shit, I shouldn't be telling you all this but … hell, I haven't slept in days. You're a nice girl, you don't fit with Jordan's way of doing things. Look, you don't want to mess around with Jordan, you know what I'm saying? Just get the hell out of here. He's letting you go easily. So go, d'you understand me?"

* * *

In the back of the Mercedes, Jasmine was separated from the man by a thick sheet of glass. It and the two passenger doors were locked. The man did not speak.

It was almost four hours to Subang Airport. On the long drive, Jasmine had time to think. Roberts had sounded nervous. He was warning her off Jordan. His cryptic words made Jordan out to be an underworld gangster. Her mind reeled. The Jordan she knew was a driven, ambitious bastard, but a gangster? Jasmine stared at the driver. The man's blow still throbbed. She looked at his solid neck and shoulders. Had he been merely overzealous in carrying out his duties or was violence his regular work? Roberts had reassured her earlier in the conversation that Jordan wouldn't have authorised him to hit her. Then Roberts had tried to hint at a more sinister side to Jordan. Which was the truth? She suddenly thought of Jordan's other 'man' – Kaw. Had he really been a personal assistant? Or had he been hired for more sinister duties? She remembered Kaw's discreet but unshakeable presence. Bodyguard or prison warden?

She tried to shake these thoughts. Luke's talk of murder and conspiracy, she *would* see sinister motives everywhere. But why not just leave a message dismissing her at her hotel? Why not wait till she got back to the office? Why the urgent interception? Was there something at the office she was being intercepted from? Or was Roberts on an agenda of his own, trying to get her off his lucrative patch once and for all? *You're a nice girl.* His patronising words riled her.

In the hard reality of the business world, Jasmine knew how to play and win corporate showdowns. The framework of the law and the sportsman's rules of ethics governed her professional life. But this "abduction" had burst into her world out of another reality – of violence and threats and underworld gangs. A cold sweat prickled her skin. Perhaps Luke had been right, after all. And she a fool all along. But, no, it was too unreal. She came back to what she knew for herself. She had worked with Jordan for many years. She knew him. Yes, he was a street kid who had fought his way to the top. But she could not believe that he would resort to gangster-type tactics. In all her career, she had never seen any evidence of it.

Jordan was panicking. That was all. This was just a clumsy attempt at damage control executed by a messenger who had been over-zealous. Everything Jordan had worked for was on the brink of disaster, Jasmine told herself. He had needed her and she had disappeared for two days. *Screwing the enemy.* No wonder Jordan was panicking. He had probably wanted to see her to get her side of the story or to bawl her out. What more would he do to her? She was surely no real threat to him in spite of her friendship with Luke. Roberts had to be trying to keep her out of the picture. That was the only scenario that made any sense to her. She was probably reading too much into what he'd said – he could've been warning her against Jordan's aggressive confrontations. *Nice girl.* Jasmine bristled still. She'd handled Jordan in such dog-fights in the past, she'd handle him again. She didn't need Roberts to protect her from her own client. Or was Roberts just scaring her so that she'd keep her distance from Roberts's prime client? Meanwhile Roberts would be reinforcing his own position with Jordan with some other cock-and-bull story damaging *her* reputation. He already had! The realisation hit her. He had got Jordan to give her face with the excuse of her "traumatic experiences". And thus he was colouring anything damaging she might publicly say in the future.

She had to talk to Roberts. Face him down and fight it out. Clear her reputation. Damn Roberts! She'd have to explain it direct to Jordan. She had turned away from Luke in the best interests of her client. To avoid a conflict of interest. She had sacrificed personal for business. Jordan had to trust her. In the confusions of all that had happened, only one thing was certain. Above all else, she was a lawyer. She clung to it with a desperate energy. Her marriage was a sham. Luke's "love" an illusion. The thought of him made her feel ill. She felt an agitation of despair and hurt. His touch and voice and smell came back to her. She had let herself love him. She had believed him when he had said he loved her. For a while, she had let the magic fool her. But she had been right to fight him off all this time. He had been using her all along. She felt the pain like a physical blow. She did not want to believe that he could do such a thing. But she could not deny what she had heard from his lips and how he had entangled love and business. The confusion of the landslide had made her turn to him – for comfort, for love. She realised how, in all their years apart and in all the anguish of her time with Harry, an unacknowledged hope of Luke's love had been her secret balm. And now there was only betrayal. It broke her heart.

All she had clung to for so long had been a false image. He had played on her feelings for him, stoked them up only to destroy everything to get what he wanted for his cause. The future lay before her like a void. Without Luke, there was nothing. A sob wrenched her. She fought to hold it down, break it apart. If Luke had always been a false image of hope in her heart, then she had always been without him. She had always had nothing and it was only now that she realised it. Jasmine held on to this thread that her cold reasoning had thrown her. She had come this far with nothing. Without Luke. She could go on alone and still make a success of her life. She fought the grief threatening to overwhelm her. She had to be practical. The future lay before her but it was not a frightening emptiness. She had her career. It was up to her to make it what she had always wanted. Harry had tried to stop her. Luke had tried to destroy it. She had battled them both and she had emerged free and alone. Her life was her own now. Her career was all she had left.

Only her work, Carruthers and her life there, only those things remained unconfused and steadfast. They had seen her through the pain of her marriage and the long years away from home and her mother. With a desperate effort, Jasmine pulled about her the fortress that had always served her so well: her passion for her work. For her, the law was unrelentingly logical, enduring as the ancient offices of her firm. She belonged at Carruthers and to an ageless tradition of reason and objectivity. The firm had embraced her, made her one of their own. They asked no questions about her past, had no interest in whom she loved or hated. So long as she did her job well, she was in for life. She was not going to let Roberts push her out. She would give him the confrontation of his weasely career. And she would win, her driven ambition would make sure of that. She would survive all that had happened, she knew it with a new certainty, and she would face whatever was to come with an energy that could not be defeated. Her work was everything, and she was not going to give it up without a fight.

*　　*　　*

Her captor helped Jasmine out of the Mercedes, his grip on her elbow unyielding. Subang Airport, just after nine in the morning. Beneath the high Moorish styled roof, taxis unloaded passengers and luggage. Porters trundled by with snakes of trolleys. An over-toasted Western tour group in batik struggled with tangles of souvenirs amid an Indian family seeing off one of their sons.

The man steered Jasmine towards the doors of the terminal building. A Japanese party pushed at them, trying to keep up with their guide. Jasmine stumbled, forcing her captor into a stern-faced woman.

The woman pushed back. Jabbered angrily in Japanese. With all her strength, Jasmine swung the bunched fingers of her free hand into the man's eye.

A yell of pain. His grip on her loosened. She pulled away and began to run, screaming. Behind her, the stern-faced woman flailed at the man. He sent her sprawling and started after Jasmine, one hand to his eye, cursing. The Japanese group were yelling.

Jasmine pushed through the mass of people, stumbling over suitcases and trolleys. She screamed, "He attacked me! Help!" Airport security police sprinted towards the chase. The man shoved an old woman to the ground, sent a business man flying. As he ran, his jacket flapped open.

Someone shrieked, "He's got a gun!"

People threw themselves onto the ground. Some ran. Jasmine was lost in the chaos. She dived into a taxi, shouting at the driver, "Go! Go! He's gone crazy! He's got a gun!"

The cab squealed out of the parking bay. Jasmine fell back into the seat.

Behind them, five security police surrounded Pang, revolvers aimed at his chest. A sixth removed Pang's gun from its holster and handcuffed him.

*   *   *

"Where's Roberts?" Jasmine strode through the offices of Seng & Mustafa, ignoring the surprised looks from the staff A security guard hurried after her.

"We not expecting you, *mem*," he said.

"Good morning," – Jasmine read his name tag – "Suleiman. I'm going to the Carruthers' offices."

"Mr Roberts – he said you're ill. The shock of the landslide. Gave you mental disturbance, he said." Suleiman kept pace with her. She was a senior lawyer and a seriously ill woman.

He was reluctant to use force. "He said don't let you pass."

"I'm not ill," Jasmine said, pausing. "Thank you for your concern. Now, I have work to do. You may go back to your station."

She turned on her heel and strode through a partition door marked "Carruthers".

The young guard stared after her, uncertain what to do. Then he walked back to his post. Ripples of whispers swept through the offices.

Only a Carruthers partner senior to Jasmine could force her to leave their offices. Roberts did not have seniority.

In the small reception area, the two secretaries stared at her in amazement. The more senior, Doreen, leaped up.

"Where's Roberts?" Jasmine asked.

"In a meeting. You're not supposed to be here."

"Who else is here from London?"

"No one, *ma'am*."

"What meeting?" Doreen hesitated.

Jasmine softened her tone. "I'm not ill. There's work to be done on the Jordan landslide. I'll be in Mr Roberts's office."

"No –"

Jasmine flashed a smile. "Don't worry, you won't get into trouble. I'll take full responsibility. When is Mr Roberts due back?"

"Four, *ma'am*." Doreen looked relieved. She offered, "He's at a preliminary conference at the Environment Commission with Mr Jordan. Benson Lee is also there, and Mr Mustafa," senior partner and head of litigation.

"Thank you, Doreen. Please bring me some coffee."

The inner office had two desks and several filing cabinets. Jasmine used this room whenever she was in Kuala Lumpur on business. She sat down at her desk by the window. The other, by the wall, was cluttered with books and papers and cigarette butts. Roberts's desk. Jasmine tried to control her rapid breathing. Cold sweat made her shiver. Roberts had been serious about keeping her out of the office. Telling them all she was crazy! But he had not been serious enough. She was here.

Doreen brought a tray with coffee and biscuits. After she left, Jasmine locked the door. She paced the office in nervous agitation. The events of that morning had been too incredible. There had to be a mistake somewhere. She moved across to the mess of Roberts's desk and sat down. Luke's words nudged at her. *You can find out the truth ... access confidential information.* She pushed these thoughts away.

But if there was nothing to find, you'd find nothing, a reasoning voice said to her. You're Jordan's lawyer, this is your office. Access whatever you want.

She looked through the papers on the desk. Leafed through the flies and documents on the floor and across the tops of the filing cabinets. She went through the cabinet drawers, pulling files on Jordan's matters. Gradually, she had assessed everything relating to Jordan's projects, methodical even in her tense state.

Nothing extraordinary.

She paced again. Eleven a.m. The latest file on the Titiwangsa project lay on her desk. It was a litigation dossier, a duplicate of the one held by Seng & Mustafa. The local firm officially had the conduct of the case as the London lawyers had no right of audience in the local courts.

Jasmine drummed on Roberts's desk. She needed to talk to him. There had to be a simple explanation for the way she had been handled this morning. An innocent explanation. She tried the drawers. Pens and stationery. Legal forms. Toiletries and a necktie.

But one drawer was locked. No key in sight.

It was just a locked drawer. Nothing special about it. She shouldn't poke into Roberts's private space. But her fruitless, roving search drove her on.

After a moment's hesitation, Jasmine fished her bunch of keys from her jeans pocket. In the bundle were an original key for her own desk in this office and a spare for the desk taken over by Roberts.

She glanced at the locked office door. Listened.

No change in the general noise level outside.

She unlocked Roberts's drawer.

Inside, she found an envelope, a bulky notebook and a rank of micro-cassettes, neatly slotted into their clip-holders. The envelope contained a thousand pounds' worth of cash in the currencies of various countries – Malaysia, Hong Kong, the Philippines – and sterling travellers' cheques in Roberts's name. That was probably why the drawer had been locked. Jasmine herself kept such an envelope in her desk in London, given her frequent business trips abroad. Shame flushed her face. What had she hoped to find, sneaking into the locked drawer?

She flicked through the notebook. It seemed to be an address book – clients and business contacts she recognised, other law firms, some personal numbers. A few strange looking numbers – too long to be telephone numbers. One caught her eye: "mca – 10.95.60.63.47.18 – w".

The first seven digits recalled the client number allocated to Jordan by her firm's accounts department for billing purposes. But it was written as if it were a European telephone number, a dot separating each pair of figures. But it was too long to be a phone number even taking into account an international dialling code and country code. Curious. She put the book back.

She was about to close the drawer when something about the micro-cassettes caught her eye. It was not unusual for lawyers to keep spare cassettes for dictation in their desks. They were often used again after the letters and memos on them had been typed. In the pause that Jasmine took to stare at these neatly slotted tapes, she saw it. The recording tabs that enabled them to be recorded over had been punched out. Whatever was on the tapes was meant to be retained.

She lifted out the first cassette and clicked it into the dictating machine on the desk. She picked up the microphone, setting the switch to "MIC". Holding the handset to her ear, she could listen privately and move about the tape by flicking the controls with her thumb.

Roberts's voice spoke clearly, giving the time and date. Yesterday morning. A click. Then a conversation – tinny and fuzzy with background noise, as if recorded in a different mode from the first words. It was slightly muffled, as if the recording were made from under cloth, a jacket, perhaps. A secret recording.

The other speaker was Farul Zain, the quantity surveyor and project manager. He spoke with difficulty – exhausted, or drugged? – and his voice cracked occasionally. With fear? Pain?

Roberts was pressing him for everything he knew about the pre-contract preparations for the tower. "I must know what you know so I can help you defend yourself. The police will grill you and then, if there's a trial, the court will grill you again. The commission will tear you to pieces. We have to make sure your story is consistent throughout ... I'm in this with you, Farul. You can trust me. I need to know the truth."

Zain was reluctant at first, his protests anxious and frightened. But Roberts persisted. Finally, Zain seemed to sob. Then, his voice quavering, he told Roberts how they – Jordan, Zain and Scott – knew that the tower would penetrate into the limestone. How Jordan insisted that the tower would be built at the height he required, regardless of the risk. "Bill said, 'Don't worry about the geophysical report. That's my problem. Your problem is to give me the tower I want.'" Zain's voice choked into a whimper. "I didn't want to do it. But he – he – has ways of persuading you, you know?"

"I know." Roberts's voice was brittle. "What was his ace?"

"My son." It was a sob. "He has someone with him now." High-pitched, panicked. "You must tell me what to say. They must never find out from me. I'll say anything to the police, just tell me what –"

Jasmine stopped the tape. Her mouth was dry. The handset was damp with sweat. Why had Roberts made these secret recordings?

She had to do something. But what?

She rewound the tape.

Make a copy, think later, her instinct told her.

She crossed to her own desk and scrabbled in the drawers till she found her hand-held dictaphone. She grabbed some tapes and, slotting one into the dictaphone, hurried back to Roberts' desk. Placing the dictaphone to the microphone, she played Roberts's tape. Bending her ear close to both instruments, she continued to listen as she recorded a duplicate copy onto the hand-held dictaphone.

The second set of tapes was an interview with David Scott, the architect. "One a.m.," Roberts's voice recorded. Last night. Roberts must have left the tapes in the desk temporarily in between this last interview and going out to the conference with Jordan.

Scott was more cautious and reticent than Zain but it was clear that he had argued with Jordan over the height of the tower. His initial design had been over fifty metres lower in height, he said, to avoid the foundation piercing the limestone stratum. Roberts wanted him to hand over those designs but Scott could not be persuaded. "They're my personal insurance policy. Jordan'll have to trust me, like on the other projects."

"It's your call," Roberts said.

"I'll say and do what I have to, to get us all out of this. For what that's worth. But Bill and I go back a long way. I'm not going to be treated like some terrified new recruit."

"But you are terrified – why else an 'insurance policy'?"

"Aren't you terrified?"

Roberts made a sound like a dry laugh. But he did not deny it. There was a knock on the door.

Jasmine jumped to her feet, dropping the recording machines. "Um – y – yes?"

"I'm going to lunch now." It was Doreen. "Can I get you anything?"

"No!" Then, more naturally, "No. Thank you. Go ahead."

Jasmine sat down again, trembling.

When the tapes ended, she put everything back as she had found it and locked the drawer.

Jasmine poured the rest of the coffee. It was cold but she drained the cup. She felt lightheaded and jittery. She stared at the pile of contracts and documents on the desk. Everything had changed. And yet it all looked the same. The knot in her stomach twisted. She had her own copies now of the taped conversations, but what was she going to do with them?

The tower had been too tall. Jordan had always known it. Known that it would pierce the limestone layer. Known the risks of instability and collapse. And he had gone ahead. Had he really intimidated Zain and Scott, perhaps even Roberts? And "fixed" the geophysical report? Jasmine felt cold. Had she heard it all correctly?

She stared at the duplicate cassettes she had made. They looked innocuous enough but anxiety gripped her. What would Roberts do if he found out she had them? Or Jordan? The encounter this morning with Jordan's thug remained vivid in her mind. If anyone found her here now … She glanced tensely at the door. Would they try to search her, take the tapes off her? Jasmine forced herself to be calm. She would get rid of the tapes before she left the building – she knew how she could do that quickly and, she hoped, innocuously. She swept up the cassettes and slipped them into her pocket.

She stood up. The original building contract lay face down on the desk in front of her. Its thick blue bulk filled her vision. She stared at it for a long moment. There was some writing on the back of the document. Handwritten. Pencil marks. Figures. The pulse of her heart flashed its veiny red veil across her vision. The pencil scratchings leaped out with each pulsing throb.

Numbers. Upside down. A sequence then a letter.

As if in a dream, she reached out and turned the contract so that she could read the sequence. Law firms handled thousands of deeds, storing them for their clients in secure vaults. The pencil marks on the back of the building contract were the reference numbers given by the deeds librarian to a document stored by Carruthers for one of their clients. It was made up of a seven-digit client number followed by the deed packet number where it was filed. Followed by a letter – the packet's location in the storage vault.

She unlocked Roberts's drawer again and pulled out the notebook. Flicking through the pages. Her hands trembling. There it was. "mca – 10.95.60.63.47.18 – w". She rewrote the number on a pad, removing the dots. "1095606/34718 – w".

Bill Jordan's client number, followed by a reference – for a file, perhaps? Followed by a letter – a deed-packet location? It was a wild card but an urgency impelled her on. She put back the notebook and locked the drawer. She tore her jotting from the pad and ripped it to shreds, throwing the fragments into the bin. Unlocking the office door, she strode out towards the lifts.

*   *   *

The deeds vaults in the basement were generally quiet. Now at lunch time, the stillness of the building gave them a deathly silence.

Here, the original signed and sealed deeds, contracts, debentures and wills held by the law firm for their clients were locked away in these damp-proof, fire-proof, flood-proof and theft-proof rooms. A complex index system catalogued the thick wallets in which the deeds were held, cross-referencing client with matter and individual items.

The deeds librarian, her uncertainty about Jasmine overridden by a shrug and nod from Suleiman the security guard, let her browse through the computer database. But the reference Jasmine had seen in Roberts's notebook was not in the system.

Jasmine did not know what it was about the coded numbers in the notebook that had hooked into her. But something impelled her to pursue her instinct. That they were not logged onto the database galvanised her more.

She went to the stacks.

The labyrinthine vaults were filled from floor to ceiling with metal rolling stacks. The air smelt of parchment and dust. She wove through the rooms given over to Seng & Mustafa deeds. In the far corner, where the lighting was dimmest, the Carruthers section began.

Working backwards on the formula she had seen in the notebook, Jasmine found section W, shelf 18. The deeds packets were all labelled with the prefix 1095606 – Bill Jordan's personal flies.

"Gotcha."

She searched for packet number 347.

The packets stopped at number 152. "Damn."

She went to packet number 003. It contained innocuous documents relating to two condominiums Jordan owned in town. She searched either side of number 003.

An unmarked brown envelope.

Inside – computer disks labelled "Titiwangsa".

Her heart racing, Jasmine scrambled at packets number 004 and 007. Nothing.

She stumbled to packet 047. Next to it two unmarked packets.

She could hardly undo the legal ribbon with her shaking hands.

Finally. Drafts, figures, graphs spilled out. Typed bundles of text and statistics. One set was a report and a series of notes that appeared to have been exchanged between Jordan and someone called Tsui Xiao Ren. The technical reports meant little to Jasmine. It was the notes that contained the sting that chilled her.

The other bundle of papers made sense of Roberts's code: "mca = McAllister". She was holding Luke's missing report.

28

"Jasmine Lian, please," the caller said. It was two thirty in the afternoon.

Doreen said, "She's not at her desk. Can I take a message?"

"Is she in today?"

"Oh, yes, she's in the building. May I take your name?"

Kidd Tan rang off. He slipped his mobile into his pocket as he walked across the secure car park at Subang Airport. "She's there," he said to Pang.

Pang had been held by the airport police all morning while the formalities were gone through. Witnesses had given conflicting stories and were impatient to catch their flights. The woman seen running from him could not be found. Kidd Tan was summoned as the director of Tan Securities and vouched that Pang was employed with the company as a private bodyguard. Pang's identification papers and gun licence had been verified, and as the weapon had been in its holster throughout the incident, the police released him without charge.

Kidd and Pang got into the Mercedes and headed downtown.

*   *   *

It was after three when Jasmine stepped out of the offices of Seng & Mustafa. After the air-conditioned interior the glaring heat hit her like a physical blow. She had walked out with the unmarked deed packets, and as they had not been on the deeds register, the librarian had let her pass. Jasmine now cradled them to her chest. She had bundled the duplicate cassettes into a parcel with photocopies of

Luke's reports and duplicates of his disks, which she'd made at an empty PC terminal. The parcel sat in the out-tray in the firm's post-room. They would be safe in case … In case what? Something happened to her? Jasmine tried to laugh at her paranoia. But she could not help glancing furtively behind her as she walked away from the office building.

The papers and disks should've been burnt in the fire at Luke's office. What were they doing in her firm's vaults? She had not had time to study the contents of the deeds packets in detail but the unanswered question was enough to make her nervy. What should she do now? She felt drained. She hadn't eaten properly since the night before. The taped conversations looped through her head. Graphs and statistics from Luke's report wove across the notes scribbled in Jordan's handwriting. She needed space to pore through the information she clutched against her. She needed time and distance. To think through the implications of it all. To think what she was going to do.

A hotel. A meal. A rest. Then – then, she'd be able to think.

The pot-holed pavement was crowded even though it was mid-afternoon. Jasmine pushed through to the kerb and squinted into the hooting traffic for a taxi. Scooters screeched by. Waves of heat and fumes engulfed her.

Suddenly, a squealing of tyres, shimmering black roaring at her. The Mercedes mounted the pavement, scattering pedestrians. Pang was out of the car even before Jasmine could grasp what was happening.

He bundled her into the back. Slammed the door against her furious battle. He slipped into the passenger seat and the Mercedes pulled out into the traffic. Another man Jasmine did not recognise was driving.

*   *   *

The heat in the converted store-room was stifling. Tan sat on the cool cement floor in his singlet and undershorts, doggedly writing in an exercise book. Four similarly brown-covered books filled in his painstaking English sat beside him. A pile of fresh books waited at his other hand. There was a pastiness to his skin and a hunted fear about his features.

He was writing it down. All of it. What happened that night with Dr Chan. What Jordan had told him to do. How he had carried it out. Everything he had done for Jordan – first contact with Wong and the other men in Kampung Tanah, the sums they were paid, the rewards they were promised, what they had to do in return. The attack on the young Indian lawyer and the head teacher and the kidnap of Wong's son. The money he himself had been paid by Jordan.

It was Tan's offering to the spirits. His actions and his life. He would burn the exercise books at the shrine, committing his paper life over to the other world. As at the annual *Cheng Beng* ceremony – the Festival of the Dead – when those of this life committed paper wealth and assets to their ancestors on the other side: paper effigies of cars and houses, televisions, microwaves and wads of "cash".

That's what he planned to do, Tan told himself And then he would have repaid his debt. A life for a life. His son would recover from the measles. No danger or illness would await the boy again – or his other son, or his wife. Or Tan himself.

But what of those lives strewn bloodily across the hillside?

Tan looked up, gasping. The toilet bowl across the floor grinned back at him. Drops of sweat slid into his eyes.

No, they were too remote. He was not responsible for them. Their deaths lay at Jordan's feet. But, he, Tan, had been the catalyst. He had killed the man who might have saved them all. Who might have stopped the construction of the tower.

Who might have stopped Jordan.

Jordan.

Tan had worked with Jordan for so long. Done so much of his bloody work. So bloody and so filthy, the stains had seeped into his very being. A guttural noise of self-disgust burst from him. He deserved his father's contempt. *Ah Teh* was right. He was filth.

He set down details of his connection with Jordan. The extortion activities in Manila. Bribery of city officials in Saigon over a retail development some years ago. Blackmail of Jordan's competitor for a hotel contract in Taiwan. You suck white cock so long, his father had said last night, you're the white man's whore.

Tan shook his head, eyes twisted shut. "No!"

He had given back two lives – the Lian woman's and the consultant's. An all those others he had helped to rescue, working side by side with the consultant. That should count for something. Tan clutched at the hope of the books already balanced. What was it McAllister had said? Give Jordan's life for all those lives that he had killed.

Tan was nodding, rocking with the rhythm. He had been sidling towards this confrontation. Jordan was his patron. To betray him would be a revolt against the established order of Tan's network. Jordan had paid him well for every task he had performed. The white man's money and favour had bought Tan's allegiance. White man's whore.

If Tan gave Jordan's life to save his own, he could not do so without endangering the Tan enterprise – Kidd, Pang, all those extended relationships that relied on the success of Tan's business. There would be shame and they would lose everything they had built up. His family, too, would suffer humiliation and poverty.

There is no shame in being poor, his father used to say long ago. Whatever you have is an illusion but who you are is the truth. Tan had not understood what he had meant.

And, now, who was he? White man's whore.

There was going to be another killing. Blood again marking the fate of the Tan family.

Kidd had never understood such things. He had always mocked their father. Always grabbed at everything he could get. Grabbing now at the chance to kill, at the money that that killing would make. The future of the Tan enterprise lay with Kidd, Tan realised.

In a moment of clarity, he saw the truth. He was sitting here, half undressed, cowering in a hut behind a brothel, almost out of his mind. His time was past. Kidd was the future. And that future, Tan saw, would be soaked in blood and devastation. "Brother against brother, blood for blood," their father had said. Seeping through the faces of his sons and their children, staining their flesh and drowning their spirits.

And he, too, would be a hungry ghost, like his father, forced out of the other world back into this one. To warn, to chide, to grieve without rest and without end. A shattering of one piece of the equilibrium would end with the destruction of the whole order of their family. As it had already brought destruction to the balance of life in Kampung Tanah.

Tan dropped his book and pen and stood up. In protecting Jordan he had thought that he was protecting himself and his family. He had been deluding himself. He could not protect them from the accumulation of the past.

It had to stop. He had to stop it.

Give Jordan's life for those lives that had been taken.

Tan picked up his notebook and looked at the words. English words. So, he had known he would come to this conclusion from the start.

He had to get word to the consultant. Warn him about Kidd. Save Kidd from himself. Stop the madness at last. They needed the consultant. He understood the balance of things. He would be their mediator.

Tan would give his paper life to the consultant. And to the executioner, Jordan's life in exchange for his own. That was the life that was owed to Dr Chan and to those nameless dead on the slopes. It was an offering that would save them all.

* * *

Luke switched off his computer and stretched. It was after eight in the evening. He hadn't slept for almost two days. He had channelled his will and mind into his work. All that day, he had plodded through the messages, e-mail and faxes that had piled up. One of the calls had been from Ibrahim, the head teacher in Kampung Tanah. Ibrahim's son had died in the landslide. When Luke spoke to him, Ibrahim explained in cracked tones that lawyers from Kuala Lumpur had come to the town. They had advised the people about their rights and talked of justice and compensation. The town was preparing a civil action against Jordan Cardale PLC and Consortium 2000. They wanted Luke to help them on the technical issues of their claim.

Luke had accepted immediately. Now that Jasmine had run back to her old life, he'd thought bitterly, neither of them would have a conflict of interest. He had spent the afternoon reviewing his existing data and surveys on the Titiwangsa Tower site. He would meet with Ibrahim in a few days.

Changing into fresh clothes – a denim shirt worn loose over T-shirt and jeans – Luke drove down into Taiping. He found Raymond and some friends at Mok's Coffee-shop Bar near the bazaar. Their loud company over food and beers distracted him from the bitterness of what had happened with Jasmine. Mrs Fung had read him Jasmine's note over the phone that morning.

It was late when Luke left Mok's Bar. Raymond and the others had already gone home to their families but Luke had stayed for another beer, reluctant to go back to his empty house. He did not head for his Land Rover. Instead, he followed the deserted streets wherever they led him, weaving a left here, a right over there. He did not notice the man who tailed him some distance behind, just out of sight. The man wore a black, visored biker's helmet and a rain mac.

Luke's walk had the deliberate invincibility of a drunken man. Tonight nothing could harm him, he thought triumphantly. He had friends, he'd had a good meal, a few beers, he'd survived a landslide. No woman, no loneliness, no assassins lurking in the shadows could harm him. He snorted a laugh. He'd been warned about assassins earlier that day – a caller on his answering-machine, cryptic and tight-voiced. He was ready for all corners.

But no one had warned him of the inconstancies of women. He had been right all these years, trying to forget Jasmine. He had been right to resist his feelings when he had first seen her again. But he had to go and fall for her all over again. He gave the thumbs up to a couple of prostitutes strolling in front of the Hotel Lucky View. It was a concrete hutch, boasting "Air Con Lounge" and "Karaoke Hostess". The women waved back, smacking kisses into the air. He laughed. "I'm a sucker like the rest of them!"

The helmet of the man following Luke flashed a moment out of the shadows. And he was gone – darting into the alley beside the hotel.

Luke's aimless wandering had brought him to the far edge of town. Behind the hotel was a warren of squat *atap* houses. The palm-thatched houses jostled against tin-roofed shacks from the last century. They were still and shuttered against the night. But beyond the quiet dark, Luke heard voices raised in excitement. Cars and scooters were doubleparked along the narrow rutted roads. Luke weaved through, craning to see where the crowd was.

In a courtyard, glimpsed through the maze of alleys off the road, figures jostled round a circle of light. Crouching, leaning in, clapping, shouting their bets. Screeching and strange fluttering.

A cockfight.

Luke aimed unevenly for the crowd, cutting along a path between two rows of houses.

It stank of waste and urine. The glare of electric lights from the cock ring plunged the tight alley into blackness. Luke felt swamped by self-pity. All his friends that night had had wives and girlfriends to go home to. He was here wading through the seamy side of town. He'd been in love with Jasmine all his life and had done nothing about it for years. Now, he'd finally won her love and what had happened? His principles and his integrity had got right in the way.

He'd held Jasmine in his arms, heard her voice purring her

love for him, he'd had everything he had longed for and he had destroyed it all for the sake of his principles. His driven, obsessive principles.

The garotte cut into his throat, jerking him backwards.

He clawed at the wire slicing into his skin. Off-balance, pinned against a rigid ferocity. The man pulled Luke out of the alley into the gutter.

Lungs and throat heaving, sucking in emptiness. Luke flailed his arms back. The man who held him was small, but surprise had given him the advantage. Luke's hands hit against the helmet as harmful to his assailant as raindrops. Blood thundered in his head. His chest fought for air. His neck pulled back at an impossible angle. Legs buckling.

Luke dropped his right arm, twisting it under his back. Entangled in the rain mac, groping against unrelenting muscle. The man jerked hard on the garotte. Blood dripped from Luke's throat. And suddenly he had it in his hand. The warm steel of his revolver. Before leaving home earlier that evening, Luke had concealed his revolver under his shirt. With an effort, Luke pulled it from his belt and jammed it into the man's groin. The satisfying click of a safety catch being released.

The man froze. Luke rammed the weapon harder into his body. The garotte slackened. Luke pulled away. The wire fell, slid to the ground. Luke twisted round, gun still aimed at his attacker. The man's hands were raised to shoulder level. But he stood his ground. Luke staggered, massaging his throat with his free hand. He sucked in desperate breaths. He gestured with the revolver, struggling for speech. "Who ... are you?" His voice was hoarse. "Helmet ... take't off!"

The man did not move.

A noise behind Luke. Voices. He spun round, gun outstretched, two-handed. A hooker and her client. Frozen. Wide-eyed. The woman screamed.

A movement out of the corner of his eye. Luke swung round. Panicked. Disoriented. The man was running down the alley, rain mac flapping.

"Stop!" Luke aimed down his arms into the darkness. Then catching himself.

Aiming high above his head instead. Firing. The shot reverberated through the night. The man threw himself round a corner and was gone.

Luke raced after him. Beyond the ringing in his ears, he was distantly aware of screaming as the cock fight disintegrated into panic. He followed the glimpse of fleeing movement through the alleyways and still streets, through parked cars, stumbling over ruts and rubbish bins. Lungs raw and heaving. He shoved past startled hookers, crashed into youths hanging out by their scooters.

Suddenly, bursting into the night market. The last of the stall-holders packing their wares. A tangle of trestle tables and generators and glaring lightbulbs. Forcing his way through. Boxes overturning. Terrified faces flashing past. Round a corner. And nothing.

A deserted street stretched left and right. Commotion behind him. Police sirens. Voices shouting in panic. Luke stood still. Listening. Sweeping his gaze up and down the shuttered shop-houses. The roar of an engine fading. Where was the man?

A movement down the block. In the shadows. Luke scuttled towards it, sidestepping against walls and pillars along a five-foot walkway. There. Squatting by the monsoon drain. A man holding a helmet and something else.

Luke shoved the barrel of his revolver into the back of the man's head. "Freeze!" he yelled. "Drop it!"

The helmet fell to the ground. A rustle. The rain mac followed. Luke reached out and grabbed the man's shoulder. Hauled him round.

An old man. Face contorted in terror. Watery eyes wide. Jabbering. "Don't kill me! I got no money! Please, spare me!"

Suddenly, behind Luke. A chorus of metallic clicks. Safety catches easing off. A voice over a megaphone. "This is the police! Drop your gun and put your hands above your head!"

Police cars screeched up, lighting the night in flashing blue, sirens whining out. Headlights caught Luke as if in crossfire. Blinded by the sudden brightness, Luke backed away from the old man. His gun clattered to the ground. He raised his hands above his head. Two police officers handcuffed him.

29

Luke was questioned and held in the police cells overnight. Detective Lam arrived from Kuala Lumpur just before dawn, his police siren wailing for three hours on the deserted highway. Luke was questioned again. A uniformed officer sat by the door. By now, the police had obtained initial accounts of the incident, including a statement from the old man whom Luke had threatened.

"Mr Seong, aged seventy-six," Detective Lam read from his notes with an air of smugness. "Couldn't sleep. Stepped outside for air. Said he saw the helmet and mac and picked them up. So, Mr Seong tried to kill you."

"No, *he* didn't try to kill me." Luke leaned against the grimy table. He spoke deliberately, trying to keep his temper.

"No one tried to kill you?"

"No. I mean, yes. There was a man." Luke sighed. "It was dark. I was chasing him."

"Mr Seong?" Lam was enjoying himself

"No. The man who attacked me."

"How do you know it wasn't Mr Seong? Did you see the man's face?"

"Goddammit!" Luke threw himself back in his chair.

Lam smiled thinly. "You always see mystery men nobody else sees."

"There *was* a man last night. And on the night Dr Chan died. I saw him again –"

"You said you didn't see his face."

"No, not last night. The man who was with Dr Chan. He was

at Kampung Tanah in the landslide. He saved my life, I don't know why. His name is Kaw, a.k.a Ronnie Tan."

Lam raised his eyebrows. "The 'murderer' of Dr Chan saved the life of the man who wants him hanged?"

"Look –"

"No, you look!" Lam shouted, his eyes hard. "What do you think I am – an idiot? You whites think you can tell us any shit and we'll believe you like kids!"

"OK, then. The people last night, they must've seen the chase!" Luke cried.

Lam was breathing hard. After a beat, he flicked through his papers and read, " 'I saw the white man. He had a gun.' 'He pointed the gun at us. He looked angry.' 'It was a big gun. I didn't see anyone else.'"

"What?" Luke slapped his hands onto the table. But he knew there was nothing he could argue with. A white man in a small Asian town, running like a maniac through the streets with a gun – nobody would remember anything else.

Lam said, "You were drunk."

"I'd had a few beers."

"The breathalyser test showed excess alcohol."

Luke threw his head back and closed his eyes.

The bruised cut on his throat stung him. He sat forward. "What about this? Did my imagination do this? Someone tried to kill me!"

Lam stared, implacable, at him. "We found nothing in the alley."

"What! A garrotte – something!"

"I think you did it yourself"

Luke shot to his feet, grabbing Lam across the table. "You're goddamn crazy! Someone tried to kill me!"

The uniformed police officer rushed at Luke, handgun drawn. Lam pulled his service pistol. The officer hauled Luke from Lam as the detective hit the panic button by the wall. An alarm sounded beyond the interview room.

"Okay, okay!" Luke shrugged off the officer, raising his hands.

"Back off!"

He sat down. In incredulous tones, he said, "Why would I injure myself and make it look like someone attacked me?"

Over the screeching alarm, Lam said, "To win the West's sympathy for your cause. Make Malaysians look bad to the world. To be a martyr for the rainforests. Maybe you fool the press but you're not fooling me."

Summoned by the panic button, uniformed officers burst into the interview room, guns drawn. Lam nodded and they hauled Luke to his feet, handcuffing him again.

Luke was charged with affray and threatening behaviour – and, for grabbing Lam, assaulting a police officer.

* * *

About the time Luke was leaving Mok's Bar, Jasmine waited in a locked room on the tenth floor of a condominium block in Kuala Lumpur. She had been there for almost eight hours. Pang and the man she did not know had brought her there that afternoon.

On the way, Jordan had called in on the senior man's mobile. The man had said, " ...and she's got some papers with her ... the consultant's report and Tsui's data ... Yes, will do ..."

He had handed the phone to Jasmine. Jordan's anger had startled her. "My instructions to you were to get on that plane. These men are my security people. You will wait at the condo. I'll deal with you when we get out of these talks."

Pang stayed with her in the apartment, watching TV on the Bang & Olufsen entertainment system in the living room. His silence continued, unnerving Jasmine the more as slow hours passed. The other man had left immediately and had not returned in all the time Jasmine had been at the apartment.

It was lavishly furnished, with the look of European grandeur and wealth. Jordan's business contacts from around the world stayed here whenever they came to the region. The block itself had been constructed by his company in a pastiche of Gothic and neoclassical styles, all Corinthian columns and fairy-tale turrets inflated to twelve storeys and air-conditioned. The Asians adored it. Jordan retained two units, this one and the penthouse for his own use.

Jasmine paced the ornate room. She wished she had not held onto the original papers and disks. Pang had taken them from her and locked them away. But at least the tapes were safe for now. Jasmine felt a twist of anxiety. How would she face Jordan when he confronted her about Luke's report? She crossed to the picture window and looked out at the lights of the city.

Jordan's contemptuous tone had shaken her. She had not been able to challenge him or stand up to him. His bullying tone had paralysed her. She felt powerless. Nick Roberts was number one now. Somewhere along the line her nerve had failed. Long before these last few days. She had stopped fighting Roberts for Jordan's work. She had stopped fighting Harry. Harry. With his bullying, which had made her feel like a guilty child again, staring up at *Ah Ba* as he screamed at her. Jasmine flashed on to terrifying images of her childhood. Her father's fists slamming into her mother, his towering bulk dwarfing her, thick arms smashing down. Jasmine's stomach knotted in panic. Jordan's bullying tone, like Harry's, had crept through her armour. It froze her and she felt unable to fight him.

She moaned out loud. "What's happening?"

Pang glanced up away from the window while the woman's back was towards him. High up on the wall, the concealed CCTV surveillance camera would be recording her image against the window. Her words should be clear in spite of the noise from the television set – they were picked up by one of four microphones hidden around the room. He wondered whether he should leave her and check the equipment. But Kidd's instructions before he'd left them to drive up to Taiping had been clear. Pang was not to leave the woman. Besides, she was unlikely to say anything of value to him, Pang thought. It wasn't his job to draw her out, just to keep her there till Jordan came.

Pang checked his watch. After eleven. Kidd would've got to Taiping earlier that evening. The drive was only just over three hours if he'd stepped on it. He would've had the whole evening to deal with the consultant. Pang stretched. He had the easy job for a change. He turned back to the television. Tan Securities had installed the best equipment for Jordan. He didn't have to go and check the monitors upstairs, he decided. On the TV monitor up in Jordan's penthouse, the black and white image of this room would be grainy through the wide-angled lens but clear enough for surveillance purposes. The time and date of the recording would be printed with the frame number. The monitor was one of a bank of screens in a utility room in one corner of Jordan's private penthouse.

Each room in the guest condominium on the tenth floor was fitted with concealed microphones and surveillance cameras. The equipment came on when noise and motion detectors revealed activity. The telephones were also tapped. Jordan had a guest apartment in every city where he had significant business interests. He had trusted only Tan's security company to wire them all in a similar set-up. Each apartment was also well stocked with liquor, pornographic videos and the telephone numbers of high-class escort agencies. In this way, Jordan learnt the secret strategies of a network of business and political contacts, and also obtained covert information that he used to bring them under his control.

Jordan and Roberts came through the front door after eleven forty. From the Environment Commission, they had gone straight to a meeting called by Dickson Loh and the Consortium directors. The discussions at Loh's Damansara house had been acrimonious, angry voices ringing out across the patio and swimming-pool. The Consortium were also being sued for compensation and investigated by the police and the Environment Commission. After six hours of talks, neither Jordan nor the Consortium had found common ground on which to make a stand against their opponents. They would now have to fight rearguard actions against each other in the spiralling chaos of legal proceedings. Roberts was strained and tense, but Jordan seethed still with fury.

In the living room, Jasmine turned from the window as Pang unlocked the door. The first thing she saw was Jordan's face. The skin was taut and pale like a death's head, his lips a gash. From the depths of their sockets, his eyes glared icy defiance. He was a cornered man but nothing – and no one – would be allowed to defeat him.

Her eyes locked on his. Jasmine stared into the hatred of her father and the contempt of her husband. But no, this was Jordan. Jordan who would do anything to stay ahead of the game. And to save himself. She felt horrifyingly afraid of him.

* * *

Jordan let the intensity of his anger penetrate Jasmine, then turned it on Pang. "What's this with locked doors and frightening Ms Lian today? She's free to move around as she wishes. You're an incompetent fool!"

Pang averted his eyes meekly.

"Now, go and get us some decent food from *Chez Max* downstairs."

As Pang slipped out, Jordan turned to Jasmine. His expression and voice were amiable. "I'm sorry if my security people have been rather heavy-handed."

Jasmine smiled weakly. Jordan's unexpected pleasantness threw her. As he had intended.

"There seems to have been a misunderstanding," Jordan went on. "We need to talk."

He led her and Roberts through to a stylish den cum meeting room and settled her at the table, solicitously pouring drinks for them all from the sideboard. The normality of the situation, like meetings they'd had over the years, disarmed Jasmine. As he played the host, Jordan handed Roberts a key. "Get the papers from the cabinet in the other room."

Roberts fetched the bundle. When he came back into the room, prickles of sweat had appeared on his forehead. Jordan had not told Roberts that Kidd had found the consultant's report and Tsui's papers on Jasmine.

Jordan snapped at Jasmine. "Where did you get these?"

"S – Seng & Mustafa's offices," Jasmine stammered, caught off-balance by the switch in tone.

"What were they doing there?"

"I – I don't know."

"How did you find them?"

Jasmine looked at Roberts. His face had a waxy sheen. His eyes jumped from her to Jordan and back again.

"Roberts?" Jordan barked. The lawyer started, blinking rapidly.

"I – I retained them," Roberts began. "After you – after we –"

Jordan had gained the upper hand by taking the offensive. In putting both lawyers on the spot, he had deflected their energy away from the real question.

"What do you –"Jasmine began. She took a breath and stood up. She made herself focus. Overcome her fear. Trust to her instinct.

She pulled on the armour she had let slip and drew herself tall. In a confident tone, she said, "I'm not playing your little power game. What's going on? This is McAllister's report, supposedly burned in a fire. How did you – or Nick – get hold of it? And these papers between you and the geophysicist Tsui. You got Tsui to fake the geological data supplied to the Consortium and the planners! What the hell's all this about?" She stared at the two men in turn, startled by her own boldness. She felt cold but held her ground.

Jordan met her eyes. So you want to play hardball, his look said. He stood up, then barked, "None of this is your damn business!"

Jasmine involuntarily pulled back. As if anticipating a blow. He saw that and smiled.

"It – it is my business," she persisted, "if you're involved in illegal activity. I'm your lawyer."

"You don't get it, do you? Nick's in charge. For the time being."
Jordan underscored this last with a long look at Roberts. Then, to
Jasmine, "You had the chance to bow out gracefully. To go back
to London with your sweet arse and career intact. But you had to
stir the shit."

"And you're up to your eyeballs in it, aren't you? The shit?"

Jordan laughed. "I've always liked your spunk. You had the
balls at one time, my girl, to stitch up the Kampung Tanah peasants
on the relocation deal. You know, they're trying to sue us now?
Roberts says those disclaimers you sneaked into their contract will
make them crawl through barbed wire and land mines each step
along the way!"

Jasmine remembered the devastation and the grief of the
survivors. She ached with shame for the legal machinations that
had once made her so proud.

Jordan was saying, with an edge to his voice, "I'd like to keep
you on my team, but it's up to you. What are you going to do?"

Jasmine felt paralysed in conflict. As a lawyer, she couldn't go
to the police against her firm's own client. And the only evidence
she had was hearsay or circumstantial. But she couldn't stand by
now and do nothing: her whole being revolted against colluding
again in his manipulations.

"JM. He's the senior partner," she said at last. "He won't let
the firm act in such circumstances."

Roberts handed her a sheaf of papers. "You might like to see
these."

They were an exchange of faxes between Roberts and Julian
Masters discussing her state of mind and her involvement with Luke.
A doctor's report was among them, diagnosing her as suffering
from post-traumatic stress disorder following the landslide, subject
to delusions and panic attacks, and all this exacerbated by her
deprived childhood and subsequent disguised life. JM's concluding
memo, transmitted a few hours before, said, "The lies of her private
life do not concern us so long as they have not affected her work
or this firm. However, the conflict of interest with the consultant is

a serious issue. (I cannot believe, though, there was malice on her part – most likely, an error of romantic judgement.) She should have no further dealings on Jordan's matters for now. In view of her untarnished record so far – and given her recent ordeal – I'm granting her six months' compassionate leave. Make the necessary arrangements and see that she is well looked after. Meanwhile, I'll handle this personally with her husband."

Jasmine sat down. Her head spun. Her pulse was racing. She couldn't breathe. They knew, they all knew, about her past. Who she really was. Harry would know now. Harry, beating her, screaming at her. She flinched at the thought. And the lies they were putting out about her. Who was this doctor? She'd never seen a doctor. There was nothing wrong with her mind.

"Dr Krishnan," Jordan said into the silence. "My personal physician here. Reliable and well respected but, like all private physicians, has his price."

"You're crazy," Jasmine gasped.

"My girl, *you're* the one afflicted."

"Who'll believe this garbage?"

"JM for one. And he's hardly a stupid man."

Jasmine sat very still. The horror of it all was sinking in. She remembered the men her mother had mentioned asking questions. And all the people who must have seen her distress after the landslide, her narrow escape from death, her and Luke together on that long, cold night. She remembered the looks and whispers of the staff at Seng & Mustafa.

No one would believe her if she accused Jordan of illegal activities, not even JM. Especially not JM now. And who would believe her if she denied ever having seen Dr Krishnan?

Jordan said with satisfaction, "I made you everything you are, my girl. I can break you any time I want."

The tone and words echoed with horrible irony in Jasmine's mind. Harry had said something close to it once. And they were both right, Jasmine knew now, with a chill. She had sold to these men both her private and public lives for all the wealth and prestige they could give her. Harry had called in the price months ago. Now Jordan held her future in his hands.

She had turned away from Luke and all the best of him within her for these men and the success they stood for. She stood now at the abyss, dust and ashes all that were left of her hopes.

"We want you to get better," Roberts said. "Let us look after you. If all goes well, you could be fine again and your career could be saved ..."

His mock-compassionate tone cracked her defences. Hopelessness overwhelmed her. She had no will any more to stand up against these men, their images tangling in her mind – Jordan, Roberts, Harry, Luke, *Ah Ba*. They had defeated her at last, with their bullying and their games, embroiling loyalty and power, love and furious violence into a seething mass until she could hardly distinguish one from another.

She crumpled into herself and began to sob.

*　　*　　*

Jordan gave Jasmine the use of the apartment for the next week. Late that afternoon, Jordan and Roberts had received notification that the police and the Environment Commission wanted to interview her as a witness at the landslide. The police had requested that she did not leave the country. "How fortunate you did not manage to leave this morning," Jordan said. Then, with a mock-paternal air, "We have all confidence in you, my girl, to be the kind of witness we all expect you to be. Nick will help you get your thoughts together."

Pang would be her escort and driver. "Go shopping, my girl," Jordan said. "Pang will put it on my credit card. Consider it therapy."

Jasmine let Pang lead her through to the dining room where he had set out the takeaway French cuisine. He stood at the door while she picked at the food. She dimly realised she had not confronted Jordan and Roberts about the taped interviews. Just as well, she thought.

Alone in the den, Jordan rounded on Roberts. "I told you to destroy those bundles. What the fuck are you playing at?"

"I – I thought we could use them – against Tsui if he ever tried to double-cross you – if – Roberts had gone pale again.

"You mean, *you* could use them. Against me. It was your little insurance policy."

"No – why –" Roberts's laugh was hysterical.

"You said I could trust Jasmine. That I should let her go back to London without a fuss. What game are you two playing?"

"We're not – I swear to you – I'm not. I expected her to go quietly, like I said."

"But she didn't."

"I didn't think she'd run off."

Jordan was like a tiger, toying with its kill. His eyes flashed in savage humour. "No, she delivered your little insurance policy to me instead."

Roberts was sweating hard.

Jordan was enjoying himself. He patted Roberts's cheek, startling him. "Timidity doesn't suit you. You're a shark. I pay you for that quality. I like sharks because they bite. They might even try to bite me. That's expected." Jordan stepped up very close to him. He could smell the lawyer's fear. "But don't forget. I always win. Try whatever little games you like. The outcome is always the same. You owe me big money. Pay your dues or – you and your wife –"

Jordan brought his hand up to Roberts's face, as if cupping a flower. He snapped his fingers. "Any time. That's all it takes."

Roberts started.

The phone rang. Jordan stepped back and took the call. It was Kidd, reporting that Luke had turned the tables on him.

"Goddammit!"

Kidd went on, "But the police arrested him. They say he was drunk, running amok with a gun. No one saw me. I've covered my tracks. No-one will believe him."

Jordan paced, massaging his temples. "Look, we can't worry over spilt fucking milk. We'll have to see what pans out. Get out of there. I need you in Kampung Tanah. There've been rumours linking intimidation episodes and bribery and the committee to me. It came up at the Commission talks. Check it out. Who's been spreading the muck, what we can do about them. What can we salvage of our 'goodwill' there."

"Gotcha. I'll head straight there."

"Roberts and I are in Singapore tomorrow. The funders and insurers are getting bloody jittery. We're meeting them for some damage control. I expect to be back in KL by midnight."

"You still holding the Lian woman?"

"She's needed as a witness in the slide inquiries."

"You want her ... out of the way?"

Jordan looked out of the window. He knew what his instinct told him to do. Get rid of Jasmine and be done with it. But there were other considerations. He said, thinking out loud, "No. She's too close. There'll be an investigation, police crawling over everyone who knew her, worked with her, the last people to see her. It'll look too suspicious – she disappears just after they want her in as a witness. No. I can't afford to risk it. But we've got her tied up on what she's going to say at the inquiries." Jordan reflected on Jasmine, sobbing wretchedly a few minutes before. She had let herself be led out of the room, a tearful woman who would do whatever he told her. She'd been a good lawyer when he needed her, but she hadn't had the bottle to last the course. Jordan said into the phone, "She's got no fight in her. She'll co-operate."

"Okay."

"Any news on your brother?"

"None," Kidd lied. "I got someone on it."

Jordan rang off. He leant heavily, both hands on the table, head lolling down. It was only a moment. A breather. And then, he looked up, his eyes clear. There was only one way he could be safe: eliminate all opponents. But he couldn't kill them all. The time for that had not come yet. So far he was staying one step ahead.

He would claw back control, he knew it. It was a matter of ball-breaking endurance and out-playing the other bastards. Bill Jordan would not lose.

30

The next morning, Luke was released on bail with Mrs Fung as his surety. In addition to his savings, she had put up all the money Jasmine had sent her over the years to cover the huge sum that had been set. Her neighbour, Mrs Bok, had brought her into town in an old Austin Morris.

The bail conditions required Luke to surrender his passport and imposed an after dark curfew on him. He was to stay with Mrs Fung and report to the police station once during the day. His gun was confiscated and his gun licence suspended. The hearing was set for the following week.

The early morning was already bleaching hot as Luke and Mrs Fung stepped out into the street. She looked frail as a ghost. Mrs Bok supported her by her other arm. Luke was subdued, awkwardly attentive to Mrs Fung, who looked exhausted and in pain.

He was saying, "Fung *Cheh*, I thank you with all my heart for doing this."

"Tsk, tsk, you are my boy," Mrs Fung said weakly. "I can do nothing else."

Luke squeezed her arm gently.

Then, she doubled over with a frightening violence. She began to vomit. A gush of bright blood spattered onto the ground.

Mrs Bok screamed.

Mrs Fung collapsed against Luke, the retching shuddering her body, her breath choked and desperate. Blood poured out in erratic bursts, marking her lips and face, splashing on her tunic, soaking into Luke's clothes.

Luke held her in his arms, shouting above the screaming, "A

doctor! Someone call an ambulance!"

People came running from all directions. There was yelling and jostling.

Luke stared helplessly at Mrs Fung as she writhed in pain, her mouth and throat stained with blood.

* * *

"Marietta!" Harry's wail howled through the flat as he stumbled in. "I need you! Marietta!"

Lights flicked on. Marietta appeared in the corridor, clumsily wrapping on a robe. "What the – Harry! It's the fucking middle of the night."

Harry staggered towards her, his alcohol-soaked features crumpling in rage and pain. He had been back in London for two days. "Help me …"

She stepped forward and blocked his path. Recollecting her authority, she said, "How did you get in?"

"Duplicate set, my love, before I gave you back the keys. I'm not bloody stupid."

"Harry, it's over. It was over when you got boringly sentimental over your little wife. Now, get out."

"No!" Harry grabbed Marietta with imploring anger. "I need you! I don't know what to do!"

He propelled her into the drawing room and pushed her into the sofa. He prowled round the room turning on all the lights, slamming the door shut. "I just need to talk. Okay? Just sit. And listen. I don't know where else to turn. I'm going crazy over this."

Marietta sighed. "Get on with it. I presume it's your wife again."

Harry flung himself on his knees in front of her. Through the anger and alcohol clouding his eyes, there was a terrible dread. He said, "She lied to me. All along. Never missed a beat. Oxford. Now. Always. I thought she was different. I believed in her. But she's just the same. Lies, secrets, laughing in our face."

"You're not making any sense."

"Don't you see? Her life was a lie all along. She's a lie. I'm married to a lie. I wanted to be free of lies, I thought I'd found something pure and untouched in Jasmine." Tears poured down his flushed cheeks. "But I'm living it all over again. Women's lies, my mother's lies, my wife's lies. My whole life is built on lies!"

Harry told Marietta what Julian Masters had told him earlier that evening. That Jasmine's real name was Jasmine Fung: her father was a small-time dealer in illegal merchandise and a child prostitute pimp; her mother was a domestic servant. She had been schooled at a national school in a small town in Malaysia and a scholarship to Oxford had been her ticket out of a life of penury and drudgery. "I fell in love with a lie! Fucking little whore, pimped by her parents, most likely! Dirty bloody Chink coolie! She fucking conned me, used me!"

Marietta began to laugh, a joyous, crowing laugh that looped around him.

Harry screamed, "What's so fucking funny?"

"That pure little wife you put up there on the pedestal, the one you threw me aside for, to worship and adore, she's just a slut like the rest of us poor girls."

He slapped her. A stinging thwack.

"How dare you?" Marietta shoved Harry backwards and stood up in one powerful surge. She towered over him.

Fear flickered over Harry's face. He had crossed the unspoken rule between them, the rule that had bound him to her over the years. She had been the one woman he'd respected with sacrosanct awe. Her dominant female power had made her the one woman he feared. It had once been a delicious fear. Now, in that instant, he saw that she might yet be the one to save him from despair.

The door opened and a young man charged in. He was blond and square-jawed. Early twenties. Wearing nothing but boxer shorts. Golden-brown washboard torso. "Marietta! Is everything all right?"

Harry stared at Marietta's new lover.

Marietta said, "Harry, this is Charlie. I told you it's over between you and me. Give me the keys and go."

Harry's roar was a cry of anguish. "You, you, too!"

Marietta's hard face stared back at him. "I never promised you eternal love, eternal faith and bullshit. Besides, you finished it between us when you decided to take that pathetic marriage of yours seriously."

Harry struggled to his feet.

The young man stepped forward. "Time you left, mate."

Harry hit him in the face. Then a blow to the gut. A knee into his falling head. He kicked his chest and head where the boy lay on the ground. It was good to see the skin breaking, blood flowing. Good to feel the unresisting flesh under his fists and feet.

"Harry!"

Harry turned and punched Marietta. Once, with all his hatred and fury exploding. He felt her jaw break on impact.

As he left Marietta's apartment, he felt a surge of power. He knew what to do now. There was only one way to treat a whore. And one thing they all deserved. He would find Jasmine and beat her to a pulp.

*　*　*

At Taiping General Hospital, Luke and Mrs Bok waited as the doctors attended to Mrs Fung. Finally, Dr Han came through. He walked them to the ward where nurses were settling Mrs Fung.

The bed seemed too big for her shrunken frame. Two tubes hung out of her elbow crease into bags of blood. Another tube fed into her chest under the collarbone. She was conscious but weak. Her eyes met Luke's but she had little strength to acknowledge him.

"We've done an urgent endoscopy. From the results, it looks like stomach cancer," Dr Han was saying. He was a grandfatherly man in his late fifties, the same Dr Han of the PTA Jasmine had petitioned those many years ago. "But I'd like to do further tests."

A movement from the bed. Mrs Fung struggled to speak. "No

tests! Take me home. It's time. I want to die at home. No more of this poking, cutting – tubes, needles ..."

"Hush, Auntie," a nurse clucked. "We'll look after you."

"No!" A dry sob croaked out. "Luke, please."

Luke went to her side and took her hand. It felt dry and cold. He spoke soothingly to her, then turned to Dr Han. "What can you be sure of right now?"

"We've given her a blood transfusion. She was anaemic, probably due to a long period of undetected internal bleeding. The sudden severe bleeding appears to have stopped. She's been given morphine to ease the pain."

"And the cancer?"

Dr Han hesitated. He did not like to give an opinion without more tests but his intuition and long experience in a small town gave him an informality a city doctor might have lacked. He lowered his voice. "It's in very advanced stages. Probably not operable."

"How long does she have?"

The doctor shook his head. "Not long. I can't say how long. But not long."

"Can she go home?"

"Well ... I'd like to keep her under observation a few days."

"No!" Mrs Fung reached up weakly. "You know I'm going to die, Doctor. No need tests to tell you what I'll die of. Die is die. Keep me here I will die. Send me home I will die. So let me die at home in peace."

Dr Han had seen many elderly patients like Mrs Fung. In his youth, he had tried with their families to keep them in hospital against their wishes. But, invariably, in the alien white wards, even as the doctors and technology fought for these patients' lives, the men and women themselves lost heart and died of soul-sadness. Now, he understood. For Mrs Fung, the shortening weeks and days – perhaps hours – were all that were left to her. He could give her nothing but soulless waiting for a little while, and maybe a little while more. But to her, nothing could have any meaning unless she could choose where and how she spent her final time in this life.

After a long pause, he nodded. "By this evening, we may be able to remove the tubes. I won't keep you here longer than necessary."

Mrs Fung smiled her thanks and closed her eyes.

To Luke, Dr Han said, "She'll need someone with her. To feed her, wash her ..."

A voice from behind them said, "I'll do it."

It was Mrs Bok. "She was good to my mother when *Ah Ma* was dying. I can repay my family's debt to her now."

Left alone with Mrs Fung, Luke took her hand. She opened her eyes. Her voice was a whisper when she spoke. "I was wrong to keep you and Jasmine apart. I thought I was doing what was best for her. But the spirits are laughing at me now. I'm so close to the gateway now, I can hear them on the other side."

"Ssh, there's no need to talk."

"Listen to me!" Mrs Fung dug her fingers into his grip. "You must make right your differences with Jasmine. She has lost her way because of me. You understand the rightness of things – it is up to you. She is your heart and you her strength. Do not lose each other." She smiled weakly. Her voice was so soft now, Luke had to lean close. She went on with an effort, "I've asked of you many things. I must ask you one more. Go to her and bring her to me. I must tell her the truth before I die. I was wrong to think that she could escape the truth. If I leave her in silence, as I had thought once was right, she will not know what the spirits know and their darkness will overcome her. I must make right with her the wrong I have done."

Luke did not understand everything Mrs Fung said but seeing her desperation, he could not refuse her.

"Please, go to her," she said.

"Today, Fung *Cheh*."

*   *   *

At the foot of Bukit Larut, Raymond Goh was waiting for Luke in civilian clothes.

"I don't go on duty yet," he said, as they shook hands. "You need some help moving your stuff to Mrs Fung's?"

"Thanks. Hop in."

Raymond swung up into the passenger seat of the Land Rover. Suddenly, on Luke's side, a scooter sped up. The visored rider shouted, "Luke McAllister?"

"Yeah," Luke said, as he turned to the voice. Froze at the faceless figure.

Raymond reached for his pistol.

The rider tossed a manila envelope at Luke, swerved round and skidded away. Luke and Raymond burst from the Land Rover and stared after the scooter. The number plate was indistinguishable.

Luke's mobile rippled.

"Yes," he snapped into it.

"You got the delivery." The same disguised voice he'd heard leaving the warning on his answering-machine. Luke stared at the envelope in his other hand. "It's papers. Go on, open it."

"Who is this?" Luke cradled the phone against his ear and opened the envelope. A school exercise book. Filled in painstaking manuscript.

"You should thank me for saving your life. Again."

"Yeah – I do. I mean it. I owe you. But how did you know?"

"You owe me, yes, you understand the balance of things. But you owe me triple. Twice for your life. And once for that pretty girl lawyer of yours."

Luke climbed back into the Land Rover, signalling Raymond to join him. "What do you want, Kaw? Or is it Ronnie Tan?" They shut the doors and wound up the windows. Luke placed the phone in the hands-free stand by the gearbox.

The voice crackled into the cab. "I can give you Jordan if you get me amnesty. His life for all those he killed on that hillside."

"Why should I believe you?"

"Read my testimony. That's just one part of it. There are seven more."

"Why me? I have no influence with the police or the

prosecutors."

"Don't lie to me! You've got Mohammed – that Planning Committee guy, ex-prosecutor – you got him listening to you. It's in the papers! You want Jordan, I know that. You and me, we can work together. You understand the way of the East, you will be my go-between."

"What do you want me to do?"

"Don't play stupid, McAllister! Your life is mine now. Get me amnesty and I'll give you Jordan."

"But –"

"I have nothing left to lose. I can take your life with me. Or that pretty girl's. One hour."

The line went dead.

As they drove up the hill, Raymond flicked through Tan's exercise book, reading out extracts. It detailed Jordan's instructions to Tan to dispose of the doctor and the intimidation of Zain, the project manager, and bribery of Tsui, the independent geophysicist. Also, the arson at Luke's office and the theft of his data.

"It's hearsay in this form, " Raymond said, as they made their way into Luke's house. "But there's enough in these allegations to start a formal police investigation."

"No!" Luke turned on his friend. "I'm not handing this over to the police. Yet. Lam will sidetrack it just like he's been sidetracking everything so far!"

"He's just one officer. Once the senior investigators get to see this, they'll override his personal crusade."

Luke did not answer. He called Mohammed on the speakerphone in the study. The older man sounded cautious. After some minutes of discussion, Mohammed said, "I'm sorry, McAllister, we cannot speak any further. I've just had news of your arrest. I cannot jeopardise the position of the Planning Committee during these investigations by close contact with an alleged criminal and radical activist."

"But –"

"You have to understand, my personal respect for you is

not enough in these circumstances. I have a responsibility to my colleagues and to the public office I represent. So far, all you have is hearsay evidence and a conversation with an unidentified man."

"But I know who he is."

"The allegations are serious ones against Mr Jordan. This mysterious man may himself be a murderer. We cannot offer amnesty just like that as a matter of public policy. Now, if you can persuade this man to bring himself in personally, then the prosecutor will decide the best thing to do on the evidence before him."

"This is one chance to get to the truth! I don't know who else to turn to."

After a pause, Mohammed said, "If the prosecutor has before him sufficient evidence – evidence that will stand up in court – then, he may – I say, *may* – considering public policy and in the interests of justice, he *may* take the necessary steps to ensure that justice is done, which *may* mean clemency for some in special circumstances. I can promise you no more than that."

"I'll get you sufficient evidence."

"One more thing. I shouldn't tell you this but you'll find out soon enough. Your arrest has been of interest to the landslide investigators. They're looking at the sabotage angle more closely. Your being in disguise that day will count against you. The police will want to talk to you again very soon."

"They know where to find me."

Luke turned to Raymond. "Lam's 'personal' crusade! I have to get the evidence on Jordan before any other bullshit gets pinned on me."

"Your man's going to call back in five minutes. We can't lose this chance."

"We?"

"I'm with you on this, Luke."

"You could risk you career."

Raymond nodded grimly. "I've known you all our lives. I've seen you go through these last eighteen months. As a cop, I say you got nothing. As your friend, I say go with your guts. I believe what you've told me and I can't stand by and see you sink deeper into the shit."

"Come on in, the swill's nice and warm."

The friends looked at each other and grinned.

* * *

"They need more information," Luke said, when Tan called back. "They need to hear it from you. They need evidence that's going to stand up in court."

"No fucking can do! I'm not giving myself up to the law!"

Luke kept talking, dredging up all his resources of persuasion and sincerity. Inching towards a compromise they could both trust. He wanted to meet Tan face to face. The voice at the end of the telephone could disappear, never call back. Luke was victim to Tan's whims this way. But, face to face, there might be a greater chance that he could persuade Tan to trust him and to give himself up. But Tan was not a fool. He saw traps in everything Luke said and refused to agree to anything. Luke was about to give up when he heard a weary tone creep into Tan's voice. He pushed on tentatively.

"Okay," Tan finally said. "Tonight. You and your one police rep. Unarmed."

"As a sign of good faith, you can choose the place."

There was a long pause. Then Tan said, "Three a.m. There's an abandoned temple ten miles east of the ridge above Old Kampung Tanah. No tricks – or you'll never hear from me again."

Luke was not surprised by his choice of location. It was difficult to get to – about five to six hours' drive, most of it through mountainous terrain on winding, narrow roads. If Luke made it on time, it would indicate to Tan his serious intentions and good faith. Its remoteness meant that Tan would know if there were any police tails. The jungle surroundings would give him cover to watch them, while he himself remained hidden, or to slip away without trace. And from what Luke had come to know about Tan, there was an aptness in the choice of religious setting close to the place of so much death.

Luke and Raymond talked for a long time, poring over a map of the Kampung Tanah region. Then Luke changed into fresh clothes and packed his tote-bag. They headed back down to Taiping.

Raymond would ensure that he got the task of checking on Luke's curfew that night as he came off shift. He would meet Luke at an agreed service station on the highway to Kuantan – the temple had to be approached from the east because of the slide impact to the west. He would wear his uniform but his colleagues would know nothing of his activities. Luke said, "If we get what it takes to nail Jordan, you're a hero. If not, you came by, found me gone and took off in pursuit of a fugitive – you bring me back and you're still a hero."

Leaving Raymond by his car at the foot of Bukit Larut, Luke headed for Mrs Fung's house. He tried the various office numbers he had for Jasmine and, after being passed to several lawyers and secretaries in the KL office, a secretary said that Ms Lian had had a nervous collapse and was being looked after at a client's home. Charming persuasion got Luke Jordan's condominium number.

Jasmine answered. She sounded dazed. There was no feeling in her voice when he gave his name. "Are you all right?" he asked.

"Yes ... No ... Who knows?"

"Why are you at Jordan's private apartment?"

"He's looking after me." She laughed without humour. "My nanny's in the other condo, I'm not a prisoner. But he'll be waiting to 'help' me if I try to leave. Reception downstairs must buzz him or something."

"What's Jordan done to you?"

"Nothing ... Oh, Luke, I'm sorry," Jasmine's voice suddenly broke. "I was so wrong about you. About everything. Now it's too late."

"No! It's not too late. It's going to be all right. I'll come for you. Tonight."

He heard nothing but her quiet weeping. "Jasmine?"

"Okay." She sounded lost. Like a little girl.

The wire-tap equipment in Jordan's penthouse switched itself off as Luke hung up

*　*　*

Luke spent the rest of the afternoon making preparations for the meeting with Tan that night. He bought electronic equipment and accessories and hunched over his mobile phone at Mrs Fung's stone-topped table. A new long-use battery stood charging in the battery stand. It was bulky but, with a talk-time of close on seven hours, it was what he needed. He accessed his voicemail company and reconfigurated his voicemail functions as well as changing the default message storage time from twenty minutes to six hours. He took the video camera from the trunk of the Land Rover and set it up on a tripod. He faced it and recorded without a break for twenty minutes.

Late in the day, a special-delivery parcel arrived for Mrs Fung. Luke signed for it. He recognized Jasmine's handwriting. Curious, he opened the parcel.

In it were the duplicate tapes Jasmine had made of Roberts's interview with Zain and Scott. Jasmine had also copied the bundles she'd found in the deeds storage. The post had dutifully brought them as she had arranged before leaving Seng & Mustafa's offices.

The parcel was postmarked the day before. A scribbled note in Chinese from Jasmine said, "Look after these for me, *Ah Ma*. If anything happens to me, give them to Luke."

Luke grinned. "That's my girl!"

He read through Tsui's papers and listened to the tapes on the dictaphone he kept in the glove compartment of the Land Rover. This was the evidence that corroborated everything he'd suspected all along. He felt a new determination to bring Tan in.

In the late afternoon, a community ambulance brought Mrs Fung home, accompanied by Mrs Bok and her husband. Luke stayed for long enough to settle the old woman. She seemed alert and relieved as they moved her from the stretcher to her bed. Mrs Bok fussed round her, issuing a barrage of instructions to her husband.

Luke bent over Mrs Fung and kissed her sunken cheek. "Jasmine will be with you tonight."

To the Boks, he said, "I've forgotten my shaving things. I won't be long."

In the Land Rover, Luke checked the time he had left. Three hours to Kuala Lumpur if he pushed it but he'd have to take care not to attract the attention of the speed cops. Allow one hour to deal with matters there. Then the long drive to the rendezvous with Tan. He would just make it. He headed for the highway and picked up speed for Kuala Lumpur.

Once there, he went straight to the railway station. He parked and went into the ornate Moorish structure. He carried his tote-bag with him. He came out empty-handed but for a greeting card and drove to a florist on the way to Jordan's condominium. Inside, he chatted to the owner, a middle-aged woman, who was captivated by his charm. Choosing a lavish basket of flowers, he pre-paid for a delivery, leaving the greeting card and detailed instruction. He gave the woman a huge tip.

"Don't worry, sir," the florist simpered. "Everything will be done exactly as you want it."

31

Harry lolled in alcoholic sleep, his mouth open, the tension in his features momentarily dispersed. After leaving Marietta's flat he had caught the early-morning Malaysian Airlines flight from Heathrow. In belligerent mood, he had knocked back the complimentary drinks, harassed the stewardesses and button-holed the other first-class passengers. He had only settled down after the captain had threatened to make an unscheduled stop in Dubai to have him taken off the plane.

As the 747 cruised over the Indian Ocean, three hours away from Kuala Lumpur, Harry seemed almost harmless in sleep. A boy emerged through the jowliness of the man, whose hopes had once promised so much happiness. In sleep, he trusted his muscular bulk and his loneliness to the cocoon of the aircraft as a child might entrust himself to his mother. But the flight would land soon at his destination and he would wake again into the years of fury that had formed him.

At about the same time, eight in the evening in Kuala Lumpur, Luke pulled up in front of Jordan's condominium block. He did not know if Jordan was there but he did not want to be seen. Through the glass frontage, the reception desk was empty but the staff door was open, revealing two figures ringed in cigarette smoke. Luke slipped out of the Land Rover and stood in the shadows by a car, pretending to fish in his pockets, while he assessed his next move.

In Taiping, Mrs Fung swallowed the last of a nutrition drink. She felt stronger than she had in a long time. Luke would keep his word. She would see Jasmine again tonight.

Mrs Bok settled the old woman and switched off the light. Out in the living area, her husband was reading the paper. He looked up at the clock on the wall. "Doesn't Luke have to be here after dark because of his curfew?"

Outside the condominium block, two Suzuki Troopers drew up. Groups of young people tumbled out, Asians and some Western youths, carrying bottles and bowls of food. As they poured into the building, the security guard glanced up from his card game in the staff cubbyhole. He did not notice the older white man behind the group.

Luke slipped away from the kids and into the stairwell. He ran up four floors and picked up the lift to ride to the tenth floor.

At the door of Jordan's guest apartment, Luke glanced round. No one else to be seen in the corridor. He did not know if Jasmine was alone inside. But he had to take the risk.

He knocked.

He heard movement and then her voice. "Who is it?"

He showed himself to the peephole in the door. The bolts slid and the latch clicked. The door opened and Jasmine threw herself into his arms.

At the bank of TV monitors in Jordan's penthouse, one screen showed them coming into the hallway, Jasmine burying her sudden tears in Luke's shoulder.

At Changi Airport in Singapore, Jordan and Roberts arrived to catch their return flight to Kuala Lumpur after a long day of meetings with the Titiwangsa project funders and insurers.

As they headed for check-in, Jordan said, "See to Jasmine's witness statement tonight."

"Tonight?" Roberts looked bleak. He was exhausted.

"We don't know when the police will call on her. We need to know what she's going to say – 'jog her memory' if she 'misremembers' things. She's had today to stew over her position. We can't leave it any longer."

"I'll see to it." But without enthusiasm.

Luke steered Jasmine into the living room, all his senses alert to possible danger. As he settled her on the sofa, his gaze swept the room. Then he was up again, moving through the apartment, checking that they were alone. Satisfied, he sat down close to Jasmine and took her in his arms. She spoke through her sobs, disjointed, hurried. Her tone was weak and uncertain. Through gentle prompting, he was able to piece together everything that had happened since she'd left her mother's house.

"... and, those poor people ..." Jasmine rambled on, tears staining her face "... I'm to blame, too – my relocation package put them right in the path of the tower collapse. They fell for the deal, even though it stitched them up on funding, on everything. They didn't see it. I was too good at my job. Now, so many are dead! They should get compensation, shouldn't they? They can't get their families back but at least money might make something right. But I stitched them up there, too!" She crumpled again into an anguish of sobs.

Luke held her. His calm anchored her distress. "The Kampung Tanah people gave up the fight because they were being intimidated by Jordan's people. Not because of your enticing relocation package. My darling, don't torture yourself like this. I've got confirmation of it – Tan bribed and bullied the town's leaders into submission."

Jasmine looked up, hiccupping to still her weeping. She seemed so vulnerable in her wide-eyed relief.

Luke said, "Compensation can't bring back the people who died. You can't change what's past but you can make the future. Don't give up just because of the mistakes of the past. Make them right again."

"I've been so wrong, Luke. I'm sorry – all the things I said about you, everything I did to damage you. I've been a monster all my life. There's nothing left now. What's the use of trying any more? He's won. You've all won. You can do what you want with me, I don't care any more."

Luke wrapped her in his arms, kissing her, stroking her hair. He let her talk on. He kept his anger close in his heart, focusing it into his determination to see Jordan destroyed. Jasmine's discoveries –

his missing report, Jordan's exchange of notes with Tsui, the taped interviews with Zain and Scott – all added to the arsenal of evidence against Jordan. But the cost to Jasmine had been severe. Holding her close to him, her broken voice in his ear, seeing her strained face, he felt a fury to settle the score against Jordan.

He could not bring himself to tell her why he had come to find her.

He stroked her pale cheeks. She drew him to her in a long kiss.

In the utility room in the penthouse, their movements played on one of the TV monitors. Pang had been instructed by Jordan to watch Jasmine, to accompany her if she tried to leave, to note any visitors. "If McAllister turns up," Jordan had said, "I want to know everything that passes between them. Put a tail on him when he leaves and notify Kidd Tan. We might be able to do the job properly the next time."

Pang was in the utility room. He had been there all day, watching Jasmine on the monitors. She hadn't tried to leave the apartment again since an attempt early in the morning. She had spent the day pacing the rooms, weeping. Pang had had little rest since he had started his surveillance duty in Taiping nights before. Bored and exhausted, he now lay on the truckle bed by the television asleep, empty bottles and burger cartons on the floor. A Jackie Chan movie was playing, loudly, on the set.

He had called in his son, a sturdy boy in his early twenties, to take a shift in watching the monitors. After the initial thrill of spying on an attractive woman, Mattson Pang had trailed downstairs and was now playing rummy with the security guard behind the reception.

Luke looked into Jasmine's eyes. He said, "About the other night ... I said some things ... I didn't handle it very well ..."

Jasmine traced his lips with her fingers to stop him. "We've both been mule-headed. Promise me one thing?"

Luke nodded.

"We won't lose each other again."

"I promise." He held her to him. The night to come hung over them. "No matter what happens. Wherever I am, we will always be together."

She returned his embrace with a desperate intensity, catching all the time they had lost. She ran her hands over every part of him, like a blind woman memorising the moment. Their desire ignited with a new urgency. Falling among the cushions, they touched with passionate fervour, forgetting everything but each other, present only to each exquisite caress and the kiss of their bodies. Jasmine felt as if her heart would burst with pleasure as every part of her opened to the brush of his lips. When he moved inside her, he seemed to touch an old, infinite longing that, rising from her very centre, up through her heart and releasing itself in a long, groaning song, left her at last contained and sighing into stillness.

Afterwards, Luke held her in his arms for a long time. Finally, he held her very still and very close, kissing her face. Then he drew apart and began to dress.

She sensed the change in his mood even though nothing in his manner or features had altered. "What is it?"

"We must get you out of here."

"But how?" she said. "There's a twenty-four hour watchman downstairs. I didn't get very far the last time I tried."

Luke said gently, "I'll find a way."

Reality faced them again as they dressed. Luke did not know where to begin. How could he tell her that her mother was dying?

In Mrs Fung's living area, Mr Bok finally stood up. "We could get into trouble if we know he's not here and we do nothing. Aiding and abetting a criminal."

"It's not our business …" his wife began.

Mr Bok picked up the phone and dialled the police station.

Luke sat down beside Jasmine, taking her hand. Speaking quietly, he told her. What had happened that morning, the course of Mrs Fung's long illness and what she had made him promise. Then he told her what Mrs Fung had said to him in the hospital. "She wanted me to come to you. To make right what had gone wrong between us."

Jasmine sat very still. This was the news that she had always dreaded. It was the moment that focused all her guilt – for obeying her mother in escaping and yet for not having the courage to have disobeyed her. For hating her mother's ambitions for her and for having lived them out. For having failed her own dreams because she loved her mother. And, finally, for having failed the old woman, after all.

She looked up at Luke. "I must go to her."

Luke nodded but he did not move. "There's something else," he said. "There's something I have to do tonight."

In Taiping, as Mr Bok waited for the line to ring, there was a knock on the door. He hung up. Husband and wife went to the front verandah. Raymond, in full uniform, was standing there.

At Subang Airport, Jordan and Roberts's flight from Singapore touched down. As it taxied to the terminal building, Jordan said, "You'll come with me straight to the apartment."

Roberts nodded without a word.

On the MAS flight from London, half an hour behind, the crew were clearing the supper trays. Harry hung over the toilet in the cramped cubicle and vomited a spray of alcohol and omelette. He washed his face and grimaced into the mirror. He had not forgotten why he had come. Digging down into his sore of anger, he stroked and prodded it till its hurt ate into him. His grimace contorted into a snarl of hatred.

Raymond left Mr and Mrs Bok with an air of determination. "There's no more you can do. Leave it to me. I'll track the *ang mo* down."

Luke told Jasmine about Tan's telephone calls and the murder, bribery and intimidation Tan had revealed in his notebook. He described the attack on him in Taiping. He told her about Detective Lam and about Mohammed's warning. And he told her where he was meeting Tan later that night.

"But how do you know it's the same man we saw on the slopes? What if it's a trap?"

"I have no alternatives left. It's a risk. But if I'm going to get anything on Jordan, I have to trust this man. He saved our lives – that must count for something."

Upstairs, in the penthouse utility room, the Chinese movie broke for the ten o'clock news. Pang woke with a start. Over the sound of the ads, he heard voices from the CCTV monitors. He scrambled up and peered at them.

Luke was saying, "Tonight could be make or break. Tan is our key if he can finger Jordan for the murder of Dr Chan and all those deaths from the collapse of the tower. I have to leave now if I'm going to make the rendezvous."

"What if –"

Luke held her gaze. "No more what-ifs. You won't lose me again, I promise. Whatever happens, you'll get word from me and you'll know what to do. The one thing you mustn't do yet is go to the police. Go to Mohammed. Straight to him. No one else."

Jasmine nodded.

"We've got to get going." Luke drew Jasmine towards the door.

Watching the monitor, Pang hissed, "Shit!" He looked round for Mattson. Not there. He headed out of the penthouse, grabbing his gun holster as he ran.

"I'm frightened. What's going to happen?" Jasmine paused in the hallway of the apartment.

"Don't be afraid." Luke smiled. "I need you to be that spunky titch of a lawyer I've always known."

She leaned up to kiss him, saying with a confidence she did not feel, "You got it."

The door burst open.

Pang exploded in, pistol drawn, his boxer's bulk filling the hallway.

*　　*　　*

In one swift move, Luke threw Jasmine to the floor and swung a sidewiping kick at Pang. His heel caught the pistol and sent it across the hall. Using his momentum, Luke hurled the weight of his body behind his crunching blow into Pang's face. As the man staggered, Luke grabbed his head with both hands and rammed it down into his shooting knee-jerk.

Stepping aside, he let Pang's unconscious bulk thud to the floor. Without a pause, he was at the door, glancing down the corridor. Empty. He slid back into the apartment and shut the door.

Jasmine had picked up the pistol and was pointing it nervously at Pang's prone form. She looked at Luke. "Jordan's security man. My 'nanny'. He must've come down from the penthouse to check up on me and heard us through the door."

"Any more of them?"

"There was another man, but I haven't seen him since they brought me here."

Luke glanced at his watch. He had to make the meet with Tan and he had spent longer here with Jasmine than he had meant to. He'd have to drive like a madman to reach the temple.

He hauled Pang into the bathroom and using leads ripped from the entertainment system, he trussed him like an oversized turkey, face down on the floor. He thrust a flannel into his mouth. Quickly, searching Pang's pockets, Luke came across the keys to the Mercedes. He tossed them to Jasmine. "Your car, madam."

He locked Pang into the bathroom. "Let's go."

Jasmine stared wildly at him. "What shall I do? What if Jordan or another thug comes after me?"

Luke gripped her and locked his gaze on hers. "You have the pistol. Use it."

"But –"

"Time is running short for both of us. There are no alternatives."

Jasmine took a breath and nodded.

Luke said, "We can only hope that Jordan won't risk his upper hand. He's got you caught even if he's not physically holding you. Whatever you might claim to the authorities, your 'mental instability' undermines it all. If he comes haring after you, guns blazing, he'll just give credibility to your version of events."

"What if something happens to you tonight?"

"The evidence will speak for itself."

"What evidence?"

"Whatever happens – I'll get word to you. You'll know what to do."

"You said that just now. What do you mean?"

Luke paused. He traced her face with his fingertips, brushed a hair from her temple. His eyes were glittering with intensity. "It's safer if you don't know what you don't need to know till the time comes. If that happens, I know you'll do what's right. Whatever disagreements we've had, whichever side we've been on, I trust you. With my life, with everything that has any meaning. Now, we've got to get going."

They rode the lift down to the second floor and then took the stairs.

The security guard and Mattson Pang were now half-way through a bottle of *arak*, a fiery local brew. The guard glanced up as a mixed-race couple sauntered arm-in-arm across the lobby and out into the car park. Later he was to tell Jordan that the man sounded South African and the couple had been talking about nightclubs to dance in that night and, no, he had not seen their faces. "They were cuddling, you know?"

Once outside, Jasmine touched Luke's cheek. "I love you," she said, and kissed him before sliding into the Mercedes.

He watched her pull out of the car park and accelerate into the darkness, then he climbed into the Land Rover and headed for the highway to Kuantan.

* * *

When Jordan and Roberts arrived, just after eleven p.m., the security guard scurried out to the reception desk, smoothing down his hair. "Quiet night, sir," he reported.

Mattson raced Jordan to the penthouse in the service lift. He stepped out as Jordan strode through the empty rooms. "Where the hell is Pang?"

Roberts, pausing by the CCTV monitors, saw a figure struggling on the bathroom floor, muffled grunting coming over the speaker.

Crashing through the bathroom door a few minutes later, Jordan hauled Pang round and yanked the flannel from his mouth.

Pang gasped, "The consultant – he was here – Secret meeting with Mr Tan. I tried to stop him – Tan's grassing on the whole damn thing!"

"Fuck!" Jordan hurled round and stormed up to the penthouse, leaving Mattson to untie his father. Roberts trotted, pale-faced, behind him.

They watched the tapes. Everything that Luke and Jasmine had said and done. Everything that they knew, Jordan now knew. He turned away and kicked the truckle bed across the utility room with a yell.

Roberts was watching the love-making again, Pang and Mattson now mesmerized beside him.

In the hall, Harry stood and listened to the sound of his wife's voice playing back. He had come straight from the airport. Jordan would know where to find Jasmine. He would give Harry whatever he needed to deal with her as she deserved. Dropping his overnight case on the floor, Harry headed for the sounds. What the hell was his wife doing making love in Jordan's penthouse?

When Harry watched Jasmine and Luke making love on the tape, his grotesque fury finally devoured the whole of him. There was a madness in his eyes as a clammy sweat made him shiver. Then a flush of fire – and his features contorted as blood pumping murderous violence exploded through his veins.

Staring bewitched at the monitor, Mattson had his hands in his jeans pockets. Dazed from *arak* and a bursting hard-on, he was in a reality of his own. "Fuck me, babe, I'm hot for you ..."

Jordan watched from the middle of the room as Harry flung himself at the boy with a roar. Harry crashed to the floor on top of Mattson. He had him by the throat, banging his head – harder, harder – against the parquet. "I'll kill you!" Harry screamed.

Pang and Roberts fought to tear Harry from the boy, grappling at his rigid arms, landing punches on his torso, trying to drag him off

They were helpless against his massive, raging bulk. Harry hurled them back, barely interrupted in his focus, fracturing Roberts's rib with a blow, breaking Pang's tooth with another.

Mattson's head was bleeding, he flailed pathetically. Harry tightened his huge hands round the boy's throat and began to crush the vice inwards.

Jordan stepped up to Harry. He had seen the final solution in the fool's jealous rage. He placed a commanding hand on his shoulder. In the voice that demanded obedience, he said,

"Stop it. Now."

As if awakened from a trance, Harry blinked and his body sagged.

"Now, I said."

Harry let go and straightened back from the boy. He looked up at Jordan.

Drawing him up, Jordan walked him to the window, an arm on his shoulder. Behind them, Pang rushed to his son. Roberts moved to a chair, nursing his chest.

In a quiet voice, Jordan said, "She's killing you, mate, isn't she? It's been hell for you all this time. Now you know for sure. She's screwing McAllister and screwing you for a laugh all along."

Harry contorted in fury. Jordan's arm contained him, reassured him. "We're in this together, mate," Jordan went on. "She's screwing you. She's screwing me, too. You heard what she's up to. She's giving my secrets to McAllister. I trusted her, like you trusted her. She's cheating on me, same as she's cheating on you."

A sob escaped Harry.

"I said before that I'd take care of McAllister. And I will. Tonight. I promise you he'll get what he deserves."

Harry looked up with gratitude.

"But what are you going to do about your whore of a wife?"

Harry cracked. "I'll kill her! She lied to me about her life – she's a fucking Chink coolie! Made me the goddamn laughing stock of this country! I'll kill her! Fucking brazen whore!"

"I'll tell you how to find her."

32

When Jasmine walked down the path to her mother's house, it was one a.m. In the still hours of the night, she had cut an hour off the usual three-and-a-half-hour drive. Still clouds hung against the sky, catching the light of the full moon. In the monochrome night, the flame tree sheltered the house, its crown sprinkled with ghostly flowers.

Harry was an hour and a half behind her. Jordan had offered him a driver and a car but in the basement car park Harry had punched the man out and grabbed the keys. He was driving a silver Jaguar from Jordan's personal fleet. In the back was a futuristic entertainment system that included a mini VCR–TV. A duplicate of the love-making segment on the surveillance tape was playing over and over again. The sound was turned up loud. He could not see the pictures but Harry's anguish-streaked eyes flicked between the sound of the love-making and the tunnelling darkness ahead.

The torment caressed him, drew into its embrace all his disappointed expectations of the years. It fulfilled his belief in himself and in his world of faithless whores. But even as each sigh vindicated his howling rage, it killed him over again.

Luke's Land Rover climbed the snaking incline eastwards into the Titiwangsa Range from Kuantan, Luke and Raymond silent in the cab.

At a rest-stop on the Kuala Lumpur–Kuantan highway, forty minutes behind them, Jordan slowed his Porsche and flashed his lights at Kidd's sports Mercedes before accelerating on. Kidd squealed out behind him in a thrust of power. He had come straight from Kampung Tanah after Jordan's call just over an hour before.

An automatic pistol lay on the seat beside Kidd. Another was in its holster under his arm.

Kidd's features were set in grim resolve. What the hell was *Tai Koh* up to? The last time that Kidd had seen Elder Brother, Tan had been in a state of nervous collapse and hardly coherent. Kidd hadn't thought that Tan would have had the lucidity to contact the consultant in secret nor negotiate an amnesty deal. Kidd swore.

Did the gibbering idiot know that he was jeopardising their whole family enterprise? How did he think he could blow the whistle on Jordan and not bring down the law on the Tans' network of dealings? Did he not care about his own business, his family?

Or perhaps he really did want to blow it all out of the water.

"Fucking bloody cunt!" Kidd yelled in Cantonese. In the last year, he had been the effective head of the family. He had taken their business to new heights. They were on the threshold of a breakthrough onto American turf. He had stitched up Jordan well and good. And, in between all this, he had taken time to buck up his brother, visit Tan's family, comfort Tan's wife and play with Tan's children. Fucking shit, he was husband and father to Tan's immediate family. And all the while, that stupid, religious, fucking fool of a brother was concerned with nothing but his own skin and soul – whatever the hell that was. He was so wrapped up in his loony head that he would destroy them all for – for what? A pat on the back by the fucking cops and a lifetime of holy retreat.

An hour later they reached the temple. It was in an isolated stretch of jungle, abandoned farms nearby. It was half-way down the valley, approachable only by foot, along an overgrown track. It had once served Chinese market-gardeners in this satellite community of Kampung Tanah. The farmers here had been the first to sell up three years before, and the temple had now fallen into disrepair, swallowed again by the vines and offshoots of the encroaching rainforest.

Kidd pulled up behind Jordan in the shadows by some trees on the trunk road. He had seen a Land Rover parked half a mile back. That meant the consultant had already arrived. Kidd stepped out of the car, shoving the pistol into his belt and touching a hand to the one bolstered under his arm. He saw Jordan emerge from his car and over the living hum of the jungle, he heard metal sliding as his client checked the magazine on his automatic. Jordan's dark shape moved towards him in the dim night. Jordan said, "Let's go."

* * *

When Jasmine had let herself into her mother's house, Mrs Bok had met her with confusion. But as they stood in the light of the living area, recognition dawned and Mrs Bok dissolved into tears. "We all haven't seen you since you were a girl! It's good that you are back now. But such a sad time."

"How is my mother?"

"She's stronger after the blood transfusion. But she's very changed because of her illness. Be strong."

Jasmine hugged Mrs Bok and thanked her, startling the older woman with her Western forwardness. "Why don't you go home to your family tonight? I'll look after my mother from now on."

Jasmine went through the house locking all the windows and doors as Mrs Bok headed down the path to her house across the road. She took the pistol out of her handbag and put it in the top drawer of the sideboard, then switched off the lights.

She slipped into her mother's room and drew towards the figure in the bed. Moonlight streamed in through open windows. As she approached, her mother turned, her eyes glittering in the dim light. "I heard your voice," she said. "I've been lying here listening to you moving around the house. Thank you for coming."

Jasmine sat down on the bed and carefully hugged her mother. Mrs Fung was thin as a waif in her arms. "I wanted to stay the first time I came back, *Ah Ma*. But I was so frightened to lose everything … I'm sorry I could not be a good daughter to you …"

Mrs Fung held Jasmine's hand to her heart. "Don't blame yourself, my little one. You did the best you could. You have been a good daughter. You still are. The best that a mother could long for."

"I'm sorry for the things I said the other night – about you and *Ah Ba*, about everything."

"We have so little time now, don't let it slip away with regrets. I blame no one – not you, not even your father. I've had a long life. And everything in it I chose for myself."

"Chose?"

"Yes, even the sadness and pain – does it seem strange? Maybe to some people it doesn't look like much of a life. But I lived it, I chose it, each step along the path. Whatever life offered me, good or bad, I went to meet it. I did my best. That is the greatest peace I can know at the end of my journey."

In the silver dark, Jasmine lay down beside her mother. They lay like they used to when she was a child, talking softly, sharing secrets.

Now that Jasmine was here at last, Mrs Fung was afraid again. Afraid to tell her the one secret she had never revealed and the one truth that devoured her from within. She gave herself to this moment with her daughter, putting off for a while longer the revelation that might finally tear them apart. When morning came, she promised herself, that would be the time. But for now, in the quiet dark, she had her little daughter back again and that was all that mattered.

Cuddled up against her mother, listening to her voice again, familiar shapes and shadows around her, Jasmine found herself talking, freeing again the girl she had always been and whom she had lost for so long. In the drive here, through the tropical dark, she had felt freed. Everything that had meant so much to her throughout her adult life lay like debris in the aftermath of the landslide – her life with Harry, her career, her brilliant work for Jordan. Everything she had built up with such will and sacrifice had meant nothing, after all, had been empty façades and baubles bought with cash and blood.

"I didn't know who I was any more," she said. "If I wasn't Mrs Harry Taunton, if I wasn't the brilliant young partner at Carruthers or number one on Jordan's legal team, I felt I was no one. But somehow, right now, it doesn't matter. I am who I've always been – Jasmine Fung, the Jasmine who tried to make you happy, who's always loved Luke. Who might've stayed forever 'that Tommy Fung's girl' but had the chance to choose another destiny. But I chose the wrong one. I made so many wrong choices. Is it too late to make a right one? Or will the right one be the wrong one now?"

Mrs Fung, stroking Jasmine's hair, staring into an internal landscape, murmured, "Too late, too early – these have no meaning. There is only ripeness. Each tree comes to ripeness in its own time. The *angsana* tree may flourish young, the flame tree comes to bloom only in the cycle of a generation."

"A long time ago, I wanted to be a lawyer of the people," Jasmine said, "but I made myself stop wanting it. There was so much else to want. And then, one day, I finally had it all. I had all the success I could ever want and I knew I had failed."

"And if you could make it come out right again?"

"I gave my whole self to something I didn't believe in. I was so blinded by Jordan's ambition and success that I didn't see what was underneath. He's a gangster and a murderer. I wanted to be a lawyer of the people and the people are dead because of Jordan. Thousands of them. As a lawyer, my duty is to my client, I told myself. As a woman, my heart cries out for the people who died and I know I have to live the truth, whatever the price might be."

"The truth ..." Soft as a breath.

Suddenly, out of the still night, a madman was shouting. It was close, slamming into them in its hatred. Footsteps on the front verandah. Banging – fists on wood.

"Jasmine! Where the fuck are you?"

It was Harry.

* * *

Jasmine stepped out into the dark living area. Harry's black shape stormed up and down the verandah, peering through the windows, hammering on the flimsy door.

"There you are, bitch! I'm going to kill you!" He rattled the window frame. His voice carried across the compound.

Jasmine opened the drawer and took out the pistol. It was leaden in her hand. Her mouth was dry, her heart beating so fast she could hardly breathe.

"I can see you, you goddamn whore! I'll kill you! I saw you humping that bastard tonight! It was *sooo* good, wasn't it?" He groaned obscenely, mimicking her sighs.

The pistol slipped from her hands. She spun round with an involuntary cry of horror. "How did you –"

"The fucking flat's wired, bitch! We fucking saw everything! Playback, slow motion, backwards, fast forward – any way you like it!"

Jasmine stepped towards the door. Luke! Jordan knew everything – what evidence Luke had, what he was planning. Where he was tonight.

The pistol lay on the sideboard behind her.

"You've screwed me all along! Fucking lied to me! This where you live? Where's Daddy-pimp and serving-wench-Mum? Did he sell you off, too, you Chink whore? I'm going to kill you!"

Working up his rage, Harry kicked at the front door. The frame splintered.

Jasmine stared wildly round for the pistol. She grabbed the standing lamp by the table and yanked out the lead.

Cracking wood. The lock snapped.

She smashed the top of the stand against the wall. The lampshade flew off. The lightbulb shattered.

A last burst and Harry hurled through.

He stopped short. The splintered glass of the bulb hovered an inch from his throat. Jasmine holding the wooden length of the lamp like an assegai. Standing firm.

"Get out!" Her voice was deep with fury. For a flash, her terror dispersed. The shame that had paralysed her for all their years together was gone. A power she had not felt for a long time surged in her.

This was her home. She would kill him if she had to.

In the ghostly light, Harry saw the new strength in her eyes. He hesitated. The authority in her voice had startled him.

She thrust the jagged glass at him. He took a step back.

Then he saw it. The lamp stand was heavy. Too heavy for her to have the advantage for long. He feinted a blow with his left arm. She jerked the stand. He grabbed it with his right and wrenched it from her. Swinging it out and then back, the base catching her hard in the midriff.

She fell heavily, winded. He heaved the stand aside. It fell with a crash, juddering the floor. He rushed at her. "I'll kill you! Bitch!"

Jasmine fought him with a terrible ferocity. Clawed at his face, jabbed his eyes. Heaving for air. Knee jerking up at him. There was no fear yet, only the strength of rage and hatred, exploding now after the years of abuse. But Harry was stronger, his huge bulk weighing down on her, immovable against her flailings. It was only a matter of time and he would have his way.

Across the garden, neighbours lay in the dark and listened to the uproar. Some came to the windows, peering out into the night. They had not heard such violence for more than twenty years. Perhaps Tommy Fung had come home.

Mrs Fung pulled herself up, clinging to the bedstead. She called out, "Someone! Help us! Help!" But her cracked voice did not carry beyond the enclosing walls.

She looked wildly around. What could she do? Call the police – but the phone was in the other room. Where was Mrs Bok? "Help …" she sobbed.

She did not understand what they were shouting. But she recognised one word. Kill. He was going to kill Jasmine, no matter what. She knew the certainty in his voice. She wept, "Someone … please … help us …"

Harry pinned Jasmine to the floor. Her mouth was bleeding where he had hit her. One arm was caught under her, searing with agony under the weight of both their bodies. He leaned his weight painfully onto her other wrist. His bulk on her was suffocating. He had pulled off her jeans and they tangled on one leg. He pinned a thick forearm against her throat. "I'll show you what you deserve, fuck you! I'll show you!"

His buttocks pistoned furiously, shunting her against the floor with each thrust. She writhed in fury, not giving up, her face contorted in tears and disgust and rage.

*　　*　　*

Mrs Fung held herself up against the door frame. In the mercurial dark, she saw the upturned furniture, the broken lamps and ornaments across the floor. Inhuman sounds tore up from the debris.

She dragged herself with an effort into the living room, leaning heavily against the sideboard. Inched her way along it. Suddenly, she felt the pistol huge under her hands.

When she saw the rape, a moan rose from the depths of her. It was as if the years had vanished and she was back on that terrible night long ago. Her husband beating her daughter, throwing the little girl to the floor, kneeling over her, leering drunk, his penis angry in his hands. "Don't you speak to me like that! I'll show you who's boss here!"

The white man's huge body in front of her now. Pale buttocks in the air. Jasmine's legs – that was all she could see of her daughter.

"You stop now!" Mrs Fung cried in English. "Stop! Stop!"

Harry did not hear the frail voice. He grunted and churned, sweating, furious, snarling.

The first shot caught him on the left shoulder-blade. He jerked backwards with a roar of shock. Even as the noise rolled across the compound, another shot exploded into the night. It smashed into his liver as he twisted round. Blood burst in sprays over Jasmine.

Mrs Fung, gun in both hands, leaned against the sideboard, each shot staggering her into it. She was no more than seven feet away from Harry.

The third bullet tore into his chest as he spun round from the impact of the second. There was a look of disbelief on his face. The last three shots thudded into his torso and caved in one side of his head.

The air stank of gunsmoke. The silence rang in the women's ears. Harry's body lay on its back, legs twisted under it, trousers down by the ankles. Jasmine dragged herself away, whimpering and sobbing for air, furiously pulling on her jeans.

Mrs Fung slid down to the floor, dropping the pistol.

The women clung to each other a long time, weeping.

Mrs Fung looked into her daughter's tear-streaked face. It was not even morning yet and the time had come.

"My little one," she said. "I want to tell you the truth about the night your father disappeared."

33

Sitting in the dark on the floor, Jasmine listened to her mother's tired voice. She was shaking and stunned by the sudden stillness of Harry's corpse. She was living out a nightmare. The furniture in chaos, moonlight streaming in, smashed glass on the floor and in the window-panes. A woman covered in blood. Weeping. But now, in living it, she felt no fear, no desire to flee as she had in the dreams. A focused alert part of her watched from within, absorbed calmly the words her mother spoke.

As her mother talked, Jasmine remembered that terrible night, all the details she had fought so hard to forget for more than twenty years. They had never spoken of it, not even the day after it had happened. She had believed for a time in London that she had escaped the memory. But it had festered inside her, infected the new life she had thought she'd made, reincarnated itself into her husband.

It had happened on a night like this, moon-drenched and beautiful. Mrs Fung had quarrelled with her husband again after dinner, Tommy Fung wanting more money for another "sure-fire business scheme" in Bangkok. In a card game earlier that day he had lost all the profit he had made on pimping four little Thai girls the month before. He screamed, in a drunken frenzy, boasting of sexual encounters with virgin girls, "A fresh young virgin cunt gives a man success in business! No wonder I fail all the time if all I get is your stinking dried cunt! In Bangkok, I get all the young girls I want. Once a year, at least, a man needs a virgin … I bring them in, sell them at good price, we live like kings for ever, I promise you."

Jasmine cleared the table, stony-faced, biting back her tears.

She did not look at her parents as they paced rings round each other, like combatants to the death. Her mother was wailing, "No, no more money! I have to feed my child. No more girls, those poor things, I can't bear it any more, I can't let you do this any more."

The beating would start soon. Jasmine, eight years old, wiry-limbed, dark from the sun, silent and burning with hatred and pain. Stop it, *Ah Ba*, stop it, she screamed inside, like so many times before. Stop it, don't hurt *Ah Ma*, not this time, please, not this time. Why did he have to be like this? Didn't he see how hard her mother tried? Why did he hate *Ah Ma* so? Jasmine's heart was bursting with agony. She could not watch them. But their raised voices pierced through her. *Ah Ma*, give him the money, just this one more time, make him love you. Outwardly, clearing the bowls, stacking the dishes, methodically, teeth clenched against her anguish, pleading inside. Jasmine moved through the kitchen like a ghost.

A solid crunch. Fist against face. Her mother stumbling against a chair, falling heavily to the floor.

Jasmine spun round, arms filled with crockery.

Her mother scrambling to her feet, sobbing as if her heart would break. Stumbling away, out of the living area. Bedroom door slamming. Go to her, *Ah Ba*, she screamed inside her head. Be sweet to her like you were yesterday with me. You gave me that doll but you gave her nothing. Go and make it all right with her now, please. Maybe there's a surprise present you got her, give it to her, make her stop crying.

She felt the hot tears pouring down her face, her breath convulsing with the sobs. Her father, turning away from the bedroom, saw her. "Don't fucking look at me like you hate me. Your mother gets what she deserves."

He sat down at the table. His anger seemed to ebb. "She doesn't understand me. Come here and give me a cuddle. I need you to love me now. You always take her side, don't you? Come and listen to your old father's side for a change."

Jasmine couldn't move. I love you both, don't you see? she wanted to say, but no sound came. She wanted to go to him, rouse him from his sorry state. Make him laugh with her again, like they'd done the day before. But she heard her mother sobbing behind the bedroom door. She wanted to climb into *Ah Ma*'s arms, stop her wretched weeping, cling to her, protect her.

Her father scowled. "Got nothing to say, girl?"

Suddenly, he stood up. "The fucking cunt's got you scared of me, hasn't she? Badmouthed me to my own bloody daughter!" Cursing, pacing angry steps by the table, working up his rage. "My own fucking daughter, got her hating me, poisoned her against me …"

He turned towards the bedroom.

No! No more! Jasmine stared in speechless anguish. Then she hurled the bowls and dishes to the floor. China smashing, fragments flying high. Hardly aware of what she was doing. Screaming, frenzied hysteria. Throwing herself at her father, her small fists pounding at him. "Stop it, stop it, *Ah Ba*! Stop it! Please, don't hurt *Ah Ma* any more! Stop it!"

He slapped her, snapping her head to the side. He hauled her up by the arms and shook her like a baby. He hurled her to the floor. Her head crashed down hard. He was shrieking, "I'm your father! You don't speak to me like that! I'll show you who's the boss!"

He fell to his knees at her feet, unstrapping his belt, ripping at his fly, pulling out his dark, erect penis.

Jasmine sprawled on the floor, terrified and fascinated. Beyond the hideous engorged penis, there was a mad brightness in her father's face. He seemed to be half smiling through the mask of his rage. It was that wildly pleased look he got sometimes when he'd played with her, the evil dragon to her vanquishing princess, the tiger to her safari Barbie. Only this time, there was an unseeing fury in his eyes that stared beyond her and it petrified her. In the one moment she might have got away, she did not move, could not. And then, his thick arm held her shoulder down to the floor and she was trapped.

His ruddy face, stinking of alcohol, was huge above her, so close she could see the beads of sweat on his pores. He was breathing hard, shaky, gasping breaths. He was on his knees still but the heat of his body burned above her. With his free hand, he scrabbled for her legs, roughly pulling them apart, angry fingers groping for her panties. She felt the scorching tip of his penis brush her belly. He rasped in a breath. She could not take her eyes off his face, contorted in hatred and rage and excitement. Her body felt like a doll's, beyond her control and will, as if all power and blood had been severed at her throat.

Mrs Fung came at him then, flying out of the bedroom, hurling herself at him, jabbing the end of her hairbrush at him. Drawing blood across his forehead, just missing his eye, jabbing into his windpipe. Hauling him off her daughter. "You do what you like to me, you bastard! Leave her alone, leave my daughter be! I'll kill you, I swear it, if you lay a finger on her again!"

He gagged, gasped for breath, clutching his throat. Sprawled on his knees, his trousers tangled, his penis dangling grotesquely. Mrs Fung stood over Jasmine, poised to fight him again. "You keep away from her!"

He glared at her and, for a long moment, their hatred locked into each other. Then, he dragged himself to his feet, buckling himself in again. Swearing and muttering under his breath, he turned away. "Aaah, you're not worth the fucking effort …"

He stumbled out into the yard. Staggering, he turned round and screamed, "I'm getting out! This time, it's for good, you lousy bitch. I don't need you, you hear me? I got friends, connections! I got women in Bangkok! Fresh young cunts! You won't ever see me again. You can break your heart crying but that's a fucking promise!"

Mrs Fung stood by the window and watched him swagger down the path, his curses ringing across the neighbourhood, fading only long after he was gone from sight.

Now, sitting on the floor with her mother, Jasmine said softly, "We cleaned up this room together, I remember. Both of us crying. You kept saying, 'It's better if he's gone, I'll kill him if he comes back.' You were so crazy, it was terrifying, I'd never seen you like that before."

Mrs Fung took a long shuddering breath.

"You put me to bed, I remember. You stayed till I fell asleep, just like when I was a baby. You sang a lullaby …"

Mrs Fung smiled through her tears. "I'd forgotten that."

"But *Ah Ba* never came back."

Mrs Fung sucked in a breath. She did not move. Then, she shook her head. "He came back. Later that night. Somehow I knew he would. I prayed that he wouldn't. But he was a coward. A weak man who wanted an easy life. There was no one out there for him, no one he could bully, no one who cared. At least I hated him – that was something like an emotion, you know? – that he didn't have to buy."

"After I put you to bed, I waited for him. I sat in the dark here and waited. I couldn't let him come back, not after I saw what he could do to you. Till that night, he had never touched you. He had had at least that much decency. But now it had started. The line was crossed. The next time, I might not be near to stop him. I couldn't let that happen to you, not ever again."

"Yes, it had made me a bit crazy. I waited for him all night. I knew what I was going to do. I got the sharp long knife from the kitchen. I cleared the furniture aside and laid out the old tarpaulin sheets from the garden. And then I sat there, in that chair, and I waited for him. It was like I'd always been waiting for that night. Till then I took the beatings, I let him do what he wanted with me. I never fought back after the first few times. I just let it happen. I waited for him to come back from his long trips, I waited dinner after dinner for him when he went out at nights. It was like all the time a part of me was just waiting for the right time to fight back."

"He finally came back, dead drunk. I learned later he'd been at his usual drinking club with his gambling crowd, running me down to them all, boasting that he was off to make a new life for himself in Bangkok. That he was leaving that night, no more henpecking, he was a free man. He had a friend waiting for him in a Lincoln sedan, they would drive up to Bangkok in style. Another one of his crazy dreams! There was no friend, no fancy big car. But when he left them all, they were sure he'd gone straight up the highway to the border. But he came home. They never knew that."

"When he came in the door, hardly standing up on his feet, he was so drunk, I stood in front of him. Made sure he saw me. Looked into my eyes. Then I stabbed him. Under the ribs, pointing upwards straight into the heart. All the way in to the hilt."

"He fell towards me and I lowered him to the ground. I'd not expected him to be so heavy. There wasn't much blood. I left the knife in, maybe that helped. I stood there for a while. I was terrified suddenly. Would I be able to get him out of the house? He was so heavy."

"But I had to. I knew I had to. I pulled him along in the tarpaulin. Out onto the back verandah. It was late now and the moon had set. The garden was just dark shapes and ghost sounds. I dragged him down the steps. It was harder going across the grass. I don't know how long it took. I thought I'd never do it. But then, suddenly, I was there, at the far end of the garden. I went to get the spade."

Jasmine stared out through the back windows. Against the lighter sky, the branches of the flame tree spread like shaggy tentacles. She remembered waking up that night long ago and hearing her mother's weeping in the garden. And the rhythmic *tchik*-pause-*tchik* of the spade. She had peered out of the window in time to see her mother's shape move across the garden to the back verandah where she picked up the flame sapling. Jasmine had watched her carry it back to the bottom of the garden. It had been too far and too dark for her to see her mother planting the sapling. But she had heard the spade again in the still night.

Afterwards, she had crept out of her room and, crouching low behind the door, had seen her mother sitting in the living area, her face in her hands, her clothes streaked dark. With soil? With blood? Her mother was sobbing as if she would never stop. Wide-eyed, not knowing what she was witnessing, Jasmine had stared in terror at her mother. But when Mrs Fung looked up, Jasmine pulled back into the shadows, unable to meet her mother's eyes. The shame of what her father had tried to do to her loomed between them. It was all that Jasmine could think about. In her eight-year-old's mind, she saw nothing of the truth, only her own guilt and shame. She could have scrambled away and she had not moved. She had not been able to choose between her father and her mother and in the end she had betrayed them both. Hated when she should have loved. Loved when she should have hated. There was no escape from her guilt. She had slunk back into bed and curled herself into a tight ball under the covers. She had not cried. She had to be strong, she'd told herself, had to build a wall around the pain. She would be strong for *Ah Ma*. Make their lives right again.

In the far distance, the wail of sirens rose from the night. Mrs Fung looked up. She did not have much time left. The neighbours must have called the police at the sound of the gunshots. Mrs Fung said, "I cleaned up then, washed the floor, wiped everything. Burned the rags next day with the dead leaves, like I do every week. No one ever found out. His friends came looking for him in the first few months – but all they wanted was the money he owed them. I paid them. His creditors came by and I paid them, too. I had to bargain with them but they let me pay over time, with interest. A few asked after him sometimes. I said he never came home that night. I said I'd be the last to know where he was.

"I put that shrine there under the tree. I pray to his spirit every day. I make sacrifices. I never forget him. I have to appease his spirit. To save us from vengeance. To let you live free of what happened."

"Sometimes, I feel sad for him. No one missed him. So long as they got their money, they never cared what happened to him. I think he knew that. That's why he came home that night."

"Can you understand now why you had to escape? Why you had to have a new life, a new name? Why you had to go far away from here, have nothing to do with me? I was so afraid for you, that somehow you would be infected with what I had done. I lived every day thinking that they would find me out, his friends, the neighbours, the police – and you would be known as the daughter of a murderer, maybe they would even think you helped me. I can face the hangman but you, you're my sweet, innocent child, you are my future and all my hope. I pushed you to escape, to forget me, to forget Luke, anything that would get you away from here. That's why I've waited here by the flame tree, to guard my secret, to keep it buried where it should lie."

Mrs Fung burst into heart-rending sobs, "You have been a good daughter! You've done everything I asked of you and more. You've sacrificed everything that you truly wanted because I asked you to. I thought that this secret would go with me to the grave. I thought that then you would be truly free. But I was wrong. The spirits on the other side laugh at me like hyenas in the dark. They know the truth and their dark power knows no bounds. Only with light can you beat them back. I won't be here to protect you and you must know the truth to fight the battles of your future. This is why I've told you now. My darling one, forgive me for what I have done to you. Forgive me …"

Even as Jasmine felt horror at what her mother had told her, she was aware of a calm strength taking root. Instead of doubt and anxiety, she grasped the certainty of truth at last. It was as if a burden she had carried was being lifted from her. Harry's unmoving body sprawled across the floor, the debris of their struggle in chaos around the room. In the dark of the shadows, it was as if twenty years had merged into one night. Her father had begun the monstrous act that night long ago, and cut through by her mother, it had hung suspended, unfinished, over them all for those long years. It was only now that she understood, as if the child she had been then could only now separate her real self from the terrible entanglement of love and hate that she had been born into. Harry had finished what had been begun more than twenty years before. She felt an overwhelming rage and indignation at what he had done to her. She hated him, loathed him with all her being. The thought of his touch made her shudder with disgust and horror. How had she not seen through his veneer to the hideous demon within? How had she chosen to love him once? She made herself look at the dark, still corpse. He was dead. And she was glad.

Her father was dead. He had been dead all this time. She felt a dizzying surge of emotion. With horror and outrage, she saw what her childish eyes had not been able to face. Her father had tried to rape her. It convulsed her with disgust. A rage she had not been able to live exploded out of the vault she had trapped it in. She hated him for what he had tried to do. She loathed him for touching her that way. Suddenly, she lived these forbidden emotions with an intensity she had never known. It was a strange, new freedom that exhilarated her even as she felt the anguish coursing through her blood. She had wished him dead that night even as she had blamed herself for making him do it. She had blamed herself because she had wished him dead. But she had not been to blame. The realisation gave her the sensation of falling. She was not to blame for her father's disappearance. She had not driven him away. With adult eyes, she saw it so clearly. She was not to blame for what he had tried to do to her. It had not been her fault. Not her fault that he had beaten her mother all the years of their marriage, not her fault that he used her as his ally when it suited him or loved her with drunken, bullying sentiment. Nor that she had loved him and missed him. In loving her father, she had not made him want to rape her. The shock of this knowledge made her tremble. In loving him, she had not made her mother hate her, had not made *Ah Ma* attack her father. Or drive him away. Or kill him. Jasmine felt the collapse of the prison she had built around her soul.

It was a terrifying, free-falling destruction of the fortress she had made for herself and also a release. She felt the abyss surround her. But the truth steadied her. The annihilation did not come. She was still there, and the pain and terror had done their worst. She had found absolution and it had come from her own soul. She clung to her mother, weeping. She was cold and shaking, as if she had survived a terrible disaster.

Mother and daughter huddled together, shaking with tears of grief and release. The police sirens pierced shrieking into the neighbourhood, flashing blue up and down the road outside. Heavy footsteps crunched down the path as uniformed police, guns drawn, poured towards the house.

*   *   *

Dawn over Taiping saw a police cordon ringing Mrs Fung's house. Teams in uniforms worked over the living area and verandah, others searched the Jaguar parked skew across the road. Neighbours crowded round the drama, wide-eyed and excited like tourists at a new spectacle. The police worked through the crowd and made house-to-house calls, taking down witness statements.

Jasmine and Mrs Fung were taken over the road to the Boks' house where Mrs Bok and her daughters fussed over them with cups of ginseng tea. They were treated for shock and Jasmine for her minor external injuries. When Dr Han arrived, he settled Mrs Fung in one of the bedrooms with a low dose of morphine. Jasmine refused to leave her mother to go to the hospital for an internal medical examination.

"They can do it here if they want. Or it'll wait," she said fiercely. She paced by her mother's bed.

Outside, she could hear the Boks being questioned about Luke. He should have been at Mrs Fung's under the after-dark curfew.

Inspector Tiong, the officer in charge, had already questioned Jasmine. "You were with him earlier last night. The …" He coughed. "The – um – tape we found in the car shows you together."

"I didn't know about the bail condition."

"Do you know where he went afterwards?"

"He said he couldn't come back with me to Taiping." A half-truth. The inspector seemed to accept that.

She could hear Mr Bok saying, "That policeman came, Raymond Goh. He said don't worry, he would find Luke."

"Goh didn't radio in. That would be standard procedure in such a case," a junior officer interrupted.

Tiong said, "Get someone down to Goh's house – is he there? Find out what happened. Looks like we got a bail-jump."

Jasmine stared out of the window at the streaming activity. Butterflies looped around the hibiscus bushes in the yard. The morning sun was bright and a breeze caught the fronds of the coconut trees. What had happened to Luke last night? Was he safe? She wanted to rush outside and talk to Tiong, tell him what Luke had told her – go and find him at the temple, she pleaded silently, bring him home, please let him be all right.

But she stayed where she was. "The one thing you mustn't do is go to the police." She heard Luke's voice again. "Whatever happens, you'll get word from me." She had to trust him. For so long, she had torn herself away from her instincts. Now, it was more important than ever that she trusted him. That she stood firm for what they had taken on together. In spite of her fear, she made herself be still.

*   *   *

The sun over the Titiwangsa Range warmed the terrace where the ruined temple perched. Raymond was half propped up against the broken statue of Kuan Yin, the goddess of mercy. His head lolled into his chest, his right leg stretching out at an unnatural angle. A bullet had shattered his pelvic bone and a bloody stain spread over his side. He held a pistol drooping in his hand.

He had handcuffed one of the Tan brothers to an iron railing by one hand. The other arm was free but useless – a deep shoulder wound bled onto the stones. The other brother was dead.

There was no sign of either Jordan or Luke.

*   *   *

"Where did you get the gun?" Tiong asked Jasmine. It was after one in the afternoon. They stood at the foot of the bed where Mrs Fung dozed. Tiong was a serious Chinese man nearing retirement, soft-spoken and meticulous. He and his wife had been customers of Mrs Fung's meals service for eight years and his children had been at primary school with Jasmine.

"I – I took it from my client's bodyguard," Jasmine began.

"Your client?"

"I was staying in KL when I heard my mother was taken into hospital. My client is Mr Bill Jordan. I was at his condominium. He has bodyguards as a matter of course. He's a rich man."

"Why did you take the gun?"

"I've already told you about my marriage," Jasmine said, looking away in shamed emotion. "My husband has been very violent – ever since he found out about my affair. I was scared. I didn't know where he was. I didn't have a licence for the gun, maybe it was foolish of me to take it but ..." She broke down. "... but he would've killed me last night. I was so frightened – it was horrible – If my mother hadn't – hadn't – stopped him ..."

Tiong took down details of Jordan's condominium and Pang's name. He would check her story. Jasmine couldn't know whether Jordan's people would corroborate it or tell them of Luke's "attack" on Pang – or wave the "mental instability" certificate at them. She would have to face whatever came up then. Right now, she'd bought a little more time.

"Inspector ..." Mrs Fung said from the bed, "are you going to take me to jail?"

Tiong turned. "I only have one last thing to clear up, *mem*, and that's this business about the gun. Otherwise – well, the neighbours all heard Mr Taunton shouting he would kill your daughter. You said you believed he would kill her. The scene shows signs of a violent struggle. The injuries on Miss Fung – Mrs Taunton – support this." He moved across and sat by her side. "At this stage, it looks like we got justifiable homicide. It depends on clearing up the question of the gun but I think we won't be making any arrests."

Mrs Fung looked at Jasmine for a long moment over Tiong's shoulder. Then she met the policeman's eyes with a steady gaze. She said, "The *ang mo* is not the only man I've killed. I killed my husband twenty-two years ago."

By four p.m. the local press had arrived in force. They clustered on the road and doorstepped the houses. "Is it true she confessed to killing her husband twenty years ago?"

"What's she like, this Fung Mei-Ling?"

"Do you remember the husband?"

"Why do you think she killed him?"

Jasmine sat with her mother, a woman police officer just outside. The Boks sat in their living room, silent with shock. Mrs Fung said, "Do not let all this upset you. It will pass. The truth can never harm you. You need to know only the right way to live with it."

A strange peace had settled on Mrs Fung. For the first time in many months, she had not felt the grinding pain as keenly. Perhaps it was the morphine. As she had told her story to Tiong, a strength navigated her words and her stricken body seemed to irradiate an old vigour. It was over at last, the secret and its torment.

An officer came in to fetch Jasmine to Tiong in the garden of Mrs Fung's house. Raymond Goh had not been found at home. His wife was distraught. The police were now on alert to find Luke and Raymond. Tiong quizzed Jasmine again about her last words with Luke. She stuck to her story.

Then, he went through with her again her memory of the night her father died. Tiong said, "You understand, we are reviewing last night's shooting after what your mother has confessed."

Jasmine nodded. They stood among the scented bursts of flowers in the garden and watched the forestry officials clear the shrine from the flame tree and set up their markers for the felling. She had never seen the flame tree more beautiful. Its feathery emerald and scarlet swayed in the breeze, glancing sunlight sparkling through the leaves. Blossom showers of red fluttered down to the grass. Supple limbs stretched up against a lapis-lazuli sky, seemed to wave to the puff-ball clouds.

She turned away as the first chain-saws roared to life. "Do you need me any more today?"

"No. But leave word where we can find you at short notice." Tiong shook her hand, as if at her family's funeral. "Thank you, Miss Fung."

As Jasmine made her way across the road, she checked her watch for the hundredth time that day. Where was Luke? Why hadn't she heard from him?

A young Malay man in an apron stood at the edge of the crowd. He held a huge basket of flowers. He had come up from Kuala Lumpur in the van parked behind him.

Journalists pressed towards Jasmine on all sides, shouting questions at her. She ducked her head and increased her pace back to the Boks' house.

Hearing the name on his receipt being shouted, the delivery-man began to push his way through to the woman hurrying to the house. He reached the gate as she strode up the yard to the door. His voice calling her was drowned among the others. He tried to push past the police guard, the basket of flowers crushing up against the uniformed chest.

"Hey, move along there, you!" the police officer shouted. "You can't come in!"

"These – for Ms Lian. I came from KL."

Jasmine turned round. She saw the voluminous basket of orchids and roses and jasmine. She went back to the gate. "It's all right," she said. "Let him through."

*   *   *

There was a card. Jasmine placed the basket on the dresser in the bedroom where Mrs Fung lay. Her mother smiled at the sight and fresh perfume.

"It's from Luke," Jasmine whispered, recognising the writing on the card.

"Where is he? Where's my good boy?"

Jasmine stared at the card. It showed a batik print of Kuala Lumpur railway station, its minarets and Moorish bulbs stylised against a sunset. Inside, Luke had written, "The road less travelled unlocks my heart." He had not signed it.

Jasmine moved across to her mother's bedside to show her the card. At that moment, Tiong came in. She slipped the card under the pillows in the guise of making her mother more comfortable.

"Who are the flowers from?" Tiong asked.

"A well-wisher, I suppose. There was no message with them."

Tiong peered at the flowers and the basket. He faced the women and said, "We've started the felling. It'll take the rest of today and tomorrow morning. Mrs Bok says you can stay here for the time being, Mrs Fung. You're not under arrest yet, *mem* – what you say is not enough at this point without a dead body. But, please, don't leave here without notifying us."

Mrs Fung nodded.

After the inspector had left, Jasmine examined the card and its envelope again. No other clue to illuminate the message. "Whatever happens, I'll get word to you," Luke had said. His message used the old phrase she had almost forgotten, their childhood signal for adventure. The Robert Frost poem came back to her. *The traveller took the road less travelled and it was that which made the difference.* Luke – always making the difference and still quoting poetry.

He had not come himself but sent word. Jasmine was afraid to think it. Something had happened to him. Something terrible. He had anticipated it. That was what he had meant. If he was all right, he would have come himself, wouldn't he, instead of sending these flowers?

Mrs Fung slipped the card under her pillows again. "What's happened to my boy?"

Jasmine moved over to the basket of flowers. She remembered how they used to leave messages in special hiding places, little gifts for each other under the roots of rain trees, taped to the underside of school desks. "Unlock my heart". Did he mean her to find a key?

She ran her hand over the basket. Outside. Inside. Nothing. She lifted the bunch of flowers out. They were spiked into a metal bouquet brush sitting on pebbles. She reached into the water and rummaged through the stones with her fingers.

There. She fished it out. It was a key. There was a red plastic toggle at its head. Attached to that on a ring was a plastic disc, the size of a small coin. A number was printed on it. It looked like a key to a locker. Was the locker number the number on the disc tag? Jasmine stared at the key. Where was the locker? What was she meant to do with it?

She picked up the card again. "The road less travelled unlocks my heart." No other message. She turned the card over. Nothing on the back but the greeting card company logo and address. Flicking the card over again, Jasmine stared at the picture of the railway station.

Railway station. A locker at KL railway station.

34

Jasmine pulled up outside Kuala Lumpur railway station just before nine p.m. Without thinking, she had given the police Seng & Mustafa as her contact address in the capital. Slipping out of the Mercedes, she hurried into the cavernous interior of the station. She found the bank of lockers.

A few minutes later, she was back in the Mercedes, Luke's tote-bag on the passenger seat beside her. She flicked on the overhead light. With trembling hands, she unzipped the bag and took out each of the items. A camcorder cassette and accompanying VCR adaptor shell. A school exercise book in manuscript she did not recognise. The photocopied papers she had sent to her mother and the duplicate tapes and disks she had made. Original data and reports Luke had compiled subsequent to the theft at his office and his recent conversation with Ibrahim.

A tap on the window made her jump.

A policeman. "You can't park here, *mem.*"

"Yes – sorry – sure." Jasmine fumbled for the ignition.

She drove along the freeways through the city for a while, disoriented, looping around and around. She couldn't think clearly. What had happened to Luke? The bag contained all the evidence against Jordan, what she had sent to Luke and what Luke himself had obtained. It panicked her. As if Luke had bequeathed his crusade to her. Where was he? Without him, she had no strength to follow through. Without him. The emptiness of those words.

She headed downtown to the business district.

Parking the car in the deserted street outside Seng & Mustafa, she peered up at the darkened building. Could she risk going into the offices again? The thought of Jordan's thugs rushing her or Roberts confronting her … Her mouth felt dry and a sick feeling rose in her stomach. She glanced at the clock on the dashboard. Time was pushing on – each moment a moment longer that Luke might be in danger. She did not know what she could do to find him, how she would help him. All she had was the bundle of things he had left for her. She had to see what was on the videotape – it might give her something tangible to act on, she thought desperately.

Jasmine looked around. The street was quiet as she would expect at this time of the night. But it was not deserted. There were passers-by, cars sweeping past. Everyone looked like they were going about their own business – no suspicious figures watching her or cars with dark shapes inside waiting for her. The building looked deserted. Jordan wouldn't expect her to come back here, she thought, not after what he'd done to her. Jasmine slipped out of the car, her heart pounding. She would risk it. Grabbing the totebag, she let herself into the building. Besides, she thought, the police knew where she was. If she didn't return, they'd be sure to send someone to look for her.

She made her way up the stairs. The offices of Seng & Mustafa were in darkness. She paused, listening. Peering into the gloom. No movement. No sound. She moved quickly to one of the conference rooms where she knew there was a VCR and colour TV. She hurried in, switching on the lights. She went to close the door and paused. What if someone came up to the office while she was here alone? She decided to leave the door ajar so she might see or hear any intruder. Then, she put the tote-bag onto the table and rummaged in it for the video cassette. She set up the VCR and popped the tape in.

On the TV, Luke suddenly appeared. In her mother's house. He was unshaven, tired, but there was a determination in his features. It was a tight close-up. She could see every crease of emotion on his face, the brilliance of his eyes. He looked straight out of the screen into her gaze.

"If you're watching me now, Jasmine, then something's gone

wrong with the rendezvous and I haven't got back in time to cancel the flowers. I hope to have seen you by the time I head out there tonight. There is so much I want to tell you face to face. To make up to you all the things that've gone wrong between us –" He looked down, rubbed his neck awkwardly. "I'm not very good at this. I guess I'll just have to make sure I see you before I make the rendezvous."

He smiled sideways at her, that old smile he always had for her. Jasmine found herself smiling back.

Luke was matter-of-fact now, going through all the information he had on Jordan and Tan, running through the arrangements he'd made to meet Tan with Raymond, his conversation with Mohammed, Detective Lam's dogged obtuseness. "So, it's all here – my testimony, if you like. You can play this tape to the authorities if it comes to that. Now, this is the crucial bit ..."

He held up his mobile phone. "I'm taking this with me tonight. I've modified it with a booster microphone. And taken out the backlit function that tells you it's on – there, it looks dead but it's picking up sound. I'm banking that the signal up in the hills will be good enough. There's a high density of cellphone base stations up there. They were a lifesaver after the slide when the rescue teams could use mobiles to keep in touch. They'll do the trick for me tonight. The phone's logged into my voicemail and it will record everything that happens tonight. So, if Raymond and I don't come back from our talk with Tan, you've got it all in digital form."

Luke gave her the access code to his voicemail and the confidential PIN number. Then he paused and, dropping his lecturer manner, he looked into the camera. "After all that's happened between us, you're still Jordan's lawyer. I cannot make you other than who you choose to be. All this that you've got now, everything I've told you – you can destroy or hand over to your client, I can't stop you."

"While the game is on and I'm in, I'll do my all to win it. If you're watching this now, then – I guess I'm out. But I've done the best I can till this moment and I will do exactly that to the end –

after that, it's not my call."

He seemed to gaze straight into her heart. "Maybe you're going to hate me for this, Jasmine. Maybe you don't want this gift I'm handing to you. But, my best girl, it's your call now. After all these years, you're still the girl I used to know and the truest lawyer you always said you'd be." He winked and grinned in his most infuriating, challenging tease. "Make the difference like you always wanted to."

He stared at her without speaking. The grin faded into a flicker of thoughtful sadness. Then the picture blinked out.

Jasmine did not move.

A sound behind her. She snapped round. Nothing. Stillness. All she could hear was her own breathing. She turned back and reached for the phone on the table. She activated the speakerphone out of habit. At work, she hated the confinement of using the hand receiver. She liked to pace behind her desk, move into the phone as if for the kill, withdraw again to reconsider, have both hands free to work, gesture, tap together. She dialled the numbers Luke had given her. The connection into his voicemail clicked and hummed. And then the playback began, filling the room.

The recording was muffled in places but Jasmine could make out the different voices. She could follow the exchanges, and everything the men said was audible. The gunshots jolted her out of her chair. She could make out Jordan's voice and another voice she did not know but who responded to the name Kidd. From start to finish, the recording lasted just over two hours but Jasmine forgot time, forgot where she was as she listened transfixed.

Behind Jasmine, the man had flattened himself into the shadows as she had turned round. Now he inched out again, moving in closer to the crack in the door, straining to hear. The sound from Luke's video cassette had drawn him to the conference room. Unseen by Jasmine, he had watched Luke with her. Now, he listened with her to the playback of what had happened at the rendezvous.

* * *

The night of the rendezvous, Luke and Raymond had parked the Land Rover up on the trunk road. There was no sign of another vehicle. Raymond left his service pistol and holster in the glove compartment. Luke was also unarmed, his mobile phone at his belt, apparently switched off.

After a short walk, they arrived at the temple courtyard. Broken statuary and pillars lay everywhere. The once ornate roof had fallen in, the dragon's head a lump against the night sky. Vines clung to every surface, shaded stones were slippery with moss. Saplings and shoots climbed out of every crevice.

A stub of a candle burnt at what was once the altar. Exchanging glances, Luke and Raymond made their way into the walled area. Three oranges, a gift to the spirits, sat at the foot of a decaying wooden tablet. Tan must have placed them there, Luke thought.

A sound behind them.

A figure with a gun on the shadowy side of a pillar. He beckoned and they moved out into the courtyard. Covering each of them awkwardly with his pistol, he patted down their torsos and backs and whipped his hand across their pockets.

In the moonlight, Luke recognised the man who had been at the landslide. He was thinner now, his eyes wilder. "Kaw. Ronnie Tan. What shall I call you?"

"Tan." Backing away to the pillar again. "Stay where I can see you. No sudden moves. What's the deal you got?"

"I told you this afternoon. No deal if you don't come in."

"Damn you! You got my notebook, I got seven more here. What've you got for me?"

Raymond said, "Show me."

Tan hesitated. Then squatted by the pillar, not taking his eyes off the two men. Picked up a pile of exercise books. Clutched them to his chest. "Why should I come in without a guarantee?" he shouted. "Right now, you got nothing on me, you got nothing on Jordan. I come in and you put a noose round my neck whatever I tell you. I'm not a fucking idiot!"

Luke said, "You want to come in, don't you, Tan? You want it to be over."

"Shut up! I want amnesty! If you can't guarantee that, then get the fuck out of here!"

"They don't know who you are. Maybe you're bullshitting. A crank who wants to be on TV. I've got to have more than I've got to get them to the table."

"Fucking crap!" Tan took a step forward, wired up with tension. The notebooks fluttered to the ground. "I'm going to kill you! I was fucking out of my head to think I could trust you!"

"You won't kill us. If you were going to, you would've done it by now."

Tan pushed the barrel of his pistol into Luke's temple. The safety catch clicking off was loud as a shot. His taut features glared wildly at Luke. Luke stared back without expression.

"Fuck you!" Tan pulled back, his scream echoing along the valley.

He sank down onto a broken pillar. He was talking loudly, incoherently. He let his gun arm fall into his lap.

Luke found a perch on a pile of stones. Raymond squatted where he had stood. Luke drew on everything he knew about this conflicted man, everything he could remember of their exchanges, everything he could surmise from what he had encountered of him. He said, almost in a murmur, "You want to make right the order of things. Return harmony to what you have dislocated. It can be done. And I will help you. I promise."

Tan grew quiet, breathing hard.

Luke said gently, "What's your connection with Jordan?"

Tan began to tell them everything, led by Luke's unintrusive questioning. He leaned his head back against a part of the pillar. The moon was beautiful that night, the jungle sounds soothing. He talked about his dealings with Jordan, the Tan underground business, his philosophy for business and life, his family, his father, how he had forced whisky into Dr Chan and set the car rolling down the road. It was a relief to speak the words, to say out to the spirits of the temple and the ghosts of Kampung Tanah, "I did these things. I murdered. I helped to murder." To say them to the ghost of his father. They seemed to fade, move away. Leave him be again.

Slight movements, just out of vision, alerted them. But before they could react, the easing of safety catches on two sides froze them.

"On your feet. Slow now." It was Jordan.

The three men did as they were told. Luke looked round. There was another man with Jordan. Both positioned on higher ground, next to a broken wall and a tree, catching their quarry in crossfire if it came to that.

"Move away, *Tai Koh*."

"Kidd!" Tan held his gun in his right hand.

"Drop it. Now." Jordan again.

Raymond stood closest to Tan on his left. Luke was at the furthest edge.

Undergrowth and saplings encroached behind him.

Tan raised his gun, pointing it alternately at Jordan and his brother. "No! I'm no white man's whore! Fuck it, Kidd, what the hell are you doing? I told you no more killing. Why are you still doing the *ang mo*'s bidding?"

Jordan and Kidd closed into the courtyard. Kidd approached his brother, his free hand outstretched. "Fucking give that to me! You're out of your head!"

"How did you know we were here?" Luke said to Jordan, eyes on the brothers.

"Latest CCTV technology, mate. Had a nice fuck before coming out tonight? Another man's wife, too – tsk, tsk. Good choice, nice tits."

Luke took an angry step towards him. Stopped in the face of the automatic pistol. Jordan laughed.

"It's fucking over, Kidd! I've stopped it all. I've stopped you!" Tan's voice cracked with hysteria. He locked pistol aim with his brother. "I've appeased the spirits. It can change now, no more blood and death on our hands, no more blood staining our family. I put it right, don't you see?"

"You're fucking loony! You might as well gut yourself! And string me up to dry in the goddamn sun!"

In his body searches, Tan had missed a small snub-nosed .357 Smith & Wesson revolver concealed inside Raymond's boot. Raymond caught Luke's eye as the brothers argued. Their expressions said nothing but Luke understood.

With a shriek, Luke threw himself into the undergrowth behind him, rolling fast. As Jordan whirled and fired in his direction and Tan twisted his head at the disturbance, Raymond dived to the ground groping for his gun. He pulled it as soon as he hit and brought his arm up to fire at Kidd in front of him.

Tan had moved into Kidd's line of fire. Tucking sideways down, Kidd, tracking Raymond with his aim, squeezed a shot as Raymond's bullet whizzed by his side.

Tan, twisting back, screamed, "No more! No more killing! Kidd!" He fired once instinctively.

Tan's bullet smashed into his brother's chest. Kidd's gun clattered to the ground. His eyes widened in shock. His mouth opened to call his elder brother but no sound came. He was dead when he hit the stones.

Kidd's shot hit Raymond in his exposed hip.

Tan froze in horror, dropping his gun. A shot behind him caught him in the shoulder. Jordan. As Tan tumbled, Raymond yanked himself half-sitting with a yell of agony and fired towards Jordan. The shot was wide as Jordan raced in the direction where Luke was last seen.

Tan was sobbing, crawling to Kidd's body. Oblivious to everything else. "Blood for blood," he moaned. "That's what *Ah Teh* said. It's finished, all finished, isn't it, now? Brother against brother ..."

Raymond hauled himself over, cursing in pain, gun in one hand, scrabbling for handcuffs with the other. He skidded Tan's pistol away and clicked the handcuffs on Tan's wrist. Tan did not resist. He hooked the other cuff to the iron railing behind Tan.

Raymond leaned against a statue, gasping in agony. He looked around the dark landscape. What had happened to Luke and Jordan?

*　*　*

Luke tumbled through the undergrowth, aiming uphill for the road and the Land Rover. But a flashing shot told him Jordan was above him, crashing down towards him. He tacked to the side, trying to shake Jordan off, but the falling ground told him he was heading ever off course.

The jungle had become overwhelmingly dense. The moonlight hardly penetrated through the layers of foliage above. There were only ghostly traces of light in the far distance, misleadingly conjuring the hope of a clearing. Hanging vines tangled Luke's head and arms, swarming roots underfoot clawed at his ankles. Running fast, directionless, coming up short against tree trunks, tumbling into rioting ferns.

Behind him, gunshots. One thudding into a tree just ahead of him. Another whistling by. Another – crack! – but it was wide.

No sound now but his rasping breath and rushing, breaking undergrowth. Behind him, like an echo, Jordan's heaving, crashing through the vegetation. Sweat soaking every pore, the dankness of the jungle dampening every part of their straining bodies.

Suddenly, nothing underfoot.

Luke slipped, tumbling, hurtling against trees and undergrowth, loose rocks kicking up, dirt and moss and rotting leaves in his nose and mouth. The ravine hurled him onto a cluster of boulders at its trough.

A bullet zinged on the stone by his arm. Winded, shaken, Luke pulled away, rolling for cover.

He splashed into rushing water and squeezed his back against a boulder. It was only then that he became aware of where he was.

Whitewater stretched across the gulley, churning like liquid silver in the moonlight. The spray stung him like shards. Rocks and boulders cluttered the shoreline where he crouched, possessed much of the waterbed, stretched up-river and down into the falling ribbon of white. The boulder he leaned against did not give him complete cover. He could see Jordan picking his way down the slope to the rocky shore. Jordan trained his pistol at Luke. Above the roar of the water, he shouted, "You're finished, mate."

Luke emerged from the boulder, hands high. He moved deliberately over the rocks right up to Jordan. The pistol touched his chest.

"There's something I've got to know, Jordan," Luke said.

"Is Lam – the detective – in your pay?"

Jordan hooted with laughter. "No, mate, he isn't! He's just a stupid Chink bastard who thinks he can second-guess the whites! What a bonus he's been!"

"He's got them all thinking I sabotaged the tower."

"I love that man! Maybe I *will* pay him for his good work."

"Like you paid Zain and Scott to keep quiet about the faulty design?"

"You'd never make a good businessman, mate." Jordan was breathing hard from the chase. But he was enjoying himself. He had all the cards now. The consultant was defeated but trying so hard to maintain a last moment of bravado. Jordan had stayed ahead of the game. He was going to win after all. "It's all about carrots and sticks, isn't it? They all get their carrots if their good – Zain, Scott, Roberts, the peasants up in Kampung Tanah. But if they step out of line, it's the good old stick."

"Anything to win."

"Goddammit! Our design was the best! It gave the stupid wogs what they wanted, didn't it? They got the tallest flagpole in the world in downtown KL, they're talking of building the longest shopping mall in the world over the Klang river in the city centre, it killed them that their once tallest twin towers in the world got overshadowed. I'm giving them the tallest pile of concrete on the highest fucking pile of rocks ever in the whole goddamn world. And built in the fastest time ever to finish first in the race with China! The tallest, the highest, the fastest, a fucking '-est' fest!

"They wanted it! It won the fucking tender fair and square! I wasn't going to let a little risk spook them all. Yes, goddammit, a tiny corner piercing the limestone *is* a little risk! And, yes, we had to cut corners to make the deadline! We would've won the race – no contest, damn it! If it hadn't been for the bloody weather, it would still be steaming ahead to its final glory. Zain and Scott got wimpy on me so I had to use the old stick – whack 'em into line. It fucking worked! You got to take risks in this business – high risk, high gain, mate!"

Luke said, "You gambled with the lives of thousands of people. They're dead because of you. You lost. And you're still going to lose, whatever you do to me!"

Jordan rammed his pistol into Luke's ribs. "You don't get it, do you? Jordan does not lose! Nobody fucking cares if you come in second, so close you can almost touch success! You're still a fucking loser! I win. No matter what!"

"You killed Dr Chan to win."

"Damn right! I got Tan to get rid of the doctor. And, thanks to Lam, I got away with it!"

"How did you get the town on your side? When I talked to them, they were gung-ho about their rights at the planning review."

"Don't you listen? Carrots and sticks. Wong and his gang of bumpkins were stupid and greedy. They were easy to buy. Fortune was on my side when the slide hit – the lot of them were killed outright. I didn't have to deal with their whingeing about what a raw deal it all turned out to be!"

In a quiet voice, Luke said, "You're a real loser, Jordan."

Even as he spoke. Luke was twisting to the side, trusting to Jordan's anger. In the breath it took for Jordan's rage to explode, Luke was swinging a fast, tight blow up to Jordan's arm. Jordan's wrist swung wide as he fired – nothing. An empty click and the pistol flew from his hand.

The two men grappled on the rocks, stumbling into the churning shallows.

* * *

The recording cut off. Sounds of a struggle and then white noise. Static. And silence.

"No! Luke!" Jasmine threw herself at the speakerphone, frantically sliding the volume control, jabbing at buttons.

The dial tone. A lifeless hum. Jasmine jabbed the buttons again. Luke's mobile must have broken in the struggle. Or tumbled into the water. But Luke – what had happened to him? Jasmine grabbed the phone up as if grabbing for Luke.

She sank down in her seat, staring at the cold phone in her hands. The silence of the room overwhelmed her. She couldn't breathe. The blood was pounding in her ears.

The man in the shadows stepped into the room. He stood behind her. In the terrible silence, his voice made her jump. "What're you going to do now, my girl?"

35

Jasmine spun round, leaping to her feet. "Nick!"

Nick Roberts stood between Jasmine and the door. He was pasty and tense, shadows under his eyes.

"Wha – what are you doing here?" Jasmine gasped.

"Working late – fortunately, it seems."

He must have been in the inner office in the Carruthers' office suite, Jasmine realised. She would not have seen any light from there if both doors had been shut. She cursed herself for her oversight. To Roberts, she brazened it out. "How long have you been standing there? How much did you –"

"All of it, my girl." Roberts shut the door and locked it. Pocketed the key.

Jasmine felt stiff and tired. The carriage clock on the sideboard showed that she'd been by the phone for two hours. She tried to clear her head. Take the offensive, her instinct told her. Don't show any fear. She rounded on Roberts. "You're in with Jordan! How could you, Nick? You play fast and loose but I never pegged you for a thug's yes-man."

"Aah, what morally upright lawyer you've always been, my girl. Life is not so simple. Now, give those all to me, and I'll take care of things from here."

"No." Jasmine pulled herself straight and tall. She had to find Luke. What had happened after the recording cut out? She had to know. "I'm going to Mohammed."

"Do you really think you can 'make the fucking difference'?" Roberts slammed onto the table. "No one's going to believe a mental case like you. You're just a hysterical woman off her rocker!"

"So let me make a fool of myself, if you're so sure of that."

Roberts took a threatening step towards her.

"I've got a copy of your secret tapes."

"What?"

"You talking to Zain and Scott. Fixing up their witness statements. And practically linking yourself directly to Jordan's crimes."

Roberts stared in panic at her. "How did you get …"

Jasmine saw his fear. She pressed home her advantage. Make him turn tail, she told herself. She described her search through his desk. "I've sent the duplicate tapes back to London," she lied. "They'll land on JM's desk today. So, even if you take all this off me, that recording is still safe. JM will come after your balls. Once Mohammed hears it, he'll start asking the right questions, I'll make sure of it. The game's over. Do yourself a favour – give it up."

"No one will believe you."

"Please. You sound like a stuck recording." Jasmine retrieved the videotape and put it back into the tote-bag. "Now, get out of my way."

Roberts grabbed her. He was sweating now. "No! You're not going anywhere!"

Jasmine shook him off. She felt a surge of fury. He was pathetic. She no longer felt afraid of him. Her voice was contemptuous. "What are you going to do, Roberts? Kill me? Come on, think about it. You kill me, you've got to deal with a dead body. What are you going to do? You've got to dump the body, cover your tracks, lie, play cat-and-mouse with the police … Are you up to that? You kill me now, maybe you buy yourself a little time but there isn't any more time, really, is there? You can't smokescreen the authorities for much longer and you know it. The police know I'm here – if I don't return to Taiping, they'll come and find me. Jordan's off out there in the jungle, now's your chance. Snatch your pecker back out of his pocket and save yourself!"

Jasmine stopped. Her outburst had startled them both. She braced herself to fight her way past him.

Roberts sat down in a chair. He dropped his head into his hands, elbows on his knees. "I owed him money. He paid my gambling debts. It's almost half a million sterling now," he said in a whisper. "He let me off the hook month by month. So long as I did what he wanted. I took on his legal work – I could wing it, pull it around in a way you never could, take the chances you never would. Get my hands dirty, you know? That was what he liked to call the carrot ..."

"And the stick?"

"He put my wife in hospital. Car crash. I can't link him directly to it but I know it was his way of reminding me of the stick. Maggie wasn't hurt seriously – whip-lash and broken ankle – but it was enough. I knew who I owed everything to." Roberts was trembling. "The recordings were my insurance policy. I thought I could use them against him, if I needed to. Hold him to ransom, you know. Play him at his own game."

"When you warned me off Jordan, you really meant it."

Roberts nodded miserably.

Jasmine pushed on. "It's over, Nick. Come with me to Mohammed. Tell him what you know. Score one against Jordan for a change. If he made it out of the jungle, he'll come for you."

Roberts looked up at her.

She said, "You'll be struck off. You'll lose your job and you'll never practise law again. Prison, probably. But co-operation is the catchword for leniency, you know that. The alternative? Stick by Jordan and one day, sooner or later, you'll be dead. Or your wife."

Jasmine held out her hand for the key. He gave it to her. She unlocked the door and strode out of the room, the tote-bag in her hand.

As she reached the street, Roberts caught up with her.

* * *

The current had swept Luke and Jordan down through the rocky channels and careered them into rocks. Fighting the thundering

469

water that swamped them, dragged them down, flung them up momentarily to the surface, Luke rammed fists into Jordan, kicked out at him, levered at Jordan's clawing hands. Jordan had him round the throat, pulled him under, forced him down.

A numbing impact on a jagged boulder broke them apart. Jordan clung to a slippery outcrop, the current, strong in the narrowing channel, sucking at him. He saw Luke flung against a succession of rocks, disappearing into the foam. Then nothing.

Painfully, Jordan scraped himself up onto the boulder. The moon was setting but there was still enough light to see the vista opening up down-river as, trembling, he stood on the precarious perch. The channel hurled into a steep fall, throwing the flying water out into space before crashing into the gulley below.

Jordan, shivering and sodden, made his way to shore, clambering over rocks and boulders.

* * *

Jasmine and Roberts reached Mohammed's home at half past midnight. It was three in the morning when Jasmine finished presenting her evidence to Mohammed, Roberts filling in the gaps where she could not. They sat in his living room in the exclusive residential area near the royal palace. Mohammed was in his sarong, a casual batik shirt pulled hastily on, but with his grave dignity they might have been in a court of law.

The TV blistered with white snow after Luke's videotape. The playback of the voicemail ended on the speakerphone. Mohammed hung up the phone and switched off the TV.

Turning, he picked up the phone again. He called the Chief of Police and the Public Prosecutor. Police were dispatched to the temple. If the team could not locate all the participants in the rendezvous, a wider search would then be called. Helicopters and dogs were on secondary alert to operate a search spiralling outwards from the temple for several miles. Extra teams would target the watercourse further down the valley on the basis of the rushing water in the background of Luke's recording.

"We'll get Jordan," he said to Jasmine. "And we'll find McAllister."

* * *

Almost nineteen hours before, as dawn rose over the jungle and the police first cordoned off Mrs Fung's house, Luke had clung limply to a rock in the shallows a few miles downriver from where Jordan had last seen him. His left leg was useless, the shin shattered against rocks when he had been swept over the sudden drop. The river had quietened along this stretch, opening out into an expanse of glassy ripples.

With a supreme effort, Luke hauled himself out of the water. He dragged himself up onto the largest boulder he could see. On its still surface, he let himself collapse. Above him, the sky began to embrace the day.

On the dank rainforest floor, daylight turned the darkness into murky green. Jordan struggled through the dense thickets and ferns. When he next looked at his watch it was ten in the morning. He reasoned that if he continued going uphill, he would eventually reach either the temple or the road near the temple or, if he were off course, one of the farms or roads near Kampung Tanah. But the ground rose and fell in stretches and in the close overhanging vegetation, he could not tell whether his overall progress was uphill or downhill. He had no idea how much distance he had covered since leaving the river.

He did not know that he had crawled to land on the opposite bank from where he had come.

By afternoon, at about the time that Jasmine had received the basket of flowers, Luke regained consciousness. The side of his face exposed to the sky was burned red. He hauled himself into a half-sitting position. Flies swarmed on his leg where the skin was broken. Blood oozed into a thickening pool.

Tearing his trouser leg into strips, Luke used them as a

tourniquet, biting back the shooting pain at each movement. He then took off his boots and socks, laying them out to dry. Exhausted, he lay back, gasping.

He unhitched the mobile phone from his belt and examined it, dialling a few numbers on it. Nothing. It was dead. He did not know when it had cut off. Probably when he'd gone into the water. The jungle stretched out on either bank. Luke felt a terrible aloneness. He put the phone on the rock beside him. "Hey, I'm here. On a rock. Somewhere down-river," he said to nothing, the sound of his own voice a reassurance across the pain of his injury and the solitude around him. "Come and get me, I know you will, my best girl. You should be getting the flowers around now. You'll know what to do. I know you will. It's not a bad point here for a pick-up, you know. I'll be the guy on the rock. Come and get me in style, Jasmine."

Up by the temple, a swarm of flies and insects had settled on Kidd's body. The stench of blood was sickening in the heat of the afternoon. Tan opened his eyes, rousing from an exhausted stupor. His shoulder jolted with pain when he tried to move. It was caked with blood and covered with flies. He tried to lift a hand to wave them away but found it trapped. Handcuffed to the railing.

The policeman was not far away. Slumped against the statue of Kwan Yin. Passed out. A gun where it had slipped from his limp hand to the ground. Tan might just reach it. He did not look over to his brother's body. Focusing all his energy on the gun by the policeman's side. Stretching, shifting his body as far as he could. Lifting his free arm in spite of his shattered shoulder. The pain like delirium. Reaching out to the black shape. Thankful for the physical agony of it, an easy pain for the brother he had killed. Tan jerked forward, making a shaft of pain dig deep into him. His fingers like claws hooking round the barrel of the gun. Pulling it back into an easy reach, then grabbing the butt.

Tan paused, gathering his strength. With a jittery hand, he aimed the gun at the handcuffs. A resounding shot. He slumped away from the railing. Free. He took the gun in his uninjured hand.

The policeman started awake. He stared at Tan, scrabbling at space for the gun he'd lost. He looked like a frightened animal. Tan stood up unsteadily, the pistol covering Raymond. Raymond tried to move but keeled over with a shriek of agony, the wound to his hip pinning him to the ground.

Tan backed away, his eyes not leaving the policeman. He paused by the staring head of his brother. Flies crawled over the open eyes. Tan stifled a sob. He knelt. Placing his gun down by his feet, watchful gaze darting to the policeman and back, he closed Kidd's eyes. Grief threatened to break him. With an effort, Tan mastered himself and picked up the gun. He turned and scrambled up the hill, staying under cover of the trees but following the track back up to the trunk road.

By now, deep in the thick jungle, Jordan had decided to make it back to the river and start again. But he had no idea where the river was. He stumbled on, cursing as the vines grabbed at him and the treacherous roots underfoot threatened to break his ankles. He was still soaked to the skin, shivering now in the dense shade. His feet squelched in his shoes, his damp clothes clung to him.

There were quick movements all around him, making him turn this way and that, shouting in anger and panic. Was it McAllister playing with him? A wild animal – did they still have tigers here? Aboriginal tribesmen? The jungle spirits of these superstitious savages?

"Fuck off!" Jordan bellowed into the jungle. "I'm not afraid of any of you! I'll get back, just you wait and see!"

Jordan's first night alone in the rainforest paled him into wild-eyed jittery anxiety. He did not sleep, afraid to sink down into the dank floor among the rustling ferns and giant plants. The closest he had been to jungle till then had been on bulldozed red earth, hard-hatted and mobile-phoned in his suit on a site visit to the Titiwangsa project. A scabby rash was beginning to form under his arms and in his crotch. His feet felt cold and itchy.

By mid-morning the next day, he heard a helicopter throbbing in the distance. He screamed and waved and crashed through the thickets, trying to get to a clearing. There were no clearings. He tried to climb a tree but fell not far off the ground. The tops of the trees towered implacable above him. He lay in the undergrowth and bellowed till he was hoarse.

The police helicopter sighted Luke easily on the top of the boulder. The rescue team winched him up and flew him to Kuantan General Hospital. Police and ambulances had already arrived at the temple and picked up Raymond. Kidd was zipped into a body bag before removal. A search for Tan was set in motion along the trunk road, moving back towards the nearest settlement, then into Old Kampung Tanah.

Jordan was weeping in frustration when the last thunder of the helicopter faded into silence.

The all embracing jungle stretched for miles on either side of him. From the sky, the green canopy lay like primeval clouds over the land.

In the quiet of the air, the teeming life of the rainforest cannot be seen or heard. The jungle embraces all beneath, succours those who seek nourishment, suffocates those who do not understand its secrets. With deceptive stillness, it reclaims each inch fought from it and each ephemeral act of defiance – the temple, the scars of earth around the tower, the defeated debris of Jordan's folly and finally, the fragile humanity of Jordan himself.

They never found Jordan.

36

Over the course of the next year, the police, in collaboration with the Environment Commission, uncovered the manipulations and deceptions behind Jordan's empire. The charges against Luke were dropped. In the investigations, he was vindicated in his professional standing. In time, his reputation flourished again.

Roberts was arrested. With the involvement of Interpol, the authorities uncovered the Tans' and Jordan's net of influence in Asia. Witnesses now came forward to reveal intimidation by Jordan, through the Tans, and evidence emerged of bribery, corruption and extortion. Zain, Scott, Tsui, the Chinese geophysicist, and members of the Tan clan involved in illegal activities were arrested. The Tans' underground client list led to further arrests.

However, Tan himself was never arrested. It was suspected that he had reached Old Kampung Tanah and taken refuge with his cousin, the owner of First Safe Limited. Through fragments of information pieced together during the investigation, it was discovered that he had been moved to the East Coast to the house of a small time gangster that owed the Tan 'firm' a favour. From there, Tan had been transported to an island close to the Thai border. He'd spent several weeks lying low in a fishing village while his wound healed sufficiently for a further move. Under cover of darkness, he had been moved on to Thailand using false papers and a hefty bribe, and then through to Vietnam via contacts in Bangkok and Saigon. After that, the trail went cold although there were to be occasional sightings of a man who might have been Tan as far afield as Shanghai, San Francisco and Johannesburg. Each time the description differed and he might have been, variously, a businessman, a short-order cook, a Cape Malay or an Indonesian. The man would disappear underground again by the time the authorities tried to pick up the lead.

Jordan Cardale PLC ceased trading and its global assets were frozen by the authorities. Consortium 2000 were cleared of any misdemeanour but under a new law passed in the light of the landslide tragedy, the development of Kampung Tanah was subject to greater environmental control. The contract was awarded to one of the Malaysian tenderers who had come in just behind Jordan on the bid. At Mohammed's instigation, Luke was invited to advise on the development with the backing of the Environment Commission and the Planning Committee.

There was a new impulse to responsible development in the region now, in the light of the Titiwangsa tragedy and several other disasters in neighbouring nations arising from grandiose, short-sighted projects. In Indonesia, smog from forest fires blocked out the sun for months, stretching as far as India and Hong Kong. The slump of the financial markets across Asia dampened the euphoria of previous years. Like the choking smoke, the economic pall woke Asians from their dream. They had thought to cheat the *tao*, to bring progress and wealth and the way of the light without its attendant dark. But in the smoky twilight of the haze, Asians were brought face to face with their interdependence and responsibilities. There was a mood-swing away from the thrusting egotism of the boom-time. The Malaysian developer, savvy to a chance to win recognition and public backing, implemented Luke's cost-effective and visionary ideas. On the cusp of the millennium, leading the way in a new Eastern concept of quality and progress, the Titiwangsa University Town was transformed into a fresh symbol for the future. It became a showcase development harmonising environmental conservation with technological advancement.

"The new design embraces the philosophy and values of the East. It is in smallness that we find the power of community and in the harmony of wind, water, sky and earth that the humans who live and work in that community find strength and well-being,"

Luke said, to the gathered dignitaries at the unveiling of the design.

The new design used organic materials and local labour, synthesising ancient Malay and Eastern art and architecture with modern functional needs into beautiful and comfortable buildings, which were the first of their kind. Enhancing instead of dwarfing human enjoyment and activity, the development blended into the tracts of jungle that were to be retained or replanted.

There would be no adventure theme park but the forests would be preserved as a new national park, with a multi-media centre that provided education on the Orang Asli, their sacred sites and history, and on the diversity of the jungle and the nation. The adventure was the jungle itself with its levels of graded trails, wilderness hikes and spiritual retreats, overseen by local rangers and guide, many from the Orang Asli tribes.

At the end of their legal battle for compensation, the people of Kampung Tanah were awarded sums out of the confiscated assets of Jordan Cardale PLC. Their community was integrated into the university town and a memorial garden with a monument by a local artist laid down at the site of the landslide tragedy.

The "mental instability" certificate on Jasmine was verified as fraudulent and the doctor disciplined. Julian Masters said to Jasmine, in a long telephone conversation, "Regardless of what we now know about Jordan, shopping your own client to the authorities is a serious breach of professional ethics. And sleeping with the other side raises a grave conflict of interest. We cannot treat this lightly. But in view of your excellent record up till then, and all the factors that have come to light, I see a future for you still at this firm."

Jasmine said, "My mother is very ill. She needs me. I can't think of my career now."

She resigned from Carruthers.

* * *

Six weeks after Luke was brought out of the jungle, he limped down the path to Mrs Fung's house on a single crutch. He wore chinos and a cotton shirt. The neighbourhood kids trailed him, laughing and mimicking his gait.

Jasmine left Mrs Fung's side in the shade of the honeysuckle and ran to meet him. She was wearing jeans and a silk vest from the local market. She fell into his arms, nearly bowling him over. Their kiss was warm and familiar. The kids giggled and she made a face at them, shooing them away. As they ran off, Luke and Jasmine turned back to each other, creases of laughter on their lips.

They sauntered arm in arm into the compound, enjoying the feel of each other. Luke had spent his first week on the Titiwangsa consultancy in Kuala Lumpur and was back for the weekend.

"I'm going to take the job with Miriam & Co," Jasmine said, smiling. The law firm in Taiping had approached her a few weeks before. They had seen her in the media after the arrest of Tan and Roberts. Pursuing their independent inquiries, they had been impressed by what they had discovered about her professional capabilities.

Jasmine went on, "It's a small firm and the senior partner is a woman. They specialise in family law, especially domestic violence cases. Also, criminal defence for women and compensation cases against corporations, employers and other Goliaths. I'll have to learn the ropes but I reckon I could be pretty good in time. Miriam thinks so."

"I have no doubts about that!"

"And it means I can be with my mother. And you."

"It makes me very happy." He grinned, nuzzling her ear.

Mrs Fung heard them coming round the house to the garden. Their happiness was almost tangible in the afternoon air. She smiled.

Inspector Tiong was charging her with two counts of murder but she knew that he knew that she would never see trial. He was taking his time in making the final arrest, dragging out the administrative aspects, double-checking every thing at a slow pace. He had to do his duty but he was a compassionate man.

He had given her six precious weeks with her daughter. It was not long but to her, every moment had been a lifetime to treasure and savour. They would be what she would take with her in the final moment.

The flame tree was gone. In its place, empty sky and compacted earth. The tree had been dismembered, its branches coming off one at a time in the felling, and the toppling of the trunk and the excavation of its roots. They were all burned in a bonfire over two days. It was gone at last, this memorial to a man she had grown to hate and a symbol of her hope for her daughter. She was free at last, truly free.

She had made right the horror of the past. Its darkness receded now to cup against the balance of the light. In the last hour, she had felt her strength suddenly ebb. She felt a calm coldness rising slowly up from the seat of her *chi* – her life energy. It was time now. Jasmine's voice came to her with a vibrant intensity and Luke's happy reply rang with an intimate clarity. She sucked in a breath suddenly and sighed. She closed her eyes, a smile lingering on her lips.

ALSO BY

YANG-MAY OOI

MINDGAME

Ambitious young lawyer Fei-Li Qwong has steered her major clients to the successful launch of their visionary sanitorium just outside Kuala Lumpur. Piers and Ginny Wyndham claim their centre for mental health and excellence will revolutionise Asia's healthcare practices. Fei is proud to be part of the team. But as Fei begins to uncover the dark reality behind the Wyndhams' public front, she finds herself drawn deep into a pall of intrigue and murder to a secret experiment that could enslave Asia under a terrifying new tyranny.

'What do you get if you cross
John Grisham with Amy Tan ... *Mindgame*'
The Independent, UK